"YOU CANNOT HIDE
FROM THE TRUTH, MILADY"

"Nor can you speak it, it would seem," she replied. "First you lie about your name. Now you try to plant suspicion in my mind with your tales. Mayhap all men of this country are bards, Chieftain, but it appears you have forgotten how to sift the truth from the husks of deception. Mayhap because you are afraid to confront it."

"Afraid?" He cupped her elbows in her hands and pulled her to him.

She pulled away. Then he caught her face between his hands, and his mouth captured hers as his fingers slipped up beneath her veil to draw her closer again. Shock raced through her, as hot and potent as the heat of a flame. Her body was as unyielding as a stone wall, but possessed a warmth that intensified the tremor roiling within her.

"I do not fear the truth, milady," he whispered, "for it is true that I have thought of doing this since your eyes met mine last night."

Her answer vanished as his lips found hers. He leaned her back over his arm, deepening the kiss until she clutched his cloak.

Abruptly her released her with a terse chuckle. "Now I have proven to you that I fear not the truth of such dangerous desires, milady. Do you?"

Books by Jo Ann Ferguson

Ride the Night Wind
Wake Not the Dragon

Published by HarperPaperbacks

Harper
Monogram

Wake Not the Dragon

⋈ JO ANN FERGUSON ⋈

HarperPaperbacks
A Division of HarperCollinsPublishers

This is a work of fiction. The characters, incidents, and dialogues are products of the author's imagination and are not to be construed as real. Any resemblance to actual events or persons, living or dead, is entirely coincidental.

HarperPaperbacks   *A Division of* HarperCollins*Publishers*
10 East 53rd Street, New York, N.Y. 10022

Cover illustration by Bob Sabin

First printing: March 1996

Printed in the United States of America

HarperPaperbacks, HarperMonogram, and colophon are trademarks of HarperCollins*Publishers*

❖ 10 9 8 7 6 5 4 3 2 1

For Marjorie Ferguson,
who has given me two precious gifts—
her son and her friendship.
Thanks, Marge.

Wake Not the Dragon

Prologue

England—East of Offa's Dyke
1277

She stood alone, among the white blossoms of the apple trees. Her shoulders were as bent as their branches, and she trembled as if a high wind were swirling around her.

Kenleigh clenched his hands at his side. It had happened again. He knew that, as surely as he knew his own name. Damn Talbot! The girl was strong-willed, but only in that she resembled her sire. In every other way, Gizela was the image of her mother, who had treated him with such kindness when he was a lad no older than the lass was now.

The man swung down from his horse and looped the reins over a branch. He walked toward her. His short tunic did not brush the high grass, but she must have heard him approaching. Instantly her shoulders beneath her dark-brown cote-hardie squared, and he took note of a surreptitious stroke of her hand against her cheek. He had never seen her weep, and she would not let that change today. When she faced him, she did not smile. She never was hypocritical with him, only courageous.

"Do I disturb you?" he asked.

She shook her head, and, when her veil fluttered back, he saw the bruise on her right cheek. He knew all too well that Talbot was left-handed, he knew only too well. He wondered what had precipitated this day's mistreatment. It mattered little. It had happened before. It would happen again, for as long as Talbot's sole child reminded him of his failure to sire a son.

"Do you wish to be alone?"

Again, she shook her head. "I am always pleased to see you, Kenleigh." She blanched, and the imprint of a hand on her cheek became more pronounced. "I mean, milord."

He took her hand, which was as tiny and fragile as a newborn bird. An illusion, he knew, for this child had been fired like a fine pot by her life. No longer as malleable as clay, she was strong, but too many sharp blows would shatter her. "I, too, am unaccustomed to the grandeur of such a title being spoken to me. I had thought my father would possess it for many more years."

"Your father was fortunate to have a son to bequeath his title to."

He chuckled. The underlying sarcasm in her young voice always amused him. "You shall get yourself into more trouble if those words were to reach beyond my ears."

"I trust you."

"I know." He seated her on a log that was as bleached as old bones. Sitting next to her, he said, "Trust me when I say that it hurts me to see you in pain."

"You are a dear friend."

"Your mother and my mother were distant cousins. We are family."

She stared down at her hands which were folded on her lap. "I would prefer to think of you as a friend, Kenleigh. A friend is more dear to me than family."

"Not all families are like yours."

"I pray not."

Pain riveted him at the grim acceptance in her voice. No, she could not be ready to cede her will to her detestable father! She had fought through all her few years. She must not capitulate now. He must give her hope to continue the battle to save her soul from destruction.

He glanced at his horse. He could not remain here to protect her as he had in the past year since he had learned of the consequences of Talbot's fearsome temper. Within the hour, he must depart to throw his lot in with King Edward on his campaign to the west, past Offa's Dyke in Wales. He smiled as inspiration filled his head. He could not be here to protect his young cousin, but his name could.

Folding her hands between his, he said, "I would ask you a question for which I would like an honest answer."

"You need only ask."

"Marry me."

Her eyes widened, and her mouth became a perfect circle of incredulity. "Marry you, Kenleigh? You are a fine lord now."

"You are an earl's daughter. Our lands adjoin. We have long been friends. It makes utmost sense." He curved his hand along her uninjured cheek. "I must leave you, and I know you have to be strong. Let my name be your shield."

"Take me with you." She shifted to face him. Eagerness stripped the pain from her expressive eyes. "The queen travels with the king on his campaigns. I shall go with you."

He smiled. "I shall ask your father before I ride to join the king."

"Father may not agree."

He understood what she dared not say, even to him. Talbot might oppose the match simply to add more misery to his daughter's existence.

Dropping to his knee before her, he said, "If he does not agree to let you join me now, I will gain his acceptance of our betrothal."

"How?"

"I know not, but, dear one, I shall not see you suffer like this again." His fingertip drew back the linen veil she had pulled forward to cloak the bruise. "I vow to you that I shall see you are protected for the rest of your days."

"But if you are far from me—"

"No matter where I go, no matter what trials life or death throw at me, this is a vow I shall keep throughout eternity." He tipped her chin up and was shocked to see tears in her eyes. "You don't believe me?"

"I do believe you."

"Then you will be my wife?"

"Yes."

As she flung her arms around him and pressed her face to his chest, he embraced her gently. He had no idea how he might keep this vow, for the journey he was about to take was laden with peril. He would find a way to honor this promise to sweet Gizela. And he would honor it with every breath, until his very last.

1

Northern Wales—1284

The spring bubbled a song against the water-worn rocks before tumbling into a languid pool. No greenery surrounded it, for the remnants of winter still clung to the uneven hillsides. The wind off the western sea held no mercy as twilight spread out of the mountain valleys and swept along the shore road.

Gizela de Montpellier dipped her hand into the cool water and drank deeply. The water was flavored with the taste of leather. For days, she had worn her riding gloves while she and her companions followed the road beside the sea, league after league, across the top of Wales. With Rhuddlan behind them, they would soon reach the king's court at the castle he was having raised in Caernarvon.

Where her husband would be waiting for her.

She sat back on her heels and gazed across the pool as her finger rubbed the ring he had given her as his bride. She had not seen Kenleigh de Montpellier in more than seven years. Then she had been but a child, and he a strapping young man riding off to enjoy his first campaign with the king. Even their wedding had not called him from the king's side, for Kenleigh, who held the title of Lord de Montpellier, had sent his most trusted servant to stand in his stead during their marriage ceremony.

Rising, she pressed her hand against her aching back. Her life at Talbot Hall had not been sedentary, but nothing had prepared her for this endless ride from her family's lands on the other side of Offa's Dyke. She lifted her heavy, murrey skirt and riding cloak, and climbed from the side of the water. The pouch and the sheathed knife at her waist, rubbed against her at every step, but she ignored them with the ease of habit. She had worn the pouch and knife every day since her eighth birthday.

The wind hit her cheeks, pulling at the linen of her wimple, but she turned to it. Never had she cowered before the wind. Its scents brought a promise of spring and a new life that must come with the defeat of the Welsh prince by King Edward. A new life for her, too— one where only the wind would strike her.

Kenleigh had guaranteed that by asking her to be his wife. Of all she remembered of Kenleigh, she remembered his gentleness most. Once he had been her haven, there to ease her fear. Now, he would do so again.

On the road, which was rutted from winter rains, a score of horses waited. Half that number of men crouched among them, seeking shelter from the cold. A single woman came forward. "Milady, you should not wander freely here," the old woman cried, her voice scratchy. "There is much danger among these hills."

Gizela put her hand out to her dearest retainer. Pomona had been her nurse before she became Gizela's bodyservant. She had replaced her mother, who had died giving birth to Gizela's only brother. A brother who had given up the fight for life only hours after he had been born. Pomona's thin cheeks were nearly as red as the stitchery on her cloak, and her hands trembled with cold.

"You can ride no farther this night," Gizela said.

Pomona huddled more deeply into her cloak, but murmured, "I shall not slow you, milady."

"Nonsense." She called to the leader of the men.

Fowler rushed to her, pressing his hand to his forelock. As always, his cheeks were as ruddy as Pomona's, but she suspected it was not from the frostiness. She wondered if the man would always blush in her company. All during the wedding rite, when he had stood proxy, he had been as scarlet as a sunset.

"Would it be wiser," she asked, "to spend the night here and to reach Caernarvon on the morrow?"

"Mayhap."

"Then you would suggest we go on?"

He shook his head, the feather bouncing on his wide-brimmed cap. "Nay, milady. If you would wish me to speak plainly— "

"I do."

"There is scant safety anywhere beyond the walls of Rhuddlan."

"Lord de Montpellier's missive asked us to come to Caernarvon," she chided softly. Pomona had told her of the men's grousing that they had to leave the thick walls of Rhuddlan to ride even more deeply into the Welsh wilderness. She did not fault them their caution, for she had seen the glares when they passed through a Welsh village. The English were not wanted in this barbaric land. However, Kenleigh had a special reason for asking her to come to Caernarvon.

She could not keep from smiling. Everyone in England knew the queen would soon be brought to childbed to give the king another child. Kenleigh had offered the queen the services of his wife at that most uncomfortable hour. Queen Eleanor had urged him to ask Gizela to visit her as soon as she arrived at Caernarvon.

Fowler bowed again, bringing her attention back to him. "I shall have a fire started, so that we might find some solace in this horrible place."

"Thank you."

He paused at her answer as he was about to step away, and, Gizela saw fear in his eyes. A shiver coursed through her. Kenleigh's men had joined him on many campaigns. She had thought fear was wrung from them, but more than one man had crossed himself surreptitiously when they entered the shadows along the road. She whispered a prayer that their fears would not come true.

The fire could not combat the cold, and the hard bread and cheese did little to fill their stomachs. Even the ale passed in its flask from hand-to-hand offered no warmth. When she saw Pomona shivering, Gizela rose to collect another cloak.

"Sit," she said, putting her hand on Pomona's thin shoulder as the old woman started to stand. "I swear your bones shall break from the cold if you move."

"You should not wait upon me, milady."

Gizela hid her smile. Pomona always insisted on doing exactly as custom dictated. How many times had the old woman advised Gizela to heed her, especially when Gizela's father was in Talbot Hall? Rubbing her cheek which had suffered her father's hand too many times, she squared her shoulders. Nothing she might have done or said would have eased her father's frustration that his only child was a girl. Three more wives had failed to give him the living son he craved. Even on the night of his death, Lord Esmond Talbot had cursed God and the wives who had denied him his most precious desire—forcing him to leave his lands to a mere daughter.

"Sit, Pomona," she ordered again. "I shall be but a moment." She waved to Fowler to remain seated as well. She would not be going beyond the glow of the fire, and the moon had risen to wash the forest in its cool, gray light.

The embroidered hem of her cote-hardie brushed the frozen ground. Sleep would not come easily tonight, although, she suspected the earth would be no less comfortable than the bed she had shared with Pomona last night in a wayside inn. Mayhap they should have stayed at Rhuddlan. No, Kenleigh had requested she join him at Caernarvon. She would try to show him, by obeying his command, that she would be a good and obedient wife.

Within her memory, she heard the echo of her father's harsh laugh. Lord Talbot had punished her endlessly for failing to acquiesce to his edicts.

Gizela shuddered as she shook off thoughts of the past. Bending by the packs that had been secured on the horses, she sought the one containing the few clothes she had been able to bring with her. The cloak of brown serge was the thickest. It would serve Pomona well.

A horse whinnied nervously and shifted against the others. She scanned the darkness. Was an animal stalking them? What sort of beasts lived within these mountains? Were there cats or bears or wolves?

She gathered the cloak, wrapping it around her arms. Rising, she froze at an unmistakable sound. A sword scraped from its scabbard. She gasped as Fowler shouted. The other men answered with a roar.

She whirled and stared at the man standing in the shaft of moonlight. He wore a bow and quiver over his broad shoulders and a long sword at his hip, but she was captured by his eyes. Although she could not see their color in the darkness, the strength of his gaze held her. He took a step forward, and the moonlight glinted off his golden hair which draped over his shoulders in the wild style favored by the barbarians of this country.

He raised his empty hands and smiled. "*Noswaith dda,*" he called, then added in English, "I bid you good evening, fellow travelers."

Behind her, Fowler said in the French spoken in his lord's manor house, "Step aside, milady. I shall deal with this cur."

Gizela took a single step backward. The stranger's smile broadened, and heat climbed her cheeks. He thought she was afraid of him. What a foolish thought! He was a single Welshman facing ten, armed Englishmen who had survived the king's Welsh campaigns.

Lifting her hand to order her men to hold fast, she replied in English, "Good evening, sir. You have chosen a chilly night to travel."

"True. That is why when I saw the flicker of your fire, I had hoped you might spare a bit of its heat for me."

"Who are you?"

"I am called Rhys." He came closer and bowed his head toward her. "Grant me the boon of this small favor, milady."

She motioned for Fowler to lower his sword. "If you come in peace, you are welcome to join us."

"Peace is what Edward wishes for *Cymru,* is it not?"

Gizela was unsure if he meant his words to be inflammatory, but a rumble raced among her men. She doubted if the Welshman understood French, for he continued to smile in spite of the mumbled insults. A single glance at Fowler brought the order to hush. The war was past. The English were victorious, so it behooved them to be generous and offer the comfort of their fire to a Welsh traveler.

The men settled themselves around the fire, leaving a wide space between them and the stranger. His smile never wavered, so Gizela could not guess if he realized the aspersions aimed at him. She draped the dark-brown cloak over Pomona's shoulders and sat next to her. Only when she looked across the fire, did she discover that Rhys was directly opposite her.

Again his gaze caught hers. Now she could see his eyes were as brilliantly blue as the hottest flames. The fire flickered its reflection within them, hiding his thoughts. Shadows from the firelight carved the pattern of his roughly sculptured features. Clean-shaven, his face was scored with the lash of the wind.

Fowler rose and came to sit beside Gizela. He drew his knife from his belt. Paring his nails, he stared at the Welshman as tension tightened every muscle.

"I hope your kind heart will not betray us, milady," he murmured.

"There was no reason to turn away a fellow pilgrim," she answered. "A lone man offers nothing for us to fear."

"They are crafty beasts."

"He is but one."

"I pray you are not mistaken," Fowler grumbled, balancing his knife on his knee. He stiffened again when the stranger reached for his own belt.

Gizela released a taut breath when the Welshman said, "I have some bits of hare for my evening meal. I would be glad to share it with any of you."

Each of the men shook his head, and Gizela sighed. She would have enjoyed something other than the coarse bread and tasteless cheese, but to accept his generosity might exacerbate the apprehension around the fire. As Rhys cooked his supper on the blade of his belt knife, she tried to ignore the enticing scents.

"I am surprised you stopped here," he said in a tone that suggested they all were long-standing comrades, "when there is an inn at the next village."

"The next village is near?" asked Pomona, peeking out from beneath her cloak.

"An hour's ride, mayhap two."

She groaned and drew back beneath her robes.

"I seldom ride," Rhys continued. "I prefer to walk these hills."

"Are you a herder?" asked Gizela.

"My duty is to guard against the dangers of the hills."

Fowler frowned. "Sheep? Goats? Is that what you herd? Where are they?"

"Safe for the night." Rhys smiled as he pulled the blade from the fire and ran his finger over the greasy pieces on it. His smile broadened as he licked his finger, then held the meat in the flames again. "I must say you have chosen a wondrous night to travel."

"Wondrous? 'Tis nearly cold enough to freeze our breaths within us."

"True, but the stars are as bright as sun-washed foam on the sea."

"You speak with the words of a minstrel," Gizela said.

"All men of this land are bards." He drew a piece of the meat from his knife and chewed on it. Glancing around the circle facing him, he smiled and hummed a lilting tune. "We sing of the law and of the old ways, teaching those who will follow what they must know."

"The ways of this land will be English now," Fowler said in English, startling Gizela, for he seldom spoke the language he considered worthy only of peasants.

"What has been among these mountains will remain."

Fowler gripped the haft of his knife. "You speak treason."

Gizela put her hand on his arm. "Let us speak of something else."

"Milady," argued Fowler, "if the king were to hear such words— "

"The king is not here."

He gaped at her as if she had taken leave of her senses. When she saw Rhys's grin, she wondered if Fowler might be right. She simply did not want to suffer through an exchange of heated words while the cold was gnawing at her bones.

"You shall find," Rhys said, his voice still serene, "Caernarvon more comfortable than this clearing."

"How do you know where we travel to?" she asked.

"Where else would you go on this road?" He pulled another slice of meat from his knife and cursed aloud as it burned his finger.

"No!" Gizela cried, jumping to her feet as Rhys held his knife and the dripping meat over his finger.

Fowler shouted after her, but she did not pause as she knelt next to the Welshman. Opening the pouch she wore at her waist, she drew out a small bag. She poured fine powder into her palm. Licking her finger, she dipped it into the powder and spread it across the red spots on his skin.

"The grease will ease the soreness, but add to the injury," she said, as she sat back on her heels. Brushing the unused powder from her palm, she drew from the pouch a narrow strip of linen. "Do not leave this on past tomorrow evening," she said, wrapping it around his burned finger. "For tonight, this will hold the herbs in place to soothe the burn."

"You are a healer?" he asked incredulously.

She smiled at his astonishment. "I only dabble with such things."

"I had not guessed that an English lord would allow his daughter such learning."

"My father and I shared a difference of opinion on that subject, it is true, but I studied as I could." She would not lay bare her past before a stranger. Tying the linen securely, she said, "That should alleviate the pain."

He wiggled his finger. "Very much. Your touch has a mystical way of healing, milady."

"It is knowledge, not magic."

"Is there a difference?" He leaned toward her, his intense eyes even with hers. "What one man calls sorcery, another knows is gained by hard work and wisdom. There are many kinds of enchantment, milady, within the mountains of this land. The ways here go back to the beginning of time, before the first memory of the first man."

"And they can be learned with hard work and wisdom?" she whispered, caught anew in the soft, potent warmth of his voice that sang through her.

"By those who believe." He touched her palm which was still dusted with the healing herbs. "The old ways say that the Lady of Llyn-y-Fan Fach was of the fairy folk, and that it was she who taught her sons the secrets that all healers heed. The secrets you have learned so well, milady."

"Nonsense!" snapped Pomona.

Gizela broke away from Rhys's gaze to discover her servant standing directly behind her. Rising, she put her hand on Pomona's arm. Pomona grasped Gizela's hand and tugged.

"You do not believe in the ways of the ancients?" Rhys asked, still unperturbed, but this time his question was for Pomona. Holding up his hand, he added, "I see the proof before my eyes."

"Milady learned her healing by long study, not by magic."

"Did I not say that the two may be one and the same?"

Pomona started to speak, stuttered, and then was silent. She tugged again on Gizela's hand with wrapping

her away from the Welshman who drew the last piece
of charred meat from his blade.

"Thank you, milady, for your kindness and wisdom,"
Rhys said, dipping his head in her direction. "I am in
your debt."

"No debt exists between us," Gizela replied. Having
this man owe her an obligation made her oddly uncomfortable. How easily he twisted words with the skill of a
master minstrel! She wanted nothing tying them
together, not even the courtesy of a debt of honor.

He stood, and she could not help stepping backward
again. Although his clothes were rough, he possessed a
regal mien that was unsettling. "The debt is mine,
milady. You cannot dislodge it by being gracious, for
that puts me further into your debt."

"Milady!" Pomona's voice held a tinge of desperation.

Gizela nodded, glad for the excuse to put an end to
this conversation. As she turned to guide the old woman
back to where they had been sitting, she stared at all her
men who were on their feet. A single misspoken word
could see more blood spilled than her simple herbs
would be able to remedy. The stench of fear hung heavy
in the air.

Gizela kept her steps slow and even. Offering Fowler
a smile, she sat Pomona back on the brown serge cloak
and drew her own over her shoulders. He scowled, for
the first time not blushing. Slowly Fowler's fingers signaled for his men to sit as well. They did not hesitate.

Silently she released her breath. Thank the heavens
Kenleigh's men were so well trained. Kenleigh! A cold
flush surged through her. Would Kenleigh share his
men's fury at her offering her herbs to the Welshman?
Old Wilda had taught her to bring solace to anyone
who had need of her skills, but the wise woman in the

stillroom had never been beyond the borders of Lord
Talbot's lands. Mayhap those rules no longer applied.

When Fowler spoke, she flinched, stunned he would
start a conversation with the Welshman. "You know
this land well?"

"As well as you know your lover's sweet flesh."

Pomona muttered under her breath, but the men
chuckled with appreciation at the quick answer. Gizela
felt Rhys's gaze upon her again. She did not raise her
eyes. She was a bride, who should think only of her
husband's caresses, not the bold scrutiny of a Welsh
shepherd.

"Do we have far to ride to reach Caernarvon?"
Fowler asked.

"Your journey shall be finished on the morrow
before the sun begins its drop to caress the western
sea." He laughed. "If all goes well for you."

Pomona whispered, "Is there danger lurking?"

"There is always danger among the mountains of this
land. You must never let that thought stray far from
your head. This is the land of your lord's enemies."

The old woman choked and pressed her hand to her
thin chest.

Gizela frowned as she handed the flask of ale to her
maid. Facing Rhys, she said, "You need not frighten her
with your tales. This land is King Edward's as surely as
England is."

"You speak with certainty, milady."

"The truth should not be heralded quietly." Not giving
him a chance to answer, she added, "Pomona, it would be
wise for us to retire for our night's rest. Even though our
journey is not long on the morrow, we will have much
to do when we reach our quarters within Caernarvon."

Gizela did not look across the fire as she assisted her
maid to pull her cloaks around her in a cocoon to ward

off the night's cold. She wrapped herself as tightly in hers and closed her eyes.

A vision of fire-hot blue eyes burst through the darkness. She opened her eyes and stared at the flames that were fading among the embers. With a shiver that had nothing to do with the night's chill, she drew the edge of the cloak against her face. Mayhap if she could shut out the night, she could shut out the thoughts that should not be hers.

She was on her way to be with her husband. The recollection of their friendship was a cherished treasure. Kenleigh would care for her and treat her well. Of that she was sure.

Then why did another man's fascinating eyes fill her head with baffling thoughts? She knew nothing of Rhys of Wales, save that he had a quick wit and cared little for the opinions of others when they did not agree with his own.

The puzzle haunted Gizela as she tried to find sleep. She listened as the men prepared for the night. The commonplace sounds of laughter and the posting of the guards were muted because of the stranger in their midst. Only Pomona's low snore brought comfort.

She watched the moon cross the heavens as the hours inched past. She did not recall falling asleep, but came slowly awake when a foot brushed her leg. Footsteps faded away along the hard ground. She lifted her head to see a familiar form heading for the trees beside the pool on the far side of the road.

Where was Pomona going at this hour? If she had heeded nothing else Rhys had said, Pomona should have listened to his warning of the peril lurking across the hillsides. She should have wakened Gizela to accompany her on her nocturnal errand.

Gizela rose, and gathering her skirts around her, she followed Pomona. Against her waist, her knife was a comfort. She whispered to the guard that she was going with Pomona, not wishing to admit that she had no idea what her servant was planning. When Pomona vanished amid the trees, Gizela did not hesitate to follow. She had seldom raised her voice to scold the old woman, but she had no choice tonight. Pomona must never be so witless again.

Even though the trees were naked under the late winter sky, their thick branches filtered out most of the moonlight, leaving puddles of shadows across the uneven hillside. The twigs rasped together like bare bones exulting in a macabre dance on All Hallow's Eve. An owl hooted, drowning out the whisper of the spring.

"Pomona?" she whispered, not daring to speak more loudly. "Pomona, answer me!"

Something moved farther down the hill toward the pool. She rushed as quickly as she dared on the rough ground. A low voice came from her left. A man's voice! Footsteps vanished into the distance. What was happening? Where was Pomona? She must find her, or—

She gasped with pain as she was shoved against a tree. As she tried to flee, her cloak caught on the sharp bark. She tugged, then reached for the ties at her throat. A blade pressed against her neck. She froze and stared at the man swathed in shadows.

"Fool! You should have stayed in your own homeland, *Saesnes*!" he snapped in heavily-accented English. He raised the knife and chuckled as he aimed it at her heart. "Welcome to *Cymru* . . . and death!"

2

Gizela's foot struck her captor's shin, and he yelped. She pulled her knife from her belt, but he grasped her wrist. Pain exploded up her arm when he slammed her fingers against the tree. The knife fell to the ground. Although he spoke neither French nor English, his curse was clear in any language as he raised his knife again.

Someone's strong fingers seized his arm and jerked it down. He whirled, trying to escape.

Gizela took a single step before her arm was caught. She moaned as another bolt of agony ran along her shoulder. She swayed. An arm swept under her knees, and she was lifted off her feet. She opened her mouth to scream.

"Do not be frightened, milady."

In amazement, she looked up. Rhys! But was he friend or foe among these shadows? She gasped. How had he been able to sneak away from the fire without Fowler or the guard who was posted taking note? She could see no sign of Kenleigh's men among the trees.

When Rhys lowered her to the ground, she cradled her aching arm in her hand. He squatted and reached out a single finger to brush her shoulder. She pulled away, then groaned as the quick motion sharpened the pain.

"Don't touch me," she whispered.

"I wish to be sure you are unharmed."

"You are not a healer."

He smiled. "You know nothing of me, milady. How can you say what I am or am not?"

Gizela was about to retort when the shadows moved behind him. She opened her mouth to cry out a warning, but his hand covered her lips.

"Say nothing," he ordered, his voice as hard as the tree behind her. "You need have no fear of Tremaine . . . now." He motioned with his head to the other man at the same time he drew his hand away from her mouth. "Tremaine mistook you for another."

"Who?" she whispered.

"You need not know." His eyes were as cold as winter ice. "The wise know when it is not prudent to ask questions." Again he looked over his shoulder. "Come forward, Tremaine, and offer your apologies directly to this lady who saved me from my own folly tonight." He chuckled and held up his bandaged finger.

Gizela drew her feet under her as the man named Tremaine rose from the deep well of shadows. She doubted if she could outrun him. He was tall, although his head did not reach the height of Rhys's. Well-favored in both face and body, he wore clothes that had seen many miles, for every fiber was woven with dust and dirt. He sheathed his knife as he came to stand behind Rhys. Folding his arms over his chest, he smiled condescendingly.

"It seems I was mistaken, milady. I should have said only 'Welcome to *Cymru*.'"

"Why did you wish to kill me?"

He shrugged. "You are *Saesnes*."

"What?"

"English," Rhys said, as he put his hand under her elbow to bring her to her feet.

She pulled away. He frowned as she rose unaided. Swaying, she clutched the tree behind her, but shrank away from his outstretched hand. "I can stand on my own."

"That is yet to be proven."

"I must find Pomona."

"She is safe and back at your fire."

Her eyes widened. "How do you know?"

"Because I sent her back there." His frigid smile returned. "I saw her, milady, but, in my rush to prevent her from hazarding herself, I failed to note you were as witless as she was to leave the security of your armed men. Fool that I am, I believed you to be wiser than that."

"I wished only to be certain Pomona was unharmed."

"She is. I assure you."

"Oh— " Tremaine hesitated when Rhys scowled at him, then said, "Chilly nights are not made for congenial conversation."

Gizela stared at both men. They were as edgy as a stag with the hounds at its heels. She was sure she was missing something— something vital—that was underlying their words, but she could not guess what it might be.

"True," Rhys said, turning back to her. "Milady, would you suffer me to check your shoulder to be certain nothing is damaged beyond repair?"

"Are you a healer?"

Tremaine snorted, but said nothing.

Instead of answering, Rhys reached toward her. She fought not to cringe away. Closing her eyes, she willed herself to stand still. She had no reason to believe he would hurt her. He had saved her tonight from his comrade. She sagged against the tree when agony rushed outward from her shoulder, but his touch was as gentle as his apology.

He drew a flask from beneath his cloak and offered it to her. When Tremaine leaned forward to see what he held, she did not reach for it.

"Do not be frightened," Rhys said. "It is wine."

"Nothing more?" she asked.

"Not much more."

She was sure this was the first genuine smile she had seen on his face. Taking the flask, she sniffed. The wine masked the scent of any herbs mixed in it. She took a cautious sip. The wine was bitter.

Rhys chuckled lowly, and she knew her face had betrayed her. "It may not be the fine wine you have known, milady, but it serves to quench a thirst and ease the miseries we suffer along the hillsides."

"I doubt if you can convince your sheep to drink this."

He took her hand and brought her back to sit on the ground. "Drunken sheep would be a herder's nightmare." Smiling at Tremaine, he asked, "Can you imagine anything worse?"

"Several things." His grim tone was as dark as the shadows.

Rhys slapped him on the shoulder. "Do not lament what cannot be changed now, Tremaine. Drink up, milady. A small sip will do nothing to help."

"I think— "

He interrupted her. "'Twas given to me by a wise old woman who knows well the use of herbs."

Gizela drank again, more deeply. Although the wine was not good, it tasted better than the ale Foster had brought with them. Its warmth spread through her, easing the strain tightening her shoulder. The two men said nothing as she took a third drink. Leaning her head back against the tree, she handed the half-empty flask to Rhys. He closed it and put it under his cloak.

He remained silent, and she stared at the heavens. The moon was falling across the sky, and the stars were brilliant on their ebony bed. She imagined them swirling like mummers at a fair and wondered what kind of music the angels would play for such a dance.

"How is your shoulder?" he asked.

Tentatively, she touched her shoulder. The anguish was still there, but it was not debilitating. Weeks had passed since Father's final explosion of temper. When the king had ordered him to remain on his lands instead of fighting the Welsh, Father had been furious, and he had focused that fury on her before he drank himself into such a stupor he choked to death on a chicken bone. Now he would never hurt her again. "It is better. Thank you, Rhys, for your healing." She giggled. Putting her hand to her lips, she gasped. She had not giggled for longer than she could recall.

He stood. "I am pleased, milady."

"Your debt to me is repaid."

"No, milady."

"But—"

Again he interrupted her. "My debts are not repaid until I have put aside the obligation."

"I release you from your obligation." She tried to stand, but her legs refused to hold her. She dropped back to the ground, astonished. "I seem to have a peculiar weakness. I am sure it will pass."

"I am sure as well."

She frowned when she heard what sounded like a stifled laugh. Blinking, she tried to see past the growing fog to the men's faces. She drew up her feet. The night was damp, but growing warmer. That would explain the mist.

"I thank you for your hospitality, milady," Rhys said, when she did not answer.

"You are leaving?"

"The night breaks your journey, but not mine." He bowed his head toward her. "I wish you well."

"Thank you." She hesitated, looking for the words she should say. Her mind was working even more poorly than her legs. "And I wish you the same, Rhys of Wales."

He chuckled as he knelt in front of her. "Here we prefer to call this land *Cymru*."

When he took her hand, she gasped again. He brought it to his forehead. The warmth of his skin surrounded her, sweeping away the cold and the darkness. The coarse caress of his fingers teased her palm as he slowly raised his eyes to meet hers. Her lips parted when his lips brushed her hand with a kiss. She was sure she had forgotten how to breathe as she stared into the fathomless depths of his eyes.

"I would know your name, milady," he whispered.

"Gizela," she answered, as she fought the sleep surrounding her. The herbs within the wine must have been stronger than she had guessed. The pain in her shoulder was now a dull thud, but her eyes refused to stay open. Mayhap she was asleep even now. Only in a dream could she be letting a stranger—a Welshman—hold her hand and press his mouth to it, leaving the sweet, tempting fire that burned in those eyes. Straining to focus on the man in front of her, she murmured, "Gizela Talbot."

"Talbot?" she heard Tremaine ask. "Not Esmond Talbot's wife?"

Rhys's voice was taut. *"What would his wife be doing here? She does not wear a widow's gorget, although I can imagine no one mourning that beast Talbot."*

Gizela was not surprised they knew her father. He had despised anything Welsh and had often gone on forays on this side of Offa's Dyke to halt the Welsh poachers who preyed on his herds. "Not Talbot," she whispered. "Gizela de Montpellier."

Rhys's fingers tightened on hers. He muttered something under his breath. Then he released her hand and stood straighter.

"What is amiss?" she asked, as she looked up at him. She wondered if he could gather a handful of the stars his head touched. Would a star burn as fiercely on her hand as his kiss had?

"Amiss?" He shook his head, and she wished he had not moved. She blinked, trying to clear the thickening fog from before her eyes. "I fail to understand your question, milady."

"You tensed at my name. Why should it distress you?"

"I know of no reason."

She was sure he was lying. She would ask him to explain. She would demand that he explain. She was Lady de Montpellier. He should respect that. She would . . . . The thought was left unfinished as a soothing darkness claimed her.

"You let her drink too much. That was stupid. How can we find out anything else from her?"

Rhys ap Cynan ignored his friend's question as he leaned Lady de Montpellier back onto the dried grass and sighed. When he had chanced upon this party of English travelers, he had not guessed Kenleigh de Montpellier's wife would be among them.

The ring on her left hand glittered, and he lifted her hand to examine it more closely. He had seen the same crest on de Montpellier's banner when the baron rode on Edward's business. He should have taken note of this immediately, instead of allowing himself to become lost in the pleasure of looking at de Montpellier's wife.

She must have no idea what awaited her. Although every word she spoke was guarded—wisdom he could appreciate while talking to an enemy—she had been open about her excitement at nearing Caernarvon.

Why was she here *now*?

He bent to examine her shoulder, and she winced, even in the midst of her drugged sleep. "Tremaine, you used her roughly. Too roughly."

"I did not touch that arm. 'Twas the other," Tremaine argued. "She held the knife in her right hand, and I had no intention of letting that wolf's whelp slice into me."

"Then how did she hurt the other shoulder?"

"Who cares?" He shook his head. "Why not kill her and have done with it? We do not need more of the English coming here."

"I have no quarrel with this woman."

Tremaine spat on the ground. "We have a quarrel with all of them."

"Even the wife of Kenleigh de Montpellier?"

"She is Talbot's daughter." His fingers toyed with the haft of his knife. "There are many among us who would relish the chance for vengeance, as you know so well."

"She is a de Montpellier now, and what honor is there in vengeance against a woman for her progenitor's crimes?" Rhys stood. A single glance at the sky told him too much time had passed. "The others?"

"They are waiting for you."

He smiled. "Then I shall keep them waiting no longer. Tremaine, my friend, I trust you will watch over Lady de Montpellier while I deal with this meeting." His smile vanished. "I wish her to be alive and untouched when I return."

"Why?"

"My battle is not with a woman. Whether she lives or dies makes no difference to our plans."

"Exactly!" He put his hand on his knife. "It makes no difference, so let me kill her before she betrays us."

"No, she lives. I owe her a debt."

He spat on the ground again. "She put a salve on your finger. That is nothing."

"She gave succor to an enemy. I owe the woman her life. Honor demands nothing less."

"Honor! Your accursed honor shall betray all of us to the English, and we shall be ground under their shoes like a hill of ants."

"Go," Rhys ordered with a sigh. "Tell Bleddyn to attend me here while you give the others the tidings of my arrival."

"Rhys— "

"Go!"

Tremaine lowered his eyes first and strode away into the trees.

Rhys stared down at the woman lying at his feet. Lady de Montpellier had no place here. Not now.

Kneeling, he reached out to touch the silken curve of her cheek that was edged by a strand of ebony hair. He pulled back his hand. This beautiful woman, whose gentleness and compassion had stirred him unexpectedly, belonged to his enemies. The gold embroidery

along the front of her fustian gown spoke of a wealth
that had been denied this land. Her father's name had
been used to inspire fear and hatred among the mountains.

He slipped his arms beneath her and lifted her
against his chest. When she moaned from the depths of
her sleep, he frowned. He had been careful not to jostle
her injured shoulder. How had she been hurt before
tonight? Although she had flinched away from any
touch as if she had been recently hurt, he had seen no
sign of any injury.

And he had enjoyed a long, slow survey of this pretty
lady while they sat by the fire. Her soft lips were an
invitation to pleasure. When the wind had molded her
heavy robe to her slender body, he had been unable to
keep from admiring every curve. The soft massage of
her breath against his face as she tended to his finger
had urged him to pull her into his arms and sample
those lips. He smiled wryly. Her men would have run
him through before he could have enjoyed more.
Mayhap it was just as well she was an English lord's
woman. He had no time for the complications a satisfying seduction of an Englishwoman could create now.
Not when so much depended on so few.

"Chieftain?"

He tensed at the young voice, but heard another
echoing in his mind. Damn Tremaine! He had nearly
betrayed Rhys earlier. Tremaine ap Pembroke should
be more cunning by now.

He smiled as he glanced at Lady de Montpellier's
face and discovered it was smooth with sleep. She had
not heard. Looking back as he set her on a mound of
pine needles and covered her with his fur-lined cloak,
he said, "Sit here, Bleddyn, and be sure the lady comes
to no harm."

The young man stared at her and swore under his breath, but finally nodded. "As you wish, Chieftain. If the English seek her here— "

"I trust you to devise a tale to give me time to return at your signal."

"The owl?"

Rhys nodded, clapped the man on the shoulder, and walked away to tend to the matters that had brought him to this lonely stretch of road. To himself, he vowed this was the night men would look back upon as the one when Welsh independence was reborn. Not even fantasies of enticing Gizela de Montpellier must interfere with that.

Sunlight struck Gizela's face, and she turned away from its harsh glare. The motion was as difficult as if she were swaddled like a newborn babe. She heard Pomona's voice. It resonated through her head, which was aching as viciously as when—

Confused, she opened her eyes and looked around. Rich fabrics in light blue and gold draped the bed where she was lying. A tapestry of a knight battling a dragon hung above a wide hearth. Around the room, several benches and a long table broke the expanse of the stone floor which was covered with rushes.

"Milady! Milady! How do you fare?"

Panic touched Pomona's voice, and Gizela turned her aching head to see the old woman's face gray with fear. Gizela reached out a hand to her. Pomona grasped it and pressed it to her forehead as she dropped to her knees by the bed.

"You're alive!" said the old woman with a moan. "Thank God and all the saints."

Gizela stared at the carved wood over her head. Rhys had held her hand to his forehead like this . . .

when? Then he had kissed it. No, that was impossible. He *had* taken the pose of obeisance to her. Or had he? She could not recall. Her last clear memory was of looking for Pomona. That had been on the road to Caernarvon. She searched her mind, but had no idea how she had gotten from that wilderness to this place.

"Where am I?" she whispered.

Pomona raised her head. "Caernarvon, milady."

"Caernarvon?" She pushed herself up to sit. With a gasp, she cupped her right shoulder in her other hand. Agony nearly stole her senses. Recollection of what had happened exploded through her head, wiping away the anguish. "Where did you go, Pomona?"

"Where? Oh, you mean when I went to get a drink of water last night."

"Last night?" Gizela asked. She stared at the sunlight streaming through the window. "What hour is it?"

"Just before sunset, milady."

She gasped in astonishment. "Sunset?" The herbs in that wine had stolen nearly a day from her life.

"Aye, milady. We arrived here in Caernarvon just past midday as Rhys suggested we would."

"Rhys!" Gizela swung her feet over the thick covers and climbed down from the bed. She pulled on the tunic Pomona held out to her, letting it settle over her kirtle. The stench of mildew clung to the wool she had worn through so many storms during their trip west. "He said he saw you among the trees and ordered you back to our fire."

"How do you know of that?"

"He told me."

Pomona again faded to a sickening shade of gray. Collapsing to a heavy bench in front of the fire, she whispered, "You followed me last night? But, Lady Gizela, why?"

"I feared for you out there in the darkness."

"I would have gone without the drink of water, if I had had any idea of endangering you, milady." She covered her face with her hands and began to weep.

Gizela gripped the upright on the bed, not trusting her knees. "You did not know I was gone?"

"When I came back, I saw your cloaks and assumed you were beneath them. You were asleep beside me when I woke at dawn. When I could not wake you, the Welshman told me you had complained of pain during the night and had taken a potion."

"You were not alarmed by his tale?"

"It was not the truth?"

She edged around the chest at the foot of the bed. "In a way. I find myself much confused, Pomona."

"That, we were told, would not be unusual when you woke."

"He had an explanation for it all, didn't he?" she whispered. When Pomona asked her to repeat herself, she asked instead, "Where is Kenleigh?"

"Lord de Montpellier does not seem to be here." She wiped away another tear. "I was told he was gone."

Gizela went to the window. "Odd he would ask me to come here when he was not here."

"Yes, milady."

Pomona's tone was so dreary Gizela shivered. She winced. She had learned, through many harsh lessons, how long the aftermath of her father's bruising blows could remain to taunt her. Three weeks had eased the pain in her shoulder to a dull ache. Biting her lip, she stared out at the courtyard below.

The castle was still under construction. Stone cluttered the courtyard, which was bare of a single sprig of grass. She could see a tower that had been raised, but others were still being built. The line of the future walls was marked by torn earth. A small cluster of houses marked the town that would one day be shadowed by the walls. Caernarvon was as raw and unfinished as the land it was to guard.

She stared at the largest tower. It was directly to her left. "What is that?"

"The Eagle Tower," Pomona said in awe. "'Tis where the queen lives now as she waits for her child to be born."

In a way, it resembled an eagle's nest. At the top of the tower flew the heraldic banner of Edward, King of England and now of Wales. The only openings in the upper walls were arrow slits and an occasional window.

"Incredible!" Gizela said. She had thought Talbot Hall was strong, but this great tower would need a massive army to overrun it. "We must ask Kenleigh to obtain the king's permission for us to visit there."

"Only the queen is here now, for, being so near her time, she was unable to travel with the king to Rhuddlan Castle."

She nodded. If her head did not ache so harshly, she would not be speaking foolishly. "Thank you for reminding me, Pomona."

"Are you ill, milady? Mayhap you should rest more."

"I would like to stay here and survey our new home a while longer."

Quietly Pomona said, "He is not within the castle, milady."

She closed her eyes, glad Pomona thought she was seeking Kenleigh. In truth, she wished to see Rhys. Then she could send for him and ask him to explain what had happened last night. Too many questions haunted her. What had happened after the sleeping herbs had overcome her? How had he returned her to her place among her men without being seen?

"I was assured you will find your rooms in the castle very pleasant, milady," Pomona said to break the silence. "Lord de Montpellier selected well, for we are away from the kitchen and charnel house. In addition, the window on the other side overlooks the River Seiont, so you will have fresh air to cleanse your rooms."

Gizela put aside her uneasiness and smiled. They had reached the end of their journey. Now her life could begin with Kenleigh. "Fresh air?" She laughed. "Pray spring is a-borning soon. That wind will seek its way through any amount of counterpanes to freeze us."

Pomona smiled. "This apartment is grand, milady. The other rooms are as fine as this one. Lord de Montpellier must have great influence and favor with the king."

"Mayhap he is with the king now." She dropped to sit on the bench by the fire. "Think of it, Pomona. We could have passed Kenleigh on his way to Rhuddlan without realizing it."

"We saw no other English travelers."

A knock on the door halted Gizela's answer. She called for it to open. A page boy, who could be no more than seven years old, peeked in. "Milady, I was told to tell you a gentleman waits in the antechamber. He requests the chance to speak with you."

"Did he give a name?"

"Sheldon de Montpellier, milady."

She recognized Kenleigh's younger brother's name, but the emptiness that opened within her was unfamiliar. What a fool all of those around her would think she was if they guessed she was disappointed Rhys was not the man waiting in the antechamber. A shepherd had no place within these walls . . . or within her thoughts.

The page boy started to turn, then he gawked at Gizela. "You really be Lady de Montpellier?"

"Yes, child."

He grinned, revealing several missing teeth. "Then I have another message for you. Queen Eleanor wants you to attend her as soon as you can present yourself, milady. Would be wise not to keep her waiting. Wide as she be getting, she is like to burst any minute with that baby."

When Pomona cuffed the lad for his impertinence, Gizela recoiled. The youngster just grinned more broadly, and Gizela said, "Tell Queen Eleanor that Lady de Montpellier will be honored to present herself as soon as I speak with my husband's brother. But her majesty can send for me before then if need be."

"Aye, milady. That babe may come at any moment. My uncle's cow was no bigger than she be." Grinning, he scurried away before he got his ears boxed again.

The door reopened in his wake, and a man walked in. His tunic and hose were a sedate black, but silver edged his belt. Gizela searched his face for any image of Kenleigh de Montpellier. She saw nothing, although she could not trust childish memory. When last she had seen her husband, she had thought Kenleigh was as tall as a giant with black hair that curled around his face. She knew he would not be that towering, for her memories of him usually put him astride his horse.

But she did not know Sheldon de Montpellier. He was older than her by only a year and had considered her useless, especially when his brother had betrothed himself to her before leaving to ride with Edward. She searched her memory. She seemed to recall Sheldon had been negotiating for the hand of the daughter of a baron in Sussex, but the baron had halted it, seeking a titled lord for his youngest.

"Milady?"

At the impatience in Sheldon de Montpellier's voice, she smiled with what she hoped would appear sincerity.

"Forgive me. Do come in and enjoy what heat there is from the fire."

The muscular man nodded. He crossed the room with a pair of long strides. His hair was as dark as Kenleigh's but she saw gray streaks through it. She was startled to realize Kenleigh might have even more silver in his hair. The paths these men traveled were hard and stole years from their lives.

Sheldon's smile pulled at a scar on his left cheek as he pointed toward a carved chair. Gizela sat, but he did not lower his lanky body to the bench.

"Milady, may I say that you look well, especially in light of your long journey here?"

"You are kind, Sheldon. I trust I may use your name."

"As you wish, milady."

"My name is Gizela. It would please me if you would use it, for we are now brother and sister." She leaned forward. "Do you bring me tidings from Kenleigh? I have looked forward to seeing him again after so many years."

"Gizela—" He grasped her hand, but she drew it back and folded it in her lap.

"Milady injured her shoulder," Pomona said when Sheldon's eyes formed slits at what he must have seen as an insult.

"Forgive me." He took a deep breath. "Forgive me for what I have done to cause you pain, and what I must do."

Gizela looked up at him. "What must you do?"

"Tell you of Kenleigh."

"What of him?"

"Gizela, he is dead."

3

"*Dead?*" *Gizela whispered.* She heard Pomona moan and begin to pray.

Sheldon nodded. Not Sheldon, she realized with another tremor of shock. He was Lord de Montpellier. He put his hand on her arm. She wondered if his fingers shook. She could not tell, for she trembled as if with a deadly fever.

"His body has been sent back to de Montpellier Court to be buried with our father."

"How?" She had to know the truth. Mayhap by hearing the truth, she might come to believe it. Kenleigh . . . dead? She drew his image from her mind. He was laughing, as she remembered he often was. She did not want to think of that laughter stilled like an ice-covered stream in winter.

"My brother was killed during a race against one of Lord Avemoor's men."

She stared at him, disbelieving what she had heard. "A race?"

Sheldon went to the table by the door. He poured wine into a goblet and brought it to her. "His horse slipped, we believe. His neck was broken." A hint of a smile tilted his lips. "Kenleigh was ever one for trying to prove his mount was the best and most swift in England."

"Was he?" She regretted speaking the words when Sheldon aimed a frown at her. Her unthinking question could be construed as an insult to Sheldon. Beyond the kindness he had shown her, she knew too little of the man she had married.

"My brother loved competition."

"Why did you send no message to me of this?" She crossed the cold floor and sat on the chest at the foot of the bed. Dear Kenleigh! Her friend and her savior . . . gone.

"I feared the messenger would meet you upon your journey, and I thought you would wish to hear the grievous account from the mouth of one who loved Kenleigh dearly."

"Thank you."

He served himself some wine. "I know you have thought little on your plans, Gizela, but I have had to think of the estate my brother left in your care. You should return there posthaste while I discuss with the king what the disposition of the lands shall be."

"Disposition? *Why should there be a question of the disposition of Kenleigh's lands?*" She did not want to speak of such things now. She wanted to try to figure out what she would do, now that her sanctuary had been taken from her.

"He was the heir to our father's lands, and, upon your marriage, you became Kenleigh's heir."

She stood and faced him. "I am familiar with the terms of the betrothal contract Kenleigh and Father signed." She recalled her father's rage at her presumption she should read it. Father had not wanted her to know Kenleigh had granted her full control of his lands upon his death.

"You need someone to petition the king on your behalf now that Kenleigh is dead. I will be delighted to do so while you travel back to England."

"No."

"No?" His brows lowered fiercely. "I understand you wish to have time to mourn Kenleigh, but— "

"I shall not return to de Montpellier Court." Standing, she raised her chin in the pose that always had infuriated her father. It was not her aim to incense Sheldon now, but neither would she cower before him and do his bidding like one of her father's beaten curs. "I have a duty to be by the queen's side when her child is born."

"That is more important than your husband's lands?"

"They have been without a lord for many years. I suspect the reeve can oversee them a few fortnights longer."

He slammed his fist onto the table, and she battled her instinct to shrink away from his fury. Curling her own fingers into fists, she met his eyes steadily.

"Gizela, you must be sensible. You are a gently-born woman. You should not be tending to such duties."

"This was Kenleigh's final request to me. As his wife, I shall not shirk my sole duty to him."

Sheldon set the goblet on the table and stormed out of the room. The door crashed closed behind him.

In the wake of his departure, Gizela heard Pomona mumbling another prayer. This one, Gizela repeated as well. Until a month ago, she had endured her father's temper. She had fought not to submit to that, as she would not to Sheldon's. Mayhap he would eventually understand. If he did not—she was not certain what she would do.

When Pomona came to her, Gizela shook her head. She did not want sympathy. Not when she needed so desperately to remain strong. "Please send for the lad who will take me to the queen."

Pomona nodded and left.

Brushing her hands against her gown, Gizela braided her hair along her back. She twisted it into place on either side of her face and covered it with gold netting. As she set her veil in place, her fingers faltered. A widow wore her gorget over her chin, so all the world might know of her grief and that she was in need of a husband.

Slowly, she raised the linen over her chin. No tears filled her eyes as she stared at her reflection. She had become a widow without ever having a chance to be a wife.

"Kenleigh," she whispered, "how can I ever repay you for all you did for me?" The gift she had been prepared to give him had been her love and a child to inherit his title and lands. She would have learned to love him, but she had no idea how to mourn a man who had been nothing but a memory for so many years. She must be strong. That he had asked of her. That she had been, and she must not fail him now.

The door opened, and Pomona said, "The boy is here to take you to her majesty, milady."

"Thank you."

"Milady?"

She gave Pomona a weak smile. "I must not make the queen wait."

"If you wish me to go with you . . . "

"Rest."

The old woman shook her head. "I shall unpack for you, milady."

"Wait. If all goes as I hope, we shall be moving to compartments closer to the queen."

Pomona's eyes brightened with pride. "I pray it shall be so. You deserve to bask in the favor of the queen."

Gizela simply smiled as she followed the wide-eyed lad out of the room. She did not serve as a midwife in anticipation of a generous reward. Nothing could equal the joy of bringing a new life into the sunshine.

The lad said nothing as he led Gizela up the steep stairs within the Eagle Tower. He motioned for her to precede him through a door on an upper floor. Taking a deep breath, for she never had been in the presence of anyone of higher rank than her father and his fellow barons, she entered the room.

The small, double window in the large room opened to grant a view of the inner bailey. The other walls, except where a huge fireplace fought back the lingering cold, were covered with brightly woven tapestries that brought forth the beauty of the queen's native land on the Iberian Peninsula.

Gizela easily guessed which among the dozen was the queen. The near legendary beauty of Queen Eleanor had not been diminished by years of marriage and numerous pregnancies. Gizela's trained eyes observed that the birth must still be several weeks away. The queen was making no concessions to her condition. Her scarlet gown of royal velvet was decorated with splendidly-colored embroidery which flowed around her as she crossed the room to talk to one of the women sitting by the hearth.

As her name was announced, Gizela dropped into a deep curtsy and waited for the queen to acknowledge her. She heard a rumble of whispers about the room.

Everyone within Caernarvon had known of Kenleigh's tragic, useless death, before she had.

"Lady de Montpellier, you are welcome." The greeting was lilted with the Castilian accent of the queen's homeland. "Do stand, and let me see you."

As she raised her head, Gizela wondered how a child of that hot and sunny country had learned to survive the constant mists and clawing dampness of this rough land edging the western sea. The queen came to her and put her hands on Gizela's shoulders. Gizela answered Eleanor's smile with her own.

"Thank you, your majesty."

"Dear child." The glitter of tears in Eleanor's eyes fell upon her cheeks as she said, "I offer my deepest sympathies at your loss, milady. Lord de Montpellier served the king well, and I know Edward shall miss his counsel."

"Thank you, your majesty," she said again, for she did not know what else to say. She dared not let the cauldron of sorrow bubble over, for it would flood her with anguish. She must be strong. Kenleigh wished that of her.

"What do you do now?"

Gizela opened her mouth to answer, then closed it. Was she presuming too much? She could not know until she said what she must. "Kenleigh wished for me to attend you upon the birth of your child, your majesty. I had understood that was your wish as well."

"Yes, but, under the circumstances, you should not feel any obligation."

"Staying busy will help."

Eleanor nodded, a smile slowly slipping along her lips as her dark eyes began to twinkle. "It is said you have a steady hand and a gentle manner during a woman's time of labor."

"You honor me with your generous words."

"I speak only what I have heard. Is it true?"

Gizela began to demur, then realized Queen Eleanor wanted her to be honest instead of gracious. "It is true, your majesty. I learned my skills at an early age and took on the role of our manor's midwife when the previous one sickened and died."

"Then I look forward to speaking to you at a more private time about this matter after you have settled into your rooms in this tower."

Accepting the words as the polite dismissal they were, Gizela curtsied again and stepped aside. To turn her back on her sovereign queen would be unthinkable. When she saw Eleanor return to talking with the ladies of her household, she was awed by the very simplicity of the scene. It could have been the household in Talbot Hall when one of her stepmothers sat with her ladies.

Gizela sent the lad to continue with his other duties. She could find her way back to Kenleigh's rooms without the page's assistance. Twilight was softening the unfinished walls of the castle when she crossed the courtyard. Night was not as long as it had been even a fortnight ago. Soon spring would bring relief from the cold and dampness.

Her smile broadened at that thought. There would be a babe within these walls soon. A royal child to continue the line of Edward and his queen. A new beginning here might be the harbinger of peace throughout England and Wales.

She should not delay in returning to tell Pomona of the queen's acceptance of her, but too many hours of sleep had left her stiff. She paused by one of the huge rocks that would be raised to form the impenetrable wall and gazed at the road leading back to Rhuddlan. She could recall nothing of the final leagues to Caernarvon.

Trusting Rhys had been foolish. He had been correct when he had said she knew nothing of him. Mayhap the pain in her head came from her bewildered brain. That would explain why she had allowed him to dose her with his herbs.

Gizela pushed herself away from the rocks when she saw specks of snow creating a pattern on her red sleeve. A winter evening was no time to be lingering in this open courtyard. Bowing her head into the strengthening breeze off the river, she hurried toward the tower.

A clump of men had gathered in the shadows to one side of the door to the tower. As she neared, she sensed they were arguing. Their bodies were stiff and their motions sharp. Hands were closed in fists, and chins jutted from angry words, as a man cursed loudly.

In shock, Gizela stared. The curse had not been in either French or English. Welsh! What were Welshmen doing within the walls of this castle? King Edward could not trust his erstwhile enemies enough to grant them freedom to enter and leave Caernarvon at will.

Scanning the inner bailey, she saw she was not the only one disturbed by the Welshmen. The sentries pacing off the hours of their watch on the wall walk, slowed as they neared the group of men who wore knee-length tunics.

Gizela hesitated. She knew of no other way to enter the tower. She could not stand in the thickening snow. She would freeze. After all, these men were surely here to negotiate their surrender to King Edward. She need not fear them.

Yet she also knew, all too well, how a beaten man could turn on those around him. When a man—or a woman—had nothing left to lose, he or she dared anything.

She took a single step. The men grew silent as they turned to watch her. Nodding in their direction, she edged toward the door.

One of the men stepped in front of her. "Lady de Montpellier, you look much the better for your rest."

In disbelief, Gizela stared at the face which she had last seen through the mist of the sleeping herbs in the bitter wine. "You! What are you doing here?"

Rhys started to reply, then paused as a lad raced up to him with a rolled parchment. The boy bobbed his head before running back toward the Eagle Tower. Without glancing at the parchment, Rhys folded it and put it within the belt of his tunic.

Something that sounded disturbingly like mirth filled his resonant voice. "Let me reassure you that I do not plot the king's downfall within his own walls."

"Do you do your plotting beyond them?"

"I do my plotting where and when it suits me to contemplate victory."

"Strong words."

"Words mean little, milady, when one fails to back them with the strength of a firm arm and a honed sword."

Gizela turned away. A firm arm and a honed sword had gained Kenleigh nothing but death in a foolish attempt to ease the hours of boredom between campaigns. *Kenleigh!* No, she would not let that grief consume her.

A finger beneath her chin tilted her face back toward the Welshman. She tugged away with a horrified cry. She did not want this man—or any other—being so bold. Rhys's tawny brows creased as his eyes narrowed, hiding the emotions she dared not read. She cared nothing about what he thought when she must not look too closely within her heart. No grief waited there, only anger that Kenleigh had proven to be as foolish as her father, who thought solely of proving he was the master of all.

"Why are you frightened of me now," he asked, "when you spoke plainly to me when we met last night?"

"When last we met you treated me with respect."

"I offer you nothing less now."

"Then do not paw me as if I were a serving wench."

His smile tightened. "It is not my habit to mistreat any woman, be she wench or a baron's lady. You mistake the ways of the English for mine."

"I suspect I have mistaken many things about you, sir." She gathered her skirts around her and pushed past the men into the tower. In the doorway, she paused only because another man blocked her way. "Is this the *herd* that you must guard?"

The men grumbled at her contemptuous words, but Rhys grinned. "You are more insightful than those who were to protect you during your journey." He glanced around the courtyard. "Or those within these walls."

"Why are you here? The king—"

"The king's men believe the Welsh are thoroughly defeated, milady. How better to enjoy their victory over us than to watch us wait upon their pleasure for the bits of power they will grant us within our own land?"

"So they give you liberty to come and go within these walls as you wish?"

His smile broadened. "You sound less trusting than your king's men who are glad to have us bring them food and provide them with workers to raise these walls."

"I have no reason to trust you."

"Wise of you, milady, although you will note we have caused no mischief."

"Yet."

"Yet," he agreed with a laugh.

"I shall not keep you from your duties, Rhys of Wales, if that is truly your name."

"I am called Rhys ap Cynan, milady." His smile was as much of a mockery as his bow. "I beg your pardon for failing to speak my full name to you during our pleasing interlude by the spring last night."

Aware of the ears eavesdropping openly on this conversation, she fought to keep from blushing. This Welshman had no more manners than his sheep.

"You have spoken your name now. I bid you good evening, sir."

"I prefer the title of chieftain," he said with another bow of his head.

She faltered as she gasped, "Chieftain? But I thought you were a . . . that is, I— "

Laughter surrounded her. Pushing past the Welshmen, she rushed along the narrow corridor leading to Kenleigh's rooms. She wished every Welshman would be consigned to hell with all due speed.

"Lady de Montpellier?"

Gizela turned only because she did not want Chieftain Rhys ap Cynan chasing her throughout the tower. *Chieftain!* How could she have been so blind? She had sensed the power he possessed, but had disregarded it. At her own peril, she realized too late.

"Yes?" she asked in her coldest tone.

"It seems it is now my turn to apologize to you, milady."

As he smiled, her heart thudded against her breast. That smile suggested the lad he had been before war had hardened him. It tempted her to lower her guard, to trust him.

"Your apology does not lessen the fact you were dishonest," she said, struggling to keep her voice serene.

He stepped closer. The brown wool of his tunic outlined the breadth of his chest, and the sleeves clung to his muscles. As she looked at his smile, it slowly faded.

"Would you have been honest among your enemies?" he asked.

"We are allies."

"The same man claims to be king of both our countries. That does not make me an ally of the English."

"You recklessly speak treason within King Edward's own castle."

He shook his head, and his flaxen hair drifted across his eyes, freeing her from their fervor long enough to release the breath she had been holding. "Not treason, milady. Only the facts as even *you*, must see them. If Edward were confident of his hold on *Cymru*, he would not have called to his side so many of his vassals, including your husband."

"Kenleigh is dead." The words burst from her before she could halt them.

"I know."

Comprehension hit her like a blow. She pressed her hand over her heart as she saw the truth in his eyes. Last night, the chieftain had known of Kenleigh's death, but had said nothing.

Her breath caught, and tears suddenly burned in her eyes. She turned away and covered her face as sobs strangled her. Dear Kenleigh! How many times had he offered her comfort when no one else had dared to gainsay Lord Talbot? The last time she had seen Kenleigh—before he had ridden away so long ago—had been in the orchard. Before he had ridden away to fulfill his liege obligations to his king and England, he had asked Father for her hand in marriage. Her father had insisted she remain in Talbot Hall, but Kenleigh had him that a match would be good for both families.

The betrothal had been signed with the marriage to take place at a date to be agreed upon when Kenleigh returned. Even though so many years had passed, Kenleigh had never forgotten. He had been a good man and a dear friend.

Leaning against the wall beside a rustic bench, she surrendered to the surge of grief. Kenleigh had saved her from surrendering to the hell within Talbot Hall by offering her the hope of eventual escape. Yet, ultimately, he had not been able to share his life with her.

"How could you let me babble on last night?" she whispered as she pushed away from the wall. "How could you not tell me the truth?"

He gripped her arms. When she cringed, he released her, but did not let her slip past him. "I vow I will not hurt you, milady. You need not fear me, but you must listen to me."

"Why?"

"Because what I have to say is for your own good."

"You have nothing to say that I wish to hear." She tried again to walk away.

His hand against the wall halted her. She whirled to go in the other direction and bumped into the steel of his arm. Pressing back against the wall, she slowly lowered herself to the bench behind her. He squatted in front of her so she could not escape.

"Go back to England," he whispered.

She stared at him in astonishment. This was not what she had thought he would say. She could not misconstrue the sincerity in his voice as he echoed Sheldon's command.

"Why?"

"You cannot be unaware of the danger lurking in the mountains beyond this castle. The Prince of Wales is dead, but the uprising against the English is not."

Her clasped hands tightened. "You speak with such surety."

"The truth should not be heralded quietly," he said, a suspicion of a smile playing on his lips as he repeated her own words.

"Why are you telling me this?"

He held up the finger that was still red where it had been burned. "I owe you a debt, milady. I would repay it by urging you to safeguard your life. Do not be the fool your husband proved to be."

She stood and pushed past him. He did not stop her. Clenching her hands, she stared along the empty corridor. The stones swallowed the light from the torches set on the walls, and it was so silent she could hear Rhys's slow breathing. "Yes, it was foolish of Kenleigh to waste his life—our life—simply to prove his horse was the swiftest in the race."

"Race? I'm baffled about what you speak of, milady."

She faced him. "But I thought you knew of Kenleigh's death."

"I do, but I know nothing of a race." He scowled. "Who told you such a lie?"

"Sheldon said—"

"It is a lie." He held up her hand to halt her retort. "Listen, milady, for I had the honor of meeting Kenleigh de Montpellier while he was on Edward's business."

"Honor?" She stared at him in disbelief. How many more ways could this man astound her? He did not hide his contempt for the English, but now spoke of her husband with respect.

He took her hand and placed it on his palm. She tried to pull away, but he stopped her by saying, "Look here, milady. England is as large as my hand, and

Cymru is your hand, smaller but with a will of its own."
He closed his fingers over hers. "England has swallowed my homeland, but *Cymru* does not cease to exist.
It is still within, possessing its own life, waiting for a
chance to spring forth." He opened his hand.

She drew back her hand and whispered, "But what
does this have to do with Kenleigh?"

"Lord de Montpellier was one of the few of
Edward's men who recognized that *Cymru* may be
annexed by England, but that it continues to exist." He
shook his head with regret. "Such thoughts may have
led to his death. Others who wish to gain power have
little use for those who preach moderation."

"Men who wish power such as you?"

Rhys chuckled, but his eyes became as hard as the
blade at his belt. "If you are suggesting I played a hand
in your husband's death, you are mistaken, milady. I
wished to see him gone from this land, not dead.
Mayhap you should look closer to those around you, to
those who had much to gain from Lord de
Montpellier's death."

"No!" Her voice rang through the corridor. "It was
an accident."

"Are you certain?"

Heat surged up her cheeks as she said, "I see no reason for this conversation to continue. Farewell,
Chieftain."

When he stepped forward to block her way, she
almost gasped out her dismay. He crossed his arms over
his broad chest as he looked down into her face which
displayed all of her amazement at his lack of manners.
"You cannot hide from the truth, milady."

"Nor can you speak it, it would seem. First you lie
about your name. Now you try to plant suspicion in my
mind with your tales. Mayhap all men of this country

are bards, Chieftain, but it appears you have forgotten how to sift the truth from the husks of deception. Mayhap because you are afraid to confront it."

"Afraid?" He cupped her elbows in his broad hands and pulled her to him.

She moaned, pulling away. When he caught her face between his hands, she raised her fists. His mouth captured hers as his fingers slipped up beneath her veil to draw her closer again. Shock raced through her, as hot and potent as the heart of a flame. His body was unyielding, but possessed a warmth that intensified the tremor roiling within her.

Her hands slowly settled on his arms. Her fingers uncurled to brush against the sturdy muscles beneath his wool sleeves. She gasped when he lifted his mouth from hers. His arm around her waist kept her from edging away, although she was unsure if she would. She wanted nothing right now but the mind-numbing enchantment of his kiss.

"I do not fear the truth, milady," he whispered, "for the truth is I have thought of doing this since your eyes met mine last night. As the fire hinted at the beauty I see before me now, I hungered for more than the food I had in my pouch."

Her answer vanished as his lips covered hers again. Her arms curved up around him as he leaned her back, deepening the kiss until she clutched onto his cloak.

When he abruptly released her with a terse chuckle, he put out a hand to steady her. "Now I have proven to you that I fear not the truth of such dangerous desires, milady. Do you?"

She hated how her hand trembled as she adjusted her veil, but she did not lower her eyes. "I do not fear admitting the truth that a mistake once made should not be repeated."

"A mistake?" He laughed again. "How simply you disregard the passion I felt on your lips!"

"'Twas a mistake."

"To feel it or to let me perceive it?" His mouth grew taut as he added, before she could shape an answer, "I have given you a warning, milady, to leave this land and return to England. I urge you to heed it."

"I shall heed it as I have your other tales."

He spat something under his breath, but said, "Heed it, Lady de Montpellier, or I fear you may not live long enough to regret it." Tipping his head toward her, he strode toward the door to the courtyard.

She watched him in troubled silence. He was suggesting that Sheldon—and Queen Eleanor—were deceiving her. Impossible! Rhys ap Cynan had proven himself a liar already.

She clenched her hands at her sides. Staying far from him would be wise, especially when her lips still tingled with the heat of his. She must never allow herself to be caught again in the glow of those wondrous eyes which saw through any pretense. Or someone might see how fascinated she was by a man who had warned her of danger, even though she suspected the greatest threat to her would come from Rhys ap Cynan.

4

Sheldon de Montpellier paced the small clearing. By the Lord's teeth, where was he? The message had stated the meeting was to take place exactly one hour past sunset. That time had passed, for the moon was claiming the sky, and stars glowed.

So it had come to this. He was waiting upon these witless churls when they should be grateful he even would condescend to speak with them. If he had not needed—

He tensed at the sound of a footstep on the hard earth. Slowly he drew his broadsword. Few allies were about at this hour.

"Lord de Montpellier, we are well met."

De Montpellier whirled and scowled. He had not expected ap Pembroke to bring a pair of his men with him to this meeting. Although his fingers itched to raise his sword, he wisely did not move. This alliance was not one based on trust. These Welsh were dolts if they thought they could overthrow Edward's rule of this blighted land without assistance.

"You are late," he said with a snarl.

"I had thought it wiser to wait until I had an answer for you." When ap Pembroke's smile grew more sly, de Montpellier tightened his grip on his sword. "'Twould be a waste of your precious time, milord, to come to you with no answer."

De Montpellier smiled and set the tip of his sword in the ground. "Speak the answer you were to bring to me."

"He will speak with you."

"Tonight?"

He shook his head. Even in the dim light, his derisive smile was cold. "He has things more important to him tonight than a *Sais*."

"This *Englishman* can gain him the very thing he wishes. He would be wise to set aside the wench who has intrigued him this evening and speak with me."

"'Tis no wench." His laugh was as cold as his smile. "The chieftain deals this night with matters of which you know nothing."

De Montpellier cursed, ignoring the Welshmen's chuckles. He had hoped for more than this when he had received the message to meet here. Yet this was more than he had had a fortnight ago. His plan, which was beyond this Welshman's comprehension, was unfolding exactly as he hoped. The best fortune he had had since his brother's death was meeting ap Pembroke. The Welshman's greed pleased him, for he could use it to reach his own ends.

Sliding his sword back into its engraved scabbard, de Montpellier said, "I will await word of the time and place for our next meeting. Be certain it shall be more fruitful than this one." He pushed past ap Pembroke's men to untie his horse's reins from around a tree.

"One more thing, milord."

"Speak swiftly, for I have no interest in remaining here when there is a pretty wench awaiting *me*."

The Welshman smiled. "Tell me of your brother's widow."

"What do you wish to know?" He mounted easily and looped the reins around his hand. "She will be my wife as soon as the king returns to Caernarvon and grants his permission for me to claim, by marrying my brother's widow, the lands belonging to my brother. In addition, the lands she inherited from Talbot will become mine."

Ap Pembroke spat on the ground and cursed. "Do not speak that name in the chieftain's hearing, de Montpellier, or you may find yourself without a tongue to repeat it."

"Your threats are useless as Talbot is dead. My brother's widow no longer bears his name, but I vow to you that before the year comes to an end, she will bear my son."

"Do not be so hasty, de Montpellier."

"What do you mean?"

He motioned for de Montpellier to bend closer. His whispered answer brought a broad smile to each man's face. They clasped arms to seal the silent vow before parting.

Tremaine ap Pembroke watched the *Sais* ride away into the night. A low laugh rumbled from his throat like a winter wind curling around the mountaintops. He had not guessed this would be so simple, but he had learned years ago to use what tools fate gave him. He had waited long for this opportunity, and de Montpellier would provide it—whether or not the *Sais* agreed to do so.

*　　　*　　　*

Chieftain Rhys ap Cynan's parting words ran through
Gizela's mind as she stood before her mirror and
brushed her hair. His threat had haunted her dreams,
nearly as much as the memory of his mouth on hers. He
was bold to kiss her within the king's castle, and she
had been as brazen to melt into his embrace, even as
she mourned Kenleigh's death.

Surely 'twas his death that had unsettled her enough to
forget herself in Rhys's arms. Yet that did not explain why
his voice, his face, his fingers upon her skin emerged to fill
her head. If she had as much sense as the king's fool, she
would banish him from her thoughts. It was impossible.
The uncompromising glow of his gaze was brighter than
the sun upon his golden hair. Each time she closed her
eyes, the recollection of the sturdy strength of his hands
overwhelmed her. The sweet temptation of his lips still
burned on hers, even though four days had passed since
he had held her as a willing captive in his arms.

"Milady?"

Shaking herself, she looked at Pomona, who was
taking a red gown from the cupboard at one side of the
grand bedchamber. The past four days had been a whirl
of activity while Pomona had made a grand parade of
moving their possessions to the Eagle Tower and the
rooms near the queen's apartment. Gizela smiled. If
Pomona had her way, not a single soul in all of Wales
would fail to understand the honor done to Lady de
Montpellier by being granted rooms within the sound
of a shout from the queen's chambers.

"Yes?" she asked as Pomona brought the gown to
her.

"Is something amiss, milady?"

"No. Why do you ask?"

"You were so deeply lost in thought. You did not
hear me speaking to you." Tears glistened in the old

woman's eyes. "I share your grief, milady. If you wish to release it . . . "

"I was not thinking of Kenleigh."

"Then what troubles you?"

Not what, she thought, *but whom.* She wanted to soothe the wrinkles of anxiety from Pomona's lined face, but she must not reveal the true course of her thoughts. "Fatigue, I suspect. The trip from England was far more grueling than I had guessed it would be."

"It does not help when you are roused in the middle of the night by one of her majesty's unthinking ladies."

Gizela smiled as Pomona dropped the dark-crimson dress over Gizela's head. The old woman brushed lint from the wool as Gizela smoothed the dress along her torso.

As Gizela straightened the sleeves which ended in wide bells at her elbows, Pomona buttoned the single button at her throat and murmured, "Milady, I would be willing to listen to whatever is troubling you."

Spinning away, Gizela snapped, "I said 'twas nothing!"

"As you wish, milady."

Regret swelled through Gizela as Pomona seemed to shrink before her eyes. For as long as she could remember, Pomona had been her staunchest ally in all the battles with her father. Never had she found it difficult to confide her fears to the old woman . . . until now. What use would it be to tell Pomona of how the chieftain was stalking her thoughts? Pomona would lambaste her—quite rightly—for being a simpleton to give heed to the Welshman's words.

Softly she said, "Pomona, you are right. I am simply tired because of that alarm from the queen's quarters last night." Putting her hand on Pomona's shoulder, she was startled and dismayed to discover it seemed as flimsy as bird's bones. Pomona had seemed old for as long as she could remember, but her servant was growing fragile. "Forgive me for raising my voice to you. I should be grateful for your concern."

"Fatigue causes us to say things we would not otherwise." She closed the cupboard door as she added, "How does the queen do?"

"Well." Gizela's relieved laugh shattered the disquiet surrounding them. "She was as startled by my arrival before dawn as I was to be routed from bed. Her ladies, in their zeal, had mistaken the pains which come late in a pregnancy for labor. I ordered warm cider to help the queen sleep, and persuaded her ladies not to surprise both of us like that. We need our rest now."

"You are worried about this birth, milady?"

Gizela twisted her hair into braids. "It is not wise to speak with certainty of the success of any birth, but especially not this one."

"You suspect trouble?"

"To lose any baby is a tragedy, but to lose the king's child at this time could be even worse."

Pomona whispered, "But this child is not the heir."

"Any royal child is a potential heir." She smiled and hooked her sash with the herb pouch around her waist. "Mayhap it shall be a healthy daughter, and it will be welcomed gratefully, but without concern of how its future will be tied to England's."

"You need not serve as midwife, milady. Lord de Montpellier would be far happier if you did not."

"Lord de Montpellier's happiness is not something I wish to consider."

Pomona's chuckle surprised her. "Well said, although you would be wise not to let him hear it."

"Kenleigh's brother has always been arrogant, which was tolerable when he had nothing to do with our lives.

Now—" She shook her head and sighed. "He speaks endlessly of the rewards our family can gain if I bring the king another healthy son. I did not learn to serve at a woman's side during childbirth for the rewards." She slowly raised her hand to her cheek and whispered, "Think how much easier my life would have been if I had not ignored Father's fury with my studies."

Taking Gizela's hand, Pomona folded it between her gnarled ones. "Milady, he is dead. He can hurt you no more."

"Nor you."

"He never struck me."

"Save when you tried to protect me." Gizela smiled. "You are right yet again. He can hurt us no more, and I can continue my studies."

"Your skill, milady, is a wondrous gift from God. I have seen you snatch a child from the grip of death. Queen Eleanor is fortunate to have you with her at this time."

"I pray she shares your sentiments after the birth. So many things can go wrong."

"Milady, you have a skill that was lacking when your mother was stricken with childbed fever. You have not lost a woman to a fever in more than five years."

"Yet I still have so much to learn."

A knock on the outer door halted Gizela from reaching for her cloak to toss over her shoulders. She grimaced, hoping it was not another of the queen's frantic women. This morning, she had looked forward to the chance to visit the stillroom and learn more from Hayes, who oversaw it. Another crisis would prevent that.

Pomona rushed back into the room with undue speed. "Milady, Lord de Montpellier wishes to speak with you."

Gizela smiled. He might bring tidings from beyond Caernarvon of how the king was ensuring peace.

Which Rhys will do all he can to prevent. The unbidden thought burst into her head before she could halt it. By her troth, she wished she could banish the handsome Welshman from her mind. A visit from her husband's brother might help.

"Pomona, bring something refreshing for Lord de Montpellier to enjoy while we talk," she said, as she walked out into the scantily furnished antechamber to greet Sheldon.

He was pacing with impatience, and she wondered what distressed him so deeply. The hem of his calf-length tunic snapped when he turned to stride back across the large room toward the window.

The apartment she had been given was more imposing than her rooms within Talbot Hall. When the walls were decorated with tapestries and more furniture was brought, nothing would rival the splendor of King Edward's newest castle. Save for Sheldon, the outer rooms were empty, because she had only Pomona with her here. There was none of the hubbub she had been accustomed to at home, and she missed the easy sound of conversations among the ladies of her household. It would be helpful to have a chance to speak with Sheldon and come to know Kenleigh's brother better.

He halted midstep as he took note of her. She returned his stare, wishing she could see more of Kenleigh in this man. Although they were of a height, Sheldon bore a greater resemblance to his mother, who had been his father's second wife. Kenleigh had always offered her a smile, no matter how grim the circumstances around them. She tried to recall if she had seen Sheldon smile once since her arrival in Caernarvon.

"Good day, Sheldon," Gizela said over the sound of the door closing behind Pomona. "I am honored you have come directly to see me upon your return."

"Return?" His eyes narrowed. "How did you know I was just returned?"

She laughed lightly. "I am the daughter of a man who often went upon forays across his lands and into Wales. I recognize the scent left upon wool by the sweat of a hard-ridden horse."

"I wish to speak with you."

"You are welcome, Sheldon." She gestured toward the bench before the hearth.

He unbuttoned his heavy cloak and shrugged it off. He tossed it onto a bench by the window. As he walked toward her, she noted his shoes were damp with mud. She wondered where he had been, for the day had dawned cool and dry.

When he held out his hands to the fire, she sat on the bench on the far side of the hearth. He cleared his throat, then faced her, the tips of his pointed shoes rearranging the rushes.

"You do my brother's memory honor, I see," he said gruffly.

She touched the fabric over her chin. Not even to Pomona would she admit how much she hated how the cloth threatened to constrict every word she spoke. "Did you think I would fail to do Kenleigh honor?"

"I had hoped not."

"When we know each other better, Sheldon, you will come to see how high my respect was for your brother."

He frowned. "We are not strangers, Gizela."

"No." She smiled, hoping it appeared more sincere than it felt upon her lips. "If we had guessed we would meet at this juncture, mayhap we would have been more interested in knowing each other better."

"I find that unlikely."

Gizela bit back her retort. If Sheldon was going to be petulant, there was little sense in continuing this conversation. Mayhap he was as exhausted as she was. With a sigh, she said, "Then we shall have a chance to know each other better now. I have been very fond of Kenleigh since I was young, and you are the only other family he has remaining."

"Only *other* family?" he snapped back. "If he had consulted me, you would not be part of this family."

"You did not approve of my betrothal to Kenleigh?" When his lips tightened, she knew he had revealed something he had not intended. "For what reason, Sheldon?"

"At that time, it was still possible your father might have a son to usurp your inheritance."

She toyed with the embroidery at the hem of her sleeve. "Kenleigh did not offer me marriage to gain my father's lands. He was willing to risk that I would come to him with the slightest of dowries." Lifting her chin, she added, "That, however, does not explain why you should feel the same way now. Upon Father's death, all he owned, save his title, is mine."

"That I know."

"Yet you still do not approve of me?"

Sheldon's smile curled one corner of his lip. "You are mistaking my words. Do not let your womanly fears fluster you."

"I can assure you that— "

He did not let her finish. "I did not come here to speak of the past, Gizela, but of the future. Of your future."

"I know you wish me to return to England, but I must stay here with the queen."

"Yes, I see that now."

"You do?" She would not have been more surprised if he had said Rhys ap Cynan had vowed his loyalty to King Edward.

She stiffened as Rhys's smile burst from her memory. If Sheldon were to learn of how Rhys had held her, he would be even more furious with her than he was now. As Lord de Montpellier, his loyalty to the king must never be questioned, especially by having a Welsh chieftain kissing his brother's widow.

When Sheldon answered, she guessed he had taken no note of her disquiet. "I must think of the future for my brother's legacy. De Montpellier Court must not fall into ruin."

"I assure you, Sheldon, I will not allow that to happen."

"You are a woman," he returned with a superior chuckle. "Even though no one would question your fervor, it is doubtful you know how to oversee a manor. I see but one obvious solution."

"Which is?"

"You shall marry me."

She laughed and shook her head. "Sheldon, I think you mistake my gracious welcome to you as my husband's brother for more. I do not know you." *And what I know of you I dislike.* She was tempted to repeat the words aloud, but refrained. It would infuriate him more. She dared not do that. His hands clenched at his sides until his knuckles bleached like bare bones.

"But I am Kenleigh's brother. I am Lord de Montpellier."

"No one would argue that."

"A titled man with few acres of ground to his name cannot do his duty to his king." He snarled a curse, then stamped toward the window.

Slowly she rose and walked around the bench, putting it between her and his anger. She was not sure it would explode, but she would take no chances. Gripping the smooth wood of the bench's back, she said, "Worry not on that issue. The king shall receive his taxes for his army without delay from both de Montpellier Court and Talbot Hall. I may be a woman, Sheldon, but I recognize the importance of such matters."

"And the matter of someone to hold those lands after you?"

"By my troth, Sheldon! My husband's bones may not yet lie in the earth." She stared at him, wishing he would relent, even a bit. "How can you ask me to remarry when I have not had time to mourn?"

"You are a rich woman. There will be many eager to turn your head with their flowery words and false promises."

"Then mayhap I should thank you for not lathering me with such."

His mouth twisted at her sarcasm. "I shall not see my father's lands in the hands of another man."

"Your concern is heartwarming, milord." Gizela took a steadying breath, then said, "I bid you good day, milord."

"I shall not be dismissed like a common page."

"Nor did I ask you to be dismissed. I asked for courtesy, milord. I have no interest in saying anything more on this uncomfortable, mis-timed subject."

"Nor do I!" He grasped her arms and tugged her against him. When a cry of pain burst from her lips, he silenced her with his mouth over hers.

Another cry filled the room, and she escaped his mouth to turn and see Pomona standing in the open door, a tray in her quaking hands. Sheldon snarled a curse under his breath, then ordered Pomona from the room.

Gizela pushed herself out of his arms. "You overstep yourself, milord, by commanding my servants."

"I wish to speak with you alone."

"I have nothing further to say to you. I shall not marry you."

He laughed. "But you shall when the king orders it."

"The king has done no such thing yet, so, until I must be forced to endure your company, milord, I would ask you to excuse yourself from mine."

She held her breath, but did not lower her gaze from his. When his hands tightened into fists, she steeled herself for his rage. She had not let Father beat her into submission. Nor would Sheldon de Montpellier.

Pomona edged away from the door as Sheldon stormed out. She set the tray on the table and winced when the door slammed. "Milady, I came back as quickly as I could. If I had had any idea Lord de Montpellier might— "

"Say no more, but hear my vow, Pomona. I shall never marry that man willingly."

"Marry a man who would say such things to you?" Pomona crossed herself and uttered a frantic prayer. "Oh, milady, do not speak of such things even in jest. Giving voice to them could bring such horrible events to pass."

"'Tis no jest." She continued to stare at the door as she whispered, "For I shall marry my husband's brother only if that is the king's will."

5

The scents of roasting meat followed Gizela as she passed the kitchen and went through the stone arch opening into the stillroom. She left the sunshine behind for the shadowed room that was cluttered with the myriad aromas of ground herbs. A single table was set in front of a smoke-stained hearth, and a pair of stools waited like patient attendants upon the bowls and buckets and stacks of herbs gathered on the table.

Over all this disarray, Hayes ruled. He was a hulking mountain of a man, who looked better suited to wrestling a bear than grinding herbs into powders. Gray hair dropped into his eyes and edged the wrinkled map of his craggy face. Scars crisscrossed his cheeks, and he walked with one twisted leg. Although she was curious, she did not ask him which of King Edward's battles had changed him from warrior to healer.

"Good afternoon, milady," he blared with his trumpet-like voice. "Why you be skulking around the stillroom when you should be enjoying the outdoors?"

She sat on one of the high, three-legged stools and smiled. "For the same reason any apprentice comes to his master. A hunger for knowledge should outweigh any other yearnings, even the yearning to savor the day's warmth."

"Never thought you would be lying to your friend Hayes," he mumbled as he pounded the leaves in the bowl.

She winced. He was too insightful, and she must hope he could not guess the cause of her distress. Keeping her voice serene, she rubbed her clammy palms on her skirt. "I was being honest when I told you I enjoy learning from you."

"Aye."

"Hayes," she asked in frustration, "how can I convince you I speak the truth?"

The pestle clattered against the bowl as he lowered himself to the other stool. He stared at the crushed leaves and took a deep breath of the minty scent. "Mayhap you be honest with old Hayes, but mayhap, not to yourself."

"I do want to learn from you!"

"Aye, that I know." A gentle smile pulled at his life-worn features. "If you not be of noble birth, gladly I would be taking you to apprentice. But this knowledge of healing is not for a lady to know. Why do you come here when Lord de Montpellier has forbidden it?"

Gizela took a deep breath as she stood. "You know much of what happens behind closed doors, Hayes."

"Nothing is secret within these walls." He ground the mortar into the bowl again. "'Twas not milord's plan to keep it a secret, I would venture, when he speaks of it loudly to any who would listen."

"Even you?"

He nodded.

"Then why have you not been honest with me?" she asked. She could easily imagine Sheldon battering this old man with harsh words. "Did he threaten you?"

His laugh startled her. "Milady, no one threatens old Hayes, for they fear what I know." He raised the mortar. "'Tis more than the knowledge of plants I know, for many dark hearts surround their majesties."

"I know that well." Her voice was taut, and she wished she could add some lightness to it. By her troth, she had hoped to put treachery behind her when she left her father's grave.

"Milady?" Raising her gaze, she met the sorrow in Hayes's faded eyes. "Milady, I did not mean to hurt you."

"You did not. Nor shall I see you hurt because you are my teacher. Lord de Montpellier does not guide my life, for he is but my brother-in-law."

"For now."

Gizela nodded. Surely Sheldon had spoken of his petition to wed her. No one would be surprised when he was granted the privilege. The Talbot lands combined with the lands Kenleigh had possessed, would make her husband one of the most powerful lords in western England. King Edward would guarantee Sheldon's loyalty by giving him her and the lands she held.

"You worry too much, my friend," she said with a smile. "Nothing shall happen until the queen's child is born."

"Mayhap . . ."

Gizela frowned when his voice faded into a fierce scowl. He stared past her, then slowly came to his feet as he reached for the sharp knife on the table. She turned, her eyes widening as she recognized the shadow in the door.

The glow of the bright sunshine gilded Chieftain Rhys ap Cynan's hair, drawing her eyes to his shoulders that nearly filled the door. His tunic was the green of a thick pine forest, and the hose following the lines of his muscular legs were the color of freshly-turned earth. Buckskin boots that reached nearly to his knees bore no decoration. He could have been created from the mountains rising beyond Caernarvon.

"What do *you* want?" Hayes growled.

Rhys smiled coolly. "I was told I might find Lady de Montpellier here, and I see I was told rightly." He bowed his head toward her. "Milady."

"Chieftain," she replied in the same polite tone. When she heard Hayes grumble, she hurried to add, "Mayhap we should speak outside so we do not disturb the work here."

Rhys stepped back to let her precede him. She was careful not to let even the trim on her sleeves brush him as she passed. The sunshine did nothing to warm the chill of disquiet within her while they walked along the curtain wall connecting two towers in silence.

"Ysolde is the healer among my clan, for we do not turn our backs on the skills possessed by our women," he said quietly. His deep voice rumbled through her like the sea upon the shore. "She was intrigued by my description of the herbs you used to take the fire from my scorched finger." He drew out a small pouch. "She asks if you might share your knowledge with her. In return, she offers you these plants from higher in the mountains."

Gizela opened the pouch at her waist and drew out a packet. "Take this to her. It is little more than ground lavender. The oils are better, but they do not travel well."

"The powders traveled well at at your waist."

Her breath burned within her as his gaze threatened to consume her in its heat. With every word, he made her aware of how close they stood. Even though it was no nearer than she would have stood beside anyone else, the warmth in his eyes made every conversation too personal.

"It is a convenient way to carry my herbs in case of the need for them," she replied, glad her voice was calmer than the beat of her heart.

Rhys drew a packet out of the pouch he held and opened it to reveal a brown powder. "Ysolde was most anxious for you to be familiar with this one."

"What is it?"

He dipped his finger in the powder. "A sleeping potion. Taste it."

She reached for the packet.

With a low laugh, he said, "Taste it, milady."

"If you would allow me—"

"Allow *me*." He held his finger out to her.

She stared at it. The very idea of such an intimate action unsettled her more than she had expected. When he placed his finger on her bottom lip and brushed it gently, she took a step away.

His eyes crinkled with amusement. "Lick it from your lip, milady. Mayhap you prefer the flavor of your flesh to mine, although I would not admit to such a falsehood. I found your lips much to my taste."

Gizela wiped her mouth clean. "If you are finished with your antics, I would gladly take the herbs."

He chuckled and, closing the pouch, offered it to her. Then he ran his finger along the linen of the wimple edging her face. His voice dropped into ebony velvet, caressing her ears as his fingertip caressed her cheek. "Edward has demanded the presence of all leaders of *Cymru* at Rhuddlan. Tell me what knowledge you have of this."

"What does that have to do with me? I serve within the queen's household, not the king's."

His hand curved along her face as he brought her mouth toward his. She should push him away, should tell him to remember his place within this castle, should walk away without looking back. Edging to the side, she bumped into the wall. She winced and rubbed her sore elbow, but halted when the fire of his eyes followed her motion. She would not let him frighten her.

"I thank you for this gift, Chieftain," she whispered. "Please pass my thanks to Ysolde."

"Milady—"

"I bid you good day, Chieftain." She convinced her leaden feet to move.

He stepped in front of her. "You have not yet answered my question."

"Because I cannot."

"I find that most odd. You are privy to the queen's most private chambers as few but the king can claim to be. Yet you wish me to believe you have heard nothing which would suggest the cause of this summoning to Rhuddlan."

"I have told you. I serve as her majesty's midwife, not as a counselor to *his* majesty." She gave him a cold smile. "Mayhap your curiosity would be satisfied if you posed that question to one of the king's trusted men."

"Such as your husband's brother?"

"Sheldon?" She shrugged, hiding her distaste at the mention of his name. "Mayhap he would know. Shall I have a message sent to him that you wish to speak with him? It might take a while to reach him, for I know not where he is within these walls."

Rhys leaned his hand against the wall not far from her head. "I care little about his present location. What I wish to know is the reason for this command to appear halfway across the country before dawn tomorrow."

"I could tell you a lie, for I do not know the truth."

"A lie? From you?" His frown became a grin. When her eyes widened at the abrupt change, he laughed. "My dear Lady de Montpellier, you have few qualifications to be a liar."

Gizela hated his condescending tone, which brought Sheldon to mind. "I should have guessed you would be well acquainted with the measure for what makes a good liar."

"A lesson every child of this land learns early."

"To lie?" She laughed sharply. "I compliment you on the fine education you give your children, Chieftain."

His fingers curled along her face, drawing her closer again, as he murmured, "We do not teach them to lie, milady, but one of the lessons taught in the Triads is what is needed by a liar: An excellent memory, a bold face, and an idiot to listen to the tale." He chuckled softly, his warm breath touching her face as beguilingly as his fingers. "I grant you the first, milady, but you have neither of the other two."

"No? Not even the last?"

He smiled. "Mayhap you are right. I am an idiot to stand here with you like this and content myself with only this caress."

She opened her mouth to answer, but suddenly he put his hands on her shoulders and claimed her mouth. She softened into his embrace as he drew her to her feet. His hard chest pressed against her, tempting her to breathe in tempo with him. When his tongue boldly grazed her lips, they parted with a sigh of indescribable delight. Her fingers clenched on his arms as he delved deep into her mouth, letting no pleasure elude him. With his cape swirling about them in the breeze off the river, she was enveloped by the craving of his fingers slipping along her back.

He whispered something when he raised his mouth. The throb of her pulse through her head masked his words.

"What did you say?" she murmured.

Smiling, he stroked her shoulder. "That I enjoy the taste of truth on your lips."

Gizela stepped out of his arms. She wobbled, for her head had grown light with the power of his kisses. "Then you should believe me, Chieftain, when I tell you I am not privy to King Edward's plans." She put up her hand, but did not touch his arm, for they had risked too much already. If someone had chanced to see her, the story could reach the queen . . . or Sheldon. She did not want to think what the consequences might be. "If you will excuse me, I should be returning to my rooms. Lord de Montpellier left a message that he wished to speak with me before the evening meal. He will not be pleased if he must wait upon me."

He frowned. "It was not my aim to focus Lord de Montpellier's well-known temper on you."

"Do not fret on my behalf." She smiled sadly. "He is eager to prove his worth as my next husband."

"Your next husband?"

"He has his brother's title. Marrying me is the sole way to obtain his brother's lands."

"And you are willing to accept this?"

"As willing as you are to accept King Edward's *invitation* to Rhuddlan."

He muttered something under his breath. When she asked him to repeat it, he smiled malevolently. "Such words are not for your ears, milady, for you would not wish me to curse either your husband's brother or your king."

"Your king as well."

"Is he?" He bowed his head to her as she stared at him in disbelief. "I wish you a pleasant day, Lady de Montpellier. Mayhap chance will avail us of an opportunity to speak again upon my return to Caernarvon."

Gizela was no longer astonished by the bewilderment surrounding her as he walked away. *This was madness.* Rhys would want more than to speak with her. His touch told her that. Yet nothing would lessen his love for this land and his determination to free it. She must remember that, for Chieftain Rhys ap Cynan would sacrifice anything—or anyone—to oust the English from Wales.

Gizela dipped her needle into the embroidery she held on her lap. Around her, conversation buzzed like a hive that had been tipped over. She had not paid attention, for her thoughts were a jumble. Mayhap she should heed Rhys's advice and return to England, albeit not for the reasons he must have for wanting her gone. To stay here and delight in his kisses when Sheldon was determined to make her his wife would be a sure route to disaster.

"If only these brutish Welsh would stay far from us," moaned one woman, her complaint catching Gizela's ear. "I know they are witless, but I wish the king would order them to stay far from us."

She bit her lip to keep herself silent. She must be cautious what she said among the queen's ladies. Glancing at the pillows where the queen usually reclined and finding them empty, she smiled. Eleanor must be following her suggestion to rest more, or mayhap she had taken note of Gizela's presence among her ladies and knew Gizela was watching her closely for any signs of fatigue.

"The king need not worry about these silly Welshmen," crowed a tall woman and laughed. "He has daunted them completely."

"Margaux," chided the gray-haired woman who sat beside the tall woman, "do not bring misfortune upon our king and his lands here in Wales with such words."

Gizela hid her smile at the admonition that could have come directly from Pomona.

"Misfortune?" Margaux laughed and shook her head so her fine veil fluttered. "Can you not see how blessed our king has been? His victories have been won all over the civilized world and here in barbaric4 Wales. Why should he be anxious about these barbarians?"

The other women joined in her laughter, save for the gray-haired woman who came over to sit next to Gizela.

"You do not find this talk amusing?" the old woman asked.

Gizela hesitated, then smiled. "I am afraid my thoughts were elsewhere."

"With the queen or your husband?"

"I am pleased the queen is resting," she answered, letting the banal serve as a shield for the truth, when she had not been thinking of either.

"Milady—" She stared past Gizela, all color draining from her face.

Gizela turned and gasped. What was Rhys doing here? He crossed the wide room as if he were the most welcome of guests. Around her, every mouth gaped open and every tongue was still. She prayed no one could hear the thunderous thud of her heart as he stopped directly in front of her. The merest bow of his head was his only greeting. She raised her gaze past the stubborn line of his jaw and tensed. As she had feared, his eyes were bright with that teasing which seemed to discern too much too easily.

"Chieftain," she said quietly, aware of the many witnesses to this unexpected confrontation. "Why are you *here* in her majesty's rooms?"

He held out his hand and smiled. "Your esteemed Lord de Montpellier has granted me the honor of escorting you to where he is awaiting you."

"Why would Sheldon ask you—?" She bit back the rest of her question when she heard whispering from the queen's ladies behind her.

"Milady?"

She looked from his challenging hand to his smile. Irritation sliced through her. How many more ways could he belittle her? She would allow no more. Quietly, she said, "I should have guessed you would be wise in this matter."

"In what matter?"

"In seeking a boon from Lord de Montpellier. Congratulations on obtaining his favor, Chieftain." She folded her embroidery over in her lap and placed it in a bag beside her on the bench.

Her smile faltered when she saw how his eyes narrowed in rage. She tensed, wondering what he might do at such a public affront. It was a lowly vassal's duty to win approval of someone with a higher rank.

"Do not confuse a boon with a simple act of courtesy, milady," he replied coldly. Again he held out his hand. "Lord de Montpellier awaits you."

She raised her fingers and put them on his palm. As his slowly closed over them, she nearly snatched them away. She was trapped by protocol and a longing she should not feel for this man. When he drew her to her feet, she realized how close they stood. A single step would bring her against the wall of his chest.

Not a sound reached her ears as he raised her hand to his lips in what should have been only a simple greeting.

There was nothing simple about it, for raw passion sparked in his eyes. A tremble coursed through her every nerve when the tip of his tongue surreptitiously grazed her skin. His thumb stroked her palm as he lowered her hand and motioned with his head toward the door.

"Milady?" he asked softly. "Will you come with me?"

She could not imagine telling him anything but yes, for she wanted more of the rapture he sent swirling through her. She opened her mouth to answer, but a murmur of whispers halted her. Squaring her shoulders, she took a steadying breath. When she saw amusement in his volatile eyes, she gathered her gown close to her. Her motion would announce to all those watching that she wished to keep as much space between them as possible.

"I will not distress my late husband's brother," she said in her coolest tones, "by delaying my arrival."

The drone of voices grew louder as she walked away with Rhys. As he led her down the stairs, he laughed.

"You seem in a good humor for a man who is amid those he is sworn to hate," Gizela said.

"I am amused by how easily you subject yourself to proprieties." He paused on a landing and brought her to face him. "And I am surprised how readily you swallowed my tale of de Montpellier sending me to fetch you. I am not his dog who has been trained to bring back the prize of the hunt for him."

"Then why did you come with such lies?"

"I liked to keep my head on my shoulders, so I devised a tale that would not send the queen's ladies into panic."

"Lies?"

"They were willing to heed them."

She backed away a half-step, then halted when her heel edged off the riser. "I thought you to be on your way now to Rhuddlan."

"I came to warn you, milady. Dexter has returned from that very castle but moments ago."

"Dexter?"

"Edward's man." He twisted a strand of her hair about his finger and bent closer to whisper. "He will bring word from Edward of his favor on de Montpellier's petition to make you his bride."

She stared at him, astonished. "How do you know of this man Dexter's errand?"

"There are those who are more than willing to speak of them to me."

"You suggest treason."

"Not to me, milady, and," he whispered as he tilted her face toward his, "that is all that matters to me. Let Edward worry about his own men."

She pulled her hand out of his and rushed down the stairs. The sound of his boots on the stone warned he was following. As they reached the lower corridor, his hand cupped her elbow.

"Chieftain, you must release me," she said, not looking at him, for she knew too well the power his smile had upon her. "Lord de Montpellier will be anxious for me to join him in his audience with the king's man."

He whirled her to face him. "He will be anxious for more than that when you are his wife. Do you wish to sleep at that man's side?"

She whispered, "That should mean nothing to you."

"You are right." He was frowning. "It should mean nothing to me, but I admired your late husband far too much to watch his widow be given thoughtlessly to his brother."

"'Tis not the widow, but the widow's inheritance that Sheldon wishes."

"Then he is even more of a dolt than I had guessed." His arm swept around her waist.

Rhys was startled when she laughed icily and stepped away from him. Her voice was as cold. "Do not baffle me with pretty words when you know your heart is much the same as his. Why do you denounce him when you would do anything—even marry *your* brother's widow—to guarantee your sovereignty over the lands you love?"

"True, but I think of you, milady. You do not deserve to be only a pawn in this game between Edward and his vassals."

"And his enemies?"

He laughed at the fury in her eyes. "What would you do if I said yes? Would you scurry away like the pert squirrel you resemble?"

"Squirrel?"

"You find that insulting?"

"I certainly do not find it complimentary."

He chuckled again when she scowled at him. "Mayhap there can be nothing complimentary between us. You need not have acted among the queen's ladies as if you find me so incredibly distasteful."

"Mayhap I was not acting."

"As I told you before, milady," he said, "the skill of lying is one you shall never master. You must learn to look a man directly in the eyes when you speak your falsehoods."

She tried to pull her arm away, but he slipped his other arm around her waist and tugged her into the shadows. He pulled her to him, delighting in the softness of her. She took a deep breath to voice her outrage, but her eyes grew wide as the motion brushed her breasts enticingly against him.

He did not resist the craving ache within him. Easily he captured her lips, giving free rein to the desire which had kept him awake long into the night. Her mouth tasted of wine, but the caress of her soft skin was even more intoxicating. Faith, but he would gladly carry her to her bed—to the nearest bed—and delve into her sweet depths.

When her slender fingers swept up his arms to comb through his hair, he bent to push aside her wimple. His mouth found the curve of her throat. Her gasp, as her hands clenched his shoulders, tightened every muscle along his body. She drew his mouth back to hers, and he longed to loosen her hair and send it cascading.

He released her with a curse she would not understand. Letting himself be enchanted by this *Saesnes* endangered all he had promised himself and his clan. When he had accomplished what some said was impossible, other women would await him. He did not need to be caught within the spell of this one.

"Rhys?"

Her soft question sent quivers through him. Fiercely, he forced his longing aside. He would not be the fool Llewellyn had been, and let a *Saesnes* destroy *Cymru*.

"We keep Lord de Montpellier waiting," he said sharply.

Gizela stared at him. "We? You truly wish to see Sheldon?" Mayhap her mind was still muddled from the power of his kisses.

"No, milady. You do. He was much anxious to have his meeting with you and Dexter when I spoke with him."

"You spoke with him? Today?"

His smile was secretive. "You are without question much like a squirrel, always poking your nose into matters that do not concern you."

"How can you say this does not concern me? I can imagine no reason why you and Sheldon should be—"

He gripped her elbows tightly. "Be wary of what accusations you make, milady, for the wrong word in the wrong ear can cost a man his head."

"Be honest with me!" How could he hold her with such desire, then twist her words to throw back into her face?

"I have been honest when I tell you that I am certain Lord de Montpellier is seeking you even now. Do you keep him waiting? That is not the way of an Englishwoman, is it? From what I have seen, your men expect you to be as finely trained as their coursing hounds or steeds."

"That is *your* impression. As Lady de Montpellier, I am a vassal of King Edward. The men of my lands are the king's upon his call. It is my duty and my honor to obey the law. Is it different here? Mayhap the women of this land follow as few rules as their men."

He did not give her the courtesy of stepping aside as he said, "Our women are far freer to seek their own lives than you, for you are nothing save chattel. Once a girl of *Cymru* reaches the age of twelve, she can decide if she wishes to marry: If she does, and her husband is found unfaithful, she can fine him ten shillings. The cost of a second offense is more. If he strays a third time, she can leave him legally. Why should we embrace the hypocrisy of English law where men have one set of rules and women another?"

"If Sheldon waits—"

He nodded to her. "I would not delay you further with my tales of this land." Taking her hand, he folded it between his. "Think of me, milady, while I am far from here. I would that this was good-bye, for you should return to England."

"You know I cannot. The queen needs me."

"Alive."

She gathered her skirts and rushed back up the stairs. She would not listen to more of his dark threats. Yet, even as she fled, she could not escape the truth.

Sincerity glowed in his eyes when he urged her to return home. His honesty must come from his fear for her. For what other reason would he speak so plainly to her? He believed the insurrection was inevitable, and, when it came, death would be a storm wind over the land, laying low all it touched.

Gizela still shivered with fear as she walked down the corridor to her chambers. When Pomona came to her, the old woman's face long with trepidation, Gizela tried to smile. She realized how horribly she had failed when Pomona whispered, "He is in your rooms, milady."

"Lord de Montpellier?"

"Yes, he and another."

Gizela opened the door and entered her rooms. With Pomona close behind her, she nodded to Sheldon, then turned to the other man who was sitting on the bench by the hearth.

He had no semblance of a warrior. Dressed in the simple robes of a monk, he could have been one save for the gold sparkling on his fingers. His lips were as thin as the hair across his balding skull, but his stomach strained his robes.

"Lady de Montpellier?" he asked in a surprisingly high-pitched voice. When she nodded, he said, "You may call me Dexter. I serve as his majesty King Edward's voice when he is involved in more important matters." He looked down his pug nose at her. "I have a message from his majesty King Edward for you, Lady de Montpellier."

"I thank you for traveling these long miles to bring me word from his majesty."

"First of all, he expresses his pleasure you are here to ease his beloved consort on the birth of his child."

"It is my greatest honor and pleasure." She could not resist glancing at Sheldon who was bouncing something from one hand to the other as if this meeting was of little import. Only the straight line of his mouth revealed his rage, for his face was otherwise blank of emotion.

Dexter nodded in Sheldon's direction, but did not speak to him. Gizela saw Sheldon tense, and she guessed he had taken offense at the motion, although she had no idea why.

"I offer you both my sympathies on the late Lord de Montpellier's unfortunate death," Dexter said with a bored sigh. "It was a complication the king did not need at this juncture when many of the Welsh chieftains have failed to pledge their fealty to him."

"I am certain it was not Kenleigh's intention to create more problems for the king," Gizela replied as she sat and clenched her hands in her lap. How dare this man speak of Kenleigh as if he had no more import than the day's weather!

Dexter stared at her as if he had not seen her before. His eyes became slits, and the boredom left his voice. "I tend to believe you are correct, milady. The late Lord de Montpellier was ever solicitous of the king's feelings on any matter."

Sheldon sat beside her. He continued to flip the item in his hands between them. Her breath caught. It was a simple gold band. A wedding band. He had come to this meeting prepared to wed her as soon as King Edward's edict was read. She would not marry Sheldon like this! With a silent sigh, she stared at the rushes twisted together on the floor. The choice of whom she would marry and when, was no longer hers.

Dexter opened a rolled parchment and began to read aloud. When Gizela managed to concentrate on what he was saying, she realized he was listing what she had come to possess when both Kenleigh and her father had died within weeks of each other. His voice droned as he described the boundaries of the lands beyond Offa's Dyke.

When Sheldon interrupted, she was astonished. "We are well aware of the possessions and obligations of Lady de Montpellier. What we wish to know is King Edward's pleasure on her marriage to me."

Dexter let the scroll roll shut with a snap. "Such a marriage would highly displease his majesty."

"What?" Sheldon surged to his feet. "I am her husband's brother. Who better than I to oversee the lands she holds?"

"The king feels he would be the best choice at this point." Dexter bent his head toward Gizela who could only stare at him in amazement. "Lady de Montpellier is so recently widowed, and our benevolent sovereign wishes no one to intrude on her time of mourning."

Sheldon swore viciously. "He ordered Lady Hoodson remarried before her husband's corpse was in the earth."

"True." Dexter stood and pointed to the rolled scroll. "Milady, I am pleased to convey to you that his majesty wishes to oversee your lands himself during this time of unrest. As close as they border Wales, he wishes there to be no questions about the iron hand holding them. Your father's reputation in this land may bring reprisals upon your manor without King Edward's name to guard it."

"I am honored," she murmured.

Dexter patted his full stomach. "Then I leave you to contemplate your good fortune while I enjoy the repast I smelled on my way into the tower."

The door had not closed upon Dexter before Sheldon shouted, *"You did this!"* He pointed at Gizela, his lips twisting with rage. "You had the queen intercede on your behalf."

"I would not speak to the queen of this when she is so close to birthing her child."

"How else do you explain Edward's peculiar decision?"

"'Tis simple. Look around you. Think of the gold it must take to build these castles. Edward needs the income from de Montpellier and Talbot's fiefs to finance his grip on Wales."

He caught her hand. His thumb pressed painfully into her wrist, and he smiled. "Enjoy it while you can, Gizela, for you shall not hold for long." He dug his finger more deeply into her. "Think of who is *your* heir."

His laughter remained as he strode out of the room to leave her staring after him, clutching her aching arm, and wondering how he would try to slay her.

6

Gizela *waved her hands* in the air, drying in the crisp breeze off the water. Wiggling her fingers, she winced. She had spent all morning pounding seeds into powder and was fearful her hands would end up as gnarled as an old crone's.

Music tickled her ears, and she paused, straining to discover where it came from and what it was. She had never heard its like, for it was delicate and assertive at the same time. Strings plucked by strong fingers sent the notes soaring.

Following the sound around a pile of stone, she stared at Rhys who was sitting on the lowest one. His broadsword remained at his side, but on his lap was the source of the music. She had never imagined a warrior could create such ethereal music which should have belonged to the fairy folk.

"What is it?" she whispered.

He looked up and smiled. "'Tis but a small *crwth*."

She laughed. "A what?"

"A small harp." He plucked one of the strings.

A note, as sweet as the first breath of spring, leaped forth. "Try it, if you wish."

She ran her finger along the smooth wood which had been polished by many hands before hers. "Have you been playing for many years?"

"That is as silly a question as if I asked you if you breathed from the moment of your birth. Music is as much a part of us as breathing."

"Will you play something for me?"

He shook his head. "Not within these walls. The music of *Cymru* can be only a dirge here."

"That lovely melody was a dirge?"

"Of lost love which will never be found." His smile returned. "There is a melody I know that is best sung near the water. Come and sit by the shore. I shall play it for you."

"Rhys, I do not think that would be wise."

"What frightens you?" He stood and placed the harp beneath his cloak. "Certainly not de Montpellier."

"Why not Sheldon? He would be glad to see me dead."

"Really? I had thought he would not dare hurt you while you enjoy Edward's favor."

She clasped her hands behind her back. "That is the very reason he wishes to rid himself of me. Edward decided—"

"To be your guardian himself." Motioning toward the gate, he said, "Do not look so shocked, milady. The word of Edward's decision was known throughout this island within seconds of Dexter's announcement. Come, milady, and allow me to teach you more about this land you soon shall be leaving." His smile became mischievous. "Think of the tales you shall be able to share with your household of the day you were serenaded along the Welsh strand."

"Rhys—"

Again he interrupted. "Let us enjoy the peace of this day while we may."

Suddenly Gizela wanted nothing but to escape from the intrigues within Caernarvon. "Yes," she said as she put her hand on his. "I would enjoy hearing this song and enjoy the peace while we may."

The last note of the song drifted into the sea, but Gizela did not open her eyes. She had not understood a single word Rhys had sung, but the sound of his voice had been as strong and rich as the waves upon the shore.

"There is no more," he said quietly.

She opened her eyes to see his smile. It was as warm as the sunshine on the water. "How beautiful," she whispered.

"Exactly what I was thinking." He brushed the corner of her veil back over her shoulder. "You are beautiful, milady."

"That was not what I was speaking of."

"I know, but I can speak of your beauty and that of the song, too." He played the harp again and sent notes rising into the sky. "That was my favorite, for it speaks of the heart of the mountains."

Her eyes widened. "That lyrical song was of those dark mountains?"

"Look away from the castle, milady. Look rather to the mountains, and see the true beauty of *Cymru*." He stood and rested one foot on the boulder where she sat. Pointing to the peaks rising above the shore, he whispered, "There is the heart of my land. The heart of my home. Such beauty should never be tamed by men who carve rocks from the hillsides to build false mountains here upon the shore."

"Yet this land has always been fortified in some way."

He smiled. "Who is teaching you the lore of my land?"

"You speak of it constantly."

"Incessantly, I fear."

"I am afraid you are right." She laughed, delighted with his teasing.

"This land is as much a part of me as my arm or my leg." He sliced his hand across his thigh. "If I were to cut this off, would it not give me pain? Would I not ache for its return to me and wish for the time when it was mine?"

As she gazed up at him, never had she wanted to touch anything as much as she yearned to caress the curve of his cheek. Roughened by the wind and bronzed by hours in the sun, it urged her to succumb to the temptation she should not feel. Many secrets were hidden within his heart, but of one thing she was certain. He wished to see all the English gone from Wales. That made him her king's enemy—and hers.

She knew that. She knew it with every ounce of her being, but she could not halt her hand from rising to his face. As he gazed down into her eyes, she stood and took a step toward him. He might be seeking the deepest secrets of her soul as if he truly were the devil's scion, as she had heard whispered. Could he know she was frightened to be alone with him like this, for he dared her to acquiesce to her yearning to be in his arms?

Fire burned along her fingertips as she brushed his cheek. An answering flare seared his blue-hot eyes, but he did not raise his arms to enfold her to him.

Stepping back, she lowered her eyes. Mayhap she had mistaken his passion for her own. She edged past the rocks toward the horses.

"I should return to Caernarvon," she whispered, not able to meet his gaze. "I need to be nearby if the queen should send for me."

As she reached for the reins, he pulled her back. His fingers tilted her face up toward his, and her arms encircled his broad shoulders. She silenced the warnings in her mind as his mouth lowered toward hers. With her breath tight in her chest, she awaited the dangerous pleasure that had filled her dreams.

Slowly he drew her to him. At the moment her breasts touched his firm chest, all thoughts of what was right or wrong vanished. His mouth caressed hers so lightly she wanted to cry out her longing.

The tip of his tongue tasted her lips, outlining them with a moist fire her rapid breath could not cool. Eagerly he explored her face and left her skin scintillating. Her hands clenched on the wool of his over-tunic as his mouth sought the heat in her pulse beating fiercely along her neck.

Whispering his name, she brought his mouth back to hers. This time, he claimed it forcefully. His arms tightened around her until every soft angle fit against his unyielding body. As his lips caressed her, she stroked the hard sinews along his back.

She gasped as his tongue moved between her lips. Her knees wobbled beneath her, and she clutched his tunic as he bent to taste her ear.

He laughed softly, his breath warming her face. He lifted her into his arms, and she stared up at him, her eyes diffused with craving.

The soft rustle of grass came up to meet her as he placed her on the ground. He held her to the earth with his mouth over hers. When he raised his lips, she gazed up at him. The golden warmth of his hair fell forward to brush her face like satin.

"Once when the mountains were young," he whispered, "Rhiannon, the most beautiful woman ever seen, was created from the flowers growing out of this earth.

Her only duty in life was to bring pleasure to the man who loved her. She was of legends, but you, Gizela, may be her resurrection." He rose to one knee and held out his hand. "Come, sweet one, and let us find a hidden bower where we can know the pleasure Pwyll found in Rhiannon's arms."

She pushed herself up and sighed. "So narrow is the gap between your loyalty to King Edward and your belief in the old ways of this land," she whispered. "Who holds your heart?"

"That need not concern you."

"No?" She stroked the grass broken beneath them. "You ask me to open myself to you, but you keep too much of yourself from me."

"I do not speak of war here, only of sweet pleasure." He brushed his lips against her neck, and she shivered. "Do not deny us what you wish for as much as I."

She stood and looked down at him. "I cannot give only part of myself to a man. If you wish to betray me as you shall King Edward—"

"Speak not his name here."

"I must, Rhys, for denying the truth is foolish. It will only bring us anguish, and I shall suffer that no more." She wrapped her arms around herself and walked toward the beach.

Rising, Rhys followed her. He admired the stern lines of her face and the strength in her gaze as she met his. Yet her cheeks were devoid of color and despair filled her eyes.

Staring out at the water, she said, "It is so difficult to believe that across this sea there is another island with people living and dying while we give scant thought to their existence. I wonder if they ever pause to consider the dilemmas we face here."

"What dilemmas?"

She faced him, her fingers locked together in front of her. With her gown whipped about her by the wind, he could view the curves he wished to explore further. She was as beautiful as Rhiannon, and, just as dangerous to those who chased her fruitlessly. He should learn from what Pwyll had suffered. Obtaining perfection was costly.

"If I could," she whispered, bringing his gaze back to her face, "I would spend every hour of my days learning from Hayes, so I might bring surcease of pain to all those who suffer."

"There are some pains you cannot heal."

"Like yours of losing this land to Edward?" Gizela asked, watching his eyes widen at her question.

"Some pains are eased by forgetfulness."

"Can you ever forget your pain?"

"Mayhap." With a laugh, he swept his arm around her and pulled her to him.

She whispered, "Do not lie to me, Rhys. What did you tell me? A liar needs a good memory, a bold face, and a fool to believe him?"

His arm kept her so close every breath forced her against him in a forbidden caress. When his finger raised her chin so she found herself staring up into his face, she was lost in the mysterious depths of his eyes.

In a breathy tone which stroked her ears as gently as his finger touched her skin, he whispered, "You quote the Triads for me, but you have no idea what you say. Do you know what the Triads are?"

"No." Her answer was as soft as his question.

With his golden hair flying back in the wind, he could have been an eagle, soaring over this land he loved. "They teach us the laws of *Cymru* that are older than the English ways. Each contains a trio of ideas."

"Such as the definition of a liar?"

"That, as well as others." He did not release her gaze as his finger roamed in a seductive path along her cheek. His other hand gently stroked her back in the same abstract design of pleasure. When his arm rose to cradle her shoulders, his low voice sent shivers coursing through her. "Another, is that there are three things which disclose the grandeur of a man's soul: What frightens him, what he tries to hide, and the very thing which he is proud to proclaim. I fear you will be hurt by the very one you profess to trust most."

"Who do I trust?"

"I speak of your king."

"Edward?"

"Why do you look so astonished, milady?" His laugh was bitter. "Has he not already gained you an enemy where you should have an ally? De Montpellier would gladly see you dead if he thought he could claim your lands."

Gizela eased out of his arms. "He is my king. I must obey him."

"Even when he uses you to gain a stronger stranglehold on this land?" His finger against her cheek brought her gaze up to meet his. "Edward cares nothing of what might happen to you as he cared nothing of what happened to your husband. If you treasure your husband's memory, leave Caernarvon."

"Why?"

"You do not belong in that horrible place."

She walked past the boulders where they had been sitting and climbed the hill to the trees. So easily his words could seduce her into believing him. She must not, for, as surely as the sun would rise out of the eastern sea on the morrow, he was her enemy. Not hers, but the king's, and more importantly—Kenleigh's.

As cool shadows enveloped her beneath the trees, Gizela glanced back at the shore. It was empty. She started to call out Rhys's name when she heard music drift to her on the wind. Turning, she looked among the trees. On a stump, his harp against his shoulder, Rhys was singing words that needed no translation, for the mournful melody spoke them clearly.

She knew she should go back to the castle. To linger here even a moment longer threatened all she must do to repay Kenleigh. Even as she told herself that, she walked toward Rhys.

He paused and set the harp back onto his knee. As he held out his hand, her breath was swift as if she had been racing mile after mile . . . or battling the desires hidden in her heart.

"Sit with me a few moments more, milady."

"That is unwise."

"Why must you be sagacious about this when you will not heed my warning?"

She knelt in the soft grasses. "Tell me why I should leave. You have given me so many nebulous reasons. Speak to me of the truth you know."

"That is something I cannot tell you. To do so would compromise vows I made from the moment of my earliest memory. You must have faith in my sincerity in speaking to you like this."

As she leaned her head against his knee, she whispered, "Why do you risk everything to tell me this? I could send to the king every word you have spoken. I would be a traitor not to."

He laughed. "Aside from the fact that you trembled when I held you in my arms, what will you tell Edward that he already does not know?"

Astonished, she gasped, "He knows of your plotting, yet he allows you entrance into his castles?"

"His men believe the Welsh spirit is broken." He tilted her face toward him. "Do you?"

"No, but I believe your hopes are futile."

"As does Edward, so you see, milady, I have no fear that anything you might say would betray me, and you need not fear playing the traitor." He drew her back up to her knees. Setting the harp on the stump, he knelt beside her. Slowly he drew back the veil covering her hair. His fingers curved around her nape as he brought her mouth to his before his whisper pierced the haze of enchantment. "Gizela, if you ever cared for your husband, return to England."

"You speak as if he were your comrade."

"Heed the warning of one who would be *your* friend this one day, if no other. Leave."

She stood and shook her head. "'Tis not that simple."

"Why not? De Montpellier's lands are where you belong, not here where—"

"Where what? Where I can serve the queen by helping her with the birth of her child?"

"Here where you are in danger!" he snapped as he came to his feet. "You are no fool. Prove it by returning to England without delay."

"I—"

Gizela whirled at the sound of hoofbeats and the sharp call of her name. Even distance could not disguise who shouted. Sheldon! If he were to discover her here with Rhys now . . .

"Do not fear, milady." He raised his voice to a shout. "You should not be so far from the castle. Do you have no sense, Lady de Montpellier? You come out here without an escort or a weapon. If—" Turning, he smiled as if he had just taken note of the horse's approach. "De Montpellier, here is your wayward lady."

"'Tis *Lord* de Montpellier now," he replied with disdain. "A title worth something, *Chieftain*." Sheldon swung down from the horse and drew his broadsword. "What are you doing with my brother's wife? Did you steal her from Caernarvon knowing the queen would be seeking her?"

"The queen?" Gizela gasped. She looked at Rhys and was astounded to see amusement in his eyes. Not the gentle mirth that glowed there when he spoke to her, but a fearsome humor that was as vicious as Sheldon's sword.

"Lord de Montpellier, what do you think I am doing with her?" he asked in a conversational tone. "I am only trying to acquaint her with her folly in wandering so far from the castle."

Gizela bit her lower lip. How easily Rhys spun this tale! Did he devise such lies when he spoke to her?

"And you chanced to meet her?"

"I was on my way to Caernarvon. She was on her way from the castle." He shrugged as he picked up his harp and put it beneath his cloak. "Mayhap you shall do better than I at persuading her to be sensible."

"What of the queen?" Gizela asked. "Is it the baby?"

Sheldon shrugged. "I know nothing of these matters, save that she is anxious to speak with you. I prefer not to be your messenger, Gizela, so prove to everyone you are not an insipid fool and remain with the queen as you have repeated endlessly is your duty."

Not giving Gizela a chance to answer, Rhys said, "I have no interest in the matters of childbirth, but I had hoped to meet *you*, de Montpellier."

"You have tidings?"

Gizela gasped, "Tidings? Of what?"

"I would prefer to discuss this far more privately," Sheldon said with a smile. "Gizela, you may take my horse back to the castle. Do not stop on your way. It would displease me deeply to discover you did not obey my orders which are for your well-being."

"But of what do you speak?"

When Rhys grasped her about the waist and swung her into the saddle, she shrieked her surprise. He laughed, then said, "Good day, milady. Hurry to the sanctuary of your castle before the night grows nigh."

She looked from one man to the other. Sheldon was grinning with what he saw as a victory over her. She turned to Rhys. He was smiling as well, but she saw the truth in his eyes. He feared for her if she remained here.

Slapping the reins against the horse's neck, she turned back toward Caernarvon. Behind her, she left what she suspected was trouble. She could not escape its tightly woven net which threatened to strangle her, for she did not know what guise it might take when it erupted to destroy all of them.

"Lady de Montpellier, I am much disturbed by what I have been hearing."

Gizela withdrew her hand from the queen's distended abdomen. The baby kicked, but was not yet ready to be born. "Of what, your majesty? I have urged you to remain serene to induce an easier labor."

"But, Lady de Montpellier, you are part of what disturbs me."

"Me?" She dampened her lips and said, "Tell me what I have done, your majesty, and I shall cease whatever it is at once. I never meant to bring you any despair."

Eleanor folded her hands in front of her. "I know you did not, but I am concerned about the time you have spent with Chieftain Rhys ap Cynan. He is too often about Caernarvon, and it seems to those who watch him most avidly, that many of his errands to my husband's castle involve you." Her lips grew tight. "This disturbs me greatly."

"It is true we have spoken often." She struggled to keep her smile in place. If she spoke the truth of what she and Rhys had enjoyed in addition to talking, the queen might banish her from her side. She did not want that to happen, for she feared the queen would need her. "Reassure yourself that our conversations deal mostly with medicinal herbs. He wishes to share with his household the knowledge I have gained of healing."

"The chieftain is not renowned for having an interest in such domestic matters."

Gizela hesitated before she answered. Someone had been spying upon Rhys . . . and upon her. Was Sheldon so determined to see her denounced that he would go to the queen with his tales? No, she could not believe even he would be so stupid. The king might become more involved in overseeing her lands if he believed she was untrustworthy.

"I know only what he has asked me, your majesty." Her smile became more sincere. "Do you recall the sleeping potion I gave you two nights ago? He brought knowledge of it to me from the healer within his household."

The queen did not smile in return. "You shall see him no more, Lady de Montpellier. Nor shall you have conversation with him. If you chance to encounter him within the castle, you shall turn and walk in another direction. I do not wish to have any of my ladies painted with the brush of a traitor's colors."

"Traitor?" Horror clamped around her throat, threatening to strangle her. What a fool she had been! Not as much as friendship should exist between those loyal to King Edward and those who would claim this land in another name. Yet, never to speak to Rhys again—? She whispered, "Your majesty, be assured that I would never betray my king."

Eleanor's stern visage softened. "That I know, but others do not know you as I do. You are kind-hearted and generous with what you have learned. You seek only to help those who suffer. You must be aware, however, there are those here within Caernarvon who would say your actions assist my husband's enemies. Therefore, Lady de Montpellier, you shall speak with him no more. Do you understand?"

She raised her chin so the sudden rush of tears would not spill onto her cheeks at this demand to prove her loyalty to her king. Never to speak to Rhys again, never to taste the delicious danger of his mouth, never to mold herself to the firm lines of his body—

"Milady?"

She knew she must falter no longer. "Yes, your majesty," she whispered. "By your command, I shall not speak to Rhys ap Cynan ever again."

7

"*'Twas you she thinks of,* milady."

Gizela raised her gaze from her knotted hands to Pomona. Her jaw ached with the tension of her clenched teeth, and every breath strained against her chest as she fought to control her fury. Shaking her head, she said, "Mayhap she thinks of me, but as a possible traitor." She surged to her feet. "Few things Father and I agreed upon, but one was loyalty to the crown. Now my fealty is being questioned."

"She wishes to protect you from others' comments."

"I never have been afraid of what others say." She laughed shortly. "Words have no sting compared to a fist. By my troth, Pomona, I would never betray my king."

"I know that, milady." She held out a mug of mulled cider, but Gizela ignored it. "Please, milady, this anger will help nothing."

She flung out her hands. "Does anyone believe I would betray my king for a sleeping potion?" Sighing, she added, "I can understand how others might be concerned by my conversations with the chieftain, but Lord de Montpellier and many of the king's other men speak with him often. Does that make them potential traitors, too? I am always careful what I say, although I suspect the chieftain knows more about the king's plans than any of us do. Why have I alone, been painted with the colors of a potential traitor?"

"Milady, milady," Pomona said with a moan. "Do not chastise yourself for what you cannot change."

Gizela sank back onto the bench and regarded her servant with a sad smile. "That is the truth, isn't it? I can rail against this injunction with all my frustration, but the truth is that I cannot change the queen's edict." She kneaded her aching head.

"So you will refrain from speaking with the chieftain?"

"I must."

Pomona rose and went to the cupboard. Opening the door, she peered inside as she said, "That aspect of the queen's ban pleases me, I must admit. It is not right you should succor those your husband deemed his enemies."

"But if I could have learned more to help a woman during—"

"Milady, you know more than any midwife I know." Pomona shoved the door closed with a crash. When Gizela stared at her, astonished at the old woman's rare show of temper, Pomona said, "Continuing on this course shall bring you only more heartache, for, no matter how much you learn, nothing you do can bring back your mother and the child who died with her. You cannot blame yourself for their deaths. Even if you had been born a son, do you think Lord Talbot would have been content with a single heir? When will you set this pain aside?"

Cold drained Gizela's cheeks. Without speaking, she rose. She heard Pomona's apology cry to her back, but she did not pause as she walked out of the room.

*   *

"You wished to speak with me, Sheldon?" Gizela asked as she closed the door from the corridor behind her. "I trust it was important if you called me to my rooms from the queen's company."

Looking up from where he was adjusting his cloak over his tunic, he smiled coldly. "I thought you might want to tell your husband's brother farewell and good luck."

"You are leaving?"

When he gave her a vicious scowl, she knew her pleasure could not be concealed. "That much should be obvious."

"When do you expect to return?"

"Do you want warning to prevent me from finding you with a lover?"

"A lover? Why would you say that? You know I have no lover."

With a laugh, he scooped up a satchel. He slipped the long handle over his shoulder. "That is hardly a surprise. Who would want a woman as unfeeling as you?"

"Certainly not a greedy man who cares only for the lands his brother did not wish him to have!"

His eyebrows lowered at her retort. Throwing the bag onto the bench, he grasped her arms. She tried to pull away, but his fingers bit into her arms.

"You will learn, Gizela, how foolish you have been to flaunt before me yourself and the fiefs you deny me!"

"I have not flaunted myself. Nor have I denied you the lands you wished. Kenleigh did that as did the king. I only abide by their wisdom in this matter. If—"

His hand rose. She put up hers to block it. With a curse, he released her.

"Belittle me again, Gizela, and you shall feel my wrath."

"I give you warning, milord. Do not raise your hand to me again, or you shall suffer the consequences."

He sneered as he picked up his satchel. "Run, if you wish, to the queen. Do you think she will care when I speak to her of the need to chastise you for your association with the Welsh? I have heard she has done much the same."

"This has nothing to do with Rhys."

"Rhys?" His eyes narrowed to slits. "Mayhap the warning from the queen came none too soon."

"You treat him like a friend. Why should I do differently?"

"He is no friend of mine."

"You seemed to welcome the chance to speak with him by the sea. Have you forgotten? 'Twas but a seven-day ago." She laughed tersely. "You seemed most anxious to be rid of me so you might speak in private with the chieftain."

"Damn you, Gizela Talbot!" He lunged forward. She tried to flee, but found herself cornered between the wall and the seat. "I should have your lying tongue cut from your mouth." He sneered, "Did you seduce my brother with your honeyed lies until you convinced him to lay down by your side and give you his name while you gave him whatever he wished?"

"Do not dirty Kenleigh's name with your false tales!" She tried to push past him, but he refused to move. "Leave me, Lord de Montpellier! Leave me, or—"

"Or what? You may hold my brother's manor lands, but you shall not rule me."

He swore viciously when she pulled his belt knife. He took a step toward her, then paused when she raised the blade.

"Begone," she whispered, holding the knife with both hands. No man would hurt her again. Kenleigh had promised his name would protect her forever, but he could not have guessed his name and legacy to her might be as dangerous as her Father's fury.

Sheldon glared at her. He backed away and grabbed his cloak and bag from the bench. Without speaking, he stormed from the chamber.

With a curse, Gizela flung the knife at the door which quivered in his wake. The knife struck the wood, then fell to the floor as the door swung open.

Pomona stared in horror as she looked at the knife and then back at Gizela. "Milady, I saw Lord de Montpellier in the corridor. He was in such a hurry, he nearly strode over the queen. What has happened?"

Sinking to the bench, Gizela clenched her hands in her lap. Never had she hated anyone as she hated Sheldon de Montpellier. She would not be his victim as she had been Father's. Let him find another way to vent his frustrations.

She ignored the frantic laughter surrounding her grieving heart. Only one living man treated her with kindness, and she was proscribed from speaking to him again.

"Milady?" whispered Pomona.

"'Tis nothing." She patted the old woman's hand.

"If you go to the queen—"

"No one needs hear of this. I will not shame Kenleigh's name."

When Pomona began to cry, Gizela sat on the bench again. She drew the old woman's face against her shoulder and let Pomona weep. As she listened to the old woman's sorrow, Gizela stared out the window. Was this the horror Rhys had warned her about? Or just its beginning?

*   *   *

Sitting on a bench by the unlit hearth in her bedchamber, Gizela listened to the call of the watch upon the wall. Starlight washed the floor clean of any color. She should rise and seek her bed, but her one try at escaping her problems in sleep had been unavailing. Leaning her head on her hand, she stared at the smoke stained stones of the hearth.

At a knock, she tensed. *Fool! Sheldon would not knock.*

"Enter." The door opened, and she dropped into a curtsy as she gasped, "Your majesty!"

The queen motioned for her to rise. "Lady de Montpellier, I would take a few moments of your time."

"You needed only to send for me," she said, pushing a chair forward for the queen.

"I recall your advice to walk as much as was comfortable." She lowered herself cautiously into the chair and sighed. "Your counsel is wise, milady, even though I must admit to a delight when I can sit quietly like this." Motioning for Gizela to sit as well, she said, "I came to say I might have been too hasty in my admonition to you last week."

"Too hasty?" Gizela had not guessed a queen might express doubt over a decision.

"I asked of you something that may be impossible within the walls of Caernarvon." She put her hands on her belly. "My husband will certainly send for all his vassals within Snowdonia when this child is born. He shall wish to show them proof of the strength of this line."

Gizela clutched her hands in her lap. Did the king have no idea, in the wake of the unsuccessful meeting at Rhuddlan, how such a command would ignite the fury smoldering within the borders of Wales? Mayhap that was his intention. If he could instigate an uprising, he could crush it and its leaders ruthlessly. Then there would be no more hints of an insurrection.

And one of the first Edward must crush was Rhys ap Cynan.

"I wish no sign of anything amiss within these walls," continued Eleanor. She pushed herself to her feet. As Gizela rose, the queen smiled. "Lady de Montpellier, although I would enjoin you from spending time beyond Caernarvon with the chieftain, you should, here in the castle, treat him as you have in the past."

"I understand, your majesty."

Eleanor put her hand on Gizela's shoulder, and her smile became as icy as the fear within Gizela's heart. "I would not wish any of my ladies to be accused of treason."

"My loyalty to the crown will never be questioned."

"I hope you are correct." She paused, then added, "And I hope I am correct in my assumption that, if the chieftain were to speak to you of matters that would be of interest to my husband, you would bring me such information with all due haste."

Gizela did not answer as the outer door closed behind the queen. The queen's comment was tantamount to an order to spy on Rhys. How could she? She wanted nothing to do with the intrigues spinning about her like a child's toy. To say nothing to Rhys was to chance betraying him into death. To reveal what Eleanor had said would mark her as a traitor and mean her death as well as Pomona's—for it would be assumed her servant had assisted her.

Rubbing her cold palms together, she paced from the hearth to the window. A sickening dread weighed in her stomach. She could not envision herself scurrying from Rhys's side—like a squirrel, to bring some seed of truth to the queen. She did not want to speak of the war that simmered so close to erupting. She wanted to be in his arms and delight in the power of passion as his mouth melded to hers.

"God's breath!" she gasped, as she slammed her fist into her pillow. To be constantly thinking of Rhys was to invite the trouble she hoped to avoid. She swept the pillow aside as frustration gnawed on her.

Her eyes widened when a small, flat piece of cured hide drifted to the floor. It must have been concealed beneath her pillow. She stared at the hide, then smiled grimly. If this was meant to betray her as a traitor, it would not have been left where she might be the first to chance upon it.

Bending, she picked it up and squinted to read what was inscribed on the material.

To Lady Gizela de Montpellier,
   You hold the life of your servant in your hand and about your throat. She is my prisoner. Her ransom is the jewelry you brought with you.
   Bring it alone to the three-sided cairn by the road edging the river before moon-set. If you fail to obey this, she will die at sunrise.

Gizela's throat closed as she fought to breathe. Pomona! The note dropped from her numb fingers. Pomona had been abducted and would be killed if she did not follow these orders.

She ran to the door and threw it open. The outer room was empty save for a single woman who was placing more wood on the fire in the hearth.

"Where is Pomona?" Gizela asked.

The woman shrugged. "I have not seen her since midafternoon, milady."

The door to the corridor opened, and two more serving lasses entered to bring fresh water from the well. They repeated what the first woman had said. None of them had seen Pomona that evening.

Gizela whirled back into her bedchamber. Again she read the note. All her jewelry for Pomona's life. Raising her left hand, she slowly drew off her wedding band. It was her only connection with Kenleigh, but her gentle husband would not wish her to sacrifice Pomona's life. If Sheldon were her husband . . . . She shuddered. He was gone from Caernarvon, and she would not wish him back, not even to help her now.

Going to the cupboard, she took out the small pouch that held the few pieces of her mother's jewelry she had kept from her father. Who could have seen her wearing these pieces and now wanted them? It could be anyone within Caernarvon's walls . . . or beyond.

Her fingers quivered as she opened the pouch. The glorious twistings of gold and gems sparkled in the dim light. How hard Pomona had worked with her to keep Father from finding these and selling them to spend for warfare against the Welsh. Now they would buy the old woman's life back from Father's enemies.

Dropping the necklaces and her wedding ring into the bag, she drew on her darkest cloak. It would hide her gown's oatmeal colored wool, making her less visible against the dark palette of the sky. She did not dare take time to change. That would draw attention to her, which she must avoid. She went to the narrow window and peered out. The moon had already passed its peak and was dropping toward the horizon. She must not delay.

Scooping up the jewel pouch, she hid it beneath the full folds of her cloak. She looked about the room one final time, for she feared she would never return. But she did not hesitate; she would gladly sacrifice her life for Pomona.

Gizela hurried through the outer chamber to the hall.

"Is it the queen?" called one of the serving lasses. "Is that why you hurry, milady?"

She did not answer. Her voice might tremble and expose too much, and she did not want to include the queen in her lies. She hurried through the corridors which were a dark maze. Only an intermittent candle marked the way.

Her fingertips on the wall guided her down the curving stairs. Avoiding the rooms on the lower floors which would be busy even at night, she skirted pools of light glowing out of doorways.

The inner bailey was empty. She glanced up at the wall where the watch marked the hours of the night. Slipping into the thickest shadows beneath the wall, she held her breath and listened. From the kitchen came the sounds of voices and laughter.

The moonlight danced on the ripples of the water as Gizela edged through a postern door and onto the narrow strip of land between the castle walls and the river. She stayed in the shadows, holding her dark cloak over her face. She held the cape tightly around her. No sign of her gown must reveal her plans. Listening, she heard the soft swish of the water and her footsteps on the soggy earth. From overhead, the voices of the men walking the watch, drifted to her. She must not let them see her. They might halt her with an arrow in her back.

At the spot where she could see the road leading along the shore on the far side of the moat, Gizela hesitated. She must climb onto the drawbridge and cross it in the sparse light. She need not fear falling, for two horsemen could ride it abreast— but she would be in plain view of the watch.

Her knees trembled like tree branches in a high wind. She forced her feet forward, but kept her pace to a relaxed stride which strained every muscle in her taut body. She hoped, even if seen by the watch, she would not be noted as anything out of the ordinary.

The crunch of dirt and pebbles beneath her slippers told Gizela she had reached the road. The moon was sinking beneath the top of the trees beyond the village. Time was growing too short. She must hurry.

Leaving the village, she ran along the road. She tightened her grip on the bag as she rounded a bend in the road. Where was the cairn? She could not recall how far it was from the castle. She scanned the night-dusted road. If she encountered thieves before she met Pomona's abductors, all could be lost.

Gizela saw the cairn beside the road and rushed to it. She put her hand to her side as a cramp stitched every breath tighter. Squinting, she tried to peer through the trees. She glanced up. The moon still hung above the mountaintops.

A hand grasped her arm. She shrieked and pulled away, spinning to face a man whose features were lost to the shadows.

"Be silent, milady," came a voice from her left. "We do not want others intruding on our business."

She held her cloak close as a short, skinny man walked from the trees. The accent on his words identified him as Welsh, but she could not see his face. Quietly, she asked, "Where is my servant?"

"She is unharmed." He laughed lowly.

Gizela stared about her as nearly a dozen other forms emerged from the darkness. She was surrounded. Although she saw no weapons, she was sure the men wore blades beneath their capes. She said nothing. Any word might mean the difference between life and death for both her and Pomona.

"You are Lady de Montpellier?" the man who had spoken before asked.

"Yes."

"Have you come alone?"

"Yes."

The man said something she could not understand. When his smile broadened and the others laughed, she bit back her fury. She would not let him goad her into doing something senseless.

"Did you bring what I asked?" he continued in English.

"Yes, and did you bring Pomona? I wish to see her."

"Do you, milady?"

"That is the agreement. The jewelry in exchange for Pomona's safe return. I wish to be certain she is safe."

"I can assure you she is." He glanced past her.

Gizela turned to follow his gaze. A hand clamped over her mouth as her arms were seized. She struggled to escape. An arm slipped around her stomach and tightened. She choked for breath. Laughter resounded in her ears. Furious, she stamped on her captor's right foot. He yelped, and his grip loosened. She tried to flee. His arm pulled her back against his hard body.

The man who had spoken, walked toward her and laughed lowly. The dim light emphasized his long nose and pointed chin. She knew she had never seen him before. "I assure you, milady, your servant is safe. Far safer than you."

She spat a curse at him, but the hand over her mouth muffled her words.

He turned and snapped what she guessed was an order. The men scattered into the trees. Fear unfurled in her stomach. Was he sending them away so he might kill her without witnesses? That made no sense. Any Welshman who was bold enough to kidnap her servant would be glad to watch an Englishwoman die.

The man leaned toward her, and she drew back. Her head struck a chest which was as hard as the rocks by the road. A gasp gushed past her lips, but only warmed the palm over her mouth. No sound escaped to betray her captors to any passing riders.

He grasped the edge of her cloak and shoved it aside. A quick tug ripped the purse from around her wrist.

"No!" she tried to cry.

Quickly he opened the bag and tipped it to pour the glistening gold into his hand. Cocking an eyebrow at her, he said, "You follow instructions very well, milady."

The hand at her mouth drew away enough so she could answer. She knew she would be silenced if she screamed. Mayhap they would kill her. Resisting the temptation to snarl at the man, she said, "I assumed you did not abduct my servant as a lark."

"But this is a lark." He smiled.

"I have done as you asked. Where is Pomona? I want to see her."

Again he looked past her. She tried to turn, but the man caught her face between his hands. When she moaned as he gripped her cheek, he said, "Do as I tell you, and you shall see her."

She pulled his hand away. "I have done as you instructed. Now you should do as you promised. Or are you a cur who cannot keep his word?"

The man snarled at her, then spat something in Welsh. Another man stepped forward. A tin cup was shoved in her direction.

She took it and sniffed. "What is in this?"

"A guarantee you will not betray us to the English."

Her eyes widened as she exclaimed, "Poison?"

The man laughed. "If we had been granted the pleasure of killing you, milady, you would have been dead long before this." He motioned with his chin. "Drink."

She hesitated. A sword was drawn with a rattle of steel. She understood. Drink it or die. If she died, Pomona would too. She would not allow Pomona to be murdered. Tipping back the cup, she drained it in a single gulp.

She heard laughter just before all sense vanished into a darkness as black as the night sky reflected in the depths of the river.

8

Gizela woke to an aching head. Even the soft sound of rushes moving beneath her as she stirred, resounded through her skull like the crash of thunder.

She forced her eyes open to the dull gray of dawn. Dawn? What had happened to the night? She drew back the blanket covering her. When her fingers brushed the front of her shift, she stiffened. Someone must have undressed her and left her to awaken in this simply-carved bed.

But where was she? She stared at stone walls. A window, as thin as an arrow slit, allowed the early light in. Overhead, the peaked roof was thatched and crisscrossed with heavy beams. Beyond the bed, a single chest was set beneath the window. Rushes covered the floor, and a shield hung on the wall beside the door.

Slowly Gizela sat. She suspected the door was barred. Her captors would not have left her here unguarded so she could escape at her first opportunity.

What a fool she had been! She had walked into what she should have known could be a trap. Touching her throbbing forehead, she sighed. At least now she had no fears of betraying Rhys or her king with any word she spoke in Caernarvon.

She looked out the window. Mountains rose with their burden of trees and rocks. She had seen the same mountains from her room in the castle, but now they were much closer. Why had she been brought here? She must discover the reason, so she could escape.

Swinging her feet to the side of the high bed, Gizela gasped. A woman was rising from a bench in a shadowed alcove. The woman wore a simple gown, and her dark braids were uncovered. The embroidery in the mantle over her shoulders contained the ruddy color of her cheeks and bright blue of her sparkling eyes. With a smile, she motioned for Gizela to rise.

"*Bore da,*" the woman said, bowing her head.

Gizela clutched the blanket to her chest. The woman spoke Welsh. That should be no surprise, but it heralded disaster for any hopes of peace in this land. If the Welsh were bold enough to abduct an English lady as well as her servant, they would dare more. What fools they were! Did they think their crimes would go unanswered? Soon more would suffer.

Gizela pulled her legs back under her as the woman stretched her hands out toward the bed. "Begone! I shall have nothing to do with Welsh outlaws."

"Milady, you need to have no fear. We are not outlaws."

Gizela gasped, "You speak English!"

"Of course." The woman's lyrical voice suggested she was singing the lightly-accented English words.

"Where are we?"

"That is not for me to tell you, milady."

"Why not?" Her head ached too much to bother with the complexities of protocol. She wondered what had been in the cup. "You have no reason not to tell me. I doubt if I shall be allowed to repeat it to anyone who does not know the truth already."

The woman glanced nervously at the door. Did she expect help, or was Gizela's captor coming to interrogate her? She turned back to Gizela and smiled, "My name is Nesta, and I am here to help you."

"I do not need help. I need answers." Her voice broke as she whispered, "Do you know where my servant Pomona might be? Is she alive?"

"Worry not." Nesta patted her hand. "Soon your questions will be answered. You are needed here, milady."

"What do you mean?"

Instead of answering, the woman smiled and asked a question of her own. "Would you care to dress?"

Gizela nodded, then looked with regret at the dull brown pattern of mud at the hem of her shift. She did not like coming before her enemies with filth coating her clothes.

Quietly she asked, "Could I have something to drink? It might ease the pain in my head."

"Your head hurts?" Nesta rushed to get a ladle of water from a bowl set on the chest. "Milady, you should have spoken of that right away. I will send for herbs to take the pain from you."

"No, no herbs." She did not want her mind muddled when she faced those who had brought her here.

When Nesta held the ladle out to her, Gizela was surprised to find the water was warm. It must have been drawn hours ago. Someone had planned this well. A shudder ached across her tense shoulders.

"Does it hurt badly?" Nesta whispered.

Anger sharpened her voice. "Your head would ache as fiercely as mine if someone had given you the choice of drinking a sleeping potion or dying."

"He would not do that."

"He? Who is this 'he'?"

Nesta glanced at the door again. "Do not ask me questions I cannot answer, milady."

"Why?"

"I am certain all your questions will be answered soon."

"But not by you?"

Nesta smiled. "Come and let me help you dress, milady." She held out a folded bundle of cloth. "I thought you would wish a clean shift."

"I would, but—"

Her laugh was as warm as summer sunshine. "No one shall intrude, milady, while you dress."

Slipping off her dirty shift, Gizela drew the other one over her head. She nearly gasped in astonishment at the softness of the material. She smoothed the linen shift along her, then looked up at Nesta as she realized it was a perfect fit.

"Turn around, milady," Nesta said quietly as she held up an unbleached undertunic. While Gizela settled it in place, Nesta laced up the back.

A gown of soft blue-green wool slid over the tunic. When Gizela reached to close the front, she discovered there were no buttons. Instead the bodice laced with simple ribbons. Was this the way all Welsh women dressed? With a pulse of shock, she realized she had never seen a Welshwoman within Caernarvon.

"I had a pouch." She ran her hands along her waist. "It was on a belt. Have you seen it?"

Nesta went to the chest and lifted off the ewer. Opening the chest, she lifted out the narrow strip of leather. "Is this it?"

"Yes." She drew the sash around her, her fingers lingering on the small pouch. When she saw her bare finger where Kenleigh's ring should be, she swallowed her fury and fear.

Nesta held up Gizela's shoes. They had been recently brushed free of dirt. Motioning for Gizela to sit on the chest, she smiled. "Now I shall do your hair for you. You shall wish to look your best when—"

"When what?"

"Come, milady," she continued, holding up a brush.

Although Gizela wanted to demand an answer to even one of her questions, she knew she would get none from Nesta. Soon Nesta's gentle strokes had the long, ebony strands flowing like a silken stream to Gizela's waist. With a few deft motions, she coaxed the hair into a single, heavy braid.

"Perfect," she announced with satisfaction.

Gizela slowly touched her hair which was smoothed back over her ears. She turned her head to look in the shield Nesta held up for her. The braid slapped her back, startling her. She had not worn her hair like this since she had been a young child.

Looking about for a wimple to cover her hair decently, Gizela froze when a sharp knock sounded at the door. When Nesta bit her lip, her smile vanishing, all the fear Gizela had tried to disregard swelled through her. Who . . . what might be beyond that door? The darkness had cloaked her captor, but now she might be coming face-to-face with a man who might have no reason to keep her alive.

When Nesta opened the door, Gizela stared at the person standing on the other side. Never had she seen such a homely man. Although no wrinkles marred his youthful skin, his nose hooked toward his pointed chin in a parody of an old man's face. Bushy brows were lowered in a malevolent expression. When he smiled, her stomach tightened in horror. Like Sheldon, he bore the scars of battle, for a puckered line was gathered beneath his left eye.

"Lady de Montpellier?" he asked.

She stiffened. She recognized that condescending tone. He must be the man who had spoken to her last night on the road. When his smile broadened, she forced herself to appear calm. She gave him a nod and said, "That you know, sir, if you keep me prisoner in your fortress."

"Not mine." He put his hand on the sword at his waist as he said, "I suspect you have many questions, milady."

"Which you shall not answer."

"No," he agreed with a superior laugh, "but I am here to escort you to the one who shall." He bowed lowly, but she realized he was mocking her when he straightened and grinned. "You are to come with me."

"I wish to see the one who ordered me brought here."

"That you may."

"May?" She shook her head. "I shall await him here."

The ugly man stepped into the room, his fingers playing with the hilt of his sword. "To meet you in this bedchamber he might find most pleasurable, milady. What would you be willing to do to save your life?"

"That, I shall not discuss with you." She kept her chin high. This pose of serenity and courage must serve her well, for she could not let any of them discover the depths of her terror.

"Discussion may not be what he wishes when he sees you here."

Nesta gasped in horror, then pressed her hands over her mouth as the man glared at her. He waved his hand, and she rushed out the door, glancing back at Gizela with distress glowing in her eyes.

"Are you pleased to frighten that gentle soul?" Gizela asked.

"She fears for you when you are not cooperative."

"I am willing to cooperate."

"Good."

"But only if you will take me without delay to the one who can explain why I am here and why I have not been allowed to see Pomona."

His brows lowered, when he said, "Come with me, milady."

"To—?"

He drew a short blade and smiled as he held it in front of her face. "Let this be your answer."

She forced any hint of terror from her face. She would not crumble before this brute, nor would she give him the satisfaction of being so defiant that he would have had an excuse to use that knife. She should save her scorn for his leader.

The narrow corridor beyond her door was murky despite the light from the morning sun flowing through a small window at the far end. When the man seized her arm, he steered her toward a staircase that dropped into a thick darkness. She wanted to ask where they led, but the glitter of cruel amusement in his eyes warned her she would not hear the truth. Praying the steps did not open into hell, she went with him.

He threw aside a door at the base of the steps. Noise cascaded over Gizela. She stared at a corridor bustling with people. They spoke with the ease of familiarity, but turned to stare in silence when the man escorted her among them. A woman stepped forward and spat at the floor in front of Gizela.

The man laughed. "Welcome among us, milady." He added something in Welsh, and a low growl raced through the corridor.

He tugged on her arm, and she did not resist. His words threatened to incite those around her to release their rage. Without a weapon, she could not fight them, and the anger in their eyes suggested they would gladly rip her apart with their bare hands.

He paused and gestured for her to precede him through an arch which was framed with rough-hewn timbers. She hesitated.

"Milady, he is waiting."

A cold shiver resonated through her like funeral bells. Her own death might await her through this arch. Closing her eyes, she uttered a silent prayer for bravery. Gizela Talbot de Montpellier would die with dignity. Without looking at the man beside her, she walked through the arch.

She stared at the room which was not too different from the great hall of Talbot Hall, save for the banner flying from the highest rafters. It fluttered in the air that swept through the windows at either end of the hall, giving life to the scarlet dragon on it. A single claw was raised as if to grasp its prey. She shivered and looked away.

Two hearths faced each other across the long room. At the far end, men sat behind a raised table. No one spoke as she walked toward them. She searched for a familiar face, but they were strangers.

Laughter rumbled to her left. Gizela faltered, then turned, sure her ears had betrayed her. In disbelief, she stared at Sheldon de Montpellier. He was sitting at one of the lower tables, a trencher of food in front of him and a woman beneath his arm.

"What are you doing here?" she whispered, for it was clear he was not a prisoner as she was.

"I could ask the same of you, milady." He stood, bent to kiss the woman soundly on the cheek, and came around a table. He carried a tankard in his hand, and she noted how uneven his steps were. He must have been drinking for hours.

"I came to find Pomona."

"She is not here."

Aware of the men watching in silence, she took a step toward him. The knife in her escort's hand halted her. Clasping her hands together, she whispered, "Pray tell me where she might be."

He took a step toward her, then wobbled. With a laugh, he dropped onto a bench. He leaned his elbow on the table. "She *might* be in hell, for all I care."

"Where you shall be if the king learns of this." She shook her head, still unable to believe what she saw right in front of her. "How could you bring dishonor upon the de Montpellier name like this?"

"I only continue the work my brother began." He laughed heartily and took a deep drink. Slapping the tankard on the table, he pushed himself back to his feet. "The work *your husband* began, Gizela."

"No," she whispered. Kenleigh had been a man of the greatest honor. He would not have betrayed his king and England in exchange for . . . . She wondered what Sheldon had traded his loyalty for and to whom. "You are lying!"

He surged toward her. When he raised his hand, another caught it.

"Here at Cadairllwyd, we treat our women with respect," said the deep voice which had filled her dreams and her nightmares.

Gizela watched, sure she must be in the midst of a nightmare at this very moment, while Rhys forced Sheldon's hand down to his side. Rhys's relentless gaze was upon her, but he said nothing more. Her eyes rose along his roughly-sculptured face to his clearwater blue ones. Amusement mixed with other emotions that she could not decipher. Too late, she realized the danger he had warned her of, would come from him.

Curse him!

Sheldon growled something under his breath and lurched back to the table.

"Thank you," she murmured.

"Lady de Montpellier," Rhys said, as serenely as if she were an eagerly awaited guest, "welcome to Cadairllwyd. You honor us with your presence. Bleddyn, I thank you for bringing Lady de Montpellier to me."

"Chieftain, you honored me by asking me to complete such a task." The homely man bowed his head and stepped back, but not before he flashed Gizela another of his satisfied smiles.

She took a deep breath, wishing that Rhys would dismiss his men who were watching this. If she asked, her request would be used only to humiliate her more when it was denied. "In the aftermath of lies and abduction, I find your greeting unamusing."

"'Twas not meant to be amusing, but to offer you welcome and let you know you are among friends."

"My friends do not kidnap me." She hesitated, then asked, "Where is Pomona?"

"Where she has always been, milady. Safe behind the walls of Caernarvon."

Gizela looked at Sheldon as he laughed again drunkenly and said, "You have the proof before you, Chieftain. She has no more wit than a pup."

"Would you like to break your fast?" Rhys asked, as if Sheldon had remained silent.

She shook her head. "It is not right to sit among my enemies and enjoy their food."

"Nor is it right for you to starve." A smile flitted through his eyes. "How can you serve your king if you are weak with hunger?"

"Must you twist everything I say?"

"Not the truth, milady." He bowed and held out his hand.

"Come. We can argue as easily while we eat."

Gizela dampened her arid lips and glanced at Sheldon who was swaying back to the woman on the other side of the table. If he spoke the truth, Kenleigh had betrayed King Edward before his brother had assumed his work. No, she would not believe Sheldon. Yet she knew so little of Kenleigh. Had the war changed him, making him eager to do anything to put an end to it?

"Thank you, Chieftain," she replied quietly.

When he smiled as she put her hand on his, she feared he would lead her to the raised table where he should rightly sit. Instead he brought her to a side table. She said nothing as he motioned for food to be brought to them. The cold glares of the servants chilled her, but she refused to lower her eyes to avoid them. Only she remained to bring pride to the de Montpellier name.

Rhys placed bread and meat on a trencher and handed it to her. Taking it, she said, "I was informed I was needed here."

He smiled as he lifted her thick braid and examined it as if he had never seen its like. "You look well rested."

"On your orders?"

"If you were asleep, you could not see the route of your travels here. It seemed the easiest way to bring you here."

"You could have tried honesty. But I would have been a fool to believe the words spoken by a man who has lied to me from our first encounter."

"Lied to you? I am not being false with you now," he said, as he let one hand settle on her shoulder. "Nor was I false with you when I urged you to return to your homeland. You did not heed me then. Will you heed me now when I tell you that you are in no danger here in Cadairllwyd?"

She longed to spit a retort back into his face, but his gentle touch unnerved her as nothing else had. As his fingers moved along her shoulder, she found herself imagining far less chaste caresses.

To hide her yearning to surrender to his touch, she whispered, "Cadairllwyd? Is that what you call this fortress?"

"In your language, it would translate as 'Old Stronghold.' That is what Cadairllwyd is, for it has been the seat of power for our clan since men first found their way into these mountains." He smiled and motioned for her to eat. "I am sure you have many questions, milady, but your food will be less palatable if not eaten hot."

Gizela considered arguing, then began to eat. She flinched each time a man stopped to speak with Rhys, for the Welsh words were a reminder of her precarious situation. The food might have been the best she had ever eaten or the worst, but she could not tell. The flavor was like sawdust in her mouth as she struggled to guess how she would escape from the results of Sheldon's perfidy. The queen needed her, so she could not delay finding her way back to Caernarvon.

When Sheldon staggered toward them, she rose. Rhys silenced the man he had been speaking with and stood as well. Flashing her another triumphant grin, Sheldon linked his arm with Rhys's. "Come, Chieftain. You wished to see what the excellent bloodlines of English stock have produced in the de Montpellier stables. Let me show you now."

"An excellent idea. Lady de—"

"Will come with us." He grasped Gizela's arm and snarled, "I consider it wise to keep an eye on my brother's wife. The lusty men of your clan might be

wooed into thinking the fire in her eyes goes deeper."
With a laugh, he added, "This is my chance to show you
my mount is stronger than that stallion you boast of."

"As you wish. First, we can take Lady de—"

"She goes with me!"

Gizela stiffened at the arrogance in Sheldon's voice.
He must be very sure of his power here to defy Rhys so
openly. She glanced at Rhys. Rage was building in his
eyes as his jaw grew taut. How could Sheldon not see?
Then she realized he was so drunk and self-satisfied, he
cared nothing for anyone else's opinions.

No hint of Rhys's anger sifted into his voice.
"Mayhap Lady de Montpellier would be interested in
seeing the beasts in the stables." He motioned toward
the door. "Our stillroom is in this direction as well.
Ysolde wishes to speak with you upon your return at the
day's end." He smiled coldly. "I failed to mention your
arrival to her before she rose in the twilight of dawn to
harvest her herbs upon the mountainside."

Sheldon jerked on her arm and stepped between them.
"My brother's wife has no interest in your stillroom."

"That is not what she led me to believe," Rhys
replied in the same calm tone.

"She is done with such work, for it brings only
shame on my family that its lady would dirty her hands
like that."

"Sheldon," Gizela interjected, "you know I have
promised to help the queen—"

"Be silent!" He faced Rhys. "Let us go to the stable."

Gizela was surprised when Rhys only nodded. She
had not thought he would suffer Sheldon's imperious
orders lightly. Murmurs of displeasure followed them
as they walked out of the great hall.

The stables, which were situated beyond the kitchen
buildings, resembled the ones within Caernarvon. She

looked past them at the walls of the fortress. Any hopes
she might have of escape were dashed. Even if she were
able to find a way through the walls, she might become
lost in the labyrinth of mountains and valleys surrounding Cadairllwyd. She had found a route to slip out of
Caernarvon. There must be a way out of this fortress.
She needed only to find it.

Rhys gave no heed to de Montpellier's boasting of
his horse's speed. He watched Gizela and smiled as she
slowly scanned the courtyard. De Montpellier had mis-
judged his brother's wife. Wit she had, and far too
much, for she was appraising the defenses of his
fortress as if she were a warrior set to storm it.

As slowly, he enjoyed appraising her. She offered an
enticing view. Her slender curves were accented by the
lacings between her breasts and the fine material of her
gown. And her hair burned with dark fire in the sunshine.

She looked at him. De Montpellier continued bab-
bling about his horse, but Rhys gave him no heed as he
stared at Gizela. He wanted to watch her eyes close
slowly as his lips descended toward hers. Then her
eager fingers would be upon him, inciting his blood to
burst into the flame he wished to quench within her.

"Gizela—"

"Here he is!" crowed de Montpellier.

Rhys did not speak the curse burning on his tongue.
He should be grateful to the *Sais* for intruding on the
treacherous temptation of his yearning for Gizela.
Mayhap he had been a fool to bring her here, but she
must not return to Caernarvon now.

"He is a fine beast, de Montpellier." Rhys rubbed the
black horse's neck.

"If you took him out of these mountains, he could
best the north wind."

"I noticed, when you rode here, he is surefooted as well." Hearing Gizela's gasp of disbelief, Rhys resisted looking at her. She should no longer be shocked at her kinsman's perfidy.

Sheldon's full chest puffed in pompous pride. "As I said, the best in my stables."

"Would you consider trading him?"

With a condescending laugh, he asked, "For what? A dozen of your poor beasts? None of them could equal him. All of them together do not have half the heart and speed of this magnificent beast."

"There are other things than horses which might interest you."

Sheldon chuckled, abruptly as sober as a priest. "And you, I trust. Shall we discuss such negotiations?"

Rhys motioned toward the stone courtyard. "Lady de Montpellier has had a very unsettling morn. She might wish some time to rest."

"Yes, I bet she would." Sheldon laughed heartily. "We would not want her to fall asleep in the middle of our conversation and disgrace her husband's family, would we, my dear Gizela?"

"Disgracing you more than you have disgraced yourself would be difficult." Gizela could not remain silent any longer as she listened to Sheldon boast of his treason. "You have brought eternal shame on the de Montpellier name."

His hand rose, then his fingers clenched into a fist. It dropped back to his side. With a curse, he glared at Rhys and stamped across the stable.

Her shoulders sagged. When a hand settled on her elbow, she whirled away. Rhys moved to halt her.

"He will not strike you here," he said.

"Thank you."

A sad smile tugged at his lips as her simple answer

confirmed his suspicions. "What sort of man do you name me, milady, that I would allow him to inflict such violence on you? Mayhap in England, his actions are legal. Here they are not. Even if 'twere not illegal, I would not sanction such brutality."

When his arm slid around her waist, she did not resist as he drew her closer. Her hand settled on his chest, and she savored the rhythm of his heart beneath her fingers. This would be so perfect if the rebellion he longed to foment was not between them. "How can I believe that when you have treated me so cruelly?"

"My intent was not for you to be hurt."

"Mayhap not yours, but your man—"

"Bleddyn."

"Bleddyn had no reservations about using terror to bring me here."

He gave her the cold smile she knew hid his true thoughts. "You have to forgive him his enthusiasm, milady. He hates the English domination with a fervor even I cannot claim."

"Yet you sent him to bring me here."

"He had orders to bring you here alive and unaware of the route from Caernarvon."

Gizela crossed her arms and cupped her elbows as she shook her head. "So I could be entangled in this duplicity which seems to be a legacy from my husband to his brother and now to me."

Bafflement threaded his forehead beneath his tawny hair. "Legacy? I do not know what you mean."

"Sheldon told me he follows in the work his brother did before his death."

"You must have misunderstood Lord de Montpellier, milady." His smile could have belonged to the dragon on the banner in the great hall, for it was savage. "Kenleigh de Montpellier was given ample opportunities to play the role his brother has chosen, but your husband's loyalties were not for sale."

Gizela lowered her eyes, for she did not want him to see the sudden rush of tears filling them. "Thank you," she whispered.

"For what?"

"I did not want to believe Kenleigh would do such a thing."

He leaned one arm on the wall of the stall and toyed with the braid falling forward over her shoulder. "You loved him dearly?"

"I had hoped to, for I owe him the debt of saving my life."

"Your life? From whom did he save you, milady?"

"From my father." She did not give him a chance to ask another question. Walking out of the stable, she looked across the courtyard.

"Gizela." He caught her hand and placed something on her palm. When she stared down at her wedding ring, he said, "I know now how precious this must be to you, milady."

"It is the only thing of Kenleigh's that I possess, save for his name," she whispered, as she slipped it on her finger. Touching the twisted gold, she sighed.

"You possess his lands."

Looking at him, she said, "The lands which Sheldon now wants so desperately, he would betray his king. The fool! But you do not deem him a fool, do you? I know how deeply you value this ground where we stand." She covered the ring with her other hand. "I suspect Kenleigh loved his father's lands as dearly, or why else would he have ridden with his vassals to fight with the king? This I do not understand."

"It is not something I could explain to you." He lifted her finger and pressed it to the center of his chest. "It is within here, milady. Every breeze, every whisper of the leaves in the trees, every blossom bursting forth from this earth, is a part of me."

She slipped her fingers around his nape as he brought her against him. His lips found hers with the ease of too many nights of longing. Straining to be even closer, wanting nothing between them but the breadth of their skin, she moaned within his mouth as his hands glided along her. His mouth stroked her neck, rising to trace the curves of her ear, each moist breath tinder for the flames inside her. When his tongue touched the tender skin behind her ear, she clutched to him, awash in pleasure.

"I have found the days without you endless," he murmured, as he flicked his tongue across her lips.

"Say nothing," she whispered. "Speak with your kisses."

He laughed huskily. "I promise you a discourse of kisses worthy of the finest bard, sweet one."

Her legs pressed against his firm muscles as their mouths met again. His kiss deepened, demanding what she longed to give, stroking her lips as she ached for him to stroke all of her. She could not imagine such rapture, but wanted it and needed it.

"Chieftain?"

All the splendor vanished at the sound of a sharp voice. Gizela stiffened as she looked past Rhys's shoulder to see Sheldon watching them. A smile twisted his lips, and fear flooded her again as Rhys went to speak with him. She wanted to shout a warning to Rhys. Sheldon de Montpellier would do anything to obtain the power he longed to possess. He had betrayed his king already, and now he had been a witness to the desire she had for Rhys. Sheldon would use that, she knew, to get what he wanted. The only question was—which of them would he betray next?

9

Gizela walked from the hearth to the narrow window of the room where Rhys had insisted she must stay. "For your own protection," he had assured her. When she recalled the hatred on the faces of those within the corridors of this fortress, she had not argued.

How many times had she paced these few steps during the hours while the sun rose and then began its tumble toward the western sea? So many questions taunted her that she could not sit and sew as Nesta did, seemingly content with their banishment to this secluded chamber.

That illusion of tranquility vanished when a knock came at the door. Nesta recoiled, her needle falling from her lap and her eyes wide. She recovered quickly and rushed to the door.

Gizela was tempted to tell Nesta that she need not hurry. That thick plank was all that stood between Gizela and the insanity surrounding her. Even though she hated being a prisoner, she appreciated every moment that she had alone to try and plan her escape.

Each time she walked by the window she looked at the guard watch set on the outer wall. She had watched them laughing, clumped together with the certainty that intruders would not come upon them today.

"I wish to speak with Lady de Montpellier," said a voice that teased her memory.

When she turned, her eyes grew wide. She stared at the man who had threatened to kill her the night before she arrived in Caernarvon. "Tremaine!"

He smiled as he held up two wooden mugs. When she took one, he bowed his head. "I am honored you remember me, milady."

"I have forgotten nothing of that night," she answered, her nose wrinkling at the odor of the ale.

"Save what was stolen from you by sleep." He glanced at Nesta, and the young woman edged out of the room. Closing the door, he came in and drew out the chair where Nesta had been sewing. He sat and chuckled. "You had no suspicions of the herbs in the wine."

Holding the cup to her nose, she sniffed. "This is unadulterated."

"True."

"Why are you here?" She saw no reason to be tactful.

"The chieftain is busy, and he asked me to speak to you on his behalf. He suggested you might have many questions."

"Will you answer them?"

He smiled. "Mayhap."

"Then I see no reason to ask them."

With a shrug, he rose. "As you wish, milady. Then I bid you a good day."

"No!" she cried, taking a step forward as he went to the door. She faltered when he faced her. This was just a game he was playing with her. She saw that in his hard eyes.

"Milady?"

"If you will, Tremaine, tell me one thing. Why was I brought here?"

His snicker was vicious. "Why do you think?"

Heat scored her face, and she lowered her eyes. If she spoke of the yearning she had discovered in Rhys's arms, Tremaine was sure to laugh more. Her heart longed to believe Rhys had ordered her brought to him because he shared that craving, but she knew him well enough now to be certain he had a reason—one that would serve him well in his attempt to defeat the English—to bring her to Cadairllwyd.

"I know not," she said quietly. "Please tell me."

"I had thought you would have guessed." He dipped his finger into her ale and sucked it lustily. "If you are here, milady, you cannot be with Eleanor when she is brought to childbed."

"There are others who can serve her."

"But do they possess your skills?" He prowled around the room. "Your husband sent for you, milady, because he knew your skills in the birthing chamber were without equal, as befits a queen."

She sat on the bench and watched him. She could trust him no more than she trusted anyone within these walls. "If all goes well, there is no reason anyone could not help."

"And if things do not go well?"

"There must be someone within Caernarvon who could help."

He laughed. "And if there is not? What if the child dies?"

She whispered, "Do not speak of such things. To bring such ill-fortune onto the queen—"

"Would serve us well." He leaned his elbow on the windowsill. "To escape the pain of her dead child, she would return to England, and surely her devoted Edward would travel with her to be certain she arrives home safely."

"And you would use his absence to start the rebellion." She held her hand to her chest. "It is a masterful plan, Tremaine."

"'Tis not mine. Rhys devised it upon learning of your identity on the road to Caernarvon." He drew his knife and jammed it into the mortar between the stones. "I urged him to slay you then, for too many of your countrymen infect our land. Instead, he persuaded me to consider his plan, which is unfolding exactly as he wished. You are here, and Eleanor has no one to help her."

Gizela rose. "Mayhap the queen shall deliver with ease."

"There are other ways to insure the child does not live."

"You would kill a babe?"

"As I would a newborn snake in its nest." His lip curled in derision as he plucked the knife from the sill. "As I would you, milady."

She set the cup on the sill beside his knife. "I thank you for your warning, Tremaine. Now, as your message is delivered, there is no need for you to remain."

"No, there is not." He dipped his head toward her and went to the door. "Have a pleasant day, Lady de Montpellier." He turned, smiling. "While you can."

Gizela cursed under her breath as he strode out and Nesta slipped in, closing the door again. Her hands fisted at her sides. No more, she vowed as she had by her father's grave. No more would she be the victim of those who saw her only as a means to an end. She must find a way to flee—before her heart's longing for Rhys betrayed her as dearly as Sheldon had betrayed his king.

*   *   *

Gizela was glad for Nesta's company as she sat on the chest and waited for the evening meal. Her hands shook as she brushed loose strands of hair back toward her heavy braid. An hour past, a lad had come with the message that Lady de Montpellier was to join the household this evening.

Nesta had kept up a steady chatter since then, which required no answer from Gizela. "Tremaine ap Pembroke serves the chieftain as his most trusted advisor. Bleddyn?" She shivered. "He is one to avoid, milady. From the time he was a lad, he has been eager to become a hero. Heroes are dangerous. They will risk anything for glory." She lowered her voice. "And he hates anything English, milady. If—" The sound of knuckles against the door brought a strained smile to her face. "That must be your escort, milady."

When Nesta opened the door, Gizela expected to see the homely soldier. Slowly she came to her feet as she stared at Rhys. Even the scanty light from the candles caught the golden fire of Rhys's hair as he tipped his head to her. Over his light blue tunic which was shorter than the ones worn by the English, he wore a cloak of midnight black. His boots accented the lean line of his leg muscles. Every inch of him announced his power within these walls.

"Good evening, milady. I trust you had a quiet day to recover from your recent adventures." He lifted her hand to his lips.

She pulled it back before his mouth could work its magic on her. No longer would she let him woo the sense from her head or give in to the fantasies she hid within her heart. Turning away, she said, "It has been a most enlightening day."

"In what way?"

She saw no reason to demur. "About why you had me brought here."

"Is it the reason I brought you here or the fact you wish to stay that unsettles you?"

"Wish to stay?" She shook her head. "Even if the queen did not need me, this is not where I belong."

"For now, milady, you belong here."

"As your prisoner?"

"If that is your wish, although, I admit I had hoped we might enjoy some pleasant times as we did along the strand."

Her heart throbbed against her breast as memory rushed forth. Her skin tingled with the need for his fingers and mouth. Yes, she wanted to cry, that was what she craved, too, but she could not forsake her fealty for the thrill of his caresses. If this was his way of twisting her to his will, she must flee with all speed.

When she did not answer, he stepped back and motioned toward the door. "I thought you would wish to be guided through the unfamiliar halls to dinner."

She almost told him she would as soon sit down with Satan as with him, but anger would gain her nothing. She must let him think she was willing to accede to his edicts. "Thank you."

He held up his hand as he swept his cloak back with his other arm. The broadsword at his side glittered as dangerously as his eyes, and she warned herself not to underestimate him.

When she put her fingers on his palm, he drew her out the door. He said nothing as they walked through the narrow corridor. Her dress rearranged the rushes strewn on the floor.

Gizela fought to keep her fingers from trembling as they entered the great hall. The banner bound to the rafters revealed the dragon of Wales with its wings open, ready to attack the English invaders.

"Our dragon shall sleep no more," Rhys said softly. "It is alive again."

"Do not forget that England's St. George has slain one dragon already."

He laughed. "But your king is no saint, despite his sojourn to the Holy Land, and our dragon hungers for the taste of English blood."

As he led her beneath the banner and the dragon's taloned claw, Gizela tried to ignore the stares of his household. Her gaze was caught by Tremaine's at the raised table, and fear flashed through her. His frown warned he wished her dead.

She looked away to be caught by Sheldon's superior smile. Too easily she understood how a deer felt when surrounded by a pack of hounds. No matter which way she turned, she was confronted by someone who would gladly use her in this struggle for power.

Rhys led her to the raised table. When he paused at the base of the trio of steps and motioned for her to climb them, she did not let her steps falter.

Sheldon did not speak as she passed behind his chair. A gracious nod of her head was her only answer when Rhys drew out the chair next to where Tremaine sat. Settling her skirt around her, she sat with her back as straight as the unadorned chair. She forced her face to remain serene when Rhys drew out the chair on the other side of her.

Her pose nearly cracked when his leg brushed hers as he sat. Even that touch, so innocent and incidental, resonated through her like the sweetest song. For the first time, she doubted she could maintain the composure that would be her shield tonight.

"Tremaine," Rhys said with a smile, "I need not introduce you to Lady de Montpellier."

"No, we are well acquainted." He lifted his knife from the table and jabbed it into the wood.

She plucked the knife from the table and dropped it in front of him. "Very well-acquainted."

He chuckled coldly and leaned forward. When he spoke to Rhys in Welsh, she suspected he wished her to feel insulted or demand a translation. Let him enjoy his pettiness, for it gave her time to scan the hall.

More than two score men sat at the tables, and she had no idea how many more might serve Rhys. She picked up a slice of bread. Without taking a bite, she lowered it back to her plate and reached for the mug set beside the trencher. She took a deep drink, hoping the honeyed wine would lessen the trembling of her fingers and loosen the knots in her stomach. She thought of what she must do and how little her life would be worth if she was caught trying to escape.

"Not hungry?" asked Rhys. He reached for one of the roasted birds set on a tray in the middle of the table. Ripping off a greasy wing, he balanced it in his hand as he waited for her answer.

She sighed deeply and squared her shoulders. There was no use pretending she was comfortable in these unbelievable circumstances. "Not very." When he smiled at her honest answer, she continued tautly, "I am tired, and I fear for Pomona."

"Why?"

"She will be sick near to death with anxiety for me." She clasped her fingers tightly. "I wish only to go home."

He arched a single golden brow. "That is what I wished for you as well, milady, but you did not heed my counsel on that."

"So you have told me." She took a hasty sip of her wine and was torn between relief and regret when Rhys turned away to answer a question posed to him by Sheldon.

Had there ever been a woman as foolish as she was? She must forget the promise of passion in his eyes and remember the vow of disloyalty he held within his heart. Her hands clenched in her lap, brushing the pouch at her side.

Slowly she smiled as she asked in what she hoped was a nonchalant voice, "More mead, Rhys?"

"Allow me, milady."

She shook her head. "I would not wish you to interrupt your important conversation with my late husband's brother. I shall pour for all of us."

Standing, she took the ewer which had been set amid the trays. She sat, shielding it from any eyes. Making certain no one saw her open a pouch on her waist, she emptied its contents into the ewer. Gizela smiled as she served Rhys and Sheldon. When Tremaine held out his cup in a silent demand, she poured him a share as well.

She watched as Rhys drank the mead and continued talking with Sheldon who seemed determined to keep himself perpetually intoxicated. A pinch of guilt taunted her, but she ignored it. None of these men would grant her any mercy, so she must be as ruthless.

When Rhys rose, she stared up at him. His motion was as graceful as the flight of the dragon overhead as he held out his hand to her. "Attend me, milady."

Uneasily she placed her hand on his palm. "Where?"

"You shall see."

"But the others are still eating."

He laughed lowly. "You have eaten less than a child. I would take you away from this place you find uncomfortable."

Gizela could not deny the warmth in his eyes, but trusting his words would be foolish. When she glanced at Sheldon, he did not look in her direction. He grabbed a bird off a passing platter and put his arm around the waist of the woman who carried the tray.

Gizela whispered, "My husband's brother may—"

"Finish his supper. You have completed yours. Attend me now."

"Rhys, I would prefer to enjoy the company of your household," she said quietly.

"You are scared."

"If wisdom is fear, then I must admit to that."

He chuckled. "As always, well said, milady. However, I have asked you to attend me now."

Knowing the words were a command, she let him bring her to her feet. The platform was not wide, and she stood so close to him his tunic grazed her dress. A single deep breath would brush her against him with an intimate stroke. Her eyes met his blue ones, and heat roiled over her. He raised her hand to his lips. When he turned it over so his mouth caressed the soft skin along her wrist, she was sure her heart had forgotten how to beat. He slipped his finger beneath the laces in her sleeve, loosening them as he drew the sleeve up her arm.

"Gizela," he whispered, "attend me now."

She stared up at him, wishing she could give him her heart and all of her being wholeheartedly, but nothing had changed. He was her enemy, the man who would do whatever he must to see the English banished from his land.

"Yes," she answered as softly, letting him lead her down from the raised table and out a nearby door.

As before, Rhys was silent while they walked along the corridor. The few servants they met pressed back against the wall to let them past. Every stare pierced Gizela, but Rhys seemed oblivious to the shock and amusement from his clan.

They passed the door opening to the stairs leading up to the room she had been given. When she started to speak, he silenced her with a frown. She reluctantly bit back her questions, for she would be wise to learn as much as she could about this fortress. Nothing must suggest to Rhys what she planned to try.

Another set of winding stairs led into an upper corridor. It was lit against the darkness with a single brand, and only one door opened onto it.

He opened it. "Milady?"

Hoping he could not hear the rapid pounding of her heart, Gizela entered. She stared at the opulently-carved bed on its round dais. It governed the whole room. Even a large hearth was dwarfed by its magnificence. She did not need to ask who used this room, for she heard the thud of a heavy bar as it dropped to lock the door.

She turned to Rhys. "I fear you have brought me to the wrong chambers. Mine are elsewhere."

"Hardly. This is where I want you. This is where you wish to be." His finger traced the curve of her cheek. When she trembled, overpowered by the potent yearnings she could not control, he laughed. "See, Gizela? You ache to be in my arms."

"What I want is unimportant," she asserted. "You are my enemy, Rhys. The only one I can welcome to my bed is the man King Edward chooses for me to wed."

"Then we shall use *my* bed."

His teasing tone warned her how much he was enjoying this. Could he guess how she longed to be in his arms? "That is impossible," she whispered as much to herself, as to him. "We are enemies."

He chuckled quietly as he swept her against him. "Your husband's brother is my ally, and he has given you to me tonight."

"You are lying! Sheldon would not—"

His finger under her chin forced her furious eyes up to meet his. "If you wish the truth, de Montpellier suggested this to show me how much he wishes to prove his fealty to his new allegiance."

"Then let him prostitute himself, not me!" She shoved his hands away. She stepped back to put more space between them. "Let any agreement you have be between you. Do not make me a part of your treachery."

"A part of our treachery?" Laughter returned to light his eyes as he sat on the high bed. He caught her hand and pulled her up to sit beside him. "Gizela, you are not a part of our plans." He slipped his fingers down her braid, loosening the hair to flow along her back. "But I want to be a part of you."

When she tried to slide off, he pushed her onto her back. The iron band of his arm held her against the mattress. She stared up at him in horror. "Rhys, I beg you—"

He bent and pressed his mouth to the curve of her neck. His words were hot against her skin. "You need not beg, for I shall be glad to give you whatever you wish."

She gasped as the fire in his eyes swept along her. Each caress of his gaze left a tingle in its wake. Quivers sucked all strength from her until her knees quaked. She was aware of every inch of his hard body only a caress away from her.

Desperately she fought to keep from reaching out to bring him against her. She closed her eyes as his fingers wove unknown patterns of delight through her hair. As he lifted a handful to press against his cheek, she slowly blinked and wondered if this was mayhap the sweetest dream. She could not ask. To speak might resurrect the truth that had little to do with this longing to be in his arms.

He brushed her lips with his. The swift touch

stripped her of all resistance to the yearning she had pushed aside too many times. Even knowing how wrong it was to want him, his mouth over hers lit the deepest recesses of her heart.

As her arms rose to his shoulders, he held her to him and captured her lips. "Let us think only of the pleasure before us. Pleasures we have imagined each time we have met." He ran his tongue along the curve of her throat, and she shivered. A wicked sound came into his voice as he whispered, "Let me prove to you that this is yet another way a Welshman is more skilled than your English."

"I shall have to take your word for that." Her back arched as his mouth moved lower to the laces on the front of her gown. She shuddered when his breath sifted through them to brush her breasts.

He drew back and frowned. "What do you mean?"

"I have never had a lover."

Grasping her left hand, he raised it. "You wear de Montpellier's ring and share his name."

She sat with her back against the pillows. "Kenleigh arranged for our betrothal when I was barely more than a child. Our wedding ceremony was done by proxy. The first time I would have seen him in many years was when I arrived at Caernarvon."

"You are a maiden?" His mouth straightened with fury. She knew it was not aimed at her when he asked, "Does de Montpellier know this?"

"He must." She laughed raggedly. "Mayhap he thought to give you my virginity as a great prize to prove his loyalty. Clearly he values me almost as much as his horse, which he would not trade you."

"This is the truth?"

"I am not lying, Rhys ap Cynan." As always, the sound of his name, which she seldom dared to speak, was delightful.

He smiled as he swept her hair back from her face. "I believe that as I believe little I hear from the lips of those who claim English birth. How alike we are, milady." His gaze held hers as he added in a breathy whisper, "And how different we are."

A peculiar expression suddenly crossed his face, and she asked, "What is wrong?"

His smile returned. "What can be wrong when you are here? Be mine, sweet one, not because of de Montpellier's scheming, but because you wish this as I do."

Wildfire scorched her mouth as he claimed it anew. Forbidden desire suffused her. When his fingers slipped over the curves beneath her laced bodice, she shivered with the craving she could not govern. Her fingers clenched the back of his tunic, then softened to splay across his firm muscles as he slowly explored her breast.

Molten need surged through her as she brought his lips over hers. She moaned into the warmth of his mouth when his finger slipped through the laces, undoing them. His rough skin added sparks to the flame within her as he teased the very tip of her breast while he pulled her closer.

When his lips lit her neck with rapture, the need to touch him became as powerful as her yearning to be touched. As his mouth coursed along the unfastened ribbons, she reached for the laces at the top of his tunic.

Suddenly he pulled away. An odd expression stole the passion from his face.

Gizela sat up. Even in Rhys's arms, how could she have forgotten that she had put the powder in the men's wine? Now, when she was here with him and his touch lit her soul, she wished there had been another way. She wanted to stay, but could not. This had been her only weapon. Yet to see him suffer as he would . . . ." Rhys?" she asked cautiously.

"'Tis nothing." His smile was strained, but his fingers played along her bodice, teasing her skin anew.

All thought was eclipsed by perilous passion. She reached to push his hand away, but her fingers curved over his, holding them to her breast as she savored the sensations which roiled through her. Raising her gaze to his, she whispered, "'Tis so wrong to want your touch so much."

"Why?" His voice softened to husky raggedness.

"You are my enemy."

"I am Edward's enemy. I would be your lover, Gizela. All you need do . . . ."

He pushed himself away from her and pressed his hands against his stomach. He reeled to the door, nearly falling.

She rushed to his side. It was too late to change anything now, even if she had the choice. Pain riveted her, as harsh as his agony. But this was her sole chance to flee, and she must not betray herself now. "Rhys, what is wrong?"

"Something is attacking my gut." He fell to one knee, his shoulder striking the door. He reached up and tried to lift the bar.

Gizela shoved it up and aside. Putting her hand against his forehead, she wiped away the icy sweat. She must give him no cause to be suspicious. "Have you been feeling ill?"

"No." He collapsed to the floor.

"Have you eaten any badly-prepared food?"

"The kitchens here are skilled."

"Then . . . ." She touched his clammy cheek as she whispered, "That leaves only poison."

"Poison?" He shook his head, then dropped to lean his head against his knees. "Impossible!"

"Let me get help." She stood. "The stillroom is near the stable, is it not?"

"I pointed it out to you when we went to see de Montpellier's wretched horse." He swallowed harshly, and she knew he was struggling not to be ill in front of her.

"I remember. Let me get your healer."

He waved toward the door.

Gizela heard sounds of sickness as she rushed out into the corridor. Closing the door behind her, she ran toward the stairs. She paused at the bottom and looked in both directions. If she recalled, the stable courtyard could be reached by a door at the end of the next hallway.

She delayed only long enough to steal a dark cloak from an empty bedchamber she passed. Pulling the hood over her face, she skulked out of the house and into the courtyard. She looked up at the windows and whispered, "Forgive me, Rhys, but I cannot stay here."

The distance to the wall was less than within Caernarvon, and the buildings within the bailey offered shadows to conceal her. Her heart leaped with elation when she saw the gate was open. Edging closer, she peered through the star-speckled darkness to discover where the watch stood on the wall. As earlier, they were gathered together. Their lighthearted voices reached her, and she pressed back against the wall as they passed above her.

Shouts came from the main building. The watch turned to look over their shoulders. She did not hesitate. Rushing through the gate, she clung to the outer stone wall. They would not see her unless they looked directly down into the shadows.

Suddenly the gates swung closed. More shouts bounced over the wall. Staying low to the ground, she ran toward the trees along the slope. She let the darkness cloak her.

10

Screams followed the odor of smoke up the mountainside. Gizela paused, staring at the column of smoke rising through the freshly budded trees. The reek reached into her empty stomach, twisting it more tightly. She had not eaten since fleeing Cadairllwyd . . . how many days ago? She was not sure if she had been trying to free herself from the mountains for three days or four. The long, hungry hours, jumbled together.

Another shriek struck her ears. She could not mistake the utter terror in the sound. Something must be horribly wrong. She should flee in the opposite direction, using whatever was happening as a diversion.

Even as she thought that, she ran, using the smoke as a guide, toward the fire. If someone was injured, she could help. In the midst of disaster, no one would take much note of her. Her clothes were Welsh, and, if she said nothing, no one would be the wiser.

She screamed when the ground suddenly dropped out beneath her. She slid on the loose scree and grabbed a tree to halt her wild crash down the hill. Panting, she inched along the steep slope to a path that edged it like lace on a fine lady's robe.

Gizela ignored the ache in her side, and the emptiness in her stomach as she raced along the path. She rounded a bend and saw a cottage in flames.

A young woman ran to her, crying out something she could not understand, and pointing to the house. No words were necessary. Someone was within it. Gizela ran around the house. As she had hoped, the front door was filled with smoke, but no flames. She took a deep breath before she entered.

Gizela plunged into the smoke. The heat threatened to force her back, but she dropped to her knees and squinted through watery eyes. A tiny form was close to a table that was already smoking. She crawled to it. With a curse, she tossed a toy aside.

A high-pitched protest came from her left. In a corner, farthest from the flames that were feasting on the wood floors before the hearth, a child crouched. She motioned for him to come to her. He shook his head, and she knew he was too scared to move.

Gizela clung close to the floor. Taking the child in her arms, she awkwardly edged toward the door. The snap of the table exploding into fire was her only warning before flames cascaded over them. Pain scorched her arm. The child screeched. She jumped to her feet and ran out of the house. She rolled the child in the dirt to put out the fire on his clothes.

The young woman came to them, sobbing. Gizela pointed to the well by the byre. The woman nodded and went to get water.

Gizela knelt beside the child and smiled. Gently she lifted his burned leg. She winced when his toes brushed her scorched sleeve, but she did not let her smile waver.

Withdrawing a packet from her pouch, she motioned for the young woman to bring the water closer. She dipped a corner of her torn cloak into it and then sprinkled herbs onto the burns on the child's legs.

The little boy screamed when she wrapped the bandage around his leg. His mother asked what Gizela guessed was a question. She did not answer, pretending to be so intent on her task she did not hear. She watched as the young woman gathered the child into her arms, embracing him and whispering into his dark hair.

Gizela handed a packet of lavender to the woman and smiled. Rising, she brushed dirt off her gown. Pain ran up her right arm, and she looked down to see angry spots of red where embers had seared through her sleeve. She had no more of the lavender with her, but she would get some from Hayes when she reached the castle.

Scanning the mountains, she saw the glitter of the sea in the distance. She must go in that direction. As she walked away, the woman ran after her, catching her sleeve and motioning for Gizela to wait.

Gizela shook her head. She could not risk staying here. The young woman started to speak, then whirled as the child cried for her. Glancing back with another twinge of envy at the love between mother and child, Gizela rushed along the road and back into the trees. She must be gone before others saw the smoke and came to help. No one must guess she had been the one to help the child.

Gizela woke to a growl deep in her stomach. She heeded it no more than she had last night when its protests had threatened to keep her awake. The pain along her burned arm had routed her from sleep throughout the night, but exhaustion from walking all day had lured her back into sleep. She stretched, wincing as she moved her arm.

"Did you sleep well?"

Gizela opened her eyes and stared up at Rhys's frown. Her first breath of delight became horror when she saw his fury. She clawed at the earth to crawl away. His broadsword pointed at her heart, and she halted.

"Will you kill me?" she asked softly.

Astonishment at her forthright question flickered through his eyes, but his expression did not alter. "Everyone should be granted the opportunity to make one mistake. You have had yours, milady. If you try to flee again, you will give me no choice but to see you dead."

"Then kill me now, for I shall not be your captive again while Sheldon betrays our king."

"Your king, milady." He withdrew the sword and held out his hand. As he brought her to her feet, he smiled coldly. "You have made your loyalty to Edward evident in your attempts to poison us."

"'Twas not poison." She looked past him to see a half-dozen men along the hillside. "'Twas quite the opposite, for the potion induces someone who has swallowed poison to expel it."

"Along with everything else in his stomach." His lips twisted as he gripped her shoulder and tugged her to him. "Tremaine will not soon forgive you."

"I do not wish his forgiveness . . . or yours."

"Or de Montpellier's?"

Her eyes narrowed. "I would see him dead before I begged his forgiveness. The crime is his, not mine."

"You have gained yourself some fearsome enemies."

"Then I count myself fortunate." She peeled his fingers off her gown, then winced as she tried to adjust her sleeve. She could not silence her moan when he twisted her so he could see her charred sleeve. "Be careful," she whispered, blinking back unbidden tears.

He said something under his breath, and she looked up at him as he murmured, "So it is true."

"What is true?"

"You paused in your flight to give comfort to a child who had been burned."

"Yes." She longed to close her eyes and let the warmth of his caress surround her as his fingers touched her cheek.

He gently ran his hand along her sleeve, avoiding the burned spots. "But you did not ruin your gown like this while you tended to him, did you?" He tipped her chin toward him. "You have the heart of a warrior, milady—to dare the fire for the rescue of a child of your enemies."

"The child is no enemy of mine. Would you have let the child die if you had stood beside an English cottage in flames and heard his mother's cries of despair?"

"I hope I never have to face such a decision, milady." He put his arm around her waist and turned her toward a path snaking along the hill. "As I hope I never have to face the decision of sending you to your death."

"I shall not make it easy for you, Rhys," she said, her voice barely more than a whisper.

Regret tainted his words. "Nor shall I be able to make your death easy for you."

With a gasp, she looked up at him. His jaw was as unyielding as the rocks along the mountains, and she knew he meant exactly what he said. He had forgiven her this one attempt to find her way back to Caernarvon. If she tried again—and she must—he would see her executed in such a way that no one would dare gainsay him again.

*   *   *

The antechamber of Rhys's rooms held only a table and a pair of benches. Two brands burned on the walls, the flare of light painting grotesque masks on the men sitting at the table. Their voices were low and intense.

Even if she understood the Welsh they spoke, Gizela doubted if she could have garnered more than a few words from their fervent whispers. The men who had been with Rhys at her capture were grouped around the table. She sat in a chair set in the corner of the room that she had not guessed existed. When she had been in Rhys's bedchamber, she had not taken note of a door which opened onto this one.

Gizela tensed when Tremaine entered. His gaze flicked toward her, then away, as if she mattered nothing to the conversation.

Rhys stood and motioned for Tremaine to join them. With a glance at Gizela, he sat again. "I had thought to see you before this," he said quietly.

"De Montpellier sensed that something was amiss, and he was pestering me to let him be part of it." Tremaine's lips curled back over his teeth. "I would gladly arrange for him to die with that English whore."

Rhys looked again at Gizela. Her face was impassive, but he noted how her fingers knitted together in her lap. Lovely Lady de Montpellier would not relinquish her loyalties, not even to save her life.

"As I told you before, Tremaine, her death will gain us nothing."

"Letting her live could destroy all we have built here." He rubbed his stomach and grimaced. "She is the whelp of that beast, and she proved she is as cunning with her tainted wine."

"She also proved she has courage. Would you have entered that burning house to save a child when you should be thinking only of fleeing?"

Tremaine fisted his hand on the table. When he fired a glare at Gizela, only her slow blink revealed she had noticed. "That is not the issue, Rhys. She escaped from Cadairllwyd."

"With the help of our own incompetence." He looked around the table. No one would meet his eyes, save Tremaine, and he was certain all the men had been equally remiss on the wall. "If for no other reason, we must be grateful she has brought our inadequate defenses to our attention."

"So you will allow her to live for *that* reason?" He pounded the table. "She must die."

Grumbles of assent raced around the room.

Rhys sighed and stood. Going over to Gizela, he said in English, "Milady, you may retire. This discussion clearly will last much longer than I had anticipated." He opened the door to his bedchamber, allowing himself no more than the pleasure of letting the back of his hand stroke her cheek. "Rest well."

"In there?"

Gizela flushed when her question was answered by coarse laughter from the table. She did not look at any of the men as she eased past Rhys and went into the room. As the door closed behind her, she went to the table. On it, a feast waited.

She sat and filled a plate with the steaming meats and soft breads. She closed her eyes, savoring the texture of food upon her tongue. Half rising, she reached for an ewer to fill her mug with chilled wine. Suddenly a hand seized her wrist.

"Sheldon!" she cried.

"Lower your voice, you fool!" He shoved her hand

away and reached for the pitcher. "Dare I drink this, or are you desperate enough to poison your own food as well?"

"What are you doing here?"

Pouring himself a generous serving of wine, he sat at the foot of the large bed. "A question I need not ask you. Have you changed your mind, sister dear? Will you relieve the chieftain's foolish longing for you in his bed and obtain me what I wish?"

"What is it you want?" she asked. Any information she had now could only help her decide what to do next.

"'Tis a small thing to ask," he continued as if she had not spoken, "for he will surely be so disgusted with your icy demeanor that he will not wish another night with you."

Standing, she shook her head as she crossed her arms in front of her. She recoiled at the unthinking motion and cradled her burned arm in her hand. "I shall not play the whore for you, milord. Nor shall I stay to watch you demean Kenleigh's name."

Sheldon's fingers curled into a fist. "You fool! You shall ruin everything if you flee like that again."

"I shall ruin nothing, save your plans to play the traitor."

"I vow that—"

"Vow nothing, for your word is worthless, milord." She turned her back on him. "Begone before someone discovers you have been here. It would not be seemly for it to appear as if you were plotting with me for another escape."

"No one would believe that."

"Mayhap not, but it would plant suspicions in the minds of those who distrust all Englishmen. Can you afford that?"

Gizela waited, not daring to breathe as she heard him take a step toward her. Then he went to the door, opened it, and was gone. She sank to the bench and pushed aside the trencher. Her hunger was replaced by fear. Rhys had been correct, yet again. He might be her only friend within the manor house.

Starlight trickled past the narrow windows as the door opened from the corridor. Rhys entered slowly. The hour was near dawn, and he had heard Gizela's footsteps in his room long after he had banished her from the outer room when he had not expected that her very presence would be an abomination to his men.

He wrinkled his nose at the stench of the candle that had burned to the end of its wick. Frowning, he saw the bed was empty. He scanned the room. His lovely prisoner could not have escaped, because Bleddyn had stood by the door all night.

He chuckled to himself as he knelt next to where Gizela was asleep on the bench. That she had refused to sleep on the comfortable mattress no longer surprised him. Nor, was he astounded to see lines of pain on her face. He raised a single finger to smooth them away.

She came awake with a cry of horror, and leaped to her feet so hastily her robes struck his face. He was on his feet before she could take another step. When she cowered away from him, he whispered her name.

Gizela blinked and looked around her. Where was she? She had been dreaming of Talbot Hall, and the dream had turned into the nightmare that stalked her.

"Forgive me for startling you, milady."

She closed her eyes and let her shoulders sag. "Oh, Rhys, 'tis only you."

He laughed. "Such a warm-hearted greeting!"

"No, 'tis not that." She drew away and returned to the bench. "I was suffering a fearsome dream."

"Speak of it, if that will help."

"No, for it is gone." She wiggled the fingers of her burned arm. "Will they allow me to live?"

"I am chieftain of this clan, Gizela."

"But you listen to the words of those who serve you. I have seen that."

He sat beside her, but did not touch her. She sensed the wall between them, as if it were as thick as the one surrounding Caernarvon.

"Your death would do nothing to help us in our cause."

"So I may live because I am incidental?"

"Do not jest, milady. 'Twas the sole argument they would heed."

Noise erupted into the room. She looked toward the door to the antechamber and was astonished to see it was ajar. When she glanced back at Rhys, his smile was gone, lost behind the wall he had raised to hide his desire. She longed to bring the passion back into his eyes as his arms drew her to him.

Softly, she said, "Close the door, Rhys."

"My men would not be happy to hear you give me orders in my own rooms."

"Please close the door, if you prefer."

The phantom of a smile fled his lips as he stood. He quietly shut the door, wrapping them in dusky silence. "Say what you will, Lady de Montpellier."

She was dismayed at his use of her formal title. It served only to put more distance between them. "What did you have to promise them so that I might live another day?"

"That you will never leave Cadairllwyd alone."

"And that I would not be alone within its walls?"

"Many eyes shall be watching for you to betray yourself."

She rose. "My loyalties shall never change."

"A dangerous stance, milady?"

"More dangerous," she whispered, "than my yearning for you?" She went to him and took his hand in hers. The beguiling sensation of his rugged skin beneath her fingertips gave her the courage to speak the truth which had been concealed for too long. "Do you know my first thought upon waking to see you on the mountainside was joy?"

"That you were no longer lost?"

She raised his hand to her cheek. "That you had found me again. Rhys, can we forget we are enemies for the rest of this one night?" She paused, waiting for him to speak. When he said nothing, she added, "The night is nearly past, so we should grasp what remains of it."

Pulling his hand away, he sat on a corner of the table. With his arms folded in front of him, he mused, "Your words bear little resemblance to your actions. You speak sweetly of passion, then flee. Do you know what would have happened if Tremaine had found you before I?"

"He would have killed me, and we could never have enjoyed this." She grasped his face. Pressing her lips to his, she dared him to assert again that she was lying.

His arms surrounded her to pull her tight to his chest. As he cradled her against him, she leaned on the hard strength of his leg. Her hands slipped along the smooth wool of his robe, exploring the coiled sinews hidden beneath his skin. A craving, more powerful than any she had known before, ripped through her. The embers of need burst into a wildfire intent on consuming both of them.

He freed her hair and combed his fingers through the ebony strands to hold her closer to him. When he tilted her face, his tongue teased her earlobe. The flurry of his breath against her became a tempest whirling to her center.

Slowly he raised his head. "My sweetest Gizela, you must be sure of this. A part of me wishes to deny de Montpellier the satisfaction of being right when he spoke of my deep desire for you."

"Which part of you?" she whispered, running her fingers up his arms. "This part?"

"No," he answered softly, brushing back her hair and gently nibbling her neck.

"This part?" She closed her eyes as she touched the hard expanse of his chest. Unhooking the clasp at his throat, she let his cloak fall to the table. She loosened the laces along the front of his tunic and delighted in his smooth skin beneath her fingers.

"Not that part."

Her breath was as ragged as his when she let her hands settle on his strong thighs. Leaning toward him so her breasts touched his bare skin, she whispered, "This part?"

"Faith, woman!" he moaned. "Have compassion for a man who would treat you with gentleness." He twisted his fingers through her hair. "How is it that a maiden like you knows these ways to drive a man mad with desire?"

"I think only of how I wish you to touch me." Her eyes closed as he brushed his mouth along her cheek. "Rhys, touch me."

His hands settled on her waist and slowly rose to cup her breasts. She clenched his shoulders, wanting to cry out as his fingers slowly slipped along her. She quivered when he teased the very tip of her breasts while his kiss claimed her mouth. As if he had never kissed her before, he tasted every inch of her lips. Not content with the flavors there, his mouth roved along the downy softness of her face. Her fingers clenched his back when his tongue caressed her eyelids, sending waves of sweetly- agonizing desire to her most intimate depths. Fighting the pleasure enough to keep a coherent thought in her head, she whispered, "The door—"

"Think no more of it, sweet one." He undid the laces at her throat, each touch promising the splendor she could find only in his arms. Against her ear, he murmured, "No one can break through that heavy bar."

"The bar?" She turned slightly to see it was firmly in place. She forgot the men in the other room when his mouth explored her shoulder as he lowered her gown. Exulting in the roughness of his whiskers brushing her skin, she swayed toward him.

Her overdress dropped to the floor unnoticed, as he asked, "Did you think I truly would have left you tonight? I have waited long for you, and now you shall be mine."

With a laugh, he tugged on the lighter material of her undertunic, tearing it. He grinned at her, daring her to protest as he threw it onto the fire.

"I soon shall have nothing to wear," she whispered.

"Then you shall be unable to leave my bed." He knelt and raised the hem of her linen shift.

She wobbled as his fingers slid up her legs to the garters holding her stockings in place, then over her knees and along her thighs. His thumbs stroked her inner thigh, eliciting sensations as fierce as a summer storm. She clutched his shoulders while he drew off her shoes and stockings.

Leaning forward, she put her hands on his face and bent to place her lips on his. Suddenly he stood, and swept her into his arms. His voice was a wordless growl as he captured her lips. Any tenderness had vanished beneath his need. He dropped her onto the bed and

knelt over her. When his arm curved around her, she
leaned against it as she pushed his tunic back from his
shoulders. She rested against the warmth of his chest as
she lowered the full sleeves past his wrists. She froze as
her eyes were caught by the naked hunger in his.

He pulled the tunic from her hands and threw it
aside. Gently he leaned her back into the pillows. Lying
beside him, she reached to touch the enticing planes of
his body. He caught her arm while his other hand settled on her knee, raising her shift along her leg.

"I want to touch you," she whispered.

"You shall, sweet one, but first I want to see your
naked3
beauty. Loving should be a delight for the eyes as
well as the body."

As his mouth descended toward her, she ached for
his lips on hers. The rapture was overpowering when he
brushed his mouth against the curve of her breast. His
finger slipped into the strap of her shift and lowered it
along her arm. She shivered with unrestrainable passion at his tender captivity. Her soft gasp became a
moan as his fingers slipped her shift ever lower.

Drawing her up to kneel beside him, he drew the
shift from her. He divested himself of the rest of his
clothes, and he pulled her to him. A soft cry burst from
her parted lips when the undeniable maleness of him
touched her. The rough heat of his chest scored her like
a thousand individual caresses, and his tongue blazed a
moist path along her breast. Her fingers splayed along
his lean hips when he teased it into his mouth.

Lingering to thrill her each time she reacted to the
undiscovered fascination of his touch, he explored her
with his heated mouth and strong fingers. Each touch
fired sparks in her until she writhed against him with a
hunger she was unable to control.

After whispering his name, she drew his mouth over hers. Daring to be as bold as he, she traced the firm lines of his body with her hands. He moaned when she ran her fingers over the hardness that would become a part of her.

He pressed her back into the pillows and looked down at her. She captured his mouth as they became one. All thoughts evaporated in the boiling cauldron of their fused bodies as the rhythms of their love accelerated fiercer, faster, more furious. Poised for one eternal moment at the very peak of passion, she sank into the loving arms of the only man who could bring her such ecstasy.

A husky warmth filled Gizela's chuckle when she whispered, "I am so disappointed."

"Disappointed?" He leaned over her, scowling.

She touched the curve of his jaw and whispered, "I failed to find which part of you did not wish to allow Sheldon to gloat over the truth."

"You shall need to continue to look, sweet one." He kissed her lightly before adding, "You are as luscious in my arms as I had dared to believe."

"As I had dreamed." Taking his hand, she pressed it to the soft valley between her breasts. She shivered, captured anew by the passion which would never remain quiescent again. Her voice trembled when she said, "My maidenly dreams, which I shall dream no more, for you made them come true."

The sound of a rooster crowing made her look toward the window. His fingers turned her face back to him. "The night is far from over, even though the sun may be touching the eastern mountains. I would have you stay here with me until the sun reaches its apex."

"And seeks the western sea again?"

"I wish 'twould be so, but—"

Bitterness filled her voice. "But you must plot the downfall of the English."

"Nothing has changed beyond this bed, sweet one," he murmured, brushing her lips with his.

When she shivered with the remnants of rapture, he drew her to him. "Rhys—"

"Say nothing, milady, but that you want me to stay with you until the sun calls me from your arms."

She answered him with her lips on his. The glory of this passion must be hers again. For a few precious hours, she could believe in the fantasy of having him as part of her life for the rest of her days. Then, when he left to involve himself with intrigue, she would have to confront the truth as she sought a way to leave him . . . forever.

11

Sunshine was inching across the large bed when Gizela woke alone. She was not surprised. Even though Rhys had spent two nights searching for her and had slept very little last night, he had been honest—as he always was—when he told her he could not linger by her side.

She buried her face in the pillows. She had been honest, too. Nothing was different, save that he had won her heart. He was everything she had vowed to hate, but she longed to be in his arms as he taught her the pleasures that had filled her dreams.

She sat up and drew her wrinkled shift over her head. Of one thing she was certain. Any vow he made would be as unchangeable as the stone walls surrounding Cadairllwyd. If she tried to escape again, nothing—not even the passion they shared—would halt him from killing her.

Nesta peeked into the room, her eyes wide as she looked about. "*Bore da*, milady. I have an oaten cake to break your fast. Would you like me to bring it to you?"

"Yes, thank you."

"The chieftain instructed me to tell you that you should say '*diolch*'. He has told us to speak only Welsh to you, so you might learn to speak it as well."

"Welsh words do not sit well on my tongue," she said quietly, as she drew her gown over her head. The wool was scratchy against her bare arms, but her ruined under-tunic had vanished in the hearth's flames.

"As the English ones do not on mine."

At Rhys's deep voice, Gizela looked past the maid to see him entering the bedchamber. His eyes glowed with a dragon's fierce fire, as they had during the night. The slightest motion of his hand sent Nesta from the room, closing the door behind her. He crossed the room in a few long strides. His fingers combed through her hair, and he brought her mouth to his.

"Did you miss me?" Rhys whispered as she leaned her head on his broad shoulder.

"I thought you would be busy with your men."

"My thoughts were not on the defenses of our walls." He laughed gently as he ran a finger along the front of her gown. "I thought only of being here with you, sweet one. When I realized my men were enjoying my bemusement, I dismissed them to tend to their tasks."

"While you tend to yours?"

"While," he said in a husky growl, "I tend to you."

Her mouth welcomed his as they entered again the succulent twilight of desire.

Tension ached across Gizela's shoulders as she walked along the lower corridor toward the door to the stable courtyard. Each time a person passed, she waited for an outburst of fury. Instead, the clan grudgingly acted as if it were not unusual for their chieftain to take an English mistress. No one spoke to her, mayhap knowing she would not understand their words, but they did not snarl at her either.

Familiar sounds greeted her as she came out into the sunshine. Shouts and the clang of a hammer on iron rang from the stables. The kitchen emitted light voices and laughter along with scents of the meal being prepared.

Turning away from both, she sought out the small building set not far from the overturned earth which would be a garden in the months to come. A tune drifted to her as she paused in the open door. She took a deep breath of the commonplace aromas that had been one of the few connections between her life in England and the one here.

Her shoes made no sound on the bare stones, but a tall, slender woman with a crown of silver hair looked up from her work at a table. Lines of age dug deeply into her cheeks, but she moved with the grace of a young woman as she smiled and said, "*Pnawn da.*"

"Good afternoon?" Gizela asked. "Can you speak English?"

The old woman looked at her, then nodded.

"I know your chieftain has forbidden all of you to speak it to me, but how can we learn from each other when I can say no more than a greeting in Welsh?"

A smile deepened the wrinkles on the old woman's face. "That is true," she said in an accent which was so strong Gizela had to repeat the words in her head before she could understand them. "Milady, sit with me and speak of what you know."

"I do not know as much as you, so I had hoped you would teach me." She sat on a bench by the door.

The old woman drew up a stool and placed her crinkled hands on the table. Quietly she said, "Milady, I have heard you have much knowledge of herbs and roots."

"Only with the ones used to relieve pain and fever of childbirth, but I am struggling to learn more."

"I am presumptuous to ask the chieftain's lady this, but we need your knowledge here in Cadairllwyd."

Gizela smiled. "Are you Ysolde?"

"Yes, and we could learn much from each other. My grandmother taught me from when I was *pedwar*." She held up four gnarled fingers. "My grandmother learned from her grandmother."

Here, at last, was someone Gizela could speak with freely, for the conversation would be of healing and life, not war.

Ysolde urged, "Sit, milady. Let us learn from each other. 'Tis not your fault you were born on the wrong side of the border."

Laughter burst from Gizela. How easy it would be if others shared this old woman's simple acceptance of the situation!

"Come," Ysolde continued. "Come, you will teach me. I will teach you."

"Yes," she said softly, "we will teach each other."

Ysolde was as good as her vow, for by the time the setting sun touched the far mountaintops, Gizela's head was filled with fascinating facts about plants she had never taken note of before today.

Entering the bedchamber she shared with Rhys, she was surprised to see him standing by the window, staring out at the mountains.

"If you want to wish on the first star to appear in the sky," she said softly, "you need wait only an hour or so."

He turned and smiled. Delight coursed through her at the tenderness she never saw anywhere but within this room.

"What could I wish for when I have almost everything I want right here?"

"Almost?" She laughed as she drew off her cloak and folded it over the bench. "Mayhap wishing on the first star could make it so."

"I see you are becoming more comfortable within Cadairllwyd."

She watched him pour wine into two pewter goblets. "Comfortable? So far only with Ysolde."

"Has she taught you new ways to poison us?" He laughed as he handed her a glass of wine.

"Ysolde's herbs are for healing, as mine are."

He shook his head. "I would not have guessed that from the posset you slipped into our mead that evening." When she glanced down at her glass, he chuckled again. "The only posset I would put into your wine tonight is a love potion to lure you back into my arms."

"You need not do that." She slipped her arm around his waist and rested her cheek on his shoulder.

He took the wine from her and set both glasses on the sill. Enfolding her to him, he smiled as he lowered his face toward hers.

The door opened. Gizela looked over her shoulder as Rhys's mouth froze into a frown. Sheldon strode toward them. With a curse, he jerked her from Rhys's arms.

"Milord," she said, fighting her anger at his interruption, "you are not within de Montpellier Court."

He pushed her to the side and took another step toward Rhys. "Chieftain, I am more distressed than you can guess at the rumors which have reached my ears. These rumors, I see now, are true."

"You need explain yourself," Rhys said, reaching once more for his wine. "Many rumors fill Cadairllwyd. I have heard, milord, of your past exploits which I suspect are the chatter of bards rather than the truth."

Gizela bit her lip when she saw the unfettered fury in his eyes. Looking at Sheldon, she clenched her hands. If he had half the wit he claimed, he would know to retreat with an apology.

Instead Sheldon said, "You have made a grave error, Chieftain."

"What error is that?"

He jabbed a finger at Gizela. "She is my brother's widow, not some common wench you may tumble whenever you wish."

"You insult Lady de Montpellier with your words, milord." Rhys's voice remained low.

"As you insult my family with the assumption you can have her." He smiled with satisfaction. "The assumption you can have her without making certain arrangements with me."

Gizela gasped, "With you? You are—"

"Lord de Montpellier," he returned. "I have nothing, save that title, but it grants me certain privileges. One is that you, *Lady* de Montpellier, should petition me for the right to bring a man to your bed. Any child you might conceive, whether it be legitimate or a bastard, still remains in line for the lands you possess." The wheedling tone returned to his words. "You, Chieftain, must have recognized that the opportunity to sire the heir to the de Montpellier fiefs does not come without a cost."

"Sheldon!"

Rhys put up his hand to silence her. "You speak of English ways, I assume."

"I speak," Sheldon said with a venal chuckle, "of the ways of Lord de Montpellier. You clearly value Gizela's company in your bed. I wish only to share in the rewards you will enjoy."

She pulled the laces on her gown tighter as his gaze swept over her. "You are despicable!"

"You are the only thing of value I have left," he returned with equal heat. "Chieftain, what are you willing to trade me for your continuing pleasure with my brother's widow?"

Gizela stared in disbelief when Rhys said, "Let us speak of this sensitive matter out of the lady's hearing. Excuse us, milady."

"No!" she cried. "I shall not be sold or bartered for. What I give, I give freely. I—"

"Excuse us, milady," he repeated, taking her hand in his. As he raised it to his lips, he murmured, "Trust me, Gizela."

Sheldon's grin grew broader, and she wondered if Rhys knew what he asked of her. No one she had ever trusted, save Kenleigh, had offered her anything without expecting something in return.

"I wish I could," she answered, but Rhys had already turned to motion for de Montpellier to go into the antechamber.

The door closed firmly, and Gizela was torn between berating them with her fury or storming out of the room. Before she could decide, the door reopened.

Rhys was chuckling as he walked in and shut the door behind him. He went to the table and picked up his wine. "Milady?" he asked, holding out her goblet, but she did not take it.

"What do you find so amusing?"

"De Montpellier is a constant source of amusement. Have you not seen that?"

"I must admit I have not." Her pain burst forth. "He laughed at the idea of trading his horse, yet he could not wait to bargain for me." Her hands trembled as she stared at the door. "Who would have guessed he considered me worth as little as his loyalties?"

"You should be honored."

She whirled to face him. "Why? Did he charge more for you to possess me than he did for you to possess any secrets Edward might have shared with him? That is no honor, Rhys!"

Framing her face with his hands, he did not let her pull away. "Do not let what he demanded concern you. He believes I shall give him what he wants."

"And you will not?"

"That is my concern."

"But to renege on a bargain—"

He laughed caustically. "'Tis no bargain to be bled dry by a *Sais* of everything my clan has fought to hold."

"Sheldon de Montpellier is as loathsome as—"

"As whom?" he asked when her voice faltered.

Gizela shook her head. She did not want to think of her father now, and to introduce his name into the conversation would add fuel to the fires of hatred. "It does not matter, Rhys."

"Do not fear. De Montpellier cannot debase what we share with his avarice." He sifted his fingers through her hair and traced her lips with his tongue. "My sweet one, think not of the ways you once knew. Let those within Caernarvon barter and beggar themselves in a quest for power. Here, let us think only of this passion we can find together."

Gizela lowered her eyes and slipped out his arms. She gently brushed the healing spots on her arm as she stared out the window.

"What draws you away from me?" he whispered, so close, his breath wafted through the hair over her ear. "De Montpellier?"

She smiled and shook her head. "I think of someone far more dear. Pomona must be ill with fear for me."

"As you were for her when you came seeking her safe return."

She stared out at the moon which was rising over the mountaintops. "Mayhap my leaving was the very thing which endangers her most. There must be questions about where I have gone that she will not be able to answer."

He drew her to the bed. Leaning her back, he placed his head on her shoulder. Her fingers twisted through his thick hair as he said, "You worry needlessly. They cannot blame your servant for your actions."

"No? You speak of Welsh ways, Rhys, not English." She sighed. "Pomona is more than a mother to me. I do not wish her to suffer."

"Are you suggesting that I sneak into your rooms in Caernarvon and—"

"No!" She looked down into his eyes. As she feared, he was only partly jesting. "Do not see this as an opportunity to revel in embarrassing Edward's men."

With a laugh, he said, "You think I cannot manage to sneak into the castle with a message for your maidservant?"

"Do not hint at such nonsense!"

"What is more nonsensical than you giving me orders, Lady de Montpellier?"

Gizela gasped as, in one motion, he rolled her onto her back. Staring at his savage scowl, she reached up to caress his hair back from his crystal-bright eyes. No longer could he daunt her, for she could feel the craving along his hard body. When he bent to press his lips against the curve of her throat, she sighed with joy.

"I shall not go if that is your wish," he whispered against her ear. She shivered as the heat of his breath stirred her deep inside. "I shall stay here with you."

"For how long?"

Regret wiped away the teasing glint in his eyes. "Do not ask, for the answer will bring you pain. For me, the subjugation of this land remains as distasteful as the day Llewellyn the Great died. I cannot turn away from the needs of my nation and my clan."

Gizela nodded, unable to speak past the despair in her throat. She swallowed roughly, then whispered, "I never would ask that of you."

"Then you cannot coddle me."

"Coddle?" She smiled, although fear scoured her heart. "I can imagine no one who would accept coddling less than you."

"But I enjoy *cuddling* with you." He kissed the tip of her nose and smiled in the moment before he captured her lips anew.

She answered his passion with her own, wanting to think only of the ecstasy awaiting them instead of the shadow of war creeping over this land.

12

Gizela stared at the open gate in the thick wall. It might as well be barred, for she could not pass through it to return to Caernarvon and her duty to the queen. She turned away as she heard the growl from the guard by the gate. There must be a way to leave Cadairllwyd, but she had not found it today. Mayhap, because she truly did not want to leave.

Light music sounded like a mountain stream leaping over well-rounded stones. Each twinkling note added to the sunshine. She walked around a clump of trees overshadowing a garden. A large man, who could claim as many years as Ysolde, sat on a wooden bench.

"Milady?" he called as he stopped playing. The luscious notes faded. "You are welcome."

"Rhys—the chieftain—"

"Loves music as much as you clearly do." He lowered the small harp to his lap. "Sit beside me, Lady de Montpellier. Your arrival is serendipitous. I would enjoy a chance to speak with you, if you are not needed elsewhere."

"I should not have interrupted."

He smiled and patted the bench. "Sit and speak with me, milady. You need not fear."

"I do not fear you. I—" She sat beside him, for she suspected she would draw less attention to herself if she talked to him for a while.

"I am Pwyll ap Cai."

"Pwyll? Like the lover of the woman made of flowers?"

"You know of Rhiannon? The chieftain teaches you well of the legends of our land, proving I taught him well to honor them."

"You taught him?"

"I serve the chieftain as his bard within Cadairllwyd. You shall learn, to a Welshman or woman, the need for a bard is second only to the need for food." Pwyll looked over his shoulder, and called, "*Bore da*, Chieftain."

"Rhys?" Jumping to her feet, she whirled to face him. Would he discover why she had walked in this direction?

"I should have guessed you would find your way here." As he took her hands in his, his gaze caught hers. A hint of a smile vanished into the deep intensity of his eyes. "Can you believe it, Pwyll? I order a bath, so milady can wash my back, and, when I return, she has vanished!"

"I left you to wash your own back," she returned, struggling to keep her tone light. "I wished to discover the source of the wondrous music I heard flowing through the courtyard."

Pwyll's laughter was as rough as metal against a file, although his voice had a velvety warmth when he spoke. "As you can see, Chieftain, I lured your lady from you with a few plucks of these strings."

Rhys looked at Gizela and stroked her cheek. It was impossible to imagine a time when he would not wish to touch her, but he suspected she might not feel the same by the dawn of the morrow. He silenced his sigh. Nothing he could do would change what must be, even if he wished to change it. "Attend me, milady."

She did not pelt him with a dozen questions when he led her to his rooms. She was learning caution and patience, hard lessons for Gizela.

A moan struck Rhys's ears. His hand went to the hilt of his sword, but Gizela pulled away from him. He shouted her name as she rushed through the next doorway. Following, he halted in the door when he saw her on her knees next to a woman whose pregnancy was well advanced.

"Hush," Gizela whispered. "'Twill be fine." Looking up, she urged, "Tell her what I said, Rhys. Please!"

He repeated her words as Gizela stroked the woman's forehead with gentle fingers. When the woman's face relaxed, he recognized her.

"Mair," he said in answer to Gizela's question. "Her name is Mair."

"Mair," she murmured, "can you stand? It will ease the pain."

Gizela waved Rhys's assistance aside as she helped Mair to her feet. "Walk about the room. I shall send you a posset. Drink it and rest." To Rhys, she added, "Is there anyone who could sit with her while I go to the still-room? Some herbs in a mug of ale will ease her pain."

"Yes, but how does she do?"

"She will be fine. The strains on a woman's body as her time nears can copy the first onset of labor." With a laugh, she said, "Trust *me* on what I know so well."

"I trust you, milady. Do what you must, and meet me before dinner in our rooms."

Her smile drifted away. "Where do you go?"

"There are matters that await my decision."

"Matters of the rebellion?"

He scowled. "Be cautious what you say, even within these walls." He kissed her swiftly.

Gizela wanted to ask another question, but Mair groaned again. Rushing back to the woman, she sighed as Rhys's footfalls vanished along the corridor. No matter what he might say, he could not—would not—trust her.

Gizela folded the edges of the piece of buckskin so none of the herbs would fall out. These would give Mair some relief from the cramping. Her fingers tightened on the packet. Queen Eleanor had suffered from the same symptoms. Did she still? If the queen's baby had been born, tidings would have reached Cadairllwyd with the speed of an eagle soaring over the peaks.

The queen had been depending on Gizela to help with the birth. Gizela paused in the corridor and stared at the timbered walls. How much longer could she stay here to exult in Rhys's ardor while the queen might lose her child and her life? Fear struck her, because she could not doubt Rhys's vow to see her dead if she endangered his clan by fleeing again. Yet, the truth of her own pledge could not be denied. She had sworn to the queen to be by her side when the child came. Not even love released her from such a promise.

Love . . . . Another icy shiver raced down her back. To love Rhys was to turn her back on everything she had known, to set aside her obligation to Kenleigh to tend to his lands, to deny what she was. Yet, it was too late to alter the course of her heart now. It wanted to belong— irrevocably and forever—to a man she should hate.

"Why do you concern yourself with such things?" she asked herself as she crossed the courtyard to the great hall. Now there was no escape for her from Cadairllwyd or the love that bewitched her. Mayhap the time would come when she would be able to choose between her loyalties and Rhys, but, for now, that choice was not hers.

Voices rumbled from the other end of the great hall as she entered. She bent to the spigot on the wooden keg by the door, then stood as she heard Rhys's voice. He was seated across the grand room, his back to her, with his trusted advisors. Laughter rounded the table, and she smiled.

Her greeting died unspoken as Rhys said, "Then 'tis agreed. De Montpellier shall be questioned about his loyalties. If he is guilty of what Tremaine accuses, he shall be put to death."

"To death!" echoed his men in a roar.

Gizela rushed out of the great hall as the men cheered the decision. Pressing her back to the wooden wall, she held one hand over her mouth. A single gasp would betray her. Was it possible? Mayhap she had misheard. No, she had not. Sheldon de Montpellier was marked for death if he expressed any loyalty to the king.

Hurrying into another wing of the manor house, she gave the mug of ale to a passing servant and made him understand that she wished it taken to Mair.

She gathered her skirts as she raced up the stairs to the rooms Lord de Montpellier had been given during his time at Cadairllwyd. Knocking sharply, she waited for an answer. None came. She almost turned away, then heard voices within.

She shoved the door open and ran in, shouting, "Sheldon, are you here?"

A woman's scream halted her, and she whirled to look at the bed at the back of the room. A naked woman was crouching against the headboard. Sheldon leaped from the bed, pulling his robe about him, and bellowed, "What are you doing in my rooms?"

"Sheldon, I must speak with you."

"I am busy."

"Too busy to know you may be killed?"

His mouth gaped, then slowly closed as he tied his robe about him. "Say what you will, so you may take yourself from here."

"They are going to question you. If you cannot satisfy their suspicions about your loyalty, they will kill you."

"They?" he asked, walking closer to her.

"The men in the great hall." She gulped, then whispered, "And Rhys."

"So you would cheat your lover from surprising me with an interrogation?" He shook his head. "Why, Gizela?"

"I wish to see no one else dead."

His fingers snaked through her hair, and he shoved her against the wall. Gizela heard the woman on the bed moan in terror, but she paid her no mind. When Sheldon raised a small blade before her eyes, she stared at him, astonished that he would focus his wrath on her.

"Why, Gizela?"

"I told you—" The knife slashed through the air over her right shoulder. When he laughed, she whispered, "Do not prove to me that you are mad! I am telling you what I have heard."

"I shall not be betrayed by you!"

"I have not betrayed anyone. Sheldon, you must leave here!"

He laughed again. "And you, Gizela, do you go with me, or do you stay with your lover to give my father's name to your Welsh bastard?"

"Gizela stays here as my guest, as do you, de Montpellier."

Gizela saw terror flash in Sheldon's eyes as Rhys's voice echoed through the room. His fingers tightened on her, and the knife quivered in his hand. When Gizela saw Rhys's blade at his nape, she understood why Sheldon did not move when a dozen men entered the room. One stepped forward to pluck the knife from Sheldon's fingers. He was pulled away from her.

"Lord de Montpellier," Rhys said without emotion, "you are to go with my men who have been instructed to ascertain the depth of your loyalty to us."

"Chieftain—"

"Do not wheedle or whine," he ordered. "Answer with the truth, or you shall find the death you are awarded shall be excruciating."

"No!" Gizela cried.

As every man turned to stare in astonishment at her outburst, Rhys waved them to silence.

She reached out to him, but her fingers faltered as he faced her. His features were as passionless as his voice. "Rhys, how can you slay—?"

"Say nothing!" Over his shoulder, he said, "You have your orders. I shall be there within the hour. You, of course, will do nothing until I arrive."

"Wait!" she cried, as Sheldon was led from the room.

"Say nothing," Rhys warned again, taking her by the arm.

Gizela knew she could not escape his iron strength. Putting her fingers to her lips to halt her plea, she watched the men leave. Not one looked in her direction.

Only Tremaine stayed behind. He walked to stand before them, a broad smile on his face. "So today it finally begins." He laughed as he locked eyes with her. "Soon not a drop of English blood shall remain in *Cymru*, save for those who yield to us. This is the glorious day when—"

Rhys interrupted fiercely, "Tremaine, you are excused. I wish to speak with Lady de Montpellier alone."

"Enjoy your *conversation* with your lady, Chieftain. An hour should give you plenty of time for any intercourse you please." His laugh remained, as he left to follow the others.

"Gizela—"

"We are not alone," she whispered, looking at the bed.

A hint of a smile twisted his lips. "Come out and begone."

From beneath the high bed, the woman scurried. She did not look at either of them as she fled.

"Let us go elsewhere, milady," he said coldly. "I wish my ears to be the first to hear how you came to de Montpellier with these tidings."

Gizela opened her mouth, but Rhys warned her to silence again. When he raised his hand, she slowly placed hers atop it. She waited for him to say something—anything—as they walked along the corridor. He remained silent until he had opened the door to their chambers. A sharp order sent the servants from the antechamber.

He closed the door and dropped the bar across it. She tensed, but dared to ask, "Why?"

"How much did you overhear?"

"Only the sentence of death if Lord de Montpellier did not prove his loyalty."

"Then you should know why I would order such a thing. Your husband's brother is a traitor who does not deserve to live."

"He betrayed you?" She sank to the bench by the hearth.

"Not completely, although 'twas only a matter of time before he brought the English here."

"But he gave you what you wanted."

He whirled to face her, his blue cape flaring out behind him like the wings of an avenging angel. "Do you know of a man named Dexter?"

"Yes, of course, I know him as you must. He is the king's man." She hesitated, then said, "He brought Sheldon the king's decision about who would be the guardian of the de Montpellier lands."

"And de Montpellier brought him information on the men amassing here as well as maps of our mountains. It is our sole salvation that the maps did not show Cadairllwyd and the other strongholds."

"How did Sheldon contact Dexter?"

"That is why Tremaine is interrogating him. We must learn that." He struck his fist onto the sill. "De Montpellier might have succeeded if I had not received word of his treachery from—" He frowned and turned away.

She rose and went to stand beside him. Putting her hand on his arm, she asked, "From whom?"

"Ask no more, Gizela, for I do not want to see you die as well. There are those who would see the de Montpellier name banished from *Cymru*." His laugh was ironic. "It is your good fortune my allies know how worthless the English consider their women. If you were of this land, you would be made to defend yourself."

"But must you kill him?"

"*I* will not be betrayed!" He drew her against his hard chest. "The decision will be made legally."

"If I—"

"Do not offer me what you know I shall not accept. You have done no wrong. Even if you sacrifice your life, it would be in vain, for a traitor cannot live."

She nodded, knowing he would not be moved. When she walked to the bench to sit, he did not halt her. Such a short time ago, she had listened to Pwyll's exquisite music. Now her heart beat with a dirge.

Hiding her face in her hands, she shuddered. She could not weep, for Sheldon deserved death for betraying King Edward. Fool that he was, he did not have the skill for double deception.

When Rhys's muscular arms surrounded her, she rested her head near his heart. She slipped her arms around him, hoping he would harbor her from the sea of madness surrounding them. His lips brushed the top of her head, and her hands slid along his back. Beneath her cheek, his heartbeat grew rapid.

"Gizela, beloved Gizela," he whispered against her hair.

She saw anguish burning in his eyes. "You did not want to order the execution?"

"I gave the order gladly." He prevented her from looking away. "Yet, I wish I never had to order another man's death. I am not a healer as you are, but, when I play the *crwth*, I am part of the song of life. It is an intricate melody that makes all of us a part of its glory. The death of even one diminishes it, but I cannot allow de Montpellier's perfidy to end the song which comes from the hearts of this land."

She put her hand over his on her cheek. As the tip of his tongue teased her lips, they parted. She moaned in soft yearning for the escape into the passion she had discovered in his arms.

When he slowly lifted his lips from hers, he said, "Gizela, you need not view what must be. If—" A shout came from the courtyard.

He rose and went to the window. She could not understand what he shouted in reply before he walked to the door.

"Wait here," he said as he lifted the bar.

"Rhys?" When he looked at her, she asked, "Will you be so eager to kill me if I leave Cadairllwyd?"

"I would not like ordering your death, Gizela."

"But you would slay me?"

Rhys kissed her cheek, then watched her eyes widen with horror as he said, "Do not make me choose between *Cymru* and you, milady."

Her gasp rang through his head as he walked down the stairs and into the great hall. He poured himself a generous serving of mead and sat in his chair in the empty room. Staring up at dragon banner tied to the rafters, he took a reflective drink. The rich flavor could not wash away the betrayal in Gizela's eyes.

His hand fisted on the table. Nothing must stand between him and his goal of freedom for his homeland. Not even Gizela de Montpellier.

At the call of his name, he watched Tremaine stride toward him. "It is done," his friend announced.

"He admitted his treason?"

Tremaine smiled. "Not directly, but it seems Lady de Montpellier was not the only one to receive a missive from him before he came here. Edward was sent a message as well. De Montpellier hoped to buy his brother's lands and wife with the information that would have destroyed us."

"He has failed."

"You do not look happy, Chieftain." He leaned one arm on the raised table. "It is unfortunate Lady de Montpellier happened into the great hall just at that moment."

"Yes."

"She will calm herself when the deed is done."

"Will she?"

Tremaine started to reply, then laughed. "Is she as dangerous in your bed, Chieftain, or have you tamed the English wildcat?"

"I would want her tamed no more than I want this land tamed by English domination."

When Tremaine climbed up and sat beside him, his friend said, "I would have thought she would be glad to rid herself of de Montpellier. Instead she went to warn him."

Cocking an eyebrow, Rhys asked, "Who can tell with a *Saesnes*? Any I have met before Gizela had no more intelligence than the oxen in the yard. She speaks of honor and obligations with the fervor of a lad taking his first sword-sworn oath."

"Her oath is to Edward."

"Unquestionably."

"Yet you let her live." He leaned toward Rhys and lowered his voice. "There are more than a few who think you are enchanted by this English witch. Bleddyn mutters that to any who will listen."

"Why should she die? She has not betrayed us."

"Yet."

"Nor will she ever." With a cold chuckle, he drank deeply and wiped his lips with the back of his hand. "If she had the opportunity, she would denounce all of us to Edward. You can be certain, she will not have the chance to leave Cadairllwyd."

"If she tries—"

"I will kill her."

"Will you?" Shaking his head, Tremaine drained his mug. "This English wench has besotted you. Kill her before you destroy yourself and all of us."

"No."

"Then you may have written our eulogy."

"Why are you so frightened of a single *Saesnes*?" Rhys looked across the room when Tremaine did. He was not surprised to see a half-dozen men standing before the arch. He raised his voice to include them. "Are you warriors, or are you timid rabbits? She is only a woman."

Bleddyn stepped forward and squared his shoulders. "Was not our last prince, the great Llewellyn, ruined by his love for a *Saesnes*? He vowed fealty to Edward to have his English bride. Will you lead us to destruction in the same way?"

Rhys came to his feet and folded his arms over his chest. He eyed the men, saying nothing until they shifted uneasily. Slowly he walked down from the raised table, crossing the room to stand before them. When they glanced at one another, disquiet on their faces, he drew his knife. He flipped it through the air. It dug deep into the table next to Bleddyn.

"That is my father's blade," Rhys said quietly. "Before Cynan ap Merin held it, the blade served his father Merin ap Olwydd. It helped provide food for their families, and it feasted on the blood of outlanders. Take it, Bleddyn ap Waljan, if you believe me unworthy of it."

"Chieftain, if Llewellyn could be cursed by a woman, can any of us be immune?"

He laughed. "Llewellyn chose his bride over *Cymru*. He let love mislead him, but do not assume I shall fall victim to the same curse." Walking to the table, he pulled the knife from the wood. He held it over his head as he shouted, "To our freedom from English domination!"

As the shouts resounded through the great hall, he turned to where Tremaine still stood alone at the raised table. His friend did not meet his eyes before he turned and walked out. Rhys cursed under his breath. They would see he was right when he won both *Cymru* and Gizela from the English king.

Tremaine threw open the door to the antechamber. "Lady de Montpellier, come with me."

Gizela clasped her hands behind her back as he held his out arrogantly. "Come with you where?"

"Your presence is requested in the courtyard below."

"By whom?"

"By Lord de Montpellier." He smiled icily. "It is honorable to grant a man his dying wish."

She held her hand over her heart, which had faltered at his words. "You ordered him killed?"

"Not my order, milady." Again he raised his hand. "Come, milady."

Shaking her head, she said, "No, I do not think that would be wise. I shall not watch your deadly pageantry."

"Do you fear your own perfidy will be revealed before this household?"

"I have betrayed no one."

"Save our chieftain when you went to urge de Montpellier to flee." For a third time, he held his hand out toward her. "Come, milady."

She hesitated, then knew she had no choice. Sheldon was her husband's brother. She owed him the obligation of not letting him die alone among his enemies.

Gizela was certain every person within Cadairllwyd stood in the courtyard beside the stable as she walked across the uneven stones. From the trees beyond the walls, the songs of the birds lilted with disregard to the dank horror inside her. She wanted to shout for the sun to flee the sky and leave the courtyard dark with shadows.

At a curse, she turned to see Rhys. His scowl was daunting, but it was focused on Tremaine. "Why do you bring Lady de Montpellier here?"

"I thought it wise for her to see what she risks *when* she betrays us."

"She will not." Rhys took her hand and drew her around the well before the stillroom. "Milady, I had hoped to spare you this sight, but, if you were to leave now, there are those—"

"Who would believe me as guilty as Lord de Montpellier," she answered tonelessly. "I shall stay. I have seen many people die, both the very old and the very young, and those in-between. Always I have been death's foe. Never have I stood in silence while death was invited to take a life."

"It is not my way either, which is why I have fought to keep you alive."

She nodded and let him lead her to a chair that was being set beneath the shade of a tree. Fury puckered the corners of his lips, and she wondered if he was angry only at Tremaine or at those who had dared to ask for her life as well. As she sat, she gripped the arms of the chair so hard, she was sure the varnish would be imprinted in her fingers.

To a chorus of jeers, Sheldon was brought forward. Pushing and elbowing their way to the best vantage point, children ran about the open area. Their elders were only a bit less boisterous as they celebrated the death of a traitor.

Her eyes focused on Sheldon as he reeled. In horror, she saw his left arm hung at an odd angle. The dried blood on his face and his broken arm told her how a confession had been wrenched from him.

"No!" she cried, jumping to her feet.

Rhys's hand was heavy on her shoulder. He shoved her into the chair. He rested the tip of his broadsword on the carved arm not far from her hand. "Be silent, milady. No one wishes to hear from you now."

"I shall not be silent!" She started to rise, but dropped back onto the seat as the sword moved in front of her. "You have tortured him!"

His cape struck her face as he stepped in front of her. She drew back, her hand against her stinging cheek as she stared at him. Leaning forward, so his low voice would not reach past her ears, he said, "Say nothing more, Gizela. I shall brook no more interruptions. Do you understand?"

She whispered, "I understand you are as beastly as all the rest of them."

His face hardened, but she did not retract her words. She had thought he was a man of honor, of decency, of compassion, but he had abused Sheldon as her father had her. She did not want him to be like her father, not at all, for she could not love a man who ruled through terror and brutality. Wanting to reach out to him, to beg him to explain why he was acting this way, she could do nothing as he stood by her side again.

Sheldon was shoved to his knees before Rhys, but he looked at Gizela. His laugh was tinted with pain. "So this is how you rid yourself of me, Gizela? Now no one can dispute your claim on my father's lands, and the king can sell you to another fool. Even though you have slept with a Welsh dog, the desire for your lands will wash the taint of your disloyalty from you."

"Sheldon, I—"

Rhys interrupted, "At this late time in your life, there is no need to insult Lady de Montpellier. We are here for other purposes."

A wave of his hand brought forth a man who bowed his head to Rhys before he began to speak in Welsh. Gizela closed her eyes. No translation was necessary. The specific words mattered little, for they sentenced Sheldon to death. Sheldon had been cruel to her, but she did not want to see him die.

Not like this.

Not with this dispassionate ritual which stripped all humanity from everyone witnessing it.

The man's voice fell into silence. She opened her eyes when Rhys spat a single word. His men swarmed over Sheldon, pulling him toward the rock set to one side of the kitchen door. She gripped the chair again. This was not the way for Lord de Montpellier to die. He should be granted a more dignified death than having his head severed from his shoulders in the same place where chickens were killed.

"Say nothing," Rhys said softly.

He put his hand on her shoulder, but she shrugged it off. She did not want his compassion. When he moved his sword so it was between her and the courtyard, she leaned back in the chair. Like Father, he would give her no chance to escape. Only Kenleigh had offered her that.

Sheldon was forced to his knees again. He growled a curse in her direction. When she flinched, he laughed. The sound ended in a gurgle as his hair was grasped and his head pulled over the stone.

The rasp of metal sliding against a scabbard filled her ears as the sun glittered off the naked strength of a broadsword. Her nails bit into the soft underside of her palms. Sheldon slumped against the stone in resignation.

Gizela watched in horror as the sword rose higher, higher, and higher into the blinding glint of the sun. All motion slowed as a great storm rushed through her head, the wind swirling loudly in her ears. The bright light reflecting off the sword flared as it swept downward. She did not see it strike, for the shadowed fog of wickedness billowed over her, stealing all her senses.

13

Nightmares captured Gizela, holding her close in talons as spiked as those of the proud dragon she had seen on the banner. She struggled, but she could not escape. The dank, cold mist of fear thickened about her. She wanted to scream for help, but no sound emerged from her strangled throat.

She forced her eyes open and looked up at the familiar hangings on the bed she shared with Rhys. She turned her face to the pillow which smelled of feathers. Breathing deeply, she wanted to wash away the reek of terror and the memory of cruelty.

"Gizela?"

Taking a steadying breath, she turned toward Rhys's voice. He placed a warm cloth on her forehead, but she plucked it off and sat up. Instantly, the room threatened to collapse into darkness. He put a steadying hand on her shoulder. She wanted to push aside his fingers, but she did not have the strength.

"Ysolde told me to have you drink this," he said, holding out a flagon.

Gizela used both hands to take the wine. She raised it to her lips, then, with a curse, flung it at the hearth. The glass shattered, spraying across the room. "Do you think I can forget your brutality with wine?"

The sympathy vanished from his eyes. "I find it impossible to believe you pine for a man who was so cruel to you."

"But you tortured him!"

"Tortured?" Astonished, his voice sharpened as he drew her to her knees on the bed. "You are mistaken."

"Am I? I saw for myself how sorry his state was."

His low chuckle shimmered through her as he stroked her face. She tried to pull away, but his arm around her waist drew her even closer.

"How can you laugh about such cruelty?" she whispered.

"How can you be so gullible?" He silenced her protest as his fingers stroked her bottom lip with a slow, sinuous delight that reached all the way to her toes. His husky voice grew softer and sought to melt the ice around her heart. "I had no reason to torture him, milady. Once he learned the futility of not cooperating, he gladly told Tremaine everything we needed to know."

"I saw—"

Again he pressed his finger against her lips. "What you *think* you saw."

"'Tis not easy to hide a broken arm."

"True, and neither will it be easy for young Bleddyn to conceal the bruises left by de Montpellier's fists against him. If you wish the truth, de Montpellier broke his arm when he took a drunken swing at Tremaine and hit the wall."

"Is that so?"

"If you do not believe what I have said thus far, why should I bother assuring you that I speak the truth?"

Lowering her eyes to look at the brooch closing the cape on his shoulder, she whispered, "Why should I believe you? You executed Sheldon without allowing him any dignity."

Rhys pressed a packet into her hand. "The sword through his neck did not end de Montpellier's life. This is what killed him."

She opened the packet and sniffed the soft powder. "'Tis poison!"

"Ysolde assured me it was a slow-working, gentle poison which makes its victims feel as if they are falling asleep. I made sure he drank it before I told him of his fate."

"Then when he sagged against the stone—"

"He was already dead."

She stared at him. The sunlight sculpted his face which had been hardened by his life of fighting. "Why didn't you tell me this before?"

"It was not my plan to have you there to witness his death. Damn Tremaine for his determination to force you to betray yourself. If I had revealed the truth in the courtyard, do you think you could have hidden it?"

"And let your clan know of your clemency to an enemy?"

He laughed tersely. "That they know all too well now, milady, for you live."

When she was about to turn away, he caught her by the shoulders. He pulled her tight to him. With wordless, tender persuasion, he wooed her lips to offer him the ecstasy waiting there. Her fingers clutched the front of his tunic as passion's primitive fire coursed through her. She answered his hungry mouth with her own. When his tongue sought between her lips, she groaned with yearning.

He pursued every shadow of her mouth. As she let her hands slip up around the firm planes of his back, she tasted his tongue with her own. His tongue withdrew, luring her to explore him anew. She did not resist the invitation to rapture, sighing with unutterable delight, as his lips caressed her face.

His mouth wandered along her cheek, pausing only long enough to graze her eyelids. He laughed as he kissed the tip of her nose. His arms nestled her close to him.

"No," Gizela moaned, drawing away. "I cannot give my heart to a man who would do such a thing."

"Your heart?"

Gizela slid off the tall bed and went to the window which overlooked the nearly-deserted courtyard. Nothing of the execution remained, although she had been senseless only a few moments.

Turning from the window, she sat on a bench. "Your household is very efficient in clearing away any signs of murder."

He showed no reaction at her emotionless tone. Instead he sat next to her and let his hands drop between his knees in fatigue. "They are very efficient," he answered. "Out of necessity. Speak to me again, milady, of this giving of your heart."

"It matters not."

"You are lying, Gizela."

"I can control my heart no more than I can control the waters upon the shore. If it is foolish enough to crave a chance to belong to you, I cannot gainsay it. Nor, must I heed it."

"Milady—"

"Stop!" she cried before his silky voice could wrap itself around her, luring her back to him. "Tremaine's advice to you is sound. You should never have allowed Lord de Montpellier to arrange for me to be brought here, when I could betray your location to the king as readily as he."

"You have no idea where you are."

"I know Caernarvon is that way." She pointed toward the hearth.

His voice deepened into a growl. "What makes you think that?"

Gizela clamped her lips closed. When her shoulders were seized, she looked into Rhys's narrowed eyes.

"I would appreciate an answer," he said. "Who revealed the truth to you?" His fingers tightened on her shoulders. "I cannot believe Bleddyn allowed you to see the route of your journey here."

"No, he did not."

His smile was cold. "I was so concerned about addling your brain that I urged them to be gentle with you. I need not have worried. 'Tis secure. You seem to know where Cadairllwyd is. The only question is, who told you?"

"You did."

His scowl etched furrows into his forehead. "Shall you lie to me as de Montpellier did?"

She shivered. "I speak the truth. Were you not the one who pointed out the peaks from the shore? Do you think they look so different here?"

He snarled what she knew was a curse.

"Will you slay me now as you did Sheldon?" she asked, barely daring to release what might be her final breath.

"If your accusations were true, Sheldon sent maps of these mountains to the king without pinpointing the location of Cadairllwyd. Which you can do, Gizela" he said, as he brought her to her feet.

Rhys watched fear bleach her face. And she should be frightened, for she alone among those of English blood, could focus Edward's fury on this stronghold. So often de Montpellier had tried to wrest this information from him, but the *Sais* had failed to garner the truth. Instead, the information had slipped from Rhys's lips as he seduced Gizela into his bed.

He had given her the information to betray Cadairllwyd to the English. Bleddyn's warning returned to taunt him. Mayhap he *was* so besotted with Gizela that he failed to see the danger she posed. The echo of Bleddyn's demand to put her to death rumbled through his head.

"Nothing has changed," he said quietly, even though he knew it was the greatest lie he had ever voiced. "While you are within these walls, you cannot reveal what you have learned."

"And if I leave, you will see me dead."

"Yes. That remains the same as well."

Pain burned within Gizela as she fought back tears. "Then have it as you wish, Rhys ap Cynan. Choose *Cymru* over me, if that will make you happy. My heart may beat with yours, but 'tis English blood within me. I cannot change what I am."

"I do not ask that."

"No?" She edged away from his outstretched hands. When glass crunched beneath her slippers, she cried, "Let the soil of this land warm you, Rhys, for I shall not again."

Grabbing her cloak from the bench, she ran out of the room. She waited for him to shout after her, but there was only silence—as endless and as deep, as the agony in her shattered heart.

"Milady?"

In astonishment, she looked up to see Pwyll. The bard drew off his wool cap and came to sit beside her at the back of the stable. She waited for him to speak, but he remained silent.

"Did you wish to say something to me?" she asked.

"You should know Lord de Montpellier's body has been returned to Caernarvon."

"So the Welsh might gloat over their victory?"

"As both a warning and a courtesy, milady. We shall not suffer traitors, but we are not animals. We believe in the God you hold dear, and we believe in mercy for those who have wronged us." He sighed, then stood. "'Twas not to speak of this that I sought you out, milady. Is it true that you are well trained in the skills a midwife must know?"

Surprised that any person in this blighted land did not know why she had come to Wales, she let pride sift into her voice. "I have delivered many babies and lost few of them or their mothers to childbirth fever."

"Then I was wisely sent to find you. Mair is in labor. Ysolde asked me to bring you, for she fears for Mair."

"Where is she?" She rose.

"Come with me."

Gizela felt each sharp glance in her direction, but said nothing while she went with Pwyll into the manor house and to a room as far from the great hall as possible. She faltered only when two men moved from the shadows to stand before the door. Ignoring Tremaine, she turned to Rhys and nodded.

"Milady," he asked, "why do you come here?"

"Pwyll tells me Mair's child is coming."

"Why do you come here?" he repeated. "This child shall be of *Cymru* as are its sire and mother."

"If I am needed to help birth a child, any child of any nation, I shall," she said with quiet dignity. "A woman's life and that of her child must take precedence over anything else, even your lust for power."

"'Tis not lust. 'Tis righteous justice."

"Chieftain, we have no time for this argument. Please let me help this woman while I can."

He nodded and stepped aside. "Go, milady. Help her. Save the child if you can, but grant solace foremost to Mair." Ignoring Tremaine's sputtering, he said, "She may be your lady's only hope."

"She is your wife?" Gizela gasped.

"She is the mother of my child," Tremaine said quietly.

"Then tell me how long she has been suffering these pains." Anger filled her when he spoke of how Mair had been struggling to give birth to this baby for more than a day. "How could you be so foolish as to wait this long?"

Tremaine's retort was forestalled when Rhys opened the door. From within, moans of agony resounded. She pushed past him and went into the room. It held only a bed and a single chair.

Ysolde rose. "Thank God, milady. I prayed Pwyll would locate you swiftly."

Gizela took Mair's hand and put her fingers on the woman's abdomen. "Can you hear me?" Gizela asked softly.

Mair's glazed gaze struggled to settle on her. She nodded. Gizela doubted if Mair could do more.

"How long has she been like this?" she asked Ysolde.

Tremaine did not give the old woman a chance to answer. "I told you. She began to complain of pains yesterday. Last night, she became like this. I sent for Ysolde then." He scowled at the old woman. "She has done nothing to help, save suggest we send for you."

As if he had said nothing, Gizela again asked Ysolde for the details of the prolonged labor. She listed what she would need to assist in this difficult birth.

"Allow me, milady." When Rhys stepped forward, quietly translating Gizela's words into Welsh, he did not look at her.

A chill slipped through her. It was as if they were strangers without even the passion of enmity between them. Dismay glowed in Ysolde's eyes as she glanced from Gizela to her chieftain, but she clearly understood what she had to do. As Ysolde went to give the orders to a servant, Gizela turned to the men. "This is no mummery, and you are excused."

Tremaine snapped, "She is my woman! I shall not have her slain by—"

Rhys took his arm. "Come, my friend. If Edward trusted her skills enough to arrange for her to guide his child into the world, you must grant her the same trust." He drew Tremaine to the door, then said, "Whatever you need, milady, you need only to ask."

"Prayers might be the best you can offer now."

"I trust your skills as a midwife." He resisted the temptation to laugh when her face softened. Quietly, he said, "That I have never questioned, as you know well."

She started to reply, but her words went unspoken as Mair moaned and her body arched with pain. Gizela rushed back to the bed.

"Mair!" cried Tremaine.

"Let Lady de Montpellier do what she can to save your lady's life," Rhys ordered. He pulled his friend out of the room.

Several hours later, the door opened and Gizela looked out. Her hair was plastered to her face in ebony ringlets, and blood marked the front of her gown. In her arms, she held a bunched blanket.

Tremaine took a single step forward. "Is it over?"

"It is over," she said in barely more than a whisper. "The child lives as well as Mair. She is weak and sleeps now." Drawing back the top of the blanket, she smiled. "Do you wish to see your son, Tremaine ap Pembroke?"

Rhys chuckled as his friend inched forward to look at the tiny bundle Gizela cradled. His smile disappeared when he looked past Tremaine to Gizela. With her eyes heavy with fatigue and the child in her arms, she never had looked so fragile and so strong at the same time. She had fought a fierce battle, and she had proven herself the victor once more.

When she smiled as Tremaine asked her a question, a sudden lurch rocked Rhys's gut. Mayhap, even now, his seed was growing within her. Then she would grow round before giving birth to his child who would suckle the breasts which were so enticing. He would hold her in his bed and watch as she slept with their son by her side. Together they would dream of the time when their child grew strong and prepared to follow his father as chieftain.

It was a tempting vision of the future, but one that was doomed never to come to pass. Until the English were gone from this land, no clan would follow any man whose blood was half-outlander.

"Rhys, come and see my son," called Tremaine, grinning so widely his cheeks threatened to snap.

He took a single step toward the child and the captivating woman holding him, before Ysolde peeked out of the room. "Milady, Mair wakes."

Tremaine rushed into the room. Gizela followed, and Rhys paused in the doorway. He smiled when she ignored Tremaine's hands and set the baby to Mair's breast.

Gizela brushed Mair's hair back from her forehead and whispered, "He is beautiful, Mair."

Mair's whisper was barely audible. *"Diolch yn fawr."*

"You are welcome," answered Gizela as quietly. Never would she grow tired of viewing the joy of the first touch of a baby's soft flesh against his weary mother's. Drawing a blanket over Mair, she looked across the bed to Tremaine. "You have seen your son, but Mair and your child need to rest. You may return when they have had a chance to sleep."

"I understand." He cleared his throat, then said, "*Diolch yn fawr*. I owe you a debt, Lady de Montpellier."

She looked past him to Rhys and shook her head. His obligation of a debt had thrown her into this morass of madness. "I cannot accept your debt, Tremaine. This is a gift given to me by God and which I must give freely."

"But—"

Rhys said quietly, "Do not argue, Tremaine. Lady de Montpellier thinks only of your lady who must rest." He raised his hand toward her. "As must you, milady."

"Mair needs to be watched."

"Which Ysolde will do." When he added something in Welsh, the old woman smiled and nodded. "Come with me, milady." His ember-hot blue eyes settled on her again as he added, "Milady, I wish you to attend me elsewhere."

Gizela knew she would gain nothing by arguing. When she put out her hand to set on his, his arm swept around her waist. She closed her eyes, leaning against him as exhaustion overwhelmed her. His arm beneath her knees lifted her against his chest.

When her stomach rumbled, he chuckled. "I suspect you need to break your fast, milady."

"I have worked long and very hard."

"So you have." He added nothing else as he carried her out into the corridor. Ignoring her half-hearted protests that she could walk, he spoke to no one.

Gizela closed her eyes and nestled her cheek against his strong shoulder, thinking she should demand he release her. She had fled from his side, and he had not followed. Did he care as little for her as he had acted yesterday? Or could he love her with the gentleness she found in his arms now?

He opened a door and set her on the floor of his bed-chamber. Her eyes widened as she saw the feast on the table in front of the bed.

"I suspected you might wish to eat," he said with a chuckle.

She took a piece of cheese and lathered butter on a slice of dark bread. When he pushed a heavily-carved chair closer to the table, she sat gratefully. He poured a glass of wine and held it out. She reached for it, but he drew it back.

"Will you drink this one?" he asked.

Her smile wavered as she looked at the hearth. In the sunlight, bits of glass still glittered on the uneven stones.

He lifted the goblet to his lips before offering it to her. "I wish to salute you, milady, for your success in saving Mair's life and her son. Tremaine shall have to relinquish his hatred in the light of his obligation to you."

"As I told him, there is no obligation."

"And as I told you, the night you shared your fire with me, you cannot set aside another's debt."

She set down her glass and rose. "Is this how you fulfilled your debt to me, Rhys? By bringing me here?"

He walked around the table and past her. With his hand on the latch, he said, "This is not how I fulfilled my debt to *you*, but 'twas the only way to satisfy an older debt now."

"To what? To seeing the English swept from this land?"

"In part."

She could not help smiling as she remembered him saying much the same, the night she had first shared his bed.

When he laughed and motioned to the table, he said, "Eat your fill, milady, and rest well . . . alone."

"You are leaving?"

He lifted her hand to his mouth. As if it were the first time he had touched her, she shivered with anticipation of what she hoped would follow. "There is much to be said between us, milady, but the time for such conversations cannot be now. I shall come back to you with all speed, for there must be some compromise that will not break your heart." His finger brushed the center of her chest, and she sighed with soft longing. "I look forward to that hour, sweet one."

She was glad he walked out of the room before she had to answer, for she did not want to lie to him. No, she wanted to lie with him. But that must never be again.

The stable was deserted, save for one man, when Gizela entered. She had waited for this opportunity for nearly the seven days Rhys had been gone to meet with his allies, and finally she had been rewarded. As her feet stirred up the hay, bringing scents of dry heat and manure, she walked to where Tremaine was brushing his horse.

"Tremaine ap Pembroke, I would speak with you," she said with quiet formality.

He glanced at her and away. "Say what you wish, Lady de Montpellier."

"You know what I wish."

He continued to brush down his horse. "If I had known, I wouldn't have needed to ask." He set the brush on the ground and folded his arms on the low stable wall. "You have come to ask me to repay you the obligation you tried to set aside at my son's birth."

"Yes."

"Then say what you wish."

"I wish to return to Caernarvon."

His brows arched, and he laughed. "Why not ask for my beating heart to hold in your hand? The chieftain would gladly give it to you before he has both our necks shortened."

"Do the men of *Cymru* think so little of a vow that they will set it aside if it involves peril?"

"How easily the name of this land rolls off your tongue!" He smiled and shrugged. "I accept your challenge, milady. After all, the Triads say three things overtake a man when he is not looking: sleep, sin, and old age. Mayhap I shall prove them wrong by ending my life upon the order of my chieftain."

"You will take me back to Caernarvon?" She wanted to trust him, but could not.

"Tonight, when the sun is gone and no landmarks give you the truth of our location, I will return you to Caernarvon."

"Thank you," she answered softly. A prick of sorrow coursed through her. Not only was she asking Tremaine to betray Rhys, but she was deceiving Rhys as well.

"Stay within the keep. I shall come for you with the setting of the moon." He picked up his brush and walked out of the stable.

She stared after him, wanting to call him back. She longed to stay here in Cadairllwyd and within Rhys's arms, without the specter of death and past vows to separate them. She doubted if that ever could have been possible, but now she had guaranteed her dreams would die as the moon disappeared behind the peaks of Snowdonia.

*   *   *

The last rays of moonlight tangled in the bushes clinging precariously to the steep crags. Lichen and ferns braved the cliffs to soften them slightly in the faint light.

Gizela huddled in her cape, looking back at the few candles which lit Cadairllwyd against the night. She stared at the thick walls and the thatched roofs of the round towers rising above them.

Tremaine stepped forward and held up a strip of cloth.

"What is that for?" she asked.

"Milady, my debt to you does not include letting you learn the route to Cadairllwyd."

Glad Rhys had not told him of her knowledge of the location of the stronghold, she stood still as he bound the cloth around her eyes. She adjusted it to prevent even the glow of the moon from reaching her.

Tremaine threw her up onto a horse, then climbed into the saddle in front of her. Ordering her to put her arms around him, he gave the steed the command to go.

She leaned her head against his back, wishing for the rich scent that was uniquely Rhys's. Hour after hour passed. The cloth scratched her face, making her skin raw. They went down steep slopes, then climbed others that seemed nearly to reach the stars. When the wind died, she could not guess which direction they had traveled.

Sleep toyed with her, for she had not rested well since Rhys left her alone. She wanted him with her; she wanted him gone. She wanted him to be the man she could love without reservation. Drifting, half-awake, half-asleep, she let the sound of the horse's hoofs lull her like a child's nursery song.

Suddenly the sure-footed beast slid. Gizela jolted awake. She tightened her arms around Tremaine. He chuckled, and she released her grip as the path grew more even.

He stopped his horse. Gizela drew off the blindfold on his command. They sat beneath the shadows of the vanguard of trees along the well-traveled road following the shore. In silence, he slid off the horse and lifted her to the ground. Looking along the road, she saw the lights belonging to Caernarvon.

"*Da boch*," he said.

"Good-bye?"

He nodded. "*Da boch* and *diolch yn fawr*." His smile glittered in the darkness. "Farewell and thank you."

"I hope the babe does well."

"He shall prosper to fight beside his father against those who would steal this land."

"Do not speak of war in the same breath you speak of your son. Pray there will be peace before he is of an age to hold a sword. If—"

She gasped when he pulled her against him. His hand covered her mouth. Fear stiffened her. He had vowed to bring her back to Caernarvon, but she had not negotiated with him to let her enter it alive. If he killed her here, no one would guess her death had been at his hand.

Then she heard a distant, familiar sound. Hoofbeats! Several horses were riding at top speed toward them. Her heart twisted, torn between hope that Rhys had followed them and the fear that he would not be turned from his vow to see her dead if she left Caernarvon.

Tremaine muttered something, then pushed her away. Swinging onto his horse, he vanished into the night.

Gizela hesitated. The riders might be English or Welsh. Dressed as she was, she could be slain by either before she could identify herself. She clung to the shadows as the riders came closer. Praying for help, she dared not move. Then they passed, fleeting phantoms vanishing back into the darkness.

She emerged from the trees and turned toward Caernarvon, not daring to look back up the mountains, for she could not weep in grief when she had gotten exactly what she wanted . . . and lost everything she needed.

14

Dawn painted the sky a rose-gray before Gizela had trudged as far as the three-stone cairn. The night had deceived her eyes, for Tremaine had left her several leagues from Caernarvon. Sunshine struck the top of the dark cape she kept over her head, as she walked through the village in the shadow of Caernarvon's half-finished walls.

The scent of baking bread and the cries of children enveloped her. Yet, everything seemed wrong. The world beyond Cadairllwyd should have changed as she had changed. She had left Caernarvon so sure of all she believed. Now, each of those beliefs had been questioned, and she was certain of nothing.

Returning to help the queen was her obligation, and Rhys now was her sworn enemy. She had seen his unwavering dedication to justice, and he would do whatever was necessary to secure Welsh rule of this land, even execute the woman who loved him.

The road became crowded as Gizela neared the drawbridge leading into the castle. She wove through the parade of carts, but halted when she saw the reason for the delay. Two guards were stopping the carts and checking them. Another guard questioned anyone who wished entrance into Caernarvon.

She stared at them. What tale could she devise to explain why Lady de Montpellier stood on this road and wore the clothes of a Welshwoman? The truth? She almost laughed at the thought. Few among the English would forgive her for surviving her ordeal. She should have died fighting her enemies, instead of helping birth another.

If she waited until nightfall, she might be able to skulk back into the castle. She turned to push back through the crowd. Grumbles surrounded her.

"Please let me pass," she said quietly.

A hand seized her arm. She was whirled to face a dusty surcoat over mail.

"Milady!" gasped a deep voice.

Gizela stared at Fowler's shocked face. The man who had defended her on her way to Caernarvon must be guarding the gates of the castle. She drew her arm out of his grip, and said as she had before, "Please let me pass."

"Milady, where have you been? Lord de Montpellier—" He gulped. "His memorial service is being held in the chapel."

"When?"

"Now." He glanced at the other guards. "Milady, they will wish to know where you have been and how you were returned to us. It was assumed you were slain along with Lord de Montpellier, although your body was not returned to Caernarvon."

"Can you take me to the chapel?"

"There will be questions."

"I am certain of that." She did not add that she intended to use the quiet time during the memorial service to devise a story that would protect her . . . and Rhys.

He hesitated, then whispered, "Can you answer them, milady?"

"Of course." She was glad he did not ask if she could answer with the truth, because that had become a rare commodity when she could not be honest even with herself.

"Come with me." Fowler was not gentle as he cleared a path through the crowd for her.

The other guards scarcely glanced in her direction when they saw Fowler escorting her. They were being kept too busy arguing with the people wanting admittance to the castle. When Fowler whispered the number of guards had been tripled in the wake of Lord de Montpellier's heinous murder, Gizela only nodded. Fowler would not easily accept the truth that the true traitor had been within the walls, the very lord to whom he had sworn his oath of fealty.

Muttering words of sympathy, Fowler left her by the door of the chapel. She drew her cloak more tightly around her. The corridors within the tower were dank and chill, but the most powerful cold came from within her. She was back where she belonged, but a hollow feeling of being a stranger haunted her.

Gizela took a deep breath and went into the chapel. Candles burned on the simple altar, lighting the small room. Daylight filtering through the narrow windows and the half-closed doors barely reached the front of the sanctuary. A single, crudely-carved statue of an unidentified saint stared down at the bits of gold and silver arranged on the altar cloth.

The priest's intoning as he sent a choking cloud of incense over the unadorned casket, halted when he stared at her. Every head in the chapel turned in unison.

Gizela looked at the black-draped coffin where Sheldon's treacherous heart no longer beat. She looked neither to the left nor the right, as she walked down the aisle between the wooden benches which served as pews. Whispers flowed out behind her like the wind in the silver birches above Cadairllwyd.

A hand reached out to her and she heard, "Milady, you live!"

She squeezed Pomona's fingers, then released them as she continued to where the priest continued to gawk at her in wide-eyed amazement. Kneeling before the priest and the casket, she crossed herself.

"Milady," the priest said, "welcome."

"Thank you." She rose. Words she must never speak burned on her tongue. Let the truth die with Sheldon! His evil soul might be facing judgment even now.

A man came to stand by Gizela's left elbow. She stared at Dexter without speaking. He appeared to be wearing the same simple robes he had donned for their last meeting. The king's man lowered his eyes before her blank stare, but said, "I would speak with you, Lady de Montpellier."

"I understand."

He waved to the priest. "This will continue later. Do not gainsay me," he added when the priest started to protest. "I speak on behalf of his majesty King Edward!"

Gizela turned to the priest who wore his distress on his face. Ice froze every word she spoke. "Father, forgive me for interrupting this memorial you have prepared. Would it be possible for the burial to take place immediately?"

He mumbled something which did not sound like an agreement, but nodded. The prestige of her late husband's title impressed even the churchman. He hurried away to arrange for the coffin to be brought to the small cemetery beyond the walls.

"Milady, the queen will wish to speak with you," Dexter said.

Argument came from an unexpected source, because Pomona rushed forward. "Milady cannot appear before her majesty until she has freshened herself from her journey."

"From where?" he demanded.

"From where I have been," Gizela answered smoothly. "What I have to say must be for the queen's ears." She smiled at Pomona. "Thank you for your concern, but I shall gladly go to the queen as I am, if she will receive me."

Dexter laughed sharply. "As I suspect you would, for Queen Eleanor's tender heart would be touched by such a bedraggled sight. Lady de Montpellier, you shall be informed when the queen will receive you."

Under other circumstances, Gizela would have shared a laugh with Pomona over being able to persuade Dexter so easily. Nothing was amusing today. Just the idea of tilting her lips in a smile seemed too onerous. She let Pomona help her from the chapel.

The empty rooms which had been hers a fortnight ago were the same. The bench, the table, the rushes on the floor, the curtains ringing the bed. Nothing had changed, save for her. She went to the window and gazed out at the mountain peaks she had admired from Rhys's bedchamber while she rested in his arms.

Pomona's happy chatter did not reach through the mist of despair surrounding Gizela. She heard the sound, but none of the words, while fresh water was brought and she washed the dirt from herself. Pomona threw the clothes Gizela had worn from Cadairllwyd on the fire.

"My best," Gizela roused herself enough to say when Pomona opened the cupboard. "I must wear my finest for this audience with the queen."

"What you wear will matter less than what you have to say."

Pulling on a clean shift, she said, "There will be many questions, I know, of where I have been."

"I know where you have been."

Gizela whirled to look at her servant. "You do? But how could you?"

"There is but one man who could lure you from Caernarvon into this lawless land." Pomona took out the scarlet gown and draped it across the bed. "You would be wise, milady, not to speak the chieftain's name within these walls."

"'Twas Lord de Montpellier who arranged for me to be enticed from Caernarvon with his collection of lies."

"What—?"

Waving her servant to silence, Gizela said, "It matters little now how he concocted that." To tell Pomona the truth that Gizela had risked herself to protect her servant would add to the pain in the old woman's eyes. "I must speak the truth to her majesty."

"About what happened to your husband's brother?"

Gizela pulled the heavy gown over her head and settled it in place. "He is dead. What more would her majesty wish to know?"

She choked out, "Milady, he was tortured before he was beheaded. What happened to him was so—"

"I know," she whispered, as she waited for Pomona to button up the back of her gown. How quickly she had accustomed herself to the ease of the clothing of Cadairllwyd and the delight of Rhys's fingers on the laces. "I was a witness to his death."

"Oh, milady, no!" Thick tears rolled along the ridges of the old woman's face.

Wanting to offer a solace she could not find for herself, she continued, "'Tis past, and I am alive."

"But your lord is dead." She hesitated as she raised her tear-filled eyes. Her voice fell to a whisper. "Chieftain Rhys ap Cynan has been accused of the crime and may be outlawed."

Cold drained color from Gizela's cheeks. Slowly she sat on the bed. "Outlawed?"

"I have heard the king is considering posting a high reward for his head. Fifteen pieces of gold."

"Rather he should have offered thirty pieces of silver for Sheldon's traitorous head."

"Milady, be wary of what you say."

Gizela nodded as she stood. "How do they know . . . why do they think Rhys did . . . I mean, Chieftain Rhys ap Cynan played a part in this?"

"You need not fear the truth with me, milady."

She stared at her maid who continued to speak in no more than a whisper. Hating the circumstances which forced her to doubt the woman she had always trusted, she asked, "Truth? What truth?"

"The truth of the love that glows in your eyes when you speak of the chieftain." She clutched Gizela's hands. "Milady, guard your heart well, for it can now betray you as no words might."

Gizela sighed as she went to draw on the wimple she had not worn for so many days. As she raised the linen to cover her chin, she sighed. Her reflection looked much as it had before she left Caernarvon. Some sign should reveal how she had found love and traded it for obligation. She turned away. If Pomona spoke the truth, and the old woman always did, the truth was visible for anyone who cared to look close enough.

Bread and meat were brought to Gizela, but she had taken only a single bite when the door to the corridor opened. Pomona rushed to it. Gizela placed the goblet of untouched wine back onto the table as Pomona returned.

"The queen requests your presence, milady." Dampening her lips, Pomona added, "If you are not ready, I can send back a message that you will be with her soon."

Postponing this meeting would not lessen her fear. "No, I shall not lie to the queen. That is not a habit to begin lightly." She looked at the mirror to be sure her hair was hidden beneath her wimple. Her fingertips stroked the material across her chin as she recalled Rhys's caress.

"Sheldon felt no misgiving about being false with his king, and this is the result."

"False?"

"I wonder if the bounty to be paid for Rhys's head is more than what Sheldon expected him to offer for the information that may yet thwart Edward's plans for Wales."

Pomona dropped to her knees and leaned against the bench, her face as pallid as the linen around it. "Lord de Montpellier did such things? If he allied himself with the Welsh, then—"

"He offered the king's man Dexter information on their fortifications as well."

The old woman crossed herself as she muttered a frightened prayer. "Milady, we must leave this accursed land immediately. If you were to return to your father's hall, we would be free of this treason."

"To go now would paint us as the same ilk as Sheldon de Montpellier."

"And Kenleigh de Montpellier."

"No!" She clenched her hands at her side. "Kenleigh did not betray his king."

"How do you know?"

"Rhys told—"

"And you believe a man who consorts with traitors?" Pomona awkwardly came to her feet. "Mayhap he devised lies to buy your loyalty cheaply, milady. Mayhap he knew you would believe any tale he told if it protected your husband's name. No one can mistake the gratitude you feel for your husband offering his name to guard you from your father's cruel hand."

Gizela shook her head, denying the logic in her servant's words. "Say nothing to anybody else of what I have told you."

"As you wish, milady."

Gizela put her hands on the old woman's arms. Looking directly into the eyes which were dulled with Pomona's fear for her, Gizela said, "No, it must be as you wish also. If it were to be known that—" She swallowed roughly and began again. "I have no wish to entangle you deeper in this."

"I shall be a part of this as long as you are."

"You risk—"

"No more than you, milady." Pomona pulled herself up to her full height and glowered as she had when Gizela was a headstrong child. "I know you must keep the secrets in your heart concealed. Whatever you tell the others, I will confirm."

"Thank you," she answered, yearning to say more, but realizing no words could express her gratitude at this unquestioning loyalty. She had forgotten such faithfulness existed when she was immersed in Sheldon's treachery. Not only his, but her own, for her rebellious heart urged her to rush back to Rhys. "I must not keep the queen waiting longer."

"Go!"

Gizela smiled gently. "I shall return to share with you what the queen says."

"'Twill be soon, milady. I know."

"I wish I shared your conviction."

"You have weathered much in your life, milady. We shall weather this as well."

Hesitating, Gizela stood in the doorway to the queen's room. She wondered how she could be honest and still protect the truth within her heart. Damn Sheldon! With his double-dealing, he had left her a legacy of bitterness along with his tarnished title.

Again, as in the chapel, whispers followed her as she entered the room. No one spoke to her. She did not blame any of the queen's ladies, for, until Eleanor forgave her, she was contaminated by the plague which emanated from the Welsh. Going to where the queen sat among a pile of pillows, she dropped to her knees.

Eleanor smiled sadly as she urged Gizela to stand. She held out her hand. "Come and sit with me, my dear friend. I have lamented the absence of your lovely face and charming company. Now Dexter has come to me with such an unsettling tale. I wish to hear what you have to say before he joins us."

Gizela sat on a small stool which had been embroidered with bright threads. "I am grateful you are willing to listen to me."

"You have served me for only a short time, milady, but your skill and kindness could not be feigned." She put her hand on Gizela's shoulder. "Rest assured Lord de Montpellier will be avenged. The barbaric chieftains of this accursed land have dared much to abduct two members of my household."

Fearing her face would betray her, Gizela stared at the bright tapestry covering the plain wall at the opposite side of the room. A bit of the truth might serve her best, but she must choose each word with care. "I was taken after Sheldon. He must have informed our captors of my skills."

"Skills?"

"As a midwife. I assisted there with a difficult birth."

Eleanor scowled, her eyebrows knitting her forehead beneath her wimple. "You defend your abductors?"

"No, milady," she said hastily, aware of the many ears ready to mistake her words and twist them to create more rumors. "I gladly assisted in the healthy birth of a baby who shall grow strong to bear arms for our king."

"For Edward?" Eleanor laughed lightly, and her ladies twittered like a chorus of birds. "Your charming innocence may be the reason they could return you here." She motioned to the door. "Go, and rest, my dear Lady de Montpellier. I shall assure Dexter you have done nothing to betray us."

"Thank you, your majesty," she hurried to say, unable to believe this was the total of the questions she must answer.

"I—" Eleanor's voice cracked as she pressed her hand to her side. Tears jeweled her eyelashes.

When Gizela put her hand against the queen's abdomen, the only sound she could hear was her own rapid breathing and the queen's. She relaxed and smiled. "Such a strong kicker will need no mail over his shoes, your majesty."

"True, but I admit to wishing to *see* him kicking than feeling it against my ribs." Eleanor took Gizela's hand. "Milady, it pleases me more than you can know to have you by my side once again."

"Nothing would have kept me from your side, your majesty." Her voice dropped to a whisper. "Or nobody."

*   *   *

Gizela listened to the fire crackling on the hearth as she stood by the window, looking up at the hills. With ease, she could pick out the serrated mountain which rose above Cadairllwyd. She had to forget that, for no one here must learn what she knew.

With a sigh, she turned away. Her fingers lingered on the soft wool blanket on her bed. She was exhausted. She should sleep, but she could not, for her dreams of Rhys would only whet her longing to be in his arms where she had found love–but was now fated to a love she could never have.

A rap against the door startled Gizela. She had not guessed anyone would intrude while she was in the midst of her grieving— Pomona was the only one who knew her sorrow was not for the most recently deceased Lord de Montpellier. Gizela gave permission to enter.

She wished she had hidden behind her guise of mourning when she saw Dexter in the doorway. Although she wanted to order him to leave, she motioned toward a bench near the raised hearth. "Please be seated. I can send for—"

He halted her by shoving the door closed and dropping the bar across it. A rigid smile inched across his lips. "We must talk, milady. We must talk alone."

"Mayhap we might do so if you will recall your manners." She made no attempt to hide her fury.

His smile broadened beneath his long nose. "I may recall that, milady, if you will recall the truth of what happened while you were far from Caernarvon."

"I have spoken with the queen. Her majesty is satisfied with my answers."

He sneered. "She thinks only of your company when her child comes."

"As I do."

"It would be a shame if you could not serve her as she wishes, but *I* must be certain as well. All I ask is for you to be honest."

"About what?" she asked warily.

He sat on the bench and tapped his finger against his teeth. "About why you live when Lord de Montpellier was returned here in pieces." Leaning forward, he locked eyes with her. "Start with the fact that you were not abducted from the castle."

"I—"

"Before you perjure yourself further, let me be honest with you. A guard on the south tower told me he saw you skulk out of a postern door on the very night you were 'abducted.'"

Gizela lowered herself to a chair and folded her hands in her lap. She would not let him see how they trembled. "I never said I was kidnapped. Sheldon was, and I went to ransom him." She met Dexter's eyes evenly. Nothing must suggest she was speaking anything save the complete truth. This small alteration would be more believable by those who were not privy to Sheldon's treason. "You need not tell me I was a fool to heed the note."

"What note?"

"One I thought was from those who had seen the chance to gain gold in exchange for my husband's brother's life." She was glad the note had been lost on the way to Cadairllwyd, for she must not complicate the situation by including Pomona's name.

"What did you give Rhys ap Cynan for your life?" he countered. "The king would not wish a half-Welsh bastard holding the de Montpellier lands."

Gizela adopted her coldest voice. "You offend me by such a suggestion. I would not bargain for my life in a man's bed." *But I would share Rhys's bed willingly, for I love him*, she silently added. "I swear on everything I hold dear, I did little save assist in a very difficult birth there."

"There? Where?"

"A fortress in the mountains."

"Where in the mountains?"

"I was deprived of my senses on my journey there and blindfolded on the way back. How would I know where it might be?"

"So you were simply released by Rhys ap Cynan."

Again she was glad she could speak the truth. "The chieftain did not release me, for another man brought me back. I believe that in being able to save the babe and the mother of his child, he obtained me my life and my freedom."

"From Rhys ap Cynan?"

"I told you—"

"You have told me lies." He stood and jabbed his finger toward her. "Your husband's name was a proud one, until the day he wed you. You shame both his name and your father's with these tales."

"I have done nothing to shame Kenleigh's name. He requested me to come to Wales to use my skills as a midwife."

"To assist the queen."

"Mayhap that was his intention, but his message to me did not specify that." She came to her feet and went to the door. Lifting the bar, she opened it. "I have told you the truth on this matter as I have told the queen. She believes me. Why should you continue to question me?"

"Because there are too many gaps in this tale. If they let you live, why did they slay Lord de Montpellier? He had much more value to them as a hostage."

She stroked the rough wood on the door. Keeping her eyes lowered, so they were shadowed by her wimple, she answered, "I was not a part of the decisions made there. For much of the time I was held in their stronghold, I remained within a private chamber."

"Yet you saw de Montpellier executed?" Dexter persisted.

"Yes."

"And?"

She stared at him. Did he wish her to describe every gory aspect of Sheldon's execution? She would not, nor would she reveal the truth of Rhys's clemency. "And what? Lord de Montpellier is dead!"

"Of what crime was he accused?"

"The document outlining his crimes was read in Welsh. I understood nothing but his name. No one translated it for me."

Dexter strode toward her. "Then they just let you go?"

"Yes, in the middle of the night near the road that leads to Rhuddlan. Two riders passed me in the hour before dawn. They were riding with all speed possible. Were they messengers to the king? If so, you can ask them. They must have seen me." She folded her arms over her chest and raised her chin. "I would have called out to them to verify my story, but little did I suspect I would be questioned so vigorously."

He scowled. "You have changed, Lady de Montpellier."

"Why do you find that astounding?" She pushed the door farther open. "I have been a witness to my husband's brother's murder." With a shiver she did not have to feign, she continued, "I cannot imagine remaining unchanged by that." She bowed her head toward him. "I must ask you to retire."

"We will talk more," Dexter said, obviously unwilling to accept defeat.

"I am sure of that."

"So am I, and—"

"Milady!" cried Pomona, nearly bowling the man down as she burst into the room. "It is time."

"The baby?" she asked. "Gather my bag. We must not delay."

Dexter blocked the door. "You cannot believe I will allow you—a suspected traitor—to attend the queen?"

Gizela took the bag Pomona held out to her. If she faltered now, more than her life might be lost. She pushed past Dexter. When he grasped her arm, she snapped, "Will you be the one to take King Edward the news of the death of his child if I am kept from assisting the queen?"

He released her, stepping out of her way. As Pomona hurried with Gizela to the door, he shouted, "This is not over, milady. I shall discover the truth, and then you shall pay for your crimes."

15

Gizela put Dexter's threats and everything else out of her mind as she rushed along the hall. All thoughts must be focused on the queen and the child. When she heard a cry from the queen's rooms, she gathered her skirts. Pomona uttered a prayer behind her. Running at the best pace she could manage, she burst into the room just as she heard someone shout her name.

"Move aside," she ordered as she shoved through the wall of women surrounding the queen. For a moment, she thought they would resist, then, almost as one, they fell back.

Gizela put her hand on Eleanor's distended belly. The muscles beneath the velvet of her skin were softening from a contraction. "Is this pain the first one you have suffered?"

"There have been a few pains before this, but not as strong as this one." Eleanor smiled weakly. "Your timing in returning to Caernarvon seems excellent, for I doubt if this child will wait much longer to be born."

"That is well, your majesty. It is time for you to enjoy the chance to hold your child in your arms."

The queen crossed herself and whispered, "I pray to God a healthy, living child shall come forth."

"You have been kicked by the baby for weeks now. Can you doubt its strength?" Daring to put her hand on the queen's shoulder, she added, "Believe in what is to come to pass, your majesty, and your faith surely is to be rewarded."

Gizela called for the queen's maidservants to come to assist Eleanor to the private chamber set aside for the birth. Motioning for Pomona to bring her bag, she loosened the laces on the top. She opened it and looked for the packet of herbs that would ease Eleanor's labor. She frowned when she could not find what she sought.

"Pomona, where is the raspberry leaf I keep in the bag?" she asked.

Her servant colored deeply. "Forgive me, milady. While you were—" She cleared her throat as the queen's ladies glanced at them. Nothing either of them said must suggest anything but the story Gizela had given the queen. "A few nights ago, I made a posset from the ground leaves when my old bones were aching. You said it would serve me well, and it did."

Gizela searched through her bag for the other herbs she wanted to have ready for the queen. "Did you use the opium and mandrake as well?"

"Nay, milady. I know they are powerful, and I would not use them without your help."

"Stay with the queen, Pomona." She closed the bag and held it out. "Guard this well. I need nothing else missing. It shall take me no more than a few minutes to go to the stillroom and gather what I need to give the queen rest. Have her reclining in a private place."

"If you will tell me what you need, I shall fetch it for you."

Gizela smiled anxiously. "It will take longer to explain than to go myself. Take yourself to the queen and assure her I shall return to her side with all haste."

Word of the labor pains must have reached every ear in the castle, for, as Gizela rushed through the hallways and down the stairs, anyone she met stepped aside to let her pass. She wondered if a message had been sent to King Edward at Rhuddlan. Even the vital meeting with the few Welsh chieftains who had pledged their loyalty to him would be interrupted by such tidings.

Drizzle filled the inner bailey as darkness swept down from the eastern mountains to swallow them in night. Gizela ducked her head into the storm. A flash of lightning scored the sky, and she flinched.

Mud clung to her slippers, slowing her and threatening to send her tumbling into the mire. She looked up and turned to her left to reach the kitchens and the still-room on their far side.

Lightning sparked. Her steps faltered as thunder cracked like a sword against a shield. Rain struck her when the wind became a mad whirlwind within the walls.

An arm snaked out of the storm. It circled her neck. Gizela took a deep breath to scream. The strong arm tightened. She clawed at it, but her fingers found no grip on the slippery wool covering it. Slowly the arm loosened. She drew in another breath cautiously, but the arm around her throat did not tighten again. She stood as still as she could, waiting to see what her captor would do. Her teeth clenched. If Dexter had set an ambush to slay her, he had chosen a poor time.

When she was pulled back against a hard body, a whisper brushed her ear. "I vowed I would see you dead if you fled from Cadairllwyd again."

"Rhys!"

He shoved her ahead of him into a half-built tower that was lower than the surrounding walls. Out of the storm, but deep in the shadows, she stared at him in disbelief. His reddish brown over-tunic with its wide slits along his arms revealed the light blue of his tunic beneath it. A hood was drawn up to conceal his strong features. Even in the simple clothes, the breadth of his shoulders and the golden hair brushing his collar could expose him.

"Are you mad to come here?" she whispered.

"I would ask the same of you, Gizela." Taking her arm, he drew her farther back into the shelter. He pulled out the knife at his belt and held it up before her eyes. Even in the dim light, she could see the brilliant, red paint decorating the wings of the dragon on its haft. "I had hoped you would not force me to slay you, sweet one, but you give me no choice when I would much rather—" With a desperate moan, he tugged her against him.

She softened as his mouth worked its magic, that dangerous enchantment that could give life to such love in the midst of hatred. When his hood fell back before her questing fingers, she tangled them in his thick hair, caught up in the storm of desire which was as wild as the one raging beyond the walls. The iron bar of his arm kept her tight to him until she was aware of every inch of his arousal.

He ripped her wimple from her head with a growled curse before kissing a path of sweet fire along her neck. He leaned her back over his arm. She swayed with the rapture, wanting to be a part once more of the intricate, intimate melody of passion.

Gizela gasped when the cold blade of his knife pressed against her throat. Staring up at Rhys, who slanted over her, she whispered, "Will you slay me without letting me explain?"

"What is there to explain?" he asked, but his voice was raw with desire. "I warned you what I must do, sweet one, and I cannot break that vow to see you dead if you tried to escape from Cadairllwyd again."

"But I did not escape. I was guided back to the road leading here."

"Do you expect me to believe such a lie?" He set her on her feet, keeping the knife beneath her chin.

"No, Rhys." She saw his surprise when she smiled, and she could not blame him, for she knew his threat was genuine. Yet, she must persuade him to look past his wounded honor. "I would not lie to you. You are no fool." She touched the front of his damp tunic and longed for his arms to enfold her. "I was allowed to leave Cadairllwyd and return to Caernarvon because I asked for the payment of a debt."

"Tremaine?" He cursed vividly. "Do you wish me to believe *he* would guide you back here where you could betray us?"

"He does not know that I know where Cadairllwyd is."

"True, but he knows better than to underestimate your well-honed wit, milady."

"Both you and he insisted the obligation of a debt to me was real." She ignored the knife as she put her hands on his arms. "Rhys, I did not want to leave *you*, but I have the obligation of a debt, too. It must be paid here."

"A debt? To that bastard Edward who will bleed your manor lands dry to finance his armies?"

Rhys was startled when tears filled her eyes and ran down her soft cheeks. He slid the knife back into its sheath as he brushed the dampness away, wishing he could retract the words that had given her such pain. When she turned away, he was certain an invisible fist had struck him in the gut. His hands stroked her trembling shoulders.

She did not look at him when she said, "This debt is one I owe Kenleigh. He offered me the protection of his name and granted me his lands so I need never fear again."

"Fear whom?"

He was not sure if she had not heard him when she continued, "The only thing he ever asked of me was to be with the queen when her child came."

"I understand."

"Do you?" Finally she faced him. Tears glittered on her cheeks, but her chin jutted with pride. "Then why do you berate me for what I must do?"

"Because I fear for you among these vicious fools, who would strangle *Cymru*."

Her fingers were closed in fists as she pressed them to her chest. "But here, Rhys, is where I must be to do as Kenleigh wished. Do not halt me from fulfilling the only vow I shall ever satisfy for my husband."

He gripped her arms and pulled her to him. "When the child is born, what then, sweet one?"

"Do you ask me to return to Cadairllwyd then?"

His thumbs wiped the tears from her cheek as he shook his head. "You must come with me now."

"I cannot."

With a sigh, he said, "I understand. Then I shall—"

She shook her head. "Do not come back here, Rhys. I have heard the king plans to outlaw you."

"Let him, for it matters little."

"Even to your friends who may be willing to sell your severed head to him for the gold he offers?"

He folded his arms over his damp tunic. "I choose for my friends only those who will not deceive me."

"As Tremaine did when he brought me back here?"

He frowned. "You speak of the fulfillment of a debt, milady. He was obligated, whether he wished it or not. If you will not come with me, then bid me farewell, Lady de Montpellier."

"Farewell?" Gizela clasped her hands more tightly on his arms. "Rhys, must it be like this?"

He stepped away and shook his head. The determination on his face shattered her heart, for she knew he would not relent on this. "I despise the very ground where Edward has raised these walls. To be here reminds me of the pain all *Cymru* must bear. When I leave here, I have no wish to return to this accursed place until I watch Edward relinquish hold of this land."

Someone calling her name halted her from speaking, although she had no idea what she might say to change his mind. She had seen the anguish this place caused Rhys. A proud man, he did not wish to stand amid the monument to King Edward's victory.

"I must go," she said, locking her fingers in front of her to keep from grasping his sleeves and begging him to reconsider.

"Go then, milady."

She took a single step, then stopped. "I shall pray for peace."

"Your prayers will be answered only by bloodshed, I fear."

"Lady de Montpellier!" the shout came again, closer.

Gizela edged to the rough doorway and peered out. She saw one of the queen's ladies rushing about the inner bailey like a frightened horse seeking its way out of the stable. She could not delay.

"Go in peace, Rhys," she whispered.

When she heard no answer, she glanced over her shoulder. She was alone. Sobs ripped from her as she hid her face in her hands.

"Lady de Montpellier? Where are you, milady?"

She swept the tears from her face. They must not be seen to reveal the grief within her. How pleased Dexter would be to denounce her before the rest of the court! No, she would not give him that gratification.

Rushing out into the wild storm, Gizela soothed the woman and sent her back into the tower, giving her a message to let Pomona know Gizela was on her way. The wind tore at Gizela's hair, and she realized she had left her wimple in the tower. She could not spend time searching for it now.

Hayes spun about awkwardly when she ran into the stillroom. Quickly he gathered what she needed and handed the small pots to her. "If there be anything else you need—"

"I shall send word." She secured the containers in her wide sleeves. It was the best protection from the storm she could offer.

"If you be needing me—"

She laughed. "I shall not send for you, for I know how you disdain such work."

His gruff chuckle followed her back out into the wind and rain. She ran to the lit tower. Again, the household scurried out of her path as she climbed the stairs to Queen Eleanor's apartment.

Gizela did not knock on the door to the queen's chambers. A woman came forward to greet her, but Gizela motioned her aside. Pomona took the containers and nodded to Gizela's quick instructions.

She kept her smile in place as she went to the door. No one must suspect there was any reason to worry. The evil humors created by such thoughts could affect the baby. At that thought, she unbuttoned her gown and let the wet wool drop to the floor. Nothing must endanger this child, not when she had sacrificed her heart's yearnings to safeguard this birth.

Gizela was amazed the smallest room in the queen's apartment had been chosen as the birthplace of the next prince or princess. Not even a hearth warmed the room. She called for blankets to be hung over the glassless window. Then she ordered all the queen's women out. She did not want them jostling her elbow in the cramped room.

"Lady de Montpellier, the queen is the one who gives orders here," retorted one heatedly.

Eleanor said, "Listen to Lady de Montpellier, my friends. Come, milady, and tell me all is well." Her face strained with the changes within her body.

The women mumbled protests as they edged through the door into the room where the fires on the pair of hearths would fight back the dampness which had seeped into the very stones of the castle.

A single woman remained in the corner of the room. Gizela gave Mary a smile, for she had been selected to be the child's nurse.

"How do you fare, your majesty?" Gizela whispered, as she saw the beads of sweat ringing the queen's forehead like a cruel crown.

Eleanor gasped, "This one wishes to be born soon."

"Good." She held up a cup. "Try to sip this slowly. It eases the pain."

Gizela continued in the calm tone she had been taught to use. When she helped the queen remove her loosened gown, Mary came to assist. Gizela hid her shock when she realized the prayers Mary whispered were not in Latin or French or English. She spoke Welsh.

Did Rhys know a Welshwoman had been chosen as the child's nurse? He could not, for he would have been too furious at such perfidy to remain silent.

The blanket at the window flapped sharply, the snap of the wool as fierce as the thunder rumbling through the inner bailey. Gizela called, "Secure that!"

Mary nodded and climbed to sit on the sill, pinning the material in place. Gizela could not keep from smiling at the obvious solution.

Dabbing the queen's forehead with a damp cloth, Gizela lowered her voice. "You are doing well, your majesty."

The queen smiled weakly, but did not speak. Her fingers clutched the tangled sheets, and a moan drifted from her lips as another contraction rippled across her abdomen.

Gizela went into the other chamber to check the posset stewing on the hearth. Dozens of questions assaulted her. She paid them no attention, but called to Pomona.

"Stay here by the door," she ordered. "It shall be easier to have you bring what I need to me."

"Aye, milady." Pomona's wrinkles deepened as she smiled. "They have little patience."

"That is their misfortune, for, as you know, a child will come only when it deems the time right."

When Gizela went back into the birthing chamber, Mary smiled from her seat on the windowsill. Gizela chuckled as she returned to the queen's side. Mayhap if those empty heads in the other room had half the sense of this Welsh nurse, Gizela could have asked for an assistant among them. As long as she had Pomona, nothing should go amiss.

The crackle of thunder made Gizela flinch, but, in her pain, the queen did not notice. While the storm faded into the distance, the contractions came closer together and more strongly until Gizela saw the gray light before dawn coming around the blanket. Still the baby had not been born.

"Music," Mary whispered, coming back to the bed.

"Pardon me?"

"Music soothes a laboring woman and lures a babe from within. Erbin, who works in the kitchen, plays the *crwth*." Color flashed on her pale cheeks. "That is—"

"I know what a *crwth* is." She wiped more sweat from the queen's brow.

"Shall I send for him?"

"Do so. It cannot hurt."

When soft music came from the door, she looked over her shoulder to see a wide-eyed lad perched on a low stool, plucking the lap harp while he stared at all that was going on. Mary came in, smiling broadly, and closed the door to a slit.

Gizela was astonished when the labor began to progress again. Curiosity taunted her. In Cadairllwyd, Ysolde had sent the bard to find her. Had he been sitting by the birthroom, strumming his harp and trying to help as the lad was?

"The babe comes," gasped the queen.

A quick examination showed Gizela the queen was correct. The baby was nearly ready to be born. The crown of its head was visible. Gizela whispered her thanks to Mary who nodded.

"Breathe lightly, your majesty." Gizela smiled at the queen. "You are doing so well."

"The baby is fine?"

"We shall know soon."

Eleanor gasped something Gizela could not understand, and she guessed the queen spoke the language of her birthland. Nodding encouragement to Mary who continued to hold the queen's hand, Gizela bent to her task. As the queen's tormented stomach muscles tightened, Gizela urged the queen to push the baby out into the world.

The muscles across the queen's belly softened again. She said soothingly, "Push as hard as you can next time."

"I have pushed so hard."

"Eleanor, push hard, and your baby will be in your arms within minutes."

The queen gave her a weak smile, then winced as she struggled to birth the child. Whispering encouragement, Gizela did not move as she guided the baby from the queen's straining body. She pulled clean cloths from the pile set on the edge of the bed, and cleaned the baby's face. Tilting it, she patted it gently on the back.

A shrill cry echoed off the high walls of the tiny chamber as Gizela announced, "'Tis a boy, your majesty! A healthy, well-formed boy!"

"He lives?" Eleanor whispered.

"Listen."

The queen's pain-lined face smoothed as the baby continued to protest his emergence into the world. Her fingers stretched to touch the infant's matted hair while Gizela tied off the umbilical cord. Again the queen whispered words Gizela could not understand. When Mary peeked over the queen's shoulder, Gizela smiled.

For one special moment, there were no boundaries between them. All of them exulted in the miracle of the birth of a healthy child.

Gizela cut through the cord. Carefully she lifted the child and wiped him clean. "He is strong, your majesty."

"He is willful," she replied, joy singing in her voice. "Be strong of will, my dear son, for in that you are like your father whose name you shall share."

Wrapping the baby in a soft piece of wool, Gizela was glad to hide her face from the queen. How many times had her father ranted because he had no son to take his name upon his death? *Only a daughter who shall submerge my name beneath her husband's.*

Mayhap she will birth the son her mother denied me, but he will not have my name either. He had repeated that endlessly, especially on the anniversary of her birth when he would seek solace in wine, and the arms of one of his many mistresses.

Begone, she told the memories she did not want to recall tonight. This was a time of joy, a time for thanksgiving, a time for imagining a future when all dreams come true.

Gizela placed the child in the queen's arms. Later the baby must be swaddled to grow strong and straight, but she suspected the queen, like every mother, would wish to count her baby's fingers and toes.

Young Prince Alfonso was the only other living son Queen Eleanor had given King Edward. There was little chance this newborn would become king because the prince was past the most dangerous years of his young life. Yet, each child was precious, because too many diseases preyed on them, often claiming their lives.

When Mary took the baby, Gizela turned her attention back to the queen. While she cleaned the bed, Gizela listened to the soft coos Mary spoke in Welsh. The words were barely heard over the rattle of rings holding the oak cradle on two upright poles.

Gizela made certain the queen drank more of the posset. Mixing opium in another glass, she watched the queen drink it. The light mixture would ease the pains left by the child's passage.

Only when the queen was asleep, exhausted from her toil, did Gizela go to the door. As she opened it, the room beyond became as silent as a tomb. She looked amid those crowded in the room. Her smile wavered when her eyes met Dexter's, but she knew what she must do. Closing the door behind her, she crossed the room to him.

"Dexter," she said, "I wish to send a message to his royal majesty King Edward at Rhuddlan Castle."

"What do you wish to say, milady?" His eyes seethed with fury, but he would not forget his place as the king's representative in Caernarvon.

"I wish to tell King Edward he is the father of a healthy son whom the queen has named Edward to honor his father."

Shouts rang through the room in complete disregard of the new baby. They muted when Gizela warned them to silence, reminding them the queen needed to rest.

Dexter nodded. "Please inform her majesty that I shall send a man posthaste."

"Thank you." Gizela started to turn away, then asked, "Whom do you send? The queen may wish to know when she rouses."

"Griffith Lloyd."

"A Welshman?"

"Who better?" he countered. "He knows the shore road to Rhuddlan as well as you know the secrets of your heart, milady. Let the Welsh who are loyal to the crown earn the king's pleasure, while those who deny our king his legal place as their overlord regret their stance."

When he smiled, she backed away. His determination to see her accused of the crimes Sheldon had committed had not lessened.

"Have him make haste," she said. "I am sure the king will want to know these tidings without delay."

"He will wish to come here, milady." His grin was savage. "Then he shall wish for answers to the questions I have posed to you. I can promise you he will not be as easy to please as her majesty, and his punishment to those who have betrayed him shall be infinitely excruciating."

16

Gizela squeezed water from a cool cloth. She set it on the queen's brow and was rewarded with a sleepy smile. When the queen closed her eyes, she sank back onto the bench.

Two days after the birth of her son, the queen was suffering from a slight fever. With what she had learned from Ysolde, Gizela had concocted a posset which granted Eleanor sleep so her body might battle this illness.

Putting her hand against the queen's cheek, Gizela smiled. She looked at where Mary was gently rocking the cradle and said, "She is cooler. I pray the fever is leaving her."

"You are a fine midwife, milady," Mary replied in her thick accent, which reminded Gizela of Ysolde.

"I simply practice the skills I was taught."

"Why?"

Gizela blinked in surprise. During the long hours of the past day while they had worked together, Mary never once had asked her such a direct question. Gizela brushed her hands against the matted wool of her stained gown as she tried to think of an answer which would satisfy the nurse without revealing the truth Gizela did not like to face.

Mary continued, "Forgive me, Lady de Montpellier, but is it the English way for a noble lady to tend to births?"

"No, but it is my way." How could she explain her yearning to prevent any woman from suffering the excruciating labor her mother had endured before dying?

"That is a good way." Her smile lit her plain face. "It would be a shame to put aside your God-given talents. He gave you these skills for a reason, and you should not turn your heart from doing what you can."

Gizela turned away. If only Rhys could have shared Mary's simple beliefs, mayhap . . . . No, she could imagine nothing that would bring them together again. He must not return to Caernarvon, and her life was among the English. She closed her eyes as her body ached for the strong caress of his hands, which would banish her loneliness with passion.

Shouts came from the courtyard. Whatever was happening in the inner bailey must not be allowed to wake the queen. She rose. Sending Mary to deliver her message would be useless, for no Englishman would heed a Welshwoman's orders.

"Mary," she whispered, "I shall return quickly. I must quiet those downstairs. You are to allow no one in here save for me or upon command of our lady." She had become accustomed to using neither the queen's title nor name, for fear the words might wake her.

"Of course, milady." Anxiously she looked from the window to the door. "If—"

"Use my name to keep them away." Gizela patted her pudgy shoulder lightly. "If they are angry, let them be angry with me."

Mary flashed her a smile of gratitude, but turned to the baby who whimpered in his sleep. As Gizela left the room, she heard Mary whisper endearments in her native language. She wondered if the queen had considered that her young son's first words might be in Welsh.

The outer rooms were deserted. Where were the queen's ladies and the men who plied them with compliments? Her bafflement became exasperation when she heard the pounding of heavy footfalls in the corridor. She rushed to caution the passersby to be quiet.

The door opened before she could reach it. A young page entered the room and intoned, "Make way for his majesty, King Edward."

"Your majesty," she whispered as she dropped in a deep curtsy. She winced as the rough stones of the floor cut through her gown.

"Rise," he ordered.

She obeyed. Her eyes widened in shock. King Edward of England possessed the same golden hair as Rhys ap Cynan. Sweat plastered his hair to his forehead, and the odor of a hard-ridden horse billowed from him. Riveting, albeit exhausted, blue eyes regarded her steadily. She waited for his next order, for she could not speak until he addressed her again.

"You are—?" he asked in the same brusque tone.

"Lady de Montpellier. Gizela de Montpellier."

He nodded, then turned to the page and the others following him. "You are excused." Only when the door was closed did he motioned for her to come to her feet and added, "I have been told you, milady, were the midwife who safely delivered my son."

"Yes, your majesty."

"How do they do now?"

Smiling, she relaxed slightly. Even a king was only a man when he worried for his child and wife. "They are well. Your new son is healthy, and your wife is recovering after a slight fever." She hesitated, then added as she would have to any anxious father, "They sleep now and should not be disturbed."

His face, which had been hardened by his years spent warring on his enemies, softened. "I accede to your learned advice, milady." Running his hands through his hair to leave it spiked at odd angles across his forehead, he smiled. "I commend your loyalty to your duty, Lady de Montpellier."

"'Twas my honor, your majesty."

"Your loyalty is doubly commendable in the light of recent events."

Gizela was spared from answering when he crossed the room and poured two goblets of wine. He offered one to her, and she accepted it with a slight curtsy. Her fingers trembled as she lifted the cup to her lips. She hesitated when he did not raise his own goblet. Fearful she had made a horrible error, she began to lower her cup.

"Please drink, Lady de Montpellier." Holding up his goblet, he added, "I salute your success in bringing forth my healthy son. I wish Eleanor had had your skills and company through all her births."

She sipped politely. "I thank you for your generous words."

"Then be as generous to me, milady, and speak the truth of the events that have transpired here during the past fortnight." He sat on one of the padded benches, but did not offer her the courtesy of motioning for her to sit as well.

She understood what he did not have to say. Even though he appreciated her efforts during his son's birth, his thoughts always must be focused on protecting those lands he claimed.

Setting her glass on the table, she folded her hands behind her back. "My efforts to save my husband's brother from death were fruitless, your majesty."

"His death will be revenged when I have Rhys ap Cynan on his knees before me." He took a sip of his wine. "What say you to that, milady?"

The temptation to lie was sweet on her tongue. When Rhys's amused voice rang through her head, telling her of the need for a liar to have a fool to heed the tale, she hesitated. Like Rhys, King Edward was no fool. Only the truth would serve her now.

Taking a steadying breath, she said, "I would wish the war to come to an end in this land, your majesty. My family has given much to secure that peace."

"That is true." His gaze drilled her. "You may have heard I planned to outlaw the chieftain."

"Yes, I heard that."

He smiled, but his eyes were cold. "There are better methods of vengeance, milady. Like you, I wish to see peace throughout this land. Other battles call me, for the Scots threaten to overrun their borders. When Rhys ap Cynan bends his knee to me, I shall know the battle here is won."

"He would prefer being outlawed to that, your majesty."

"You speak with intimate knowledge of the chieftain."

She matched his chilly smile. "I have come to see the pride within these people. In that, they are no so different from those of us who were born on the other side of Offa's Dyke."

"True, milady, and the time shall soon come when the Welsh shall acknowledge me as their rightful liege as do our countrymen." He rose and picked up the glass she had set on the table. Lifting it, he said, "Drink to my victory, milady, and to the victory of my allies. Drink to the death of my enemies. Our enemies."

She took the glass in both hands and sipped, not daring to disobey.

He took the goblet from her. Emptying it in one gulp, he smiled. "I vow to you, milady, that you shall never forget the part you will play in bringing the Welsh dragon to heel."

Rhys leaned against a pillar at the side of the great hall of Caernarvon and watched the others. No one spoke in the grand room where the banners of King Edward commanded every corner. Faith, but he had vowed never to return to this accursed place. A message had been delivered to him that Edward wanted all chieftains of North Wales to wait upon him at Caernarvon. Even so, he would not have returned here, save for the rumor Edward had devised a way to defeat the chieftains. He could not allow that to happen.

Most of the faces in the room he recognized. Many he considered allies. Other faces belonged to the insidious Englishmen who had stormed into his homeland and demanded its subservience to their treacherous king.

It was said Edward had been outrageously delighted with the tidings of another son. So much so, that he had knighted the messenger Griffith Lloyd and bestowed on him lands which should have belonged to a clan allied to Rhys's.

Gizela! He could not doubt she had helped assist the child into the world. His hands closed into fists at his sides as he realized her errand across the rain-swept courtyard must have been on behalf of the queen.

Bleddyn's warning rang again in his ears. He should not have trusted an Englishwoman, who had used a life debt to force Tremaine to escort her from Cadairllwyd. His anger at his friend had dimmed when Tremaine had asked if Rhys would have done differently when she came with her request. The honor of satisfying a debt would demand nothing less.

Faith, this had become too intricate. He could denounce Gizela for her quick wit that had enabled her to slip out of Cadairllwyd. He could hate her for her assistance to the queen in bringing forth this child which was certain to be a nettle in all Welshmen's sides. He could vow to banish her from his life, but, when he returned to his bed that was empty without her, the longing to hold her overwhelmed him. It denied him sleep and the chance to dream of her.

Rhys cursed under his breath. In spite of their exhilarating hopes of independence from their English overlords, all had come to naught. The English king had commanded them to attend him, and, like dogs, they had heeded their master.

He turned to leave, but a low voice mumbled, "What think you of this, Rhys ap Cynan?" The short man's nearly bald pate glistened in the sunshine flowing through the open doorways at either end of the great hall.

"I think we must be cautious when dealing with the lion in his lair, Bran ap Gwydion. Do you speak for us today?"

"What words I choose shall make little difference." He scratched his cheek which was covered by a rough field of gray bristles. "You know what this means."

"Aye. Edward has found a way to humiliate us once more."

"Mayhap for good."

"You are right."

Bran's aged eyes grew large in his wrinkled face. "Do my old ears fail me? Are you, Rhys ap Cynan, ready to cede your very soul, along with your lands, to this English interloper who dares to call himself King of *Cymru*?"

"I said nothing of that." He folded his arms over his chest in a lackadaisical pose he doubted fooled anyone. Once again, he scanned the room. "I said only that I agreed with your assessment. Whatever the king does here today will have no bearing on my clan. We are of the rocks and hills of *Cymru*. We shall be a part of this land long after the dust of this outlander king has been swallowed by the earth. *Trech gwlad nag Arglwydd.* Stronger is a country than a lord. How long will Edward hold our land?"

"You speak treason."

"To this king?" He shrugged. "Mayhap. To *Cymru*? Never!"

The older man nodded, but glanced around them. Mumbling a farewell, Bran scurried away like a frightened bird.

No one else approached Rhys. That did not surprise him, for many of the chieftains no longer could afford to battle the English or be aligned with those who refused to allow an end to the rebellion. He understood all too well their dilemma.

Young men had been slain and fields scorched. Lands could not be sown when no one was left living to tend to them. The past winter had seen much sickness and starvation. When their women were stolen or raped and killed by the king's men, no children could be born to replace those lost to the war.

Children . . . . A slow smile drifted across his lips as he thought of Tremaine's son lying in Gizela's arms.

There had been a softness about her he had never seen before as well as a sense of triumph. Never before had he wanted to tangle his life with any woman's as he had from the moment he saw her, fresh from her victory in bringing the baby into the world.

The double doors at the rear of the great hall swung open, halting Rhys's thoughts. He tensed, his hand dropping onto the haft of the blade at his side.

Edward entered with all the pomp the English court enjoyed. Rhys had to admit that, in this King of England, the Welsh had a worthy adversary. Edward had honed his battle skills in the Holy Land, and now he hoped to strengthen his death grip on *Cymru*.

In a high-pitched voice, a page announced the king's many titles as Edward's men-at-arms swarmed into the room. They lined the walls, holding their weapons openly. Rhys heard his countrymen's rumble of disquiet.

Fools! Had they thought Edward invited them here to salute them with his best wine? No, the Englishman intended to prove to the Welsh his sovereignty over them. A single word would lead to the slaughter of all the Welsh leaders, but Edward would not give it. To kill them all now would lead to an uprising throughout *Cymru*. Edward could not risk that.

King Edward called from the low dais, "Who speaks for you?"

"I speak for my countrymen," answered Bran ap Gwydion as he stepped forward and inclined his head, offering the respect due a worthy adversary, not a liege.

"Then speak of your allegiance to the King of Wales."

"We have no need for a king to rule over us. Even Llewellyn ap Gruffydd bore no more than the prestigious title of Prince of Wales, your majesty."

"But I am a king. I do not aspire to possess the title of a mere prince." A rumble rushed about the room at the affront.

Rhys remained silent. Nothing had been said yet that was different from any of the other times Edward had exchanged words with the Welsh chieftains. Watching Bran consult with his advisors, Rhys folded his arms over his chest and rested his shoulder on the wall. He was ready to pull his knife if the war of words became one of weapons. He would not leave his clan as leaderless as Llewellyn had left *Cymru*.

When Bran looked again at Edward, no one in the room spoke. The old man's voice remained steady. "We of *Cymru* are a proud people, your majesty. We find it impossible to bend our head to a foreign king. As foretold in the ancient legends, we need a leader born of our land. The great wizard Merlin promised us the coming a king whose homeland is ours. A king who speaks neither English nor French, but speaks the language of this land. A king who understands the ancient traditions and respects the strength found in our mountains and rivers."

Edward's lips tightened in rage. At the back of the hall, a slow smile spread across Rhys's face. Bran possessed more courage than Rhys had guessed, for even Llewellyn ap Gruffydd had acknowledged Edward as his liege before rising in rebellion.

Edward turned to speak to one of his men, then strode from the room. His soldiers blocked the doors.

Rhys reached for his blade. This might be the signal to slay them. If he were about to die, let the English die with him. He was about to pull the knife when a door opened. Edward entered, followed by a woman who walked with a bowed head. She must have been waiting in the corridor beyond the doors.

With a silent curse, Rhys realized he was watching a carefully designed mummery that was being played out for Edward's benefit. But what did Edward wish to prove? The cry of a baby told him too well. Faith, but they were fools!

And he was the greatest of them all, he realized when Edward stepped aside so he could see the woman holding the baby. Gizela! He took a pace forward, his hand sliding again to his knife. Her gaze met his across the room, and he halted as if he had run into a wall of the thickest stone. The sorrow in her eyes was for him. She could not halt what was about to happen any more than he could. Jamming one fist into his palm, he bit back his curse as she handed the baby to her king.

Edward held up the wailing child. The swaddled baby screamed his outrage more loudly. "I give you what you have petitioned for. A prince born of Wales. A prince who speaks neither English nor French, but whose first words shall be uttered in your native language. Do you swear loyalty to this newest prince of your land? Do you swear loyalty to my son who shall bear my name?"

No one answered. Except for the baby's cries, silence clamped onto the room. When the king's lips twisted in fury, he repeated his question to the sound of his guards drawing their broadswords.

The man next to him reached for his sword. Rhys put his hand on the man's arm to halt him. If the Welsh chieftains bared their weapons, they would die. Edward could claim the Welsh had attacked first. Mayhap that was what the king wanted.

It could not end like this. The rebellion must live on, and it must grow strong. The time for victory was ahead of them, but, if they fell victim to Edward's treachery now, that victory would be lost.

Rhys pushed through the press of his allies to meet the king's icy stare. Behind him, the other chieftains waited to see what he would do. If they thought past their pride which was piqued at being duped by Edward, they would have known what Rhys did. The only way to save themselves was to play out this charade.

"Chieftain Rhys ap Cynan," said Edward, a smile returning to his lips, "I had hoped to see you here."

"To shorten me by a head?" He heard Gizela's gasp when he answered in French as unaccented as the king's. By now, she should understand why he did not admit to such a skill on the night they met and her men had been ready to slay him.

Edward chuckled. "The thought is tempting, but, without proof of your crimes, I had preferred the idea of speaking with you here today. And I have no proof of your crimes, Chieftain." He glanced at Gizela who was once again staring straight ahead. "Not yet."

"Honesty and honor go hand-in-hand."

When Gizela looked at him, Rhys fought the longing to pull her into her arms and comfort her. Never had he seen such grief on her face, but her obligation and duty imprisoned her within this drama as did his.

Edward's smile grew. "Such honor and honesty deserve a reward. Do you agree, Chieftain?

"Aye." He would say no more until he gauged the course of Edward's thoughts. The English king certainly would offer no reward to any Welshman within this hall, especially Chieftain Rhys ap Cynan.

"And you, Lady de Montpellier?" He put his hand on her elbow and drew her forward. Rhys saw her stiffen when Edward raised his voice. "Let it be known by one and all that Lady de Montpellier has served my queen and me well in bringing forth this child. Know all of you who stand within this chamber that, in return, Lady de Montpellier has been betrothed to my distant cousin Lord Paien of Ponthieu."

No one in the room was more astonished than Gizela, for she gasped, "Betrothed?" She clamped her lips closed when Edward turned to her.

Rhys clenched his hands beneath the sweep of his cape to keep from reaching out to her and urging her to hide her shock. He glanced back at Edward. The English king was smiling broadly, and well he might. He had guaranteed his hold over the de Montpellier and Talbot manor lands by offering them to an ally. In addition, Edward had removed the threat of Lady de Montpellier's questionable allegiance by arranging to send her to her new husband's lands on the continent near Flanders. An excellent decision, and Rhys would have congratulated Edward on his wisdom if he could have spoken past his fury.

"Lady de Montpellier?" Edward asked.

"Thank you for your kindness," she whispered with a swift curtsy.

Edward placed the baby in her arms and motioned for her to move forward. "You see, Chieftain, the rewards offered to those who remember their obligation to the English throne. Do you come to prove your fealty as Lady de Montpellier has done?"

Only the vow to repay Edward for this mockery gave Rhys the strength to kneel before the crying baby Gizela held. He reached up to take the child's hand. His fingers brushed Gizela's, and he heard her intake of breath. The sound, which was too soft to reach other ears, sent a pulse of longing through him. He gazed up at her. Even though she wore a strained smile, he could see the anguish in her eyes. He had threatened to expel her from his life when last they spoke, but now she would be gone irretrievably.

His gaze remained locked with hers as he pressed the child's tiny hand to his forehead. Tears filled her eyes as his voice rang throughout the hall saying, "To this babe, who is born of *Cymru*, I pledge my allegiance and the allegiance of my clan."

"Rise, Chieftain Rhys ap Cynan," ordered Edward with a victorious smile. "Both my son *and* I accept your oath of loyalty on behalf of yourself and your clan."

"Both my clan and myself, shall endeavor to keep the vow made to your son, your majesty."

The king's smile dimmed. Rhys waited for him to speak, but he would not be coerced into ceding the freedom of his clan to this outlander. He *had* seen the reward Edward offered those who did his work. Gizela had been traded for the money her husband's lands would bring the English monarchy.

"So be it," Edward said. "Are there any others among you who are wise enough to follow Chieftain Rhys ap Cynan's lead?"

Rhys moved aside to watch his allies bend their knee to the baby. Each man repeated the words Rhys had spoken. When he reached the back of the hall, Rhys was not surprised to see Bran waiting for him.

"That was wise," the old man said.

"That was the only choice we had." Rhys laughed icily. "Except for death, of course. My clan does not need a martyr. I can serve them better by continuing to battle the king."

"What if this son takes the throne?"

Patting his friend on the shoulders, he said, "Let tomorrow deal with tomorrow's worries, for the other son is hale in England. As for myself, I cannot wait for the day Edward's son succeeds him, for we shall be rid of this cunning cur who makes every effort to destroy us."

Rhys did not stay to see the rest of the Welsh chieftains announce their fealty. He strode past Edward's men. One moved to halt him, but was ordered back. Now that Edward had half a victory, the English would wish the chieftains out of Caernarvon with no delay.

The courtyard was deserted, and a dreary rainstorm ruined the April day. The weather was the perfect match for Rhys's spirits. A few quick questions gained him the information he needed so that he could be standing by the door to Gizela's chambers when she returned.

Her face was as colorless as the sleeves of her undertunic. Gizela faltered when Rhys stepped from the shadows to open her door for her. By now, he should have been halfway to Cadairllwyd.

She was pleased with the serenity of her voice as she said, "Good afternoon, Chieftain. Have you decided to wait out the storm here?"

"Something as harmless as rain does not unsettle me." He went with her into the antechamber and looked at her face which was alternately lit and shadowed by the faint light from the embers in the hearth. "I have managed to survive much more today."

"I did not know that was what he planned." She flushed. She should not be admitting this to Rhys.

He swept a hand around her nape and brought her face close to his. Bitterness filled his voice. "He said nothing to you of how he intended to use the child you drew out into the world? You did not see his whelp as the tool to tear away the last bit of pride remaining to *Cymru*?"

"How can you ask that of me? I am a midwife. I did what I could to safeguard a life. What that child chooses to do with his life or what he must do to satisfy the dictates of his father is something I cannot concern myself with as I fight to welcome him from the womb.

Birthing this child was no different from when I helped Mair."

"True," he said, "for you turned that birth to your advantage as well."

"I had no choice."

"You could have stayed with me."

Her heart contracted painfully at the open yearning in his voice. "I wanted to, Rhys. God alone knows how much I wanted to."

He swept her against him. His kiss was deep and hard. She answered it with all her longing, wanting to savor every moment of the love she should not know. Her fingers relished the strength of his chest. With her breath shallow and swift in her ears, she tasted the sweet flavor of passion within his mouth.

He growled a curse and drew away. "Gizela, I want you back at Cadairllwyd in my bed where we can enjoy this ecstasy until we are sated."

"You know that is impossible."

"Your obligation to your husband is complete."

She wrapped her arms around her as she turned to the fire. "The king has given me to another man. I cannot disobey his edict."

"So you would go to a man you do not know and share his bed and give him sons? Will you yearn for him as you yearn for me?"

"Do not talk of love," she said softly.

"Love? Do we speak of that?"

Determined no sign of her anguish would be visible, she replied, "You speak of little else, Rhys ap Cynan. Your love for your clan and your love for this land have obsessed you until it will ultimately betray you."

"As it has betrayed you."

She nodded and sank to the bench. "I do not even know where this Ponthieu is, Rhys."

"Nor the man you shall take for your husband."

She put her hand out to him. "Even if I knew him well, I would not wish to marry him."

"Because he would take you so far from your home?"

"Because I love you."

When he stared at her as if she were mad, she was tempted to say he was right. He was leaving forever. She might never see him again. The words her heart sang each time she looked into his blue eyes should have remained within her.

He clasped her face in his hands. "Do not love me, Gizela, for you want all of my heart. I cannot give it. Not while honor compels me to do what I must for *Cymru*."

Putting her hands over his, she whispered, "Can *Cymru* offer you this?" She brushed his lips with hers.

"Gizela—"

"Tell me no lies, Rhys. Even though I have been a fool to believe you might love me as I love you, the truth is that you cannot change your dedication to seeing this land free. Just know that I shall love you with every breath until my last."

She gave him no chance to answer as she rushed into her bedchamber. Pomona looked up as the door opened, but said nothing when Gizela shut it behind her and leaned against it, her eyes closed as she fought to keep from flinging it aside and rushing back out to Rhys's arms. If she loved Rhys, she must let him go— for her love for him made him a target for King Edward's frustration.

For so many years, she had been seeking someone who would love her as she longed to be loved. Mayhap she had found that man, but she would never know.

17

The breeze off the water was rich with scents, but Gizela took little note of them as she stared at the freshly turned earth. Nothing marked the ground where Sheldon de Montpellier's body lay. She turned from his grave and walked back to the castle. Mayhap she should give the order to have his body returned to de Montpellier Court, but the idea of him lying next to his brother, when Sheldon had been ready to betray everything Kenleigh had fought for, sickened her.

Let Sheldon stay here in the earth of the land he had wanted so badly to possess! Let his bones rot to enrich the soil that was no more filthy than his soul. She would not think of him again.

Hayes handed Gizela two packets of herbs. Cocking his head to the side, he frowned. "You be too different, milady."

"So I have heard over and over." She sighed as she balanced the packets on her knees while she perched on the high stool.

"I hear you be leaving Caernarvon."

"Yes."

"When?"

"At dawn tomorrow."

He put his hand on her shoulder and looked her directly into her eyes. "Do you run to or from?"

Gizela did not try to demur. "I am going home until Lord Paien comes to claim me and my lands."

"He be a lucky man." He spread out his arms. "You bring the knowledge you have gained here to his manor house."

"I suspect he will be much more impressed by the combination of the Talbot and de Montpellier fiefs."

"True."

She laughed. "Hayes, I shall miss you. Your honesty always reminds me that my problems are of little concern to anyone beyond myself."

"On that, you be wrong." He sat on the low bench he preferred and gazed up at her. "The king took a personal interest in your life." He wagged his finger in her face. "Now you need to be watching over your new lord's lands and tenants, and you must learn more to be a great healer. You have learned from me and from the Welsh. You shall learn more in that land you go to."

Slipping from the stool, she picked up the packets. "I hope Lord Paien is more congenial to the idea of my work than the most recent Lord de Montpellier was."

"Your husband spoke of you with pride."

"Did he?"

"Aye, and so has the chieftain."

She did not need to ask which chieftain Hayes spoke of, for she knew Hayes was as anxious as she was to learn more about the herbs of Wales. "You have spoken with Rhys?"

"Nay." He scowled. "I speak not to the enemies of my king." His face smoothed. "But I did see his pride in you when he spoke with you here that day." Standing, he patted her arm. "I shall pray you find peace, milady."

"Is that likely?" She smiled. "Thank you for answering the questions I have had. What you have shared with me, I shall teach to those in the stillrooms of de Montpellier Court and Talbot Hall before I go with my husband. I hope peace and happiness are yours, Hayes."

"As you say, milady, 'tis unlikely, as long as I remain among the queen's retainers. The king may wish her to travel with him when he defeats the Scots."

Gizela squeezed his hand before walking out of the stillroom. That farewell had not been easy, but, at least, she had had a chance to tell him good-bye. She looked at the mountains beyond the walls. As easily as if the tip of the peak were lit by a beacon in the deepening twilight, she picked out the one overshadowing Cadairllwyd.

"Rhys," she whispered, knowing her voice would never reach him. He had made his choice. Now she must accept it, whether she wished to or not. Even though she longed for Rhys to speak of love to her, she would not change him. His unfailing honor was as much a part of him as the warm skin that delighted her fingers.

Her rooms were deserted when Gizela returned to them. She smiled sadly. Pomona had been working hard all day gathering together what they would take back to England. The men who had traveled with her into Wales would return also. They must be eager to enjoy the comfort of the Great Hall. Their meals, until they reached England, would be sparse fare heated over a fire along the road.

Taking a candle from the antechamber, she went into her bedchamber. It was if she had returned to her last hours at Talbot Hall. The room was stripped of anything which suggested she once had lived here. Pomona had packed everything, save for the linens on the bed. By sunrise on the morrow, even those would be gone, and her stay in Caernarvon would be simply a memory to treasure within her shattered heart.

She set the candle on the deep windowsill. Kneading her hands, she folded her arms on the sill. She did not need to leave on the morrow. She could stay. She could hope Rhys would return, that Edward would change his mind, that her life might not be mired in despair.

Footfalls sounded behind her. Recognizing them, she called, "Pomona, I am within."

Her servant came in, carrying another candle. "Milady, you should not be here in the dark. If you wish me to bring you something to eat, I—"

"What is it?" She turned to see Pomona's quivering finger pointing to the bed. With a gasp, she stared at the blade embedded in the headboard. The red scales of the dragon were painted on the haft. With its pointed tail raised high in contempt and its wings ready for flight, it proclaimed the Welsh clans' refusal to accept the rule of the English.

"Rhys!" she whispered.

"No, milady, do not speak his name." Pomona reached out to snatch the knife. "Let me rid us of this wickedness." She moaned when Gizela's hand halted her from pulling the blade. "Milady, do not touch it. It is evil. Let us leave now."

Knowing her servant's advice was wise, Gizela plucked the knife from the oak. She caught the piece of buckskin that was about to tumble onto the pillows.

"Milady, please—"

She looked across the bed at Pomona's face which was blanched with fear. "Bring the lamp closer." She cradled the knife in her hands as if it were a baby. She gasped as she ead what was written on the buckskin.

Come. Sick. River road.

The message was simple. Trust Rhys to find a way to get to her without compromising his allies . . . or her. Biting her lip, she touched the letters. Rhys must be very ill if one of his men had risked his life to get this to her. What if he were dying? She shook her head to negate her fearful thought. She must help him.

"What is it?" Pomona asked.

"He is ill." She reached for the pouch holding her herbs. "I must go to him. If Ysolde could tend to this sickness, he would not—"

"He?"

"Rhys."

Pomona grasped Gizela's arms. "Milady, have you addled your wits? You cannot leave Caernarvon to give succor to the king's enemies. *You* will be outlawed."

"Should I let the man I love die because I fear that?"

"Love?" Pomona folded her hands over her chest. "Milady, he has bewitched you."

"Yes," she said softly. Slipping the pouch of her herbs onto her belt, she flung her cloak over her shoulders. "From the moment I saw him along the road, he has worked his spell upon me. I will not let him die."

"Milady—"

"Pomona, you must stay here and keep anyone from entering this chamber until I return." She embraced her servant. "You are the only one I can trust within these walls."

The old woman sighed and nodded in resignation. "One thing I must ask. Will you be coming back?"

"I vow to you, I shall return as swiftly as I can. Our trip should be delayed no more than a few days. If you must lie, speak of an unsettling sickness. Let them think I suffer a fever. No one will wish to come in here then."

"There is nothing I can say to persuade you to listen to good sense?"

"Too long I have listened to good sense, and my sole reward has been to be exiled from England by the king's order to marry." She glanced toward the window and the mountains beyond it. She tied the embroidered strip closing her cloak over her gown. Hiding the dragon knife beneath her cape, she turned to Pomona.

"Stay safe, milady," she whispered.

"I wish you the same." She lifted the latch on the door and looked out to find the outer chamber was still empty.

"How will you slip out of the castle?"

With a taut smile, Gizela said, "The hour is early. With the gates open, I need only devise the tale that I have been called into the village to assist with a difficult birth. That will give credence to the lie of me suffereing a fever, for I could be set upon by an evil humor while helping to bring forth the baby." Her fingers tightened on the latch. "The king's announcement before the chieftains made everyone aware of my skills. Who would have guessed I would use them like this?"

She did not give Pomona a chance to reply. Hurrying down the stairs and out into the inner bailey, she greeted each person she met as if nothing were amiss. At the gate, she greeted the guard. She smiled when he acknowledged her with a nod and no questions. When the sour scent of ale struck her, she glanced toward a pile of dirt near the inner wall. His flagon must be waiting for him there. He wanted only to get rid of her.

As she crossed the drawbridge, Gizela pulled her dark cloak around her. Her hood concealed her wimple, so no one could guess if she were English or Welsh.

Night covered her in an ebony mask as she left the village behind her. She glanced back at the castle. It glowed like an earthbound star. Would she be able to return? Her steps faltered as she wondered if she wanted to go back to marry a man she did not know. She must not think of that now. All her thoughts should be focused on reaching Rhys and curing him of the disease he suffered.

More quickly than she had thought it would take, Gizela reached the cairn. She slowly turned about, looking for her escort. If she had the time, she might find Cadairllwyd on her own, but every moment was precious when Rhys fought for his life.

Minutes passed, then an hour.

"Where are you?" she whispered to the night as the passage of the second hour was marked by the spinning of the stars overhead.

Mayhap English riders had come along the road and persuaded the Welsh to leave. No, that was impossible. Any of Rhys's men would risk death to get him the help he needed.

A twig cracked, cutting through her like a scream in the night. Before she could move, a hand caught her arm. A knife emerged from the darkness in front of her face. Looking along the brawny arm, she stared at a stranger. Only his short tunic suggested he might be Welsh.

"Who are you?" she asked. "Can you take me to Cadairllwyd?"

"You dare much, woman, coming here."

"I—" The tip of another knife pricked her spine.

A hand reached around her to pull the dragon knife from her belt. Three more men stepped from the trees.

She knew none of them. Her breath grew uneven and strained as she tensed. If these were outlaws, she could die at their hands while Rhys died in his mountain fortress.

The man holding the knife said, "Speak your name, woman."

"If you sent me the knife of Rhys ap Cynan as a message, you know my name well. If not, there is no need to speak it."

A chuckle from the shadows warned her more men lurked there.

The man snarled, "Your English wiles do not amuse me. Why do you loiter where no *Saesnes* is welcome?"

"I was informed Chieftain Rhys ap Cynan is deeply ill." She shuddered, more in fear for Rhys than herself. "I have knowledge of healing herbs."

"Do you think we need your English knowledge?" sneered the man as he ran the flat of his knife against her cheek.

She winced at the cold caress, but said, "If you are of his clan, you do him ill by delaying me. Or do you wish to lose your chieftain who dares to confront King Edward? Mayhap you truly wish to bend your knees to the English king, and the chieftain's death will grant you that."

Another man stepped from the shadows. "Can you heal him?"

"Tremaine!" Relief surged through her.

No smile marred his face. "I asked if you thought you could heal him?"

"Your message did not say what he suffered, but I shall try."

"If you fail, you will die."

Gizela did not hesitate. "I understand that."

"Mayhap you wish to slay our chieftain, even if you have to sacrifice your life." He fisted his hands on his hips. "We understand Lord de Montpellier has been hailed as a hero, milady. Do you aspire to such martyrdom?"

"No. Does your chieftain?"

"What do you mean?" he demanded as the knife was pressed to her cheek again.

She kept her chin high. "By wasting time in this worthless conversation, you threaten Rhys's life. Every minute may be precious. His death would deal a serious blow to the rebellion."

Tremaine motioned, and the men sheathed their weapons. Walking toward her, he suddenly smiled. "Forgive me, milady. I had to be sure you were sincere about this."

"Do you think I would have chanced coming here alone if I had been faint-hearted?" Anger burned within her, but she ignored it. "Tell me how Rhys fares."

"He will be much better when you arrive with your medicines." He took her arm and steered her along the rough ground toward a stand of trees.

Her eyes widened when she saw a familiar mount among the horses. Sheldon's horse! She glanced at Tremaine, but could not read his expression here in the shadows. Had he brought the horse as a reminder of the fate of traitors or was it merely coincidence? She would not give him the satisfaction of asking.

He assisted her onto the back of the tall stallion. Adjusting her skirts around her ankles, she took the reins. He mounted and signaled to his men. They surrounded her.

"Follow me, milady," Tremaine ordered.

"Like this?"

"How else did you expect us to bring you to Cadairllwyd?" Even in the darkness, she could see the challenging glitter in his eyes.

Gizela glanced back toward the road. By letting her ride without a blindfold to the fortress, Tremaine guaranteed she would not be allowed to leave again. At least, not while she lived.

"'Tis your choice, milady," he added when she did not move.

"You know 'tis no real choice. I cannot let him die."

"The choice is yours. Come with us or not."

She nodded and hit her heels against the horse to guide it deeper into the trees. Behind her, she heard Tremaine's triumphant laugh.

Tremaine hurried Gizela through the deserted hallways of Cadairllwyd. She guessed he had had the corridor cleared. Did he wish no one to know she was here? That made no sense, unless nobody, save the men he had brought with him, knew she was within the fortress. A hint of fearful laughter escaped from her lips. If she failed and Rhys died, Tremaine would be certain she did not have long to mourn before her execution, which would be as public as Sheldon's had been.

As she had asked a half-dozen times during the ride through the night, she whispered, "Can you tell me what he is suffering?"

"He is ill," he answered as he had before.

"Does he have a fever?"

"I do not know."

"How do you expect me to help if you will not tell me what is wrong?"

Tremaine smiled at her. "You are the healer, milady. 'Tis for you to decide how to tend to the chieftain." He paused in front of the door to Rhys's chambers and faced her. "Think well, milady, of what it will cost you to enter this room and not cure him."

She reached for the latch. His hand halted hers, and her frustration burst into anger. "Leave off, Tremaine. I tire of your taunting. As you have brought me here to attend to your chieftain, step aside so I may do so."

"I would that you had stayed away. Your poison has infected this household enough."

"I have no intention of murdering him."

"I am sure you do not, for you would not give me the pleasure of seeing you dead." He moved aside and gestured for her to open the door.

"You are not coming in?"

His smile broadened. "You have no need of my help. If it would please you, I shall send for Bleddyn to sit at the door. Whatever you need, he can bring you."

"Better you should send for Ysolde."

"She could not cure the chieftain of this sickness. Mayhap you can."

Gizela did not answer as she opened the door. Coldness inched through her as she crossed the empty antechamber. Where were his servants? Horror nearly halted her midstep. If the illness had struck others, the whole fortress might be in danger. How ironic it would be if the Welsh were devastated by a fever instead of their English enemies!

"Rhys?" she called softly as she opened the bed-chamber door. She received no answer. The darkness within the room was illuminated by a lone candle on the table near the window. Insects fluttered about its flame, daring their lives for a moment of its glory. As she went to the high bed, she had sympathy for them. She risked everything she was, to come here. Yet, like the moths drawn to the candle, she would chance anything to savor the potent fire of Rhys's kiss one more time.

"Rhys, are you awake?"

Again no reply answered her whisper. She loosened her cloak and set it on a bench. Reaching for the pouch of herbs, she put her hand on the bed and leaned toward the pillows heaped against the headboard.

The bed was empty!

She frowned, then pressed her hand over her heart which beat fast with fear. Was she too late? Had he died and been taken to his grave? If—

The door closed behind her. She whirled. A form emerged from the shadows. She opened her mouth to scream. The sound came out in a gasp.

"Rhys!"

He stepped into the light of the single candle. His chest was naked beneath his loosely tied robe. His strong legs were as bare, but she did not pause to delight in the view of his brawny form.

Rushing to him, she raised her hand to his forehead. It was not hot with fever. She touched his cheek, then the pulse in his neck. All was as it should be, yet—

"You should be in bed," she whispered.

"Aye." His arm curved around her waist, bringing her up against his chest. The heat she had expected to feel on his brow burned into her neck as he pressed his mouth to her skin.

She closed her eyes, reveling in the splendor she had feared she would never know again. Then, with a cry, she pulled away. "How could you lie to me like this? I have been frantic with fear for you. Did you think of that before you devised this prank?"

"I knew you would come if I were ill."

"But you are not!"

"But I am." He put his hand over his heart. "I ached deep within me, Gizela, to know that at dawn on the morrow you would be leaving *Cymru*."

"How did you know that?"

"As I know of other things within Edward's castle." He smoothed her hair back from her face. "With the dawn, you and your enticing eyes would have been lost to me for all time. That thought sickened me until I was as weak as a nursing babe."

"But you deceived me! You and Tremaine." She crossed her arms over her chest to prevent her fingers from reaching out to caress his skin. "Did you pause to think when you created this lie, of the consequences to me if I answered your summons?"

His fingers slipped along her shoulders before sweeping down her back to urge her closer. Fury burned in his voice. "I thought long on those consequences before I sent the message to you, sweet one, but my decision was simple. I would not see you a pawn in Edward's hands."

"Rather I should be one in yours?"

"You are in my hands." His laugh was muted against her mouth.

She was unable to breathe as his fingers stroked her with slow passion. Within her, a liquid longing roiled. His breath burned against her ear as he loosened her braids to free her hair to flow through his fingers. What he whispered in her ear she could not understand over the frantic beat of her heart. Only the craving existed, tempting her to forget sense as she melted against him.

Slowly, as slowly as he explored each surface of her skin, the tantalizing touch of his lips moved upward along her chin to taste her cheek. Sampling the corners of her mouth, he moaned his desire as he captured her mouth anew.

Unable to deny him what she craved for, she quivered beneath the eager assault of his tongue against her mouth. She answered his passion with her own, delighting in the flavor of his mouth.

Raising his lips from hers, he whispered, "Tell me that you want me as I want you."

"I want you, but—" Her voice faded as he took her right wrist and drew her fingers toward him.

She could not escape the glorious glow of yearning in his eyes as he led her fingertips along his chest. Her hands tingled as the heat of his body surged onto her skin.

He laughed. "Do you fear touching me because you will discover you can feel sweet passion again? Do you fear this time desire can be forever?"

"You speak of love."

"Do I?" Refusing to relinquish her hand, he pressed it against the soft wool covering his thigh. He guided her fingers along his leg. Husky need softened his voice. "Can you touch me and disavow the pleasure we both feel?"

Her breath burned roughly in her chest as her fingers were scorched by rapture. The hard sinews beneath her palm lured her closer with a magical melody which had no form. Eagerly her mouth met his, for every bit of her waited to share in the joy.

When he leaned her back onto the bed, she could not resist the yearning which swirled between and through them, their need becoming one, as their bodies craved to be. Her hands swept up along the strength of his back as his tongue demanded all the succulent secrets hidden within her mouth.

His fingertip moved across her breast. When she moaned in soft pleasure, he smiled down at her.

He slowly unbuttoned her gown. Slipping his fingers beneath the material, he explored her breast which was covered so enticingly by her shift. She surrendered to the sensations which whirled over and through her, fastest and most fiercely where his fingers touched her.

His lips followed the neckline of her gown as he lowered it. Entwining her fingers through his hair, she fought the savage need which stripped all strength from her. Refusing to let this joy be forbidden, she slid her hands beneath his robe. His rough skin enticed her even more.

His gasp urged her to lure him into the thickening mist of passion. Sitting up, she lifted her gown over her head. He ran his finger along the front of her shift.

With a soft moan, he drew the sleeves along her arm. "Are you ready to cure me, healer?"

"I fear it shall not be a quick healing," she whispered, "but I shall share what I know of its cure, if you will tend to me."

His eyes glowed. "I should have known you would not yield your will without some condition."

"You do not want my will." She smiled as she loosened the sash on his robe.

"So true. I want your lovely body entwined around me."

His arm brought her tight to him as he tasted the desire on her lips. Pushing aside her shift, he smiled when she murmured his name in near desperation as her bare skin brushed against him. With slow delight, he traced the lines of her body with his fingers and his gaze.

She needed no urging to do the same, but he shook his head as she reached to draw his robe from him. Leaning her back into the pillows, he knelt over her. The robe fell aside, and he did not need to urge her to touch him.

She stroked the warmth of his chest. As her fingers moved lower, she traced an eager path along his abdomen. She watched the deepening pleasure on his face. He tipped her mouth toward his as she dared to touch him with a boldness born of her own need to be caressed.

She took his right hand in hers and pressed it to the warm valley in the center of her chest. As his lips enticed hers, she led his fingers along her. Her heart throbbed in an uneven rhythm beneath his touch when he stroked the sensitive skin of her breast. Moaning against his mouth, she quivered. His ragged laugh raced through her.

As his lips followed his fingers, his breath burned her, scintillating, scorching, stripping away any remaining resistance. Lightly his tongue teased the tip of her breast. Her hands settled on the firm strength of his hips as she enticed him silently to the rapture they both craved.

"Not yet," he murmured against her, each word swelling into her and increasing the ache of longing. "I have waited too many nights to hurry now."

Her answer was silenced as his fingers found the soft silken texture of her legs. Trembling, she moaned his name desperately as he stroked upward to discover her most intimate pleasures. he sweet prelude of teasing caresses vanished into the desperate need. Agonizing and wanton, the frenzied craving overtook her as she moved with the rhythm of his touch.

Tremulously, she drew him over her, wanting him to share this wild obsession. She opened her eyes to see his face so close to hers. His gaze met hers as he brought their bodies together, melding them with the fire of their burning passion. Matching his motions, she lost herself in the escalating ecstasy. Faster, more fervently, they sought the ultimate enchantment. Poised on the apex of passion's perfection, she surrendered herself in the moment before the world vanished into the heated flame that consumed her and the only man who could share this glory with her.

Yet, even within that quintessence of joy, was the pain of knowing she still could not win his heart from the hatred that stood between them and love.

18

Rhys stood and wiped his dirty hands on his tunic. He stretched as he looked over the open field perched between two soaring mountains. The sunlight streamed in an unbroken cascade over his head, for no trees clung to the rocks thrown in an incomprehensible pattern between the low thickets and lush grass.

Faith, he loved this land. His clan had held these mountains since before the beginning of legend. Letting his gaze follow the highest peaks, which were as raw as if they had just

been born, he rubbed his hand against his lower back. His training as a warrior had not included spending a day in a high meadow harvesting plants for the stillroom.

A slow smile tilted his lips as he admired the way Gizela's gown followed her slender curves while she reached for more samples to put in the large bag beside her on the ground. In the past fortnight, as spring had crept into the high reaches of this land, he had exulted in the warmth of her love. Her face was the first thing he saw when he opened his eyes in the light before dawn, and he drifted to sleep with her cheek soft against his shoulder.

She had not spoken of leaving again, although he knew her thoughts often drifted to her servant who might no longer be within Caernarvon's growing walls. Rather, she had seemed content to spend her days working with Ysolde and her nights in his arms.

Now he had everything he wanted. When she had told him he would have to choose between *Cymru* and her, he had seen that as a challenge. There had to be a way to keep Gizela with him as well as hold onto the lands of his fathers. Chuckling, he decided he had tweaked the English lion's nose doubly.

"What is so amusing?" Gizela asked, looking up at him. "Mayhap the soil on your face, Chieftain?"

He wiped his sleeve across his face and squatted beside her. "Simply happy. Are you nearly finished?"

Gizela smiled as she balanced the bag in her hands. "Ysolde told me to get all the butterbur root we could, and I think we have found what we can here today." She shook more dirt from the roots of the plant she had plucked from the earth. "This should help us ease fevers when the cold weather returns."

He slipped his arm around her and drew her to her feet. "I enjoy hearing you speak of our future together." He kissed her lightly, then laughed as he brushed the earth from her cheek. "Have you found contentment with us?"

Putting her arms around his waist, she laughed. The sound caressed him like a million tiny bubbles floating on a mountain stream. "It would seem others have grown more content with me being here in Cadairllwyd. Bleddyn did not snarl at me this morning, and if he can accept me, there is hope others will."

"It seems he has acceded to the inevitable."

"How romantic you are, Chieftain! Is that the bard's skill I have heard you brag of?"

With her chin cupped between his thumb and forefinger, he tilted her face up so he could see the love glittering in her eyes. "I speak of that young fool, Gizela, not of myself. Do you question my longing for you?"

"No."

When she added nothing else, he urged, "But?"

"No buts, Rhys."

He took the bag from her and held her hand as they climbed down the steep hillside. "I have seen you staring out the window toward Caernarvon. Why?"

"I think of Pomona." She smiled sadly as her honest answer confirmed his conjecture. "I had thought I was honest with her when I told her I would return."

"Impossible."

"Who is to say what is impossible?" Gizela halted when they reached the base of the hill. She put her hand on his arm and faced him. How could she make him understand the grief that thwarted her happiness? The king would not vent his frustration on an old woman, but, without Gizela, Pomona had no one within the castle. "Rhys, you still can enter Caernarvon, for there has been no proclamation to outlaw you. If you were to speak to her—"

"What is now only suspicion in Edward's mind would be substantiated. Being deemed a traitor is not something you should consider lightly."

She shivered. "That I know all too well."

He entwined his fingers with hers as they walked along the path leading from the high meadow. She smiled when she heard his light-hearted whistle echo off the hillsides. Slowly she was beginning to understand the attachment he had to this untamed land, for she, too, delighted in the wild storms that played about the unforgiving heights. In comparison, the rolling hills surrounding Talbot Hall seemed lifeless.

When the trail widened so they could walk side-by-side, Rhys said, putting his hand to his back, "I fear you shall wear me out with this gathering."

She swept her arms around him and massaged the firm muscles along his spine. "This was not how I planned to tire you today."

"I shall never tire of that, Gizela. If—"

When he did not continue, she looked up to see his jaw tightening with fury. She turned to follow this gaze. A thick cloud of smoke edged up the mountain, not far from a village. Once before she had seen such a deadly cloud along the hillsides. Then she had rushed to the aid of a child in a burning house.

"Oh, no! Fire!" She gripped his hand. "That cannot be Cadairllwyd. 'Tis too close."

"No," he growled with rage. "They have chosen to strike a less protected target."

"Strike?" Horror clamped her throat closed as if she had breathed in all the smoke. "The English?"

"Who else would set Treystwyth aflame?" He drew the knife with the red-winged dragon, which had been returned to him. "Stay close, milady. There is no telling where the English might be now."

She took the bag, knowing he could not be burdened with it. Sticking as near to him as his shadow, she edged into the trees.

The curving path descended into the valley. The reeking odor of smoke seeped along the stream and the village. As they neared Treystwyth, Rhys slowed, his thumb stroking the haft of his knife. He looked at her, and she nodded, knowing what he did not have to say. Any rock or bush could shelter an enemy.

His enemies, not hers. She swallowed the fear in her throat. No, the English were her foes now as well, for to be discovered here with Rhys would seal her fate as a traitor. No one would give her the chance to speak of love, a love which knew no boundaries.

"Oh, dear God!" she whispered when Rhys drew her out onto a rock overlooking the village.

Below them, the village was outlined in flame. Thatch roofs offered tinder for fires which leapt from one cottage to the next, like a malevolent child bent on destruction. Screams struck her ears.

"Rhys!" she exclaimed, keeping her voice low. "Look! There!" She pointed to where horsemen rode wildly along the village road.

The strident sound of metal screeched in her ears. She stared at the broadsword in Rhys's hand. When he looked at her, She saw his eyes were filled with a hatred as hot as the flames below. She whispered, "Please do not do this."

"Do what?"

"Throw your life away by rushing into that hell alone." She cringed when she heard another shriek from the village. "Please, Rhys! We must go and find help."

"Say nothing," he hissed, as he pulled her down behind a rock. "Stay here."

"Where are you going?"

"To help."

"Against so many?"

His lips drew back in a feral smile. He pointed up the hill. She squinted into the sunshine, then saw the furtive motion he had. Fear clamped around her, cutting off her breath—then she realized the men skulking down the hill were Welsh. Bleddyn and a half-dozen men inched toward them. Rhys motioned to them.

Without a greeting, Bleddyn said, "I should have known you would see the flames, too." He scowled at Gizela. "'Tis the English."

"I count nearly a score of English soldiers on horseback and afoot."

"That is what the messenger from Treystwyth said before he died of the wounds inflicted on him by those beasts." When Gizela whispered a soft prayer, Bleddyn's scowl deepened as he continued in Welsh, "If those damned English have found hidden Treystwyth, they will certainly discover Cadairllwyd. You can be sure how they found their way here. Only one person could have given them the information."

Rhys answered in the same language, "If you speak of my friend Tremaine, you should have proof of your words before you utter them."

Bleddyn's eyes grew round, then narrowed with fury. "I did not mean—"

"We have no time for that now." Rising, Rhys motioned with his broadsword toward the burning village. "My blade wishes for the taste of English blood. I shall not deny it a banquet." Beneath the cheer from his men as they drew their long weapons, he added to Gizela in English, "Stay here, sweet one. I will return for you when it is safe."

The men were racing down the steep hillside before Gizela could protest. Clenching her fists on the rock, she watched them swerve between the boulders and the brush clinging to the hill. The screech of the battle cry struck her ears, and she folded her hands and bent over them. She could not pray when her mind was caught in a mesh of fear.

Something exploded in the village, sparks striking the trees. New leaves burst into flames. They would drip fire on anyone beneath them.

"Rhys," she whispered, "be careful."

Even from her aerie, she heard shouts. The warriors must have found each other amid the smoke and fire. In astonishment, she watched some of the English ride away, careening down the hill like a runaway cart. Not all of them—for she had counted only a dozen before the smoke obliterated the scene from her view.

She coughed as the smoke tickled her throat. Rising to her knees, she tried to see the village. A man's hand seized her arm. She screamed as she was twisted away from the rock.

"Where is Rhys?" Tremaine demanded.

She put her hand over her heart as she stared into a familiar face. "Tremaine, where have you been?"

"Does that matter now?" he snapped back. "Where is the chieftain?"

"In the village."

He muttered something under his breath so swiftly she could not guess if he spoke English or Welsh. Then he asked, "Alone?"

"No, Bleddyn brought some men." She pointed to the path leading down the hill. "They took that route. If—"

"Silence! What do you know of fighting?"

Another wave of smoke halted her answer. Coughs ripped from her, tearing at her insides until she thought they would be shredded completely. She sagged to the ground, her eyes watering, her breath ragged. Wiping tears from her eyes, she glanced at a small bag he was carrying. The symbol embroidered on it looked familiar, although she could not tell for certain in the billowing smoke. When he leaned past her to look down the hill, she saw the glitter of gold through the loose laces at the top.

"Where did you get that?" she asked.

He shoved the small bag back into the pouch at his waist. "Why worry? 'Tis nothing that can help us now."

"But gold—"

"Is useless unless it has been hammered into a blade." He grasped her hand. "Come, milady."

"I am to stay here." She tried to pull her hand out of his grip. "Rhys told me that."

"The chieftain may have changed his mind when he sees the death below."

"Have you been there already?"

His laugh was frosty. "Do not display your ignorance for my enjoyment, milady. If I had been there, would I be here now? I heed only what I heard from the man sent to alert us in Cadairllwyd." He jerked her to her feet. "There will be those who need your skills with medicines."

Grasping her bag, she followed. The smoke swallowed them, and she depended on him to guide her. Blinking could not ease the pain in her eyes as the gray cloud grew thicker and hotter. She winced when an ember struck her gown. Batting it out with her hands, she did not slow.

Gizela stared about in horror as they reached the path cutting through the middle of the village. Not a single building had been left standing. What was not still burning or turned to ashes had been knocked to the ground. Rubble cluttered the road, each pile topped with a burning memorial to the lives lost there.

The English soldiers had vanished. Not even a dog wandered along the streets, and the sole sound was the crackling of the fires which were dying along with the victims of the raid.

Suddenly forms appeared out of the smoke. Tremaine's hand was on his sword, when Gizela cried, "Rhys! You are safe!"

He drew her within the arc of his embrace as she stared up at his face which was darkened with smoke and soot. His voracious kisses repudiated his low voice when he whispered against her cheek, "You did not think a few English bastards could lay me low, did you?"

Releasing her, he sighed with fatigue and wiped the back of his hand against his brow. "Tremaine, I thank you for guarding my lady."

"She was reluctant to obey orders," he said with a smile. Before Gizela could speak, he added, "How fare the others?"

"No one from Cadairllwyd was hurt, but there are dead and injured among those of Treystwyth." He looked at Gizela. "Will you help?"

"How can you ask that?"

"Because the men who killed here rode with orders given by Edward."

Shocked, she said, "Rhys, my loyalties have never prevented me from helping those needing my assistance."

"And where are your loyalties now, milady?" Motioning to the burning village, he said quietly, "You see what the English have done. This is why we fight, Gizela. This is why I cannot bend my head to that English bastard who dares to set up his son as the next ruler of *Cymru*. He strips us of the pride we have in our homeland."

"You ask me to betray my king. If I do, I would be no better than Sheldon."

"Are you with us?"

"I shall not fight the English."

Tremaine laughed darkly. "Dare you hand her a sword and bow? She might aim it at us."

Ignoring him, Rhys said, "You have knowledge we need desperately."

"Knowledge?"

"Of healing and of life." He drew her away from where Tremaine stood, motioning for his friend to go to assist the others who were seeking through the ruins for anyone who might be alive. Leading her away from the flames, he paused when the rumble of the fires smothered the keening of the mourners. "Are you with us?"

She shook her head. "Not with your alliance, but I will not betray you, Rhys."

"That is not enough."

"For you or for your clan?"

His face hardened into a scowl. "We are one and the same."

"I love you, Rhys," she whispered, putting her fingers up to his cheek. The grit left by the smoke scored her skin. "That must be enough for you." She lowered her eyes and turned away. "I know you cannot say the same to me, so mayhap you cannot understand."

He whirled her back to face him. "I understand there will be questions, Gizela. Questions of loyalty that you must answer without hesitation. You—"

"Lady de Montpellier!" Bleddyn ran toward her. "Lady de Montpellier, we need your help."

"I shall be right with you," she shouted back.

He nodded and vanished back into the storm cloud of smoke.

"If Bleddyn can accept me as I am," she whispered, "why can't you, Rhys?"

"I want all of you with me." He tilted her face toward him.

"You have all my love."

Another shout kept her from saying more. Rhys took her hand and led her into the very heart of the destruction. Hardly a dozen stones sat atop another. Goods were strewn about, most trampled and useless. A few people wandered in the ruins, their steps as uneven as sleepwalkers.

"Is this the price you are willing to pay?" Gizela whispered. "Edward has the strength to destroy all of this land."

"'Tis not just the land he wishes to destroy." He knelt by a shape in the shadows of the demolished wall.

Gizela turned away as sickness crawled up from her stomach. The stench of death overwhelmed her, and she fell to her knees. She covered her face with her hands so she would not see the young body, contorted and charred in death. Sobs ripped from her. Too many were dead—people who did not care about honor and obligation and had asked for nothing but a chance to live in peace.

Rhys drew her to her feet. She pulled away and shook her head as she pointed to the dead child.

"Is this," she cried, "worth even a single rock on these hills? Is this what you want for all of *Cymru*, Rhys?"

"This is war."

"How can you let it go on? How can you let more suffer?"

"Have you asked Edward the same question?"

Her face grew cold as she imagined posing such a question to the king. "I need not, for I know what he would say."

"He would say this is his by God's will." He snorted and drew her along the road. "He does the devil's work in the good Lord's name."

"Yet, you would drive the English away as cruelly." She saw more burned corpses by a ruined cottage. Hastily she looked away. "Is this what it must be like? How many more must die before you are satisfied?"

"Enough that the English learn we shall not be conquered."

"So you will die instead of bending your knee to the English?"

"If necessary."

Gizela said nothing as she rushed to where Bleddyn was kneeling beside an old man. She drew out her pouch and poured a numbing herb into her hand. When Rhys came to stand behind her, she did not look up at him. She loved him with every ounce of her being, but she hated the pride that might destroy everything he wished to possess—including her love.

Gizela opened the door to the bedchamber and paused. Standing, silhouetted in the window, Rhys looked down the long shaft of an arrow. Her heart cramped with fear as she imagined him sighting it on an Englishman while another of Edward's men took aim on him.

When he turned, he did not smile. "You have been long at work, milady."

"There were many who sought assistance from Ysolde and me. Now it would appear you plan to give us more healing to do."

"You have heard?"

"That you have sent messages to the other chieftains to arrange a parley for a counter-attack on the English?" She nodded, then bit her lip as fear filled her. "Oh, Rhys, do you know what you are inviting down upon your heads?"

"Aye, but if we accept the attack without retaliation, Edward will deem us weak."

"Let him," she whispered.

"Then they will attack again and again and again—until there is nothing left of *Cymru*—save the legends sung in secret by the bards. We cannot risk that." He smiled. "Gizela, you look upon this as a woman. You cannot understand the protocol of war."

"No?" She went to him and took the arrow from him. Tilting it so the head was against his chest, she said, "The force of this being driven into a body tears apart the heart and expels every bit of air through the holes of its thrust. Like a broken bottle, the body deflates and dies." She cracked the arrow across her knee and threw it to the floor. "Now it is no more dangerous than kindling to keep this room warm against the winter. It eases the body instead of destroying it."

"Gizela—"

"Nay, I have more to say." She faced him squarely and raised her chin to meet his startled eyes. "You may wish to forget I am the daughter of Lord Esmond Talbot. By my troth, I myself would wish to disavow any connection with him, but the truth is I grew up in a household of warriors. I know what war does to a man, how it makes him think he is as grand as an archangel when he is no more than a beast. I ask you, as I asked you this afternoon, will you put an end to this before the soil of this land is washed into the sea with the blood of the Welsh?"

"No."

"Then you all shall die."

"You have so little faith in me?"

She shook her head. "This has nothing to do with faith. This has to do with facts. Edward is ringing this land with castles, the ones he captured from your prince Llewellyn, and the ones he builds. How long do you think he can hole up in Rhuddlan while he waits for his barons to raise an army more terrible than any hell could spew forth?"

"Honor—"

"You speak often of honor, but how many dishonorable acts have been done in the name of honor? Was the attack on Treystwyth an act of honor? Armed knights against farmers? Yes, the day was won by the English, but for what purpose? I asked you before, Rhys, and I shall ask you again. Does a single rock along these hillsides matter as much as the life of one child?" She took a steadying breath and said more calmly, "I pray you believe honor is worth its cost when this land lies in ruins in the wake of a war."

He caught her arm before she could walk away. He lowered his head so that his hair fell forward to brush her shoulder. "Why are you running away from me, Gizela?"

"I am not running away."

"You find no honor in revenge."

"None." She raised her eyes to meet the challenge in his as he seated her on the bench by the bed. "Vengeance would gain me nothing, save an existence as low as the beast who injured me."

Rhys stroked her arm as he sat and leaned her head against him. From within the depths of his chest, she could hear the rumbling echo of his voice. "Today the Welsh suffered and died. Tomorrow it will be the English."

"And on and on and on until all are gone." Rising, she walked to where his broadsword leaned against the hearth. She touched the carved hilt which was nearly level with her eyes. "I do understand the protocols of war, Rhys. To hold, a leader must defend what is his. That was among the earliest lessons I was taught."

"As I was." He stood and took her hands, drawing her back to him. "We are what we are, milady."

"Although I know you wish I had been born of this country, I am not. I can give you my heart except for the part that belongs to England and always will."

He shook his head. "I would have you as nothing save what you are. You give me clarity to question the old ways. In these days when those ways die around us, we need wisdom to accept the changes of the future."

"Then rethink what you are doing."

"Nay," he whispered as he brushed her cheek with a heated kiss, "I wish to think only of what I am doing right now."

With a grin, he pulled her to him. His hands traced the curves of her body, lighting every inch with the yearning which became the sweetest agony she could imagine. Her gown fell away before his eager attention. As her fingers roved along him, she gloried in his eager mouth moving over her.

When her body strained to be nearer to his, he swept her into his arms and lowered her back onto the pillows. Lying beside her, he unhurriedly tasted her skin, teasing her to the very brink of insanity. The tempest of desire flowed around her, carrying them both past the boundaries of infinite ecstasy.

The door opened and closed in the twilight before dawn. Gizela reached out to touch the empty pillow on the other side of the bed.

"Stay safe, my love," she whispered, although Rhys was gone. "Stay safe and come back to me."

19

"*Come.*"

The single word intruded into Gizela's dreams. She shook her head. She did not want to wake. The evening had been long while Rhys consulted with his allies. Even though she had stayed awake to greet him when he returned to their rooms, he had wooed her curiosity from her with his fiery kisses. She wanted to linger in the dreams of that sweet love a while longer.

For too many nights while Rhys rode through the mountains to convince his allies to join this gathering at Cadairllwyd, she had found no sleep. Now she could soothe her fearful heart in knowing he was safe within the walls of the fortress once more.

"Gizela!"

She smiled. Here was the voice that filled her dreams with the glories of rapture. Opening her eyes, she smiled as she held up her arms to draw Rhys back into the bed which was draped in darkness. He could make the dream of rapture come to life.

"Come." He ripped back the covers. Ignoring her cry of astonishment, he snarled, "Edward's men are amassing beyond Cadairllwyd's walls."

"The king's men are here?"

"We have been betrayed. Someone must have alerted Edward to our location and the parley here."

"Do we fight?" She stared at the broadsword he was buckling over his hips. Fear pinned her to the mattress.

With a mirthless laugh, he tossed her clothes to her. "The warriors of this clan are scattered across the mountains to give Cadairllwyd warning of any attack." His lips twisted as he pulled his bow and quiver over his shoulder. "I wonder which one betrayed us."

Gizela pulled her simple gown over her linen shift. "They may have been ambushed and killed."

"What does it matter? We have no choice but to flee."

"Flee?" She never thought Rhys would suggest retreat. "You are surrendering Cadairllwyd to the king's men?"

"Not exactly," he said and chuckled. He went to the window and signaled out of it. When he turned back to her, he tossed her a heavy cloak.

"What are you planning?" she asked.

He drew her toward the door even as she was trying to pull on her slippers. "You soon shall see. Ask no more questions. We must leave while we can."

"Leave? But if Cadairllwyd is surrounded—"

He silenced her with a swift kiss. As she gripped the front of his tunic which might soon be awash with his blood, he whispered, "Trust me, Gizela. Stay close, so you do not get left behind."

Terror threatened to paralyze her. The situation must be far worse than he suggested if they were retreating without a single arrow put to string. "Are you leaving because of me? I will stay by your side if you wish."

"You would fight Edward's men?"

"I would tend to those who are wounded."

He stroked her cheek and opened the door. "I pray we shall have no wounded, and the English can tend to their own." He chuckled again. "If there is any among them left to tend."

"What are you going to do?"

"What is needed to be done. If all goes well, milady, they shall think twice before they attack a Welsh settlement again."

Giving her no time to ask more questions, he led her out of the room. The corridor was deserted. A single torch burned along the wall. He plucked it from its holder to light their way. The walls glistened strangely, and she wrinkled her nose.

"What smells like rancid lard?" she asked.

"An ancient weapon which the English will not suspect."

A shout came from the courtyard. Rhys's strides lengthened. She ran to keep up with him.

Only when they reached the large common room in the heart of the fortress did he slow. "One minute," he ordered.

Gizela dropped to a bench near the door and tugged on her shoe. Straightening, she watched Rhys go to his men who were clustered near the table where they gathered for each meal.

"Is everything set?" she heard him ask.

"As you ordered," Bleddyn answered.

"The other chieftains?"

"They understand what we do."

Rhys nodded. "Good. Then go."

Bleddyn drew his sword and jumped up onto the table. He cut through the ropes holding the dragon banner in place. The men caught it as it fell. Folding the banner, they handed it to Rhys. He bowed his head to them and tucked it under his arm.

"Go," he ordered again, pulling his own sword. The men set theirs across his in a complex pattern which rang with steel. Lifting his sword, he swept theirs up. "When next we meet, my friends, Edward will be the poorer many men. Let him know the Dragon of Wales wakes."

With a cheer, the men raced out of the Great Hall. Turning, Rhys held out his hand to Gizela as graciously as if they were about to go for a leisurely walk through the garden. "We must go."

"Where?"

"We have prepared for this exigency. No clan can be so proud that we fail to learn the lesson from Llewellyn ap Gruffydd's mistakes in dealing with Edward. They are too many for us to meet them in open combat. There are other ways." Regret sifted into his voice as he looked around the hall. "And other places."

Gizela whispered, "Rhys—"

"No time now, sweet one."

He pulled her out of the Great Hall, not giving her a chance to commiserate with him. Mayhap it was just as well. She wondered what she could have said to ease his pain at losing his home.

Gizela's foot slipped. Her hand went to the wall to support herself. She pulled it back in shock. Oil dripped from her fingers.

"What is this for?" she cried.

"To guarantee Edward's men do not return to him with an account of this day."

She stared at him in horror. If the whole building were as soaked with oil and lard as this passage, a single spark would turn it into an inferno.

"Vengeance?" she whispered.

"Justice," he said tautly, drawing her out of the keep.

The courtyard was nearly deserted. When she rounded the heavy stones of the huge hearth in the kitchen, she gasped as she saw a trap door in the floor. She watched a lad scramble down a ladder.

"What is it?" she asked.

"A passageway to the chance for revenge."

A man knelt by the trap door. "Few who should go, remain," he answered to Rhys's sharp question. "The young ones are helping the old, as you taught, Chieftain."

"Good. Gizela, you must go."

"Has Ysolde come out yet?" she asked.

The man shook his head. "She went to pack her medicines in the stillroom."

When another man rushed up to them, he spat a flurry of orders in Welsh. Rhys nodded and motioned him down the trap door. He added something to the man by the door, then turned on his heel to go out of the kitchen. He was drawing his sword as he left.

The man by the door gestured for Gizela to climb down the ladder.

"No," she said, "I must go and help Ysolde. She may need assistance in carrying her supplies."

"Milady," began the man, then he shrugged. "Stay, if that is your wish. 'Tis your life you gamble." To the others clumping behind Gizela, he commanded, "Come with me. Now!"

Gizela raced out into the courtyard. A single man was shouting orders, but she ignored them, for she guessed they were to other warriors she could not see.

The stillroom was empty.

"Ysolde!" she cried. Was the old woman hidden by the shelves?

She got no answer. Skirting the table, she saw the door to the garden at the back was open. She ran to it, then froze as she stared at the sickening sight in the midst of the overturned earth.

Ysolde lay in her own blood, an arrow buried deep in her neck, fresh herbs beneath her slack fingers. Forcing her feet forward, Gizela knelt by the old woman. Her trembling fingers could find no pulse. Leaning her head against Ysolde's chest, she heard no heartbeat.

"No!" she cried. "No, not you, Ysolde. You are not a warrior!"

Something buzzed past her ear. When an arrow bounced off the stone wall behind her, Gizela jumped to her feet and fled into the stillroom. Another arrow struck the door frame. She collapsed against the table, then pushed herself to her feet.

She lurched back out in the courtyard. When Rhys ran toward her, she saw shock on his face.

"Gizela, you should have—"

"I needed to be sure Ysolde was safe." She gripped his arms and whispered in a broken voice, "She is dead, Rhys. In the herb garden."

"Dead? How?"

"An arrow. Two more were fired at me."

His shout sent three men racing toward the stillroom. He turned her toward the kitchen. "Go, Gizela"

A dull thud rang through the courtyard.

"What is that?" she cried.

"Edward's men are determined to break the gates down." He glanced over his shoulder as the battering ram struck the gate again. "Go, Gizela!"

She shook her head. "I shall not leave without you."

He grasped her shoulders and steered her toward a ladder. "If you love me, go."

"What of you? If the king's men—"

Capturing her lips, Rhys erased every protest from Gizela's mind. Her arms slid around him as her fingertips sought to memorize the shapes of his body. When he drew her away, she feared she never would touch him again. With a sob, she clung to him.

"Go," he whispered. "I shall come to you in no time."

Tears blurred the sight of him walking resolutely away. She took a step to follow, then paused as a man ran toward her.

"Tremaine!" she cried. "Are Mair and the baby safe?"

He drew her away from the ladder. "I saw to that immediately. Come. I shall help you, too."

She pointed to the ladder. "Rhys wanted me to go this way."

"There may be trouble at the end of the tunnel. If—"

Bleddyn burst around the hearth, his sword in one hand and a bucket in the other. "What are you still doing here? The chieftain wants all of us gone."

When Bleddyn stepped onto the ladder, he said, "Do not loiter here. They are nearly through the gate."

Gizela tugged against Tremaine's hand. For a moment, she feared he would not release her. Then he did, and she nearly tumbled into the hole. Bleddyn steadied her, glaring at her as well as Tremaine.

Gingerly she stepped onto the top rung of the ladder. Bleddyn's shout urged her to hurry. She did not dare. The ladder swayed with every motion. Feeling her way down the thin branches lashed together with long sinews, she clutched onto the sides as it rocked. Hands settled on her waist and lifted her to the ground.

She smiled her thanks at Pwyll. Although she wanted to ask the bard why he waited here, he asked, "Who remains behind you?"

"Tremaine." She pointed to where he was climbing down. "Rhys and—"

"The fool!" Tremaine spat.

The bard said, "There is no time to argue. Follow the glow of the brands and watch your step. Listen to the instructions of the man at the end of the tunnel."

"I shall wait for Rhys," Gizela said quietly. "I will not leave without him."

Tremaine snapped, "Do not ruin everything with your bleating, milady. Go with Pwyll and have Bleddyn lead the others to safety."

"No, I shall stay and wait here for Rhys."

He opened his mouth to retort, but his words went unsaid as Rhys rushed down the ladder. Rhys's eyes narrowed when he saw Gizela. He grabbed her hand and said, "Let us go while we can."

As they followed the twists of the tunnel, the roof became lower, so she had to bend at an uncomfortable angle to walk. Dampness chilled her through the thin fabric of her gown. Voices came from in front of her. Friends or foe? She could not tell, for they were distorted. She watched the glow of the torches ahead of her.

Suddenly the ceiling opened, and she could stand. In front of her was a ladder, the twin of the one beneath the kitchen. She scrambled up it. Hands grasped her wrist and pulled her out. She was swung out of the way as if she were a sack of flour.

Falling to the ground, Gizela struggled to stand. A hand on her shoulder kept her close to the earth so she offered no target to the English. She twisted to see Tremaine and Rhys climb out of the hole. Beyond them, she could see the walls of Cadairllwyd. She realized they were near the top of the cliff overlooking the stronghold.

Rhys motioned for her to go with Pwyll. The bard led her to a rock where four women crouched. They gathered her in like a hen pulling a recalcitrant chick under her feathers. None of them spoke as they stared at the buildings below and listened to the hushed voices of the men and the shouts of the English.

When Rhys grasped her hand, he led her at a rapid pace along a path only he could discern along the rise. The others followed in a grim parade.

Dawn clawed its way over the horizon as they clambered higher up the rocky outcropping behind the fortress. They clung to the sparse shadows which shrank with the arrival of the sun. Mair's baby whimpered, but was silenced.

Gizela saw most of the clan sheltered behind a pile of boulders the size of the gates to Caernarvon. Caernarvon! Her breath caught beneath her ribs with a pinch of pain. By fleeing like this with the Welsh, she was severing all links with her homeland. No, she corrected herself, that tie had been ripped asunder when she returned to Cadairllwyd and denied the king his wish of seeing her married across the channel.

Rhys called quietly, "Here is perfect." A quick motion dispersed his men along the ridge. His voice was a rumble when he spoke to the other chieftains. They nodded and went to follow his orders.

Gizela noticed Tremaine rubbing his palms on his tunic. *With fear? Why should he be frightened now?* She looked back at Rhys. Was it possible his plan could fail? If it did, the Welsh rebellion could die here, even before it was born, for the strength of the land stood together on this mountainside.

Tremaine strode forward. "Rhys, this will not work. We must—"

"Have no doubts, my friend." With a satisfied laugh, Rhys called Bleddyn, "Do you have it?"

The homely man held up the bucket. His smile deepened as he bent and pulled a mound of twigs together.

Carefully he tilted the bucket to release a canister. He opened it, and the glow of embers brightened the morning. Along the ridge, the clan's warriors drew their quivers off their backs with a precision which told Gizela they had practiced this often. Only Rhys did not move as he stared down onto the thatched and shingled roofs of his home.

Inching forward while Bleddyn passed the canister along the hillside, Gizela put her hand on Rhys's arm. He gave her a swift smile and slipped his arm around her waist. It tightened when an ear-shattering crash and the sound of cheers announced the English had broken down the gates. King Edward's soldiers flooded into the courtyards and ran into the buildings.

Rhys did not raise his voice, but its quiet authority filled the morning. "Bleddyn, give the command now."

Gizela watched, horrified, as the each man fit an arrow to string. Their oily tips glistened in the sunrise the moment before they dipped them into the coals they had taken from the canister.

Bleddyn shouted, and a flurry of arrows cascaded down onto the thatch roofs. A second command sent another firestorm into Cadairllwyd.

Fires erupted throughout the fortress, swallowing it in one greedy gulp as oil and lard flared. Screams came from within the walls, but the Welsh archers released more fiery arrows into the trees and grass around the fortress to envelop it in fire. The blazes sealed the doom of the English inside Cadairllwyd.

"For Treystwyth," Rhys murmured.

Gizela could not speak as she watched flames spear the roof of the keep. Slowly her gaze went to Rhys. He had destroyed what he loved to prevent the English from claiming. Horror threatened to strangle her. He had ordered the destruction of his home, the place he loved most, in order to defeat his enemies. She had dared to love Rhys as she had wanted to love her father, yet feared Rhys would be no less brutal in his determination to attain what he wanted.

Rhys frowned when he saw the stricken expression on Gizela's face. He took a step toward her, but she whirled to go answer the need for her skills in tending a small injury. So many questions she must have. So few answers he could give her.

"You now have guaranteed Edward will outlaw you," Tremaine said, as he came to stand beside Rhys and watched the flames.

"I care little what Edward's law deems me. The laws of *Cymru* are what I heed now."

"And your lady?"

Rhys tore his gaze from the fire to look at Gizela who was tending to a cut on a child's hand. "What of her?"

"She will be outlawed as well. Her death at the hands of the English will not be as swift as your hanging, Rhys."

"For them to slay her, they must first possess her." He folded his arms over his chest. "That will not be."

Pwyll approached and dampened his lips, then said, "Forgive me for intruding, Chieftain."

"You know I value your counsel." He smiled at the bard who had set aside his *crwth* to join the archers on the hillside. "Speak openly."

"The English may not be the only ones wishing your lady dead." His hands flew about to emphasize his words. "Not all the chieftains, who answered your call to this ill-fated meeting, are pleased to have an Englishwoman among us. I have heard Ysolde is dead."

"Aye," Rhys said. "Gizela found her in the garden behind the stillroom. Slain with an arrow that somehow found its way into the fortress."

Tremaine shook his head. "Are you certain it came from without?"

"We have all seen," Pwyll added quickly, "how often Lady de Montpellier works there. Mayhap she was the target instead of Ysolde."

Rhys arched a brow, then looked back at the fire. "She spoke of two other arrows being fired at her."

"By whom? How many would wish to see Lady de Montpellier dead?" Pwyll shuddered. "Even the name she obtained along with her husband's lands is abhorrent, for it reminds us of the man who would have betrayed us to Edward."

"Then there is but one thing to do. Rid her of that name."

Tremaine laughed shortly. "Would you have her be called Lady Talbot? Speak that accursed name among these people, and you shall witness her being torn apart by those who have suffered Talbot's brutality. You know that well, Rhys."

"I know she would be known as only 'Gizela' if she were my wife," Rhys said quietly.

"Wife?" gasped Tremaine, his eyes widening. "Have you lost your wits? If you take her as your wife, Rhys, you may lose the support of every man here. Those who grumble that you have a *Saesnes* for your mistress will question your sanity if you graft her into this clan now."

"Now would not be the right time, but it is an option if the time were to come when I must." His jaw grew taut as he said, "I shall surrender neither *Cymru* nor my lady."

"Then you may lose both."

After hours of walking up steep mountainsides, Gizela could not hide her dismay when she saw the number of people ahead of her. They were grouped around the mouth of a broad cave near a river. It was the perfect site, easily defendable and with all the fresh water they needed, but she knew they had little food and fewer supplies.

When she entered the shadows, her dismay grew. Even though a short pile of blankets stacked against one wall and a handful of pans set by a fire pit showed that preparations had been wisely made, the cave was cramped and cool and damp. For the summer, they could live here. When winter arrived, this cave would offer scanty shelter. She hoped Rhys had a plan to survive through the killing cold in the highlands.

When a cup was pressed into her hands, she took a deep breath of the broth. She wondered how the women of the kitchen had managed to heat this so quickly. She plucked a slice of bread from a tray held out to her.

"Thank you," she said as she dipped it into the steaming broth.

"No butter," announced one of the women, and they all laughed.

A flush climbed Gizela's cheeks. She hoped the dim light prevented them from seeing her reaction. Putting her food on the tray, she walked out of the cave.

Hot tears abruptly saturated her eyes. She did not look back as she walked along the creek. The splash of the water took a mournful tone as she looked across the mountains which were glowing in the first light of the day. In the valley, the shrouds of smoke marked the graves of Edward's men.

How had they found Cadairllwyd? Mayhap they had captured someone from the village, but what she had seen of the attack suggested the English soldiers had killed without mercy. No one had been given a reprieve, even for an inquisition. The traitor must have been within the walls of Cadairllwyd. Had he or she been the one to kill Ysolde?

A shiver shook every bone along her spine, despite the warmth of the day. Dear Ysolde, who had thought only of giving a surcease of pain. She had died in agony. And for what? The traitor might still be preparing to denounce them to the English.

Pausing to sit beside a still pool enclosed in a nearly perfect circle of stone, she stared at the brook as it followed its serpentine path toward the valley floor.

Rhys's hand settled on her shoulder, she did not flinch, for she recognized his touch immediately. Rhys sat next to her and leaned her head against his shoulder.

"Do you come here to mourn?" he asked.

"Yes."

"For whom?"

She sat straighter. "For Ysolde, of course."

"For no one else?"

"Who else was slain?"

He smiled grimly as he gestured toward the valley. "Two score of Edward's men if fortune was with us."

"By my troth," she cried, setting herself on her feet. "Why do you mock me with this?"

"I need to know where your heart resides, Gizela." He stood and gathered her hands into his. "Speak to me of the truth, for the time has come when you can no longer hide behind my cloak. War is here, and each of us needs to trust the other."

"I shall never betray you."

"Aye, I know that, but others are not so certain. You may be called publicly to answer for your birth."

"I know." Drawing her hands out of his, she clasped them behind her back and stared down into the valley. "I thought you would be busy with the chieftains."

"They are eager to break their fast before we use our jaws for talking."

Gizela laughed, surprising herself as much as him. "You need to be a diplomat as well as a warrior, Rhys."

"That is, unfortunately, true. This alliance is a jealous one, for many men hope to lead it, and only one shall."

"You?"

He shrugged. "I do not aspire to such if I am not the best man to lead us into victory against the English. We cannot let petty differences divide us when we never have needed more to be united in common accord."

Gizela sank back onto the rock. "And if you fail to bridge your differences?"

"We cannot. We must not fail this time, or we all may be banished as far from *Cymru* as you were to be."

"Then you would die, for you take your life from these rocks."

Tousling her hair, he sat with his back against the boulder and his arm draped on her knees. "Mayhap I shall leave all this warring behind and sail far from here as Madoc ap Owen Gwynedd did a century ago."

"Where did he go?"

"Who knows? Farther than the land of the Irish. Mayhap as far as the end of the world. He returned with tales of a strange land on the opposite shore of the wide ocean. Poor, unfortunate Madoc."

Her eyes widened. "*Poor, unfortunate Madoc?* I thought you envied him."

"Why should I envy a prince who had to cross the huge ocean to find his heart's desire when I found mine here?"

"In these hills."

He shook his head. "In your eyes, my love."

"My love?" she whispered, afraid to believe what her ears told her.

"I love you, Gizela, as I love these rocks and the glory that is *Cymru*." He tipped her mouth so close, his lips brushed hers as he spoke. "Be my wife, Gizela."

She did not hesitate. "No, Rhys, I shall not marry you."

"You love me, don't you?"

She smiled sadly as she rose. "More than I love anything or anyone in this world, and, for that reason, I shall not marry you." She tangled her fingers in his silken hair. "Why do you ask me now, Rhys? Because you fear for me?"

He stood and enfolded her to him. "sweet one, there already are questions of how Edward's men found Cadairllwyd and why Ysolde died. They will not be silenced easily, for they gnaw at the alliance like a cancer."

"And you shall exacerbate the wound if you take me as your wife." Slipping out of his arms, she whispered, "You told me but moments ago, this alliance is doomed if it is not united. I shall not let you doom it and yourself by saving me."

She did not let him give her a chance to answer before she ran along the stream toward the cave. Her heart had been given the very thing it wanted and she could not accept it.

20

Rhys tapped his fingers impatiently on his knee as he listened to the debate around him. The chieftains were trying to uncover the truth of the attack on Cadairllwyd and to find the traitor who would be rewarded with death. Or, that had been the announced intention of this meeting when it was called.

It had not taken long for the topic to turn, as he had anticipated, to Lady Gizela Talbot de Montpellier. Faith! The fury was no less than he had envisioned, but he might have been able to curb it if he had been able to announce Gizela had forsaken her ties to England and Edward to join with them as his wife. Instead she might die, for the rage focused on her and those connected in any way with her.

Tremaine prowled about the clearing like a cat. "'Tis true."

"You brought her to Cadairllwyd?" asked Bran ap Gwydion, who had taken again the role of spokesman for his fellow chieftains.

"On the orders of Chieftain Rhys ap Cynan."

Bran frowned. "Is this true, Rhys?"

"Aye, I gave the order for her to be brought."

"And the order that she be allowed to view the route from Caernarvon to Cadairllwyd?" Bran looked back at Tremaine. "Why didn't you give her the sleeping potion as you did the previous time?"

"Rhys urged me to see no harm came to her, not even from my own hand."

Rhys scowled. "This chatter gains us nothing. Gizela never left Cadairllwyd save when she was with me. She could not have taken the information to Edward."

"Mayhap it did not pass from her hand directly into his," Llyr ap Adwr said. The thin man smiled coldly. "She is a beautiful woman. If she seduced one of your men as easily as she seduced you, Rhys—"

He exploded from the ground to grasp the man by the throat. Llyr fell back, choking, then pulled his knife. Rhys knocked it to the ground. Gripping the man's chin, he pulled Llyr's head back painfully. His gritted teeth strained every word as he snarled, "Speak no more of my lady, Llyr ap Adwr."

"Rhys, leave off," ordered Bran.

Rhys sighed and stood. His foot shoved the knife toward Llyr before he returned to where he had been sitting.

Bleddyn edged closer to him. "Chieftain, if you wish, he shall not live to see the sunset."

"You would kill a fellow Welshman because he insulted Gizela?" he asked, astonished.

"Nay, for his insult to you, Chieftain." His lips curled into a satire of a smile. "He insults your manhood with his suggestion that she would seek another, when you have her busy in your own bed."

Rhys resisted grinning. Trust the young buck to see Llyr's words in such a light. Quietly he said, "Let there be no blood spilled needlessly among those of us who are allies, Bleddyn. If your sword thirsts for blood, let it be English blood that quenches it."

His yearning to chuckle vanished as he listened to the argument among the chieftains. Even though many of the men looked to him to protest, Rhys sat with his arms folded and his face impassive. To speak now might do more harm than good. Upon the wrong word leaving his mouth, the chieftains would unite. As long as the controversy continued, Gizela remained unaccused of betraying them.

When Tremaine asked permission to address the group, Rhys tensed. Tremaine had made no secret of his enmity for Gizela.

"Bran?" Rhys called.

"Tremaine speaks first."

"For himself," Rhys argued, "not for our clan."

"Tremaine, do you agree?"

Nodding, Tremaine said, "I speak for myself, for I am not the chieftain. Gizela Talbot de Montpellier—"

A growl of fury met her name, and Rhys fought not to reach for his knife. Tremaine had damned her with no more than the recitation of her name. Even though no man loathed Esmond Talbot more than he did, Rhys would not let her be executed simply because she had the misfortune to inherit her father's name.

"—was born in England, raised in England, and," continued Tremaine, "is the widow of an Englishman. Her husband's brother was executed by my chieftain's order as a double traitor. Yet I ask you to grant her clemency."

Gasps ringed the clearing. Rhys frowned. This was not what he had expected from Tremaine. Mayhap his friend had depths he had not seen.

"Do you have a reason for your request?" asked Bran.

"She has shown her support for our ways by coming among us and healing those who are sick and tending those who suffer." He laughed tersely. "And, as we know well, she is but an Englishwoman who knows nothing of the ways of her king. Englishwomen are raised merely to serve their husband's needs."

Llyr stood. "And that is what worries me. Is she serving her husband even now? Has she not been betrothed to the king's cousin? What if he sent her here to gather information as we sit and ponder like old women beside the fire?"

Cheers of assent met his words.

Rhys came to his feet. "I have asked to speak, Bran."

"You spoke at the beginning, and I believe you have nothing new to say." When Rhys scowled, Bran rose, saying, "These are your lands, Rhys ap Cynan, and the duty is yours. I trust you will do as you must to make your forefathers proud of you as we return to our own clans."

The men left the clearing, save for the warriors of Cadairllwyd. They looked at each other uneasily as they waited for Rhys to speak. As the silence grew, heavy and disquieting, Bleddyn stepped forward.

"Chieftain—"

"Say nothing," Rhys interrupted in a monotone. "Go and do your tasks. I shall tend to this myself."

Tremaine remained behind when the other men left. "Rhys, I am sorry my words did not help."

"I thank you for your attempt. You are the one I know I can always depend on."

"I can vow that will never change," he said before Rhys walked away from the clearing.

Reaching the cave, Rhys strode across the ground which was already worn with the feet of his clan. He did not look back at the men drifting away across the hillside. The chieftains did not doubt his fidelity to the ancient laws.

He paused in front of the door of the cave. "Are you busy?"

Gizela lowered the pestle into the wooden bowl. "How did the meeting of the chieftains go? What did you decide?"

"Can you leave here? I wish to speak with you alone."

Gizela tried to read the emotions in his eyes, but his face was as blank as the stone walls of the cave. "Yes."

He pulled her into his arms and found her lips with ease. Without releasing her fingers, he led them around her waist and held them behind her back. In the prison of his embrace, she wanted nothing but this joy. The tip of his tongue teased her lips open, adding to her passion. When she moaned with the longing that resisted anything but gratification, he bent to tease the velvety skin directly behind her ear.

"Come with me," he whispered. Gizela held his hand as they left the cave. They walked slowly along the steep hillside. The few low blades of grass caught at the long hem of her dress.

The muted sounds of the clan near the cave were replaced by the remote bleats of the sheep in the higher meadows. Even that comforting noise vanished into the distance as she heard something she could imagine only as a fierce wind blowing along the mountains. Yet, no storm clouds marred the cobalt perfection of the crystal sky. Only sunlight rained down on them.

When Rhys halted by a large stone and motioned for her to sit, she whispered, "Is this where you shall slay me?"

"You are insightful, milady."

She shook her head. "I saw the temper of the chieftains each time they looked at me." Arching her brows, she said, "The only thing I find odd is that they did not wish to watch."

"They trust me to do what I must." He ran his fingers through her hair. "They see it as my honor as well as my obligation."

Taking his hand, she guided it to her temple. "Here," she whispered.

"Here?"

"Here is where the blow should fall, if you do not wish me to suffer."

He knelt beside her. "I would not have you suffer, my love, but I do not understand why you speak like this."

Her fingers curled along his strong jaw. "I merely echo what Father told me on the many times he threatened to kill me."

"Your father threatened to kill you?" he choked.

"Why do you act surprised? What have you called Esmond Talbot when you did not think I heard? One of the hounds of hell?" As her thumb brushed his face which was rough with the wind, she whispered, "So many times he told me how a single blow there would put an end to the misery he suffered each time he looked upon me."

"How could any man be miserable when he looked upon your beauty?" He kissed her questing fingers lightly. "If I had a daughter as lovely and giving as you, I would be thankful every day of my life."

She drew her fingers away. "But only if you had a son as well to aspire to your title." She sighed deeply. "I know you hate my father for what he did to *Cymru*, but his greatest crimes were within his own hall. He killed my mother and two other wives in the effort to have a *living son. Even his mistresses gave him only living daughters, but none of them survived past infancy. Only me, and I* was a daily reminder of his failure to sire a son."

Rhys smiled gently. "His failure has been my pleasure, Gizela."

When she did not smile in return, his faded.

"You still do not understand, Rhys. Esmond Talbot refused to be considered a failure, so he must put the blame elsewhere. The failure belonged to his wives when they did not conceive quickly— or to me—when they lost the child or their own lives. Even my study to become a midwife and to help birth a healthy son for him did not meet his approval."

"He was mad."

"Mayhap, and his madness was vicious."

"He hurt you?"

"Many times."

Disgust filled his voice. "He never raped you, did he?"

"What would that have gained him?" She laughed mirthlessly. "If I could have given him a legitimate son, I suspect he would have no reservations about using me. I could not, so he simply took out his frustration on me with heavy fists and the vow to see me dead." She closed her eyes and whispered, "Then I found a way to put an end to it."

"You convinced Kenleigh de Montpellier to marry you so you might escape your father's heavy hand?"

"Kenleigh was kind to me from the first time I recall him visiting Talbot Hall. He asked me to wed him, for he had hoped his name would bring me haven." She looked at him and gathered his hands between hers. "Who would have guessed it would bring me here to where I must hurt the man I love?"

"Hurt *me*? How?" His fingers closed into fists over her hands. "I would give almost anything, my love, to repay your father for what he did to you."

"It is over." Her smile was more sincere. "That is what has been my salvation. It is over, save for what I have done to you." She hesitated, and then said, "I have among my herbs several that, when mixed together, will result in death. If I were—"

"Come with me, Gizela." He drew her to her feet. "It is not your duty to kill yourself. 'Tis my duty to see you killed, my love, but no hour was put upon your death."

"You cannot expect the chieftains will be amused by such a subtle method of skirting the law. You can no longer avoid the choice. You can no longer have both me and *Cymru*."

He folded her hands against his chest. "Do you beg me to kill you now?"

"Of course not."

"Then come with me." He seized her hand and tugged her along at a pace near a run.

The uproar became louder. They rounded a bend in the stream. Rhys's delighted laughter filled her ears as she gazed at the waterfall falling in wild abandon down steep cliffs.

The first fall was the longer of the two, but was obscured by the trees surrounding the upper pool. A verdant forest of ferns as high as her waist edged the lower basin and climbed the steep slope. The lower falls sang out their melody, a deeper undercurrent to the song of the stream. The water coming down the side of the cliffs looked like strands of carded wool—soft, silken, and straight.

"'Tis magnificent," she whispered.

"'Tis called *Pistyll Mynyddfan*."

"What is that in English?"

He laughed, the sound as wild as the waters. "Simply a lofty mountain waterfall."

"Whatever its name, 'tis lovely. It should belong in heaven."

"Have I never told you this land is as close to paradise as any mortal can dare lay claim?"

"I believe you may have once." She was astonished when she could smile. She never had imagined her last hours could be like this, but now she could envision no better way to spend this time than laughing with Rhys. No, she could think of one finer way.

Her skin tingled with longing as Rhys walked down the easiest slope and held out his hands to her. Putting her hands on his shoulders which were below hers, she let him lift her down to stand beside the pool. Mud oozed into her shoes, but she took a deep breath of the pungent greenery and forgot the mire. He dropped to his knees and dipped his hand into the water. After he had drunk deeply, he cupped his hands together and offered her some of the crystalline water.

"Thank you," she said as she sat on the ferns which sparkled with spray. "Thank you for everything, Rhys."

He said nothing when his wet hands drew her face toward his. There were no words which could say what she read in his eyes. The fiery longing became more potent with every chance they had to satisfy it. She closed her eyes, eager for the touch of his lips on hers.

Soft laughter brushed her ear as he pushed aside her heavy braid. His tongue brazenly tickled her earlobe. The sound careened through her like a fever, setting her aflame with the desire only he could bring to life and only he could sate. With her arms around his shoulders, she urged him closer and ever closer.

When he leaned her back in the plush bed of soft ferns, the plants rustled their welcome over the roar of the water and her heart's frantic beat. Again she waited impatiently for his lips to touch hers. Slowly her eyes opened to see him smiling down at her.

"You smell of mint and other less pleasing things," he said with a chuckle.

"What kind words, Chieftain."

Sitting back on his heels, he said, "'Tis the lot, I fear, of a man who wishes to love a healer."

"Let me wash my hands."

"I was jesting with you." He caught her shoulders and leaned her back into the ferns. "What do I care for the odors on your gown when soon I shall toss it far from you?"

"No," she whispered, slipping from beneath him. "I want this time—this last time—to be so wondrous, I shall dare hell to savor a moment of its memory."

His fingers on her arm halted her. "My love, you speak of your death with such acceptance. Why?"

"Do you wish me to rail against it? What good would that do?" She sighed. "I do not want to die."

"There is still much to be said between us on that."

"Is there?"

"Yes, much. I do not want you dead. I want you by my side for the rest of my life."

"That is where I wish to be, but—"

He kissed her deeply, and she let him draw her into his arms. There she could forget the pain. "Do no fear. Trust me, Gizela, and think only of ecstasy."

"A fine way to think," she whispered. He must have some way to save her from the sentence of death. She must trust him.

"And I shall think only of ecstacy, when you smell sweeter."

She loosened her shoes and pulled off her stockings. Stuffing the heavy leggings into the shoes, she pretended not to see the holes. They would not last through the month. Pushing that thought out of her head, she raised her skirts nearly to her knees.

"I thought you were washing your hands." Rhys laughed.

"Why ruin my shoes?"

She tested the water with her toes. With a shiver, she drew her foot out of the pool. She smiled over her shoulder to where Rhys reclined against the fern covered slope.

"Does this water never get warm?" she asked with another exaggerated shiver.

"Never." His gaze stroked her bare legs beneath her kilted skirts, but his voice remained light. "This cataract has its birth in the very depths of *Eryri*. Within high mountains, where even the sun's heat cannot reach, this stream keeps the sea cold to the rim of the world."

Gizela laughed as she eased her foot back into the icy water. "Must you always sound like a bard when I ask you nothing more than a simple question?"

Folding his hands beneath his head, he smiled. "The plight of even the most uneducated Welshman when he discusses the land holding his heart."

"And giving his soul its fervor?"

"I think you are beginning to understand."

"Maybe. I—" With a cry, she fought for her balance on the slick stones of the pool.

Her feet slipped out from beneath her, and she dropped to sit in the water. Rhys's roar of laughter was louder than the cacophony of the falls. Shaking her hands in disgust, she glared at him.

"You should be careful, Gizela," he said in mock concern. "The bottom of that pool can be slippery. If you fail to take caution, you—"

"Enough!"

She ignored his chuckle as she stood. Her gown was soaked from the waist and weighed as much as the rocks along the precipice. When Rhys continued to laugh, she reached for the laces which closed at the back of her waist. A single tug loosened them to leave her dress gaping.

His laughter faded as he sat up. The beguiling fires burned in his eyes as she lowered the gown along her shift. Flicking the garment to the ferns not far from where Rhys watched, she ran her fingers through her braid to free her hair.

When she reached for the clasp holding her simple undergarment closed, desire erupted to every inch of Rhys's body. He found himself on his feet and at the edge of the pool without realizing how he had gotten there. He thought only of the golden skin emerging from beneath the linen as she lowered the thin sleeve along her arm.

Kicking off his boots and ripping his stockings from his feet, he splashed into the pool and pulled her nearly naked body against him. He gave her no chance to speak before his mouth captured hers to demand exactly what she wanted to give him.

Her hands swept up through the tawny jungle of his thick hair. A moan escaped from her as he sought past her lips. The water seeped from her to add to the heat growing between them. Her leg brazenly rubbed against his as he tightened his arms around her.

He drew her from the pool. Her undershift fell away to be thrown atop her other clothes. As she reclined back into the soft bed of ferns, he stripped off his own garments. The hunger aching within him, refused to wait any longer. He must be against her, skin to skin. His eager moan brushed her lips in the second before he pressed her more deeply into the ferns.

When he rolled onto his back, he brought her to lie atop him. Drawing her mouth toward his, he delighted in the half-light of her thick hair streaming along both of them.

She laughed with unfettered happiness as he tickled the curve of her waist. The sound faded into the glorious pleasure as the yearning returned stronger when she moved against him, her soft skin burnishing his rough body. His hand settled on her hips to press her more tightly to him.

Lying beside him, she let her fingertips slowly explore the breadth of his chest. His hands drew her mouth to his as she touched him. The rough and silken textures of his skin seared her fingers. When her mouth discovered his intriguing flavors, she smiled to hear his sharp pants of pleasure. Each graze of her mouth against him stoked the fire within her until it was as hot as any smith's furnace.

With a groan of near desperation, he pushed her onto her back. Held between his firm body and the delicate fingers of the ferns, she reveled in the fiery kisses he showered on her. The slick stroke of his tongue explored the gentle upsweep of her breast until she moved enticingly with the rhythms of their love.

"Not yet," he whispered against her sensitive skin. The heat of his breath evaporated the moistness and added to the heated river flowing within her. As he moved over her, she became lost in the rapture.

Her cry of joy matched the tremor rocking her as he dared her to control what was no longer controllable. Whispering his name, she urged him to release her from the splendid anguish, but he laughed softly.

As she ceded all of herself to the enchantment, they were one. Together, they soared to the very essence of their craving. For one eternal moment, they possessed ecstasy, knowing that forever they would possess love.

The song of the water over the stones drifted through Gizela's mind, but she thought only of how Rhys's hair was so soft against her fingers. With her eyes closed, the fading bliss burst back to life when he kissed the length of her neck gently.

"I love you," she whispered. As his fingers stroked her forehead, she opened her eyes to see his tender smile.

"I love you, too, sweet Gizela."

Reaching up to touch the sandy texture of his cheek, she knew she must share with him the words billowing on a sweet breeze through her heart. "Rhys?"

"First let me speak to you of what I must."

"Rhys, I—"

He put his finger against her lips to interrupt her. "Let me say this first." He drew her up to sit beside him on the crushed grass which bore the imprint of their bodies. Plucking a leafy strand from her hair, he said, "I wanted to tell you this before the others learn of it. Word has come to me that Prince Alfonso has been ill."

"King Edward's son?" Her eyes widened in horror. "Of what?"

"That is of no concern." Grimly, he added, "What matters is that the child you helped Eleanor birth may soon be heir to the English throne."

"A Welsh-born prince who speaks neither English nor French," she whispered in awe. She wondered if the king had had some prescience of his older son's illness when he enacted that infuriating charade. The leaders

of all the Welsh clans had sworn allegiance to the newborn prince, who now could be king.

Rhys stood. As the sun dripped down his hardened
physique, he scooped up his clothes. He tossed her
gown to her as he pulled on his undertunic. The
moment his head appeared through the wide neck of
the shirt, he said, "That, as much as the fact
Cadairllwyd was overrun, is why the chieftains demand
your death."

"Because I helped birth a child?"

"That child is claimed to be Prince of Wales. No one
will accept this fallacy Edward has thrust upon us.
Mayhap the child was born here, but he is no more of
Cymru than—"

"I am?"

"Faith, Gizela. Will you let me finish before you
assume the worst? You may not have been born here,
but you hear the songs of this land singing in your
blood."

Sitting next to her, he pulled on his boots. As he tied
his sash about his waist, he paused and loosened it.
Sliding off a leather sheath, he pressed it into her
hands. Slowly she withdrew the knife with the dragon
haft.

"Do you wish me to use this to put an end to my
life?" she whispered. Without speaking, she slipped the
long blade with its etching of a dragon back into its
case. "I cannot, for I would cut short not a moment of
the time I have with you."

"You are not listening. I told you before I do not
want you dead. I cannot slay you, Gizela."

She closed her eyes and whispered a soft prayer.
Without looking at him, she asked, "Will you give the
task to Bleddyn? He would gladly see me dead."

"I shall give the task to no one."

"But the chieftains—"

He stood and brought her to her feet. With his hands clasped behind her waist, he said, "I cannot allow anyone to take your life, because of a vow I made before I met you. That vow kept me from speaking as I had wished among the council of the chieftains."

"A vow?" She searched his face. "To whom?"

"To your husband."

"To Kenleigh? What did you vow to Kenleigh?"

"I believe it is time you knew the truth about what Kenleigh de Montpellier was doing in *Cymru*."

21

Shocked, Gizela whispered, "What was Kenleigh really doing in *Cymru*? What do you mean?"

"Listen to yourself, sweet one." He lifted her hand to his lips. The warmth of his mouth on her skin lessened the bonds of fear around her. "You have come to speak the name of this land with the ease of one born here. Mayhap because you were fated to be a part of this land from the moment you took your first breath. Kenleigh de Montpellier was simply the means for you to come here."

"That is true, but I do not understand what you mean when you speak of Kenleigh. He came to ride with King Edward's men."

"But he was unlike most of them. Kenleigh de Montpellier was willing to listen to any man, even if he did not agree with his opinions. We spoke often of ways to bring peace here."

"You and Kenleigh were friends?"

"We might have been friends if not for the determination of Edward to hold this land."

She smiled. "And yours to keep him from grasping it."

"Aye." He drew her to him. "Think of poor Edward sitting in the tower of his grand castle and lamenting about how I have taken a fair prize from him when I won you."

"Lamenting is not what I imagine. Rather, I think of his ire that I defied him so openly when he thought he was honoring me with such a marriage."

"Do you honestly believe he cared about you when he gave you to a man you have never met?"

"No," she whispered. "He cared nothing for me, but I had hoped he would wish to honor Kenleigh's memory."

His eyes were dim with sorrow. "Well it would be that he should honor your husband. Kenleigh de Montpellier was respected by all who knew him save his brother, who despised him for being the elder."

"Even Father granted him respect."

"I had never imagined Talbot and I might agree on anything, but I am wrong yet again, for I respected Kenleigh de Montpellier, too."

She stopped by the edge of the water. "Tell me about the last time you saw Kenleigh, Rhys. It has been so many years since I spoke with him." She sighed. "I find it difficult to recall his face, save for his gentle smile."

Instead of answering, Rhys put his finger to her lips and drew her along the stream to where a clump of trees curled shadows on the uneven water. The first twinge of fear vanished when she saw the mischievous twinkle in his eyes. She understood why when he drew her around the trees so she could see a familiar form coming down the hillside.

Tremaine paused in midstep as his eyes locked with Gizela's. He started to speak, then faltered. Clearing his throat loudly, he said, "Well met, Rhys. Milady."

"Speak with honesty," Rhys replied, chuckling. "You are astonished to see Gizela walking by my side."

"I had thought you would obey the edict of your fellow chieftains."

"You, more than any other living man, should have known that was impossible." He raised Gizela's hand so her wedding ring glistened in the sunshine. "I could not kill Lady de Montpellier."

Tremaine's eyes narrowed. "So you would honor that debt over your obligation to your clan?"

"Which debt?" Gizela asked when Rhys simply nodded.

"A debt that is mine, milady," Rhys said.

"To me?"

He smiled. "Do not flatter yourself that I have saved your life because you bandaged my finger."

"Then which debt?"

Before he could speak, hoofbeats echoed along the stream. Rhys grabbed her hand, pulling her into the water. Her feet slid on the stones, but she kept her footing. They splashed out on the far side.

Tremaine leaped across and shouted, "They are close, Rhys!"

"English?" she asked.

"Our horses died in Cadairllwyd," Rhys answered grimly. To Tremaine, he added, "Take Gizela and flee. I will give you time."

"No!" she cried, grasping his arm as he drew his sword. "Come with us."

He shoved her toward Tremaine as the shadows of the riders burst forth from the trees. "Keep my lady alive, Tremaine. If God wills it, I shall meet you back at the cave."

"Rhys—"

"Go with him!" he fired back at her.

Tremaine tugged on her arm and pulled her into the shadow of the bushes higher on the ridge. No more than the space of three heartbeats passed before riders rode into the clearing on the far side of the stream.

Gizela blinked back tears of frustration and fear as she heard the leader call for a halt. She recognized the design on his surcoat. King Edward's men! He shouted to Rhys who stood by the edge of the water. Rhys's answer was to raise his sword.

"Stay still," hissed Tremaine. "They do not see us."

"Are they blind?"

"They think only of the quarry before them. The prize is high for the man who brings Rhys ap Cynan to Edward."

She moaned with despair. Drawing her feet beneath her, she gasped as Tremaine jerked hard on her arm. His hand clamped over her mouth when she fell back onto the soft earth.

"Do nothing to betray us, milady. I have no wish to die here today."

Rhys did not move as the leader of the English warriors shouted and rode across the stream. Would he just let the man ride him down? He must not sacrifice his life like this. He must—

Rhys raised his broadsword higher. Metal rang through the afternoon, its resonance bouncing off the nearby hills as the leader's sword struck his. Rhys spun to face the rider as the horse wheeled in the narrow clearing. Shouts urged the Englishman on.

Gizela clenched her hands until her nails ripped into her palms. Her prayers were muffled against Tremaine's hand. She stiffened when he tensed as the leader called an order in French. "Search the hillsides. This renegade may not be here alone! I want anyone you find brought to me alive. They shall face the full force of the king's vengeance. 'Tis time these barbarians learn—"

"I am here alone, *Sais!*" shouted Rhys in the same language. "Do you think I would not hunt in my own lands by myself because I fear some herd of Englishmen who clump together like frightened sheep facing the mighty strength of the wolf?"

"Lay down your sword, cur, and respect the will of your betters!"

Rhys adjusted his grip on his sword. "Coward!" he roared. "You will not face me alone, Englishman? Do you fear your blood will nurture the soil of this land?"

"Surrender!" shouted the Englishman again. "Surrender or die."

"Surrender *or die?*" *He laughed. "Rather I would guess it is surrender and* die."

The rider looked past him, and Rhys risked a glance behind him. Closing in an arc were nearly a dozen of King Edward's men. Each carried a bare sword ready to cut into him. Silently he cursed. The quiet along the mountain had deceived him. That, and his yearning to share the truth with Gizela. Now, she might never hear it from him.

As he gritted his teeth and balanced firmly on his feet, he did not let his gaze stray toward where Tremaine had taken Gizela. He doubted they had gotten far before they had to seek a place to hide from English eyes. One life lost at the hand of Edward's men was all he would allow this day. Tremaine knew their clan needed a leader more than two dead heroes. He would see Gizela was taken back to the cave.

Gizela . . . . If he died here, she would join him in death before the day's end. He alone, stood between her and the command of the chieftains. He must fight the English and win.

With a shout, he rushed forward. The rider raised his sword, but not in time. Rhys's blade drove deep into the man's gut. Rhys pulled the bloody length from the Englishman. He pushed him from the horse and leaped into the saddle. The horse neighed, frightened by the odor of death. He twisted the beast's head and shouted the battle cry of his clan.

The Englishmen scattered before him like dried leaves on a breeze. His sword found another victim. The man's howl was a triumphant song in his ears.

Gizela flinched as a body fell into the stream. She strained to see. Was that Rhys or did he still live? Tremaine's arms were a prison, and she could not move. With a curse, she jabbed her elbow into his stomach. His breath burst from him as she pulled away.

She jumped to her feet. She could not let Rhys fight this alone. Tremaine caught her and swung her to the ground. She pushed herself up, but his knife flashed in front of her eyes.

"Tremaine," she whispered, "we must help him."

"If you betray our location, the English will have no chance to slay you," he spat. "Because I will see you dead first."

"Are you so afraid of the English?"

His mouth twisted, but he glanced over his shoulder as a victorious shout sounded. He turned back, the knife still before her as she collapsed against the earth. The shout had been in French.

"No, not Rhys. Do not be dead, my love," she whispered.

Tremaine seized her arm and drew her up to sit. "We must go."

"Rhys—"

"You cannot help him by being captured, too."

"Captured?" She struggled to look past him.

On the ground Rhys sprawled, the point of a sword against his back as his captor wiped blood from his mouth. Three Englishmen were lying in widening scarlet pools. The rest of the soldiers stared at the man beside Rhys, who was scanning the clearing.

Gizela held her breath as his gaze swept toward them. She was sure his gaze touched hers, but it must have been only her fear. He continued to look about the clearing. If he had seen her, he would be giving the orders even now to rout her and Tremaine from their hiding place.

"He lives," whispered Tremaine nearly soundlessly against her ear. "They do not want to kill the great Rhys ap Cynan so easily, I can assure you. None of Edward's men would deny their king that pleasure he had when he ordered Llewellyn's brother David drawn and quartered."

"If we—"

He pressed his hand over her mouth again. She moaned against his clammy flesh when Rhys's wobbly arms and ankles were lashed together. The soldiers congratulated each other on their good luck in capturing such a prize as they tossed him over the back of a horse and bound him in place.

Hot tears scorched her cheeks. She should be proud. The Englishmen were frightened of an unconscious man. That was a tribute to Rhys's fearsome reputation. But she could not feel anything but fear. Tremaine spoke true. Edward's vengeance would be appalling.

Gizela froze when a soldier poked his broadsword into some of the shrubs beside the stream. He raised his blade to slice through the next one. A shout from another man halted him in mid-swing. He grumbled as he stamped back to his horse.

Tremaine's hand slowly lifted from her lips as the Englishmen rode off, seeking their way farther down the mountainside. He turned her to face him. With the same low, intense tone he had used the day Cadairllwyd was destroyed, he whispered, "Milady, we must be unseen when we return to our allies."

"I know," she managed to gulp. "Tremaine, we must—"

"Warn the others first." His stern voice became laced with far stronger emotion as he said, "I promise you that you shall see him again. On my sword-sworn oath, I vow that to you."

"In death?" she whispered. "Slay me now, Tremaine, so I might escape this pain."

"I shall not slay you."

"But the chieftains—"

"*My* chieftain has a reason to keep you alive. While he lives, I must obey that."

"And if Edward executes Rhys—" Her laugh was tinged with tears as she stood and stared along the stream. "What will it matter if I live or die then?"

"I hope it matters little to you, milady, for death will be yours."

Tremaine led her across the stream. He paused, bending to pick up the knife Rhys had dropped. Holding it out, he asked, "Do you want this?"

"No." She did not add she had the knife Rhys had given her beneath her gown. With a sob, she grasped the knife from Tremaine. She threw it into the stream. It crashed against the rocks.

Cursing, he rushed her along the path. "You fool! Do you want to alert every Englishman in *Cymru* to us? Do not let your grief mislead you. We are in more danger now than we have ever been! Once they get Rhys back to the castle, they will be determined to wring every fact from him."

"He shall never betray us!"

"Not intentionally perhaps."

She jerked her arm away. Staring at him as if she had never seen him before, she gasped, "Not even unintentionally. Tremaine, what is wrong with you? Rhys is your friend and your chieftain. How can you say such things?"

His mouth worked, but no sound emerged. He herded her along the steep path leading away from the stream. When she started to demand an answer, he hushed her. Frustration ate at her. This was no time to be doubting Rhys. They needed to work together to find a way to free him.

At the top of the hill, he put his arm around her quivering shoulders. "Forgive me," he said, staring at his shoes. "'Twas despair speaking."

"I know."

Voices drifted along the path to them—Welsh voices from the cave.

"Wait here," Tremaine ordered.

"Why? I should—"

Bleddyn rushed across the clearing. Jabbing a finger in Gizela's direction, he demanded, "Why does she still live?" He pulled his knife. "Did the chieftain give you the task? Was your stomach too squeamish to do as you were ordered? If you could not slay her, I shall."

Tremaine snapped a single word in Welsh. The younger man froze. When Tremaine motioned for Bleddyn to come with him, he added, "Milady, wait here."

"Tremaine, I wish to—"

"The council of the warriors of this clan is no place for a *Saesnes*."

Gizela lowered her stiff body to the ground and watched them walk away. Glances came in her direction, but no one spoke to her.

Tremaine came to stand in the middle of the clearing before the opening to the cave. "Heed me!" he shouted. Raising his hands, he motioned for quiet as the warriors gathered behind him. "Heed me well, for the words I speak are so bitter I do not wish to utter them ever again. Our chieftain has been captured by the king's men."

Gasps of shock crackled like summer thunder. Two women by the cave fell to the ground weeping. Others crossed themselves as they whispered prayers.

Bleddyn raised his sword over his head and shouted. The other men echoed by his words. Clanging their swords together, they called the words over and over.

Gizela closed her eyes. She did not know the exact meaning of what they were shouting, but she recognized a battle cry. Fools! Did they think they could batter their way through Caernarvon?

Bleddyn's voice was rising to a frenzy. The other men were stamping their feet as they struck their blades together.

When Bleddyn motioned toward the trees, Gizela could listen in silence no more. She jumped to her feet and cried, "Do not throw away your lives! You are too few to assault Caernarvon directly."

"Would you have us leave him there to die?" asked Bleddyn.

"No," she said, crossing the clearing to stand in front of him. She drew the knife Rhys had given her. The winged dragon seemed to take flight as she raised it over her head. "The dragon has woken from its slumber. Do not kill it with stupidity."

He sneered. "Do we follow a *Saesnes* against Edward's might? It would be easier to slit our throats before that English bastard can remove our heads from our shoulders for us."

"I do not ask you to follow me. I ask you to listen."

"You are a *Saesnes*!" he snarled.

Tremaine put his hand on her arm. He locked eyes with Bleddyn. "She is the chieftain's woman. She has a right to be heard."

"Aye, she is the chieftain's woman. That means only that she is pleasing in his bed. Her kinsman was a double traitor. She may be no better. Do we follow a whore's leadership?"

She held the dragon knife out to Tremaine, who might be her only ally among the hotheaded young warriors. "I have no wish to lead you. All I wish is for Rhys to be returned unharmed. Why are you standing about lamenting like frightened children when you could be making plans to save him?"

A tall man stepped forward and growled, "Rid us of her, Tremaine. You know the orders of the chieftains. Expunge this sickness from the soul of our clan. We need no *Saesnes* betraying us."

"Slay her!" shouted another voice. "How do we know she did not arrange for the English soldiers to capture our chieftain today?"

Tremaine snapped a word she had never heard. Silence clamped over the clearing. "Heed me," he said again. "Our only concern now is our chieftain. We shall get our vengeance for this insult when we free the blood from those who guard Caernarvon."

"Are you sure he will be taken there?" Pwyll asked as he moved closer to Gizela. With his hand on her shoulder, the bard displayed his feelings clearly. He would stand with her and the chieftain. "Did we not hear Edward has returned to Rhuddlan?"

"The road to Rhuddlan is long," Gizela said softly. "They would not wish to give Rhys a chance to flee."

"True," Tremaine answered, "and I recognized the leader as one of the men at Caernarvon."

"When were you there last?" she demanded fiercely. "Rhys never brought you with him while I was there."

Tremaine's lips twisted in a frown as he took her arm and led her away from the others. A sharp order kept anyone from following. "Mayhap I am wrong, and they will take him to Rhuddlan Castle, but I would bet my life on them imprisoning him in Caernarvon."

"'Tis not your life you gamble."

"No." He sighed and clasped his hands behind the fullness of his tunic. "You are correct. 'Tis not my life. 'Tis the life of a man who trusts me as much as he trusts you."

Bitterness sharpened her voice. "For the trust he has in me, his clan has denounced Rhys as a moonstruck fool. Do you think they will follow you if they see you aligned with me? God's breath, I never knew what it was like to be spurned when I could help."

"Then help me. You know Caernarvon well."

"Say what you wish with candor."

"'Tis simple. We both know an assault on Caernarvon is futile, even though the walls are unfinished. What I need is for you to sneak me into Caernarvon."

She turned away and clenched her hands by her side. "You ask me to betray my king. Even though you have probably been outlawed, you must know a way we can get in."

"I ask you to save Rhys's life."

Pain ate through her, but she nodded. On this one thing, she and Tremaine must work together. Yet, to betray her king would mean losing everything she had. No, everything she had was lost if Rhys died, for her life was with him now. She closed her eyes, wishing she could take back her cold words when he had asked her to be his wife. Mayhap, if they could free him, he would ask her again.

"When?" she whispered.

"We cannot wait long." He glanced toward the cave. "I can leave with the dawn."

She shook her head. "'Twould be better to leave with sunset, for the way into the Caernarvon is best sought when only the stars light the way."

"I will await your answer at sunset tomorrow, milady." He smiled icily. "Who would have guessed that Rhys ap Cynan's life would depend on the daughter of one of his enemies? Think well on your decision, milady, for you hold his life in your hand now."

"Are you certain?" Gizela stared at Bleddyn, then looked up at the dim light filtered through the rain. Behind the clouds, the sun must still be high above the mountains.

The young man shook his head, scowling. "Tremaine left me this message for you. You are to meet him below the falls. He wishes to speak with you immediately. He said it cannot wait until sunset."

She clasped her hands to hide their trembling. "That cannot be right. Mayhap the order was garbled before it reached your ears."

"He gave me this message himself, Lady de Montpellier."

"If he told you—" She silenced her own protest. She must not let Bleddyn suspect what she and Tremaine planned. He would insist on joining them, and she could not trust the young man who would gladly see her dead.

"Mayhap you do not wish to acknowledge Tremaine ap Pembroke as our chieftain, Lady de Montpellier. Otherwise, you would not question his request."

"Do you go with me?" She wished Tremaine had been honest with her about what he planned. Mayhap he already had told Bleddyn of the scheme to sneak into Caernarvon.

He snorted. "Whom do you fear? Your English allies?"

"Not my allies any longer. Do you doubt I have been outlawed?"

"If you wish to remain here—"

Gizela walked past him to the entrance to the cave. She shivered as she stared at the steady rain. The night would be cool in the mountains and miserable by the sea. Mayhap the horrid weather would be their collaborator in this mad strategy to free Rhys.

"I will go."

Pulling her cloak over her shoulders, she went out into the rain. The dirt of the well-traveled path had become mire. She fought her way upward along the ridge toward the waterfall.

She did not pause as she reached the spot where Rhys had met his enemies bravely. Rain struck her face like dozens of small needles, each intent on penetrating her skin. On every step, mud splashed up to seep through her ruined stockings in a frigidly- clammy caress. The sound of the waterfall urged her to succumb to tears as she recalled the rapture she had discovered with Rhys there. She must think only of how soon they would be together once more.

She turned away from the falls and struggled up the hill to the meadow above it. When she reached the meadow, she was not surprised to see it empty. Tremaine most likely would be waiting under the trees along the brook where the rain would not be as fierce.

Relief coursed through her when she saw a man materialize from the deepest shadows beneath the cliff. She rushed toward him.

"Tremaine! Did you want us to leave early because of the storm? If all the hills are as muddy as this one, we should leave. There is no time to spare. If—"

The flat edge of a cold blade inched up along her throat until it reached the underside of her jaw. She did not dare to breathe. A simple upward motion would kill her. She could not see her captor. Did he ride at Edward's orders, or was he a Welshman who was determined to carry out the chieftains' order of her death?

When the man stepped from the dusk by the cliff, her eyes widened. She recognized him instantly. He was the man who had held the sword to Rhys's back. At her gasp of astonishment, the knife pricked the underside of her chin.

He walked to her. Ripping the cloak back from her head, he ignored the water running in rivers along his scarred face. Rain dripped on her as he tilted her head back. Slowly he smiled.

"Greetings, Lady de Montpellier," he said with a slight nod. "We are well met on this dreary day. I am right pleased you are here exactly as we were told."

"Rhys would not betray me."

"He will betray many more important things than your location, milady, now that we have you to assist in his questioning." Looking past her, he nodded.

Her hands were wrenched behind her. "Stop!" she cried. The men laughed as chains were wrapped around her arms, tightening until she moaned. Closing her eyes, she prayed her arms would not break at her shoulders.

Her captor released her, and she swayed as she fought the agony searing along her back. She was steadied, so she could face the man who had greeted her.

With the tip of his finger, he forced her chin up so she could not avoid his eyes. "Lady de Montpellier, I arrest you in the name of his majesty, King Edward." A smile curled on his lips. "The charge is treason."

22

By the time the gates of Caernarvon appeared out of the darkness, Gizela had succumbed to a state of numbness which was shot through with lightning-hot pain each time she moved. She swayed with the motion of the horse on the uneven road. With her hands manacled, and her feet lashed together with a rope beneath the horse, she had no hopes of escape.

How ironic that Tremaine had been right when he said Rhys would be held in this castle! Her captors were bringing her to Caernarvon, so she could be judged along with Rhys. No, not just to die beside him, but to betray him into confessing more than he would wish. She must be strong to handle the torture they would force her to watch, for she knew he would not cede his will easily, not even for her.

And Tremaine? Was he alive or dead? She had not dared to ask, for she must not reveal anything about the Welsh refugees to the English.

Tears blurred the weak light which was glittering off the wet walls as she prayed Rhys was still alive within

Caernarvon. She did not trust these Englishmen to be honest with her. She hoped Tremaine had been right as well when he assured her King Edward would oversee the execution of Chieftain Rhys ap Cynan himself. Then Gizela de Montpellier would die. Esmond Talbot, the demon of Welsh nightmares, would have his final triumph over his daughter when she gave her life for loving one of the Welsh he had reviled.

When they rode over the drawbridge, the leader of her captors spoke softly to the guard. In surprise, the ruddy-haired man stared at her. Gizela met his gaze without emotion. As soon as they entered Caernarvon, she relinquished any hopes that Tremaine and the others would save her. Without the information she had, they would not be able to find their way about the castle without divulging their errand.

The guard motioned for them to enter, but continued to stare at her as if she were a ghost. In the rain, the inner bailey was as empty as her heart. Her eyes rose to stare at the magnificent Eagle Tower. It no longer offered sanctuary, for it might be the gateway to death. Her heart caught painfully when she realized she might be denied the chance to see Rhys again. He could die never knowing he had betrayed her with a single unguarded word, for she could imagine no other way the Englishmen could have found her.

Or, had the traitor who had led Edward's men to Cadairllwyd pointed out where she and Tremaine could be found—just as he had pointed out where Rhys might be captured?

When the horses were halted near the door to the Eagle Tower, the ropes were slashed from her ankles. Gizela was yanked from the horse. Her knees collapsed beneath her. With a soft cry, she dropped onto the hard stones. Blood oozed down her knees when she was pulled to her feet. She could not silence her moan when her captor seized her aching arm. He spun her about, nearly rocking her from her feet again, and shoved her toward the door to the tower.

The corridor was as deserted as the courtyard, and few brands burned along the walls. When she was led up the familiar stairs, Gizela swallowed the tears in her throat. She was scared, more scared than she had ever been, and she had no idea how she could free herself from the fate awaiting her upon the king's command.

Suddenly Pomona raced forward. "Milady!"

The man pushed her back. "Out of the way, old woman."

When Pomona started to protest, Gizela shook her head, motioning for her to be silent. Pomona must do nothing to create more trouble now. Gizela looked back to see Pomona huddled with her hands over her face, her shoulders quaking like the sea in a storm.

Although she had dared to hope Kenleigh's name would delay her hearing until the king returned to Caernarvon, she was not surprised when she was ushered into a small chamber. As he had the day he announced the king would assume guardianship of her and her lands, Dexter sat behind a carved table.

"Lady de Montpellier," he said, motioning for her to be brought forward, "I am grieved by what has come to pass, but not surprised, I must say. I knew you would prove to be as foolish as your husband."

She did not answer.

"Remove her manacles, Lytton," he ordered.

The scar-faced man obeyed, then withdrew, closing the door behind him.

Gizela winced as she rubbed feeling back into her fingers. Hot, prickling cramps ached along them when she fisted her hands. When Dexter held out a goblet of wine to her, she used both hands to take it. She did not trust her fingers. Taking a deep drink, she gratefully sat on the bench by the table. As her wet dress clung to her, she shivered in the dank air in the tower.

"Thank you," she whispered, as she took a second sip.

"Do not thank me," he said, the acidity returning to his voice. "I would have ordered you hanged in front of the gates as a warning to others. You are fortunate our gentle queen has a tender spot within her heart for you."

"Her majesty knows of this?" Her fingers clenched the goblet. Because of her admiration for the queen, she hated having ruined herself in Eleanor's eyes.

"She was informed of Lytton's mission to retrieve you from the mountains." He shook his head. "How your father would have rued this night!"

"Damn my father!" she said, coming to her feet. She threw the goblet at the hearth, not caring that the wine sprayed across the stones. "I never pleased him while he lived. Why should I care if I please him now?"

"Or please your king?" Dexter walked around the table and stopped in front of her, his fingers laced together over his wide belly. "Do you still consider Edward your lawful liege, milady?"

"Of course."

"You have not given your loyalties to the Welsh along with whatever else they demanded?"

Heat seared her cheeks, while Gizela asked, "Is Chieftain Rhys ap Cynan here?"

"Where else?" Dexter poured another goblet and set it on the table. When he reached for a third cup, she frowned. If he saw her bafflement, there was no sign in his voice as he continued, "This is the site of some of his most heinous crimes. Can you imagine any place better for his death than here? The king will be pleased, for it shall fit his idea of perfect justice."

"And the king will be his judge?"

Dexter chuckled. "What need is there for a trial when we all know so well what that barbarian has done?"

"He deserves a trial and the right to refute the evidence against him."

"Lady de Montpellier's heart remains as gentle as ever."

At the familiar voice, Gizela stood. In disbelief, she watched Tremaine walk forward and pick up the third cup. He tilted it toward Dexter with a smile, then turned to her.

She stared at him. He wore a longer tunic in the English style, and a thick gold chain dropped along the front of the wool. Not a hint of rain dampened his hair. Pressing her hand over her heart, she realized he must have left the mountain sanctuary before the storm began.

"Is Bleddyn with you on this plot to betray those who trusted you?" she asked.

Tremaine laughed. "Milady, you need not prove your ignorance with such questions. Young Bleddyn shall be as dead as his chieftain soon, for he will never bend his knee to King Edward."

"*King*?" Her fingers tightened into fists before she could scratch out his lying eyes. "How easily hypocrisy rolls off your tongue."

Dexter stepped between them. "Tremaine is a friend of England, milady, as your father was."

"Two treacherous vipers who hunger for power!" she snapped back. "What price did they pay you to betray Rhys, Tremaine? If you settled for just the gold about your neck, you received less than was promised to Sheldon." Her eyes widened. "No, 'twas much more, wasn't it? The gold I saw in your purse when Treystwyth was burned was English gold. You sold your countrymen into hell for a few pieces of gold!" She closed her eyes, willing the horrible memories of appalling death and ruin from her head. She must think clearly of what was happening now.

"I am, as I always have been, King Edward's loyal subject, and it is my honor to be able to serve him in this small way," Tremaine answered. But she did not believe his assertion. "I want peace among the hills of my homeland. Rhys ap Cynan wants nothing but war, when we could obtain so much for our clan, if we lived in harmony with the English."

"You care only about advancing yourself, Tremaine ap Pembroke! If it means betraying your chieftain, you will feel no remorse, will you? You care little that you have betrayed not only Rhys, but your whole clan!"

His smile did not waver as he crossed the room and put his hands on her shoulders. When she tried to shrug them off, they became talons which cut through her wet robes into her aching muscles. "My dear Lady de Montpellier, you are distraught. I cannot be betraying my rightful leader when my only lord is King Edward."

"That's ridiculous! I heard you tell Rhys just—"

"Be careful of what accusations you make, milady." While Tremaine faced her, Dexter could not read the truth in his eyes. "I am the king's man although I am of Wales."

"Yes!" she snapped. "You are a *Waelisc*." He flinched when she used the Welsh word for outlander. "No true son of *Cymru* would do as you have."

He chuckled. "What spirit, milady! 'Tis a shame you allowed yourself to be entangled in this intrigue. 'Tis no game for a woman."

Gizela's gown ripped as she wrenched herself out of his grip. Putting her hands on her torn sleeve, she faced him squarely. "That is the first honest thing you have said in this room, Tremaine. It is true. Intrigue is not a sport for a healer. Fool that I was, I let Rhys's trust for you smother my impression of you as a gutless dog."

He raised his hand, then lowered it, glancing like a guilty lad in Dexter's direction. "Take care what you say."

"Why? Shall we not speak of how you completed the work Sheldon was supposed to do? Did you deceive Lord de Montpellier as well and take his information to gain this man's favor?" She pointed to Dexter who laughed.

"I did what I must." Tremaine lifted her heavy braid and smiled. "My only failure was constantly underestimating what an excellent ally you were, milady. When Dexter needed me to bring him the information Sheldon was to provide, I let you convince me to bring you here. Then you and Rhys could not control your lust long enough not to play into my plans to provide a scapegoat for the destruction of Cadairllwyd." With a laugh, he said, "I spoke to the chieftains to spare your life, milady, because I knew you would be needed to induce the chieftain to reveal all he knows to the king's inquisitors."

"You—" She choked on the words she found impossible to speak. "You killed Ysolde, didn't you? So the chieftains could not kill me during the escape?"

"I needed you alive." He walked away from her, sipping his wine. Abruptly he turned, his eyes dangerous slits. "You may be assured, milady, if I had wanted you dead, my first arrow would have found its mark."

Dexter interjected, "The king has decided to give you a reward commensurate with your work, Tremaine."

He smiled coolly. "You will be informed when he arrives before the week's end."

"Week's end?" Gizela sank to the bench again. "The king will be here so soon?"

"Why should he delay his pleasure in seeing his enemies executed?" Tremaine glanced at Dexter.

Dexter smiled and left the room.

Pain twisted through her. "You have secured the doom of those who call you brother."

"I think of a better life for them."

"They will not think this a better life." She fought to keep her chin high. "Will you go back and lure them into the king's hands? Or must they die beneath the sword and flame?" "Rhys chose well when he selected you, Gizela." He held out his hand. "You are two of a kind, so dedicated to what you see is right, that you cannot see the prizes awaiting all around you."

"Where will you take me? To Rhys?"

He laughed as if she had made the greatest jest. "Mayhap the king will be clement enough to spare you from watching Rhys's death, but he requires that Rhys sees you while he is being questioned. To protect you, he will give the new king the truth."

"Then where do you take me?" she asked, not letting him guess the depths of her pain at his cruel words.

Tremaine took her hand and placed it on his arm. When she would have pulled away in disgust, he clamped his fingers over hers, pinning them to his sleeve. He gave her no time to say more as he led her out of the room.

His chuckle resounded up the stairwell as he said, "I assume you have dozens of questions."

"Only one."

"Speak it."

"Why?"

"Ah, the simplest question." He paused at a curve in the stairs and stepped toward her. When she backed into the wall, he smiled. "Why did I lead the English to where I knew Rhys would be at a time when he would do anything to protect you? Very simple. In exchange for delivering Rhys to him, Edward will give me you, Gizela."

She shook her head. "You made an error there. I have been arrested for treason as well."

"Is that so?" He laughed. "A small jest I knew would unsettle you."

"Unsettle me? You beast!" she cried.

He shrugged. "Those among the English who do not know you as well as I, cannot believe you have been anything save a pawn in this. After all, you are only a woman. Look about you. Do you go now to a cell?" He flung out his hands. "I take you to your chambers, milady, where you can enjoy the comforts you have been denied in the mountains."

"But why do you want me? I would have thought you would be the first to denounce me. You despise me."

"Aye, but I do not despise your wealthy estates which you inherited from that fool you wed."

"The very man you convinced Rhys to execute!"

His hand stroked her icy cheek, but became a claw on her shoulder when she tried to pull away. "Of course. The whole thing was so deceptively simple I nearly laughed while all of you played your parts exactly as I wished." With another laugh, he hit the side of his hand sharply against the wall only inches from her head. "Chop. No more de Montpellier, although I owe him a debt for teaching me how easily murder can gain a man what he wishes."

"I do not understand you."

"No?" He leaned closer. As she tried to evade him, he whispered against her ear, "Would you understand if I tell you that de Montpellier's greatest crime was fratricide?"

"He killed Kenleigh?" she whispered, unable to believe what she was saying.

"De Montpellier saw the opportunity that would be his when his brother was dead. How unfortunate for him that Edward saw the same opportunity!" He gripped her face and turned it toward him. "Yet Edward will be so grateful at having the chance to execute Rhys ap Cynan, he will gladly give me you and the lands you hold."

"I shall tell him—"

He forced her mouth beneath his. Moaning as her head was pressed against the unyielding wall, she tried to pull away from his cruel touch. Glaring down at her, he could not hide his shock when she jerked her head out of his grip and laughed.

"I will denounce you before I give you Kenleigh's lands."

"Do so, and you shall watch someone dear to you put to a slow death."

"Rhys—"

"Not him, for he is already marked for death. Your heroic lover has refused to answer any questions, no matter what torture was inflicted on him." When she turned her face from his malevolent smile, he pulled her up the stairs and threw open the door to her chambers. "Look well within, milady, and see one who has suffered too much because of you already. Would you see a poor old woman die for your treason?"

Gizela whispered, "Pomona? No, you must not bring her into this."

"Too late." He shoved her into the room.

When the door slammed in her face, she whirled away. "Damn you!"

"Milady, milady, you are alive!"

Gizela forced her anger deep within her as she held out her hands to Pomona. The old woman fell to her knees before her, weeping against Gizela's ruined gown. Slowly she sat on the bench beside the hearth.

Hot tears of pain fled down Gizela's cheeks. All she had done, all Kenleigh had done, all Rhys had done, had led to this moment when deception had cost her any chance of saving the man she loved.

She could do nothing to help him. If Tremaine had his way, she would view Rhys's execution on her way to be wed to his greatest enemy. She shuddered with horror as she imagined Tremaine demanding his rights as her husband. He would want a child to solidify his claim on her lands. He would be as determined and as brutal as her father about having a living son.

"Hush, milady," Pomona murmured. "Do not weep when your tears will bring no release from your suffering."

"How can I not cry when Rhys is going to be executed and there is nothing I can do to stop it?" She stood. "I shall find a way to help him. I know not how, but I must, even if I give my life in return."

"Do not throw your life away. Patience, milady." She smiled sadly. "How many times have I told you that? Have patience."

"The king arrives before week's end. Mayhap if I were to speak to the queen—"

"There are always other ways."

Raising her head, she whispered, "Other ways? For what?"

"To save the one you weep for. Is that not what you want?"

Gizela drew away. To speak of the truth within her heart would leave her vulnerable. If she voiced them—

Softly Pomona said, "I am your true friend, milady. I pray you do not doubt that."

"No," she answered, clasping Pomona's hands again, "I do not doubt that in my heart." She put her fingers to the center of her chest. "It simply aches so deeply that I dare not heed its urgings. How can I save Rhys? Everyone he has trusted has betrayed him."

"Save for you."

"Will you help me, Pomona?"

"Help you free him?"

"Yes."

Pomona whispered, "You know how impossible that is?"

"Aye." She wiped the tears from her cheek. "But what do we have left save for the impossible?"

23

The creak of the opening door woke Gizela from her fitful sleep. Starlight crept past the narrow opening in the wall to wash over her bed. She sat up. "Pomona?"

"Aye." The old woman rushed to the bed at the best speed she could manage. "I have heard the tidings. The king will arrive by midday."

"Dear God!" She clenched the blankets, fearing she would be ill.

"But that is not all I have heard." Pomona bent toward her and whispered, "The chieftain is being held in a chamber two floors above this one."

"In this tower?"

"The next one."

Gizela swung her feet off the bed. Pulling on her slippers, she looked at her servant. "From whom did you get this information?"

"Hayes."

Her eyes grew wide as she slipped from the bed. "Hayes! How does he know?"

Pomona took Gizela's hands and drew her to sit on the chest by the bed. "My dear lady, you must be strong when I tell you what he told me."

"He took healing herbs to where Rhys is being kept?"

"That is so."

"What sort of herbs?"

. The old woman smiled. "He told me you would ask that, and that I should tell you the herbs were for healing a small, inconsequential wound."

She pressed her hands together and bowed her head over them as she fought the horror racing through her. Had Rhys been tortured, or had he hurt himself trying to escape?

Taking a deep breath, she stood. "Then the time has come."

"Milady, think long on what you plan."

"I have thought long on it, Pomona. If I do not try, Rhys will be executed and I may be forced to wed the man who betrayed both him and my husband's brother. Mayhap even Kenleigh. If I fail, Rhys and I shall die. If I succeed—"

"You will be outlawed for the rest of your days. You never will be able to claim the lands that are yours."

She laughed wryly. "How many times have I chided Rhys, telling him not a single stone in these mountains is worth more than a life? Do you think I consider two collections of dirt and stone on the far side of Offa's Dyke more important than Rhys's life?" She held out her hands. "Are you with me, Pomona?"

"Aye, milady, and may God have mercy on our foolish souls."

Climbing the shadowed stairwell within the other tower, a heavy bag slapping against her, Gizela reached back to help Pomona up the steep steps. So far they had been fortunate, meeting no one in the halls which were usually empty in the middle of the night. She could not depend on good fortune to continue, for the worst was ahead of them.

She tightened the simple cloak around her. Pomona had brought clothing suitable for a serving lass, for they hoped no one would think it unusual for the two of them to be about in the hours before dawn.

A choking foulness struck her. With her hands over her mouth and nose, she climbed toward the floor where Rhys was imprisoned. This odorous tower must open onto the charnel house. Taking a deep breath to calm herself, she nearly gagged on the reek of human waste.

Fury threatened to undo her. Damn Dexter and Tremaine for leaving Rhys in this horrible place!

"'Twill be all right, milady," whispered Pomona when they stopped on a landing, one floor below where Rhys was reported to be kept.

"Only when it is over."

Her servant smiled. "Tell me what you wish me to do."

"Take this." She slipped the bag from her shoulders.

Kneeling down on the floor, she opened the bottle of wine and mixed in the ground lettuce and oil of roses she had had Pomona bring from Hayes's stillroom. The excuse that Gizela was unable to sleep had prevented Hayes from asking questions. Gizela hated deluding her friend, but the deception would save him, if by some chance, she succeeded. Then Hayes could honestly tell the king he had no idea of her plans.

"You must get him to drink as much of this as possible," she said, handing the bottle back to Pomona.

"Him? The chieftain?"

Letting wickedness sift into her laugh, Gizela said, "The guard. Make sure he drinks as much as he will, as quickly as he will."

Pomona nodded. Squeezing Gizela's hand, she hurried up the steps.

Gizela heard someone shout and tensed, but the sound of Pomona's calm answer drifted to her along with a man's chuckle. Inching up the stairs, she peered around the corner to see a tall, obscenely obese man sitting on a stool that strained to hold him.

"Wine?" he crowed as Pomona held out the bottle.

"Why should the soldiers on the wall get all the good wine?" Pomona asked. She glanced back at Gizela, then hurried to say, "I cannot stay long. If I am gone when he wakes, milord will miss me."

"Along with this bottle of wine." He opened it and took a deep drink. "Why did ye bring this?"

"My son shares the duty up here." Pomona's nose wrinkled. "When I came to see him, I discovered how foul it was. No man should have to be here unless he is a criminal. Drink what you wish, for I cannot stay."

He tilted the bottle back. Wine flowed out of his mouth and over his chin. Gizela clenched her hands. If too much of it ended up on the front of his tunic, the herbs might not work as she had planned.

The guard tossed the bottle back to Pomona who caught it easily and tilted it upside down. Only a few drops fell to the stone floor.

"Shall I bring more tomorrow night?" Pomona asked.

The guard slapped his wide thigh. "No need. By tomorrow night, the king will be sure there is no prisoner to guard."

Pomona mumbled something and hurried to the stairs. She preached as if she was going all the way down, then eased next to where Gizela stood in the shadows.

Minutes passed, each one as precious as the light coming through the arrow slits while the moon sank toward the western sea. When Gizela heard a heavy thud, she drew the knife in her sash before she peeked around the edge of the stairwell. The guard sprawled on the floor like a beached boat.

"Now!" she whispered, slipping the blade back into her belt. She had not asked Pomona where the old woman had stolen it, and she did not care. As they scurried up the stairs, she asked, "Pomona, do you know where Rhys is being kept?"

"He is the only prisoner here."

"Then let us look for a locked door."

Gizela ran along one hallway, then went in the other direction. Her breath came in sobs, for no door was barred closed. She had no idea how much wine the guard had swallowed, so she could not guess how long he would sleep.

She gasped when she saw a barred door at the end of the second passage. Bending, she put both hands against the bar. She strained, gritting her teeth. She could not move it. When she saw Pomona coming toward her, she motioned her to hurry. Together they raised the thick plank. They lowered it carefully to the floor, not wanting to alert anyone on the floor below them.

She threw open the door. "Rhys, are you within?"

"Gizela?" Shock strained Rhys's voice, then fury as he demanded, "Gizela, are you mad?"

With a soft cry, she ran to be enfolded in his arms. His beard brushed her cheek as he drew her against him. Raising her gaze to his face, she saw lines of strain. Blood was dried on his forehead and down his left cheek. Her fingers trembled as she touched his face. She did not want this to be another dream which metamorphosed into a nightmare.

Rhys whispered, "sweet one, you should not be here. If they were to discover you had come back to Caernarvon, your life would be worth as little as mine."

"They know. They—"

"Milady," called Pomona. "You must leave now. The guard is stirring."

Rhys grabbed Gizela's hand and motioned for Pomona to follow. Gizela pulled away. Taking Pomona's hand, she smiled when Rhys did the same. Together they sped the old woman down the stairs.

The dark stairwell went round and round in the heart of the tower. Each step brought more odors until it took all her strength not to gag. How ironic that Dexter's plan to torment Rhys by putting him in this horrible tower, made it easier for them to escape! No guards wished to linger near the stench. At the bottom of the stairs, Gizela gestured for them to keep within the shadows. She peered out at the inner bailey.

"Where now, milady?" Rhys asked.

"You want my advice on the protocol of war?" She delighted in the chance to tease him once more.

"I want your advice, sweet one," he whispered against her ear, sending shivers of yearning through her, "on how to escape from here with our skins intact so I might enjoy yours next to mine."

Pomona murmured, "There are guards on the posterns and all gates. They are ordered to halt and question anyone."

"We must go past them swiftly so they cannot stop us," Rhys said. Shall we steal a horse, milady?"

Hearing the tension beneath his jesting, she nodded. "Come. I will take you to the stables. We can steal horses so all of us—"

"Not me," Pomona whispered.

Gizela looked at the old woman whose face was ghostly in the faint light. "What?"

"I am not going with you, milady, for I would only slow you."

"We will help you," Gizela said. "Pomona, come with us."

She lifted Gizela's hand to her forehead and bowed. "Years ago, when I saw the misery your father was determined to inflict upon you, I vowed never to leave your side until I could be sure you would never be hurt like that again." She placed Gizela's hand in Rhys's. "Now I know you have another who will protect you and cherish you as I had dreamed Lord de Montpellier would."

"Thank you," he said, bowing his head to Pomona.

"I have waited many long years to see milady aglow with joy, Chieftain." She smiled sadly. "I will not be false and say I do not wish she had found a man among the English, but I shall not deny her the happiness you have given her. Guard her well."

"You can still come with us," Gizela said.

"Go!" She glanced over her shoulder, then kissed Gizela's cheek. "Go in peace, milady." She held up the wine bottle she still carried. "There are still enough dregs left within this wine to support my tale of how you put me to sleep while you freed the chieftain."

"But what will you do, Pomona?"

"I shall return with Lord de Montpellier's men to England, and I shall live out my days in Talbot Hall where I was born. It will be all right, milady." She gave Gizela a shove toward Rhys. "Go while you can. I shall pray for your happiness."

Gizela whispered, "And I for yours."

"Thank you, Pomona," Rhys added. "You do your lady proud with your dedication and sacrifice."

Blinking back tears, Gizela hurried by his side into the thinning darkness along the walls of the inner bailey. She looked up. The stars were fading, and dawn soon would be upon them. They must hurry. By the time the sun was at its highest, Edward would be here to watch Rhys's death.

"There," said Rhys, as he pointed to the opposite curtain wall. "At least three guards walk that wall and as many on this side. I have been regaled with tales of the strength of the English contingent."

She pulled off her cloak and flung it over his shoulders. "Wear this, Rhys, and they will see you as one of the English."

"A frightful thought."

She smiled. "One of your final thoughts if we do not succeed." She pointed to the stable on the other side of the bailey. "Let me go first. I shall get horses."

"How?"

Patting her pouch, she said, "I can devise a compelling story of the need to tend to an ill stable lad."

I wish you many fools to heed your tale," he whispered.

"Wait until you see me with the horses, then come."

"I shall not wait long, for I shall not leave you to face trouble alone."

Her fingers curved along his cheek. "My love, I can never be alone when your heart beats along with mine."

His fingers sifted through her loose hair as he captured her lips. His mouth threatened to free the savage need within her, so she drew back. She must be able to concentrate on her task.

Gizela said nothing as she stepped out of the shadows and walked across the bailey. She waited for the call to halt, but, as she had hoped, the watch took no note of a lone serving lass crossing the courtyard.

A single brand lit the stable, its light glittering on leather and the water in the buckets by the stalls. Gizela ran to the closest horse. She smiled when she saw it was sturdy. Throwing a blanket over its back, she untied its halter and brought it with her as she reached for the next horse's halter. Her smile broadened when she saw Rhys strolling toward her as if he had nothing on his mind save stoking the fires on the kitchen hearths for the morning meal.

"A good choice," he whispered, pulling off the cloak and handing it to her. As she tied it around her neck, he added, "I saw the main gate is open. They dare not close it in anticipation of Edward's arrival. Isn't it perfect that his vanity and love of pageantry, shall be our salvation?"

"Yes, isn't it?"

Gizela whirled at the unexpected sound of another man's deep voice. She gasped and stared at Tremaine. He raised his sword as he advanced toward them.

"Tremaine!" Rhys held out his hand. "To have you fight beside me is—"

"All wrong," Gizela cried. "Rhys, do not heed him. He will kill us both!"

"Gizela, he has risked his life to save me—to save both of us—from the mockery of English justice."

"He is not your friend! He betrayed you to the English!" She gripped his arm. "Rhys, you must see the truth. He has betrayed you. You told me once, every leader must be wary of treachery. He persuaded you to slay Sheldon, then betrayed you to the English in order to obtain de Montpellier Court."

Rhys looked at his friend, confusion threading his forehead. "Do you wish me to pose the question to him so he might deny it?"

"Why should I deny it?" Tremaine laughed. "After all, your English whore speaks the truth."

"Whore?" Rhys took a single pace forward. He halted when Tremaine raised the broadsword to the level of his heart.

"Do you know a better name for her?"

"The one I offered her as my wife and the mother of my children is one I hope she now will accept."

"She will give you no children, Rhys. You may rot in hell knowing I shall let her live long enough to bear my son who shall one day hold both de Montpellier's manor lands and those belonging to Talbot." His laugh was exultant. "How many times have you vowed to take from Talbot all he treasured in retribution for the death of your father? Did you think I would be the one to fulfill that vow?"

"Your father?" cried Gizela. "My father killed your father?"

Tremaine's wicked laugh threatened to sear her soul. "Tell her, Chieftain. Tell her how her father practiced his hideous tricks on Cynan ap Merin until there was little left of your father to bury. Little in one piece, that is."

Gizela clenched her hand on the horse's blanket, fighting not to be sick. "I did not know," she choked. She put her hand out to Rhys, but could not reach him. "Rhys, I had no idea."

"I know, sweet one." Although he did not turn to her—and his face would be implacable before his enemy—she could sense his gentle smile in his voice. "I had hoped you would never know."

"Yet, you allowed Talbot's daughter to live," taunted Tremaine. "From the moment you saw her, you were her captive, bewitched by the daughter of Satan himself. You should have slain her that first night."

"You know I could not."

"Because of your honor?" Tremaine sneered, "What honor is there in letting her live?"

"You know I pledged to Kenleigh de Montpellier as he took his final breath that I would protect his wife with my life. It was little to pledge to a man who had been our last chance for peace in this land."

"Before Sheldon killed him," Gizela whispered.

"De Montpellier murdered his own brother?" Rhys gasped.

"You did not know?" she asked.

"When a friend lies dying, my thoughts are solely of giving him comfort. Gizela, I vow to you that he died with little pain. All his thoughts were of you in his last moments, as mine are now." He reached for her, but Tremaine kept the sword between them.

"And this is how you satisfied the vow to Kenleigh de Montpellier?" Tremaine asked with another laugh.

Rhys's gaze held hers as his hand closed on the empty sheath at his waist. "I had hoped to persuade Gizela to return to England, but she did not heed my warnings of the danger within Caernarvon. So I took her from here to protect her in Cadairllwyd."

"I thought you wished me to be far from the queen when her babe was born," she whispered. She looked at Tremaine. "Why did I believe you?"

Rhys answered beneath Tremaine's laugh, "You believed him because you did not dare to trust your heart which urged you to trust me."

"And you believed me when I offered to help you get your English witch back, giving me the chance to plant all the suspicion I needed to bring both of you to ruin." Tremaine's derisive chuckle was low enough not to call attention from beyond the stable. "Believing me was imprudent of you, Chieftain. Have you not seen the truth? Gizela Talbot de Montpellier brings only death to those who covet her and what she possesses."

"What she possesses?" He turned to face her. "What care I for English soil? My heart belongs here in *Cymru*. Let Edward have what is his."

"Even de Montpellier's estate?" With a derisive laugh, he kept the sword in front of Rhys. He swung it toward Gizela when she tried to edge away. "You are more a fool than I had guessed. I thought you had considered the riches you could gain by wooing this whore into your arms. You have ever been an absurd ass."

"What must I say to persuade you?" Rhys took a step forward, but froze when Tremaine pressed the point of the sword to the buttons on the front of Gizela's gown. Her face washed of all color. "Take de Montpellier's lands," Rhys said, "if that is your wish! Gizela and I shall make our home here in *Cymru*."

"Your home will be hell! I wanted those lands, and I have worked long to gain them for myself." His smile wavered as he shook his head in feigned sorrow. "You should have listened to your whore. Of course, there are things she could not tell you, such as my intention to help de Montpellier betray *you* to the king. Her arrival in Caernarvon changed my plans. Now I shall have the lands of our clan in addition to the reward Edward gives me for slaying two escaping traitors. Say farewell to your whore, Chieftain." He balanced the broadsword easily in his hand.

"Let her go," Rhys ordered. "You may have my life, but free her."

"No!" She reached toward Rhys. "Do not bargain with this man who has no honor."

"Silence!" Tremaine scowled at her, and she raised her chin in what defiance she could muster. "You are a fool, Chieftain! I do not plan to kill her unless you make it necessary." He pressed the end of the sword against the laces holding her cloak around her neck. "That is unfortunate, Chieftain, for I would enjoy watching you witness her death before you join her in the afterlife."

Gizela breathed shallowly. Each breath might be her last as the sword rose to her throat. She looked from its expanse to Rhys. His hands fisted at his side. He did not dare to move. If he did, Tremaine would drive the blade into her.

"I love you," she whispered.

Tremaine chuckled again as he caught her gaze. "How endearing! Say *da boch* to your lover, milady." He swung the sword toward Rhys whose face bore no more expression than the stone walls around them.

As Tremaine raised the sword, Gizela fumbled with the pouch at her waist. She cried, "Tremaine, look out!"

He froze, then whirled to her. He opened his mouth, but choked when she hurled the herbs in the pouch at him. The tip of the sword clattered to the floor as he clawed at his eyes. He took one step toward her, then another. Lifting the sword, he snarled, "I shall see you die, English witch. If—"

He collapsed to the earth. The sword fell beside him. She stared at Rhys who was lowering his fists to his sides. He shook his fist which had struck Tremaine. "Faith, but his head is hard!"

Gizela grasped his arm as he knelt beside Tremaine. "Leave him."

"I must be sure he is not in danger."

"He would have killed you!"

"He is my cousin, Gizela. I am not your father. I cannot punish those who are not what I wish them to be. Let him stay with the English if that is his wish." He smiled. "He is breathing. Come, my love. Let us be gone."

He lifted her onto the horse. The beast shifted, uneasily, but Rhys calmed him with a murmur. Turning, he prepared to mount. He smiled and brushed his hand against her cheek.

Suddenly a groan burst from his throat. She screamed. Rhys fell against the horse, his fingers stretched across her thigh. Slowly he slid to the ground.

Hearing Tremaine's victorious laugh, she pulled the knife at her side. She could not let Rhys die like this. She swung it at Tremaine.

He jerked her from the horse. She raised the knife, but he knocked it from her hand. She backed away, cradling her stinging hand. When he lifted his sword toward her, she moaned at the sight of Rhys's blood on the long blade.

"You killed him!" she cried.

"I hope so." He smiled as he drove her toward the stable wall. Lowering the sword, he gripped the front of her gown. He dragged her to him. "English whore, you will pleasure me now."

"No!"

"You will say only 'yes' to me." His mouth ground into hers.

She fought him. Her nails cut into his hand holding onto her gown. With a curse, he raised his hand to strike her. She used her knee against him. His curse was a howl as he bent in pain toward the floor. He did not release her. Falling hard, she fought to hold onto her senses.

"You shall pay for this," Tremaine growled through gritted teeth.

Something moved behind him. She had no time to react. The knife swept down with eye-blurring speed.

Tremaine shrieked and fell to one knee. She scrambled away from him as he pulled the knife from beneath his ribs. Pushing himself to his feet, he turned to face Rhys. He lurched forward one step, then crashed again to the ground. This time he would not rise again. Scarlet filled each indentation in the stones.

Gizela ran to Rhys. He held his hand to his side, but she could see blood flowing through his fingers. "Come," she cried, "we must go."

"The watch must have been alerted by this commotion," he said. His voice was a weak shadow of its usual strength.

"Can you mount?"

He nodded.

"Get on the horse."

"Gizela—"

"Trust me," she whispered.

He reached to touch her cheek, but pulled his blood-stained hand back. "I do trust you, sweet one. Trust me."

She took his hand between hers. "I trust you, Rhys, as I have trusted no one else in my life."

Gizela did not wait to see if he could get on the horse. She ran through the stable, untying the horses. She slapped them and sent them fleeing out into the bailey. Shouts came from the walls. Would it be enough?

She ran back to the horse where Rhys was struggling to sit upright. He must be hurt worse than he wanted her to know. They might need more time to clear the gate. Whirling, she pulled the brand from the wall. Touching it to the pile of hay nearest her, she tossed it back farther into the stable. Fire feasted on the dry hay.

Gripping the reins, Rhys held out his hand to Gizela. She clasped his wrist, and a quick tug pulled her up behind him. Wrapping her arms around him, she pulled the reins from his hands.

The horses burst out from the smoke. Shouts echoed from every direction as the horse raced at full speed toward the gate. Men rushed past them to put out the fire. She urged the horse to go faster. Every second within the walls increased the chances of an arrow in their backs. Her cloak snapped behind her like the wings of the mighty Welsh dragon.

Shadows claimed them as they rode through the wall. Across the drawbridge, they fled. Shouts chased them. Arrows struck the road. Gizela tightened her grip on Rhys as the horse raced along the rough road, past the range of the strongest bowman.

When Rhys suddenly pulled on the reins, Gizela rocked into him. "Rhys, we cannot stop here."

"Help me down."

"What?" She looked over her shoulder. "They will send pursuit. They will catch us in no time."

"If we stay two on a single horse." He smiled weakly. "They shall never find us among my hills."

She nodded and slid to the ground. With his hands on her shoulders, he eased himself off the horse. He motioned toward the horse. She struck its haunches and, with a shriek, sent it at a full run along the road.

"We must go before they discover our ruse," Rhys said, his voice growing weaker on every word.

She put her arm beneath him so he could use her shoulder as a crutch. Climbing the stones along the hill, she was panting by the time they had reached the trees.

"Forgive me," he whispered. "I did not want to believe Tremaine would betray me."

"I know, for I never was willing to believe that my father would hurt me again." She brushed his hair back from his cheek. "We want to believe those we love the most are good and kind and honorable. 'Tis sad when 'tis not so."

He brought her face toward him. "But 'tis wondrous when it is so. Come, my love, and let me prove that to you."

"For the rest of our days."

His rakish smile startled her as he added, "And all our nights, my love."

Epilogue

**Mountains above Cadairllwyd
1285**

Gizela stood alone by the fire. As the door opened, the wintry wind swirled the flames in a wild dance. Her smile was soft and welcoming as Rhys reached across the narrow floor to take her hands.

Hungrily, he claimed her lips. The memory of their sweet flavor had healed him when he lay near death in the wake of Tremaine's treachery. Her lips' gentle touch had soothed him during the endless fortnights of recovery. And the yearning to know this tempting treat once more had sustained him during the long hours of facing the truth with his fellow chieftains.

As her slender fingers coursed along him, like gentle rain on parched earth, he drew back with regret. "It is over," he said, pinning her hand to the frosted front of his tunic.

"I cannot be sorry," she whispered. "The rebellion almost stole you from me once. I do not wish to fear that every day of my life."

He arched a single golden brow. "It died for the lack of a leader. No one is willing to bring Edward's wrath down upon them now that young Prince Alfonso is dead and the child we pledged our allegiance to will be the King of England, as well as our prince. We cannot rise against our own prince."

"Rhys—"

"Say nothing, dear wife." He looked about the rough hut and smiled. "This is too precious to me. Let Edward have his grand schemes and his fortresses along the sea. Here in the mountains, we shall live free as we always have."

"Come. Let me get some stew to warm you."

"Stew is not what I wish to warm me on such a long, cold night." When she smiled an invitation he would never refuse, he reached for the door. "But, first, my love, a caller awaits without."

"You left someone out in the night?" Gizela pushed past him to lift the latch. She swung the door aside and cried, "Pomona!"

The old woman threw off her snow-dusted cloak and embraced Gizela, weeping against her neck. Gizela hugged her and tried to soothe her, as Pomona had soothed her through so many nights of pain.

"Come," Gizela whispered. "Come and sit by the fire."

"The cold despises my old bones, milady."

"What made you come here now?"

Pomona smiled as she touched Gizela's stomach that was growing rounder. "I know you are the midwife, milady, but I have learned much with your help. I thought you might need me by now."

Taking Pomona's cloak, Gizela carried it to a simple peg by the door. She smiled at Rhys and whispered, "Thank you."

"I have seen you pining for her."

"So you went into Caernarvon?"

He shook his head. "Into England." He flashed a smile at where the old woman was holding her hands out to the fire. "She had returned to your father's house, which was simpler to enter than Edward's castle."

"But you vowed never to set foot on English soil."

"How could it be English when it belongs to you, my love? You are unquestionably of *Cymru* now." He swept her into his arms and kissed her heartily.

"Pomona will—"

"Understand I have been far from you for far too long, my love." Slipping his wet cloak off his shoulders, he threw it atop the bench and laughed. He scooped her up in his arms, ignoring her gasp of astonishment.

He carried her into the other room and placed her on the bed which had been too empty without him. Leaning over her, he held her in place with the rapture of his lips. He chuckled again as he put his hands to her waist.

"Pomona noticed right away, sweet one."

"I am certain you bragged of this child to her on more than one occasion. You are an intolerably proud father."

"I might have mentioned it once or twice." He stroked her stomach. "Not to brag, but because I knew Pomona would wish to be here." He laughed. "Her slender lady looks as round as a barrel."

"You must take part of the blame for my increasing girth."

"I gladly take the full blame." Smoothing her hair back from her forehead, he whispered, "I want no one else to take credit for this child we share. He shall grow up strong and free in this land of his forefathers."

Drawing his lips toward hers, she whispered, "Why are you chattering when I wish only for you to think of keeping me warm?"

"Gladly, my lady."

Gizela smiled. She had finally found a love as strong and true as the heart of a dragon.

Let HarperMonogram Sweep You Away!

Once Upon a Time by **Constance O'Banyon**
Over seven million copies of her books in print. To save her idyllic kingdom from the English, Queen Jilliana must marry Prince Ruyen and produce an heir. Both are willing to do anything to defeat a common enemy, but they are powerless to fight the wanton desires that threaten to engulf them.

The Marrying Kind by **Sharon Ihle**
Romantic Times *Reviewer's Choice Award–Winning author.* Liberty Ann Justice has no time for the silver-tongued stranger she believes is trying to destroy her father's Wyoming newspaper. Donovan isn't about to let a little misunderstanding hinder her pursuit of happiness, however, or his pursuit of the tempestuous vixen who has him hungering for her sweet love.

Honor by **Mary Spencer**
Sent by King Henry V to save Amica of Lancaster from a cruel marriage, Sir Thomas of Reed discovers his rough ways are no match for Amica's innocent sensuality. A damsel in distress to his knight, Amica unleashes passions in Sir Thomas that leave him longing for her touch.

Wake Not the Dragon by **Jo Ann Ferguson**
As the queen's midwife, Gizela de Montpellier travels to Wales and meets Rhys ap Cynan—a Welsh chieftain determined to drive out the despised English. Captivated by the handsome warlord, Gizela must choose between her loyalty to the crown and her heart's desire.

And in case you missed last month's selections . . .

You Belong to My Heart by **Nan Ryan**
Over 3.5 million copies of her books in print. As the Civil War rages, Captain Clay Knight seizes Mary Ellen Preble's mansion for the Union Army. Having been his sweetheart, Mary Ellen must win back the man who wants her in his bed, but not in his heart.

After the Storm by Susan Sizemore

Golden Heart Award–Winning Author. When a time travel experiment goes awry, Libby Wolfe finds herself in medieval England and at the mercy of the dashing Bastien of Bale. A master of seduction, the handsome outlaw unleashes a passion in Libby that she finds hauntingly familiar.

Deep in the Heart by Sharon Sala

Romantic Times *Award–Winning Author.* Stalked by a threatening stranger, successful casting director Samantha Carlyle returns home to Texas—and her old friend John Thomas Knight—for safety. The tender lawman may be able to protect Sam's body, but his warm Southern ways put her heart at risk.

Honeysuckle DeVine by Susan Macias

To collect her inheritance, Laura Cannon needs to join Jesse Travers's cattle drive—and become his wife. The match is only temporary, but long days on the trail lead to nights filled with fiery passion.

Harper Monogram